P9-CLB-440

image comics presents

For SKYBOUND ENTERTAINMENT
Robert Kirkman - CEO
David Alpert - President
Sean Mackiewicz - Editorial Director
Shawn Kirkham - Director of Business Development
Brian Huntington - Online Editorial Director
June Alian - Publicity Director
Rachel Skidmore - Director of Media Development
Mike Williamson - Assistant Editor
Michael Williamson - Assistant Editor
Dan Petersen - Operations Manager
Sarah Effinger - Office Manager
Nick Palmer - Operations Coordinator
Lizzy Iverson - Administrative Assistant
Stephan Murillo - Administrative Assistant

International inquiries: foreign@skybound.com
Licensing inquiries: contact@skybound.com

WWW.SKYBOUND.COM

IMAGE COMICS, INC.
Robert Kirkman – Chief Operating Officer
Erik Larsen – Chief Financial Officer
Todd McFarlane – President
Marc Silvestri – Chief Executive Officer
Jim Valentino – Vice-President
Eric Stephenson – Publisher
Corey Murphy – Director of Sales
Jeremy Sullivan – Director of Digital Sales
Kat Salazar – Director of PR & Marketing
Emily Miller – Director of Operations
Branwyn Bigglestone – Senior Accounts Manager
Sarah Mello – Accounts Manager
Drew Gill – Art Director
Jonathan Chan – Production Manager
Meredith Wallace – Print Manager
Randy Okamura – Marketing Production Designer
David Brothers – Content Manager
Addison Duke – Production Artist
Vincent Kukua – Production Artist
Sasha Head – Production Artist
Tricia Ramos – Production Artist
Emilio Bautista – Sales Assistant
Jessica Ambriz – Administrative Assistant
IMAGECOMICS.COM

THE WALKING DEAD, VOL. 1: DAYS GONE BYE. Sixteenth Printing. Published by Image Comics, Inc. Office of publication: 2001 Center St., Sixth Floor, Berkeley, California 94704. Copyright © 2015 Robert Kirkman, LLC. All rights reserved. Originally published in single magazine format as THE WALKING DEAD #1-6. THE WALKING DEAD™ (including all prominent characters featured in this issue), its logo and all character likenesses are trademarks of Robert Kirkman, LLC, unless otherwise noted. Image Comics® and its logos are registered trademarks of Image Comics, Inc. No part of this publication may be reproduced or transmitted, in any form or by any means (except for short excerpts for review purposes) without the express written permission of Image Comics, Inc. All names, characters, events and locales in this publication are entirely fictional. Any resemblance to actual persons (living and/or dead), events or places, without satiric intent, is coincidental. For information regarding the CPSIA on this printed material call: 203-595-3636 and provide reference # RICH – 622421.

PRINTED IN THE USA

ISBN: 978-1-58240-672-5

ROBERT KIRKMAN
CREATOR, WRITER, LETTERER

TONY MOORE
PENCILER, INKER, GRAY TONES

CLIFF RATHBURN
ADDITIONAL GRAY TONES

INTRODUCTION

I'm not trying to scare anybody. If that somehow happens as a result of reading this comic, that's great, but really... that's not what this book is about. What you now hold in your hands is the most serious piece of work I've done so far in my career. I'm the guy that created Battle Pope; I hope you guys realize what a stretch this is for me. It's really not that hard to believe when you realize that I'm delving into subject matter that is so utterly serious and dramatic...

Zombies.

To me, the best zombie movies aren't the splatter fests of gore and violence with goofy characters and tongue in cheek antics. Good zombie movies show us how messed up we are, they make us question our station in society... and our society's station in the world. They show us gore and violence and all that cool stuff too... but there's always an undercurrent of social commentary and thoughtfulness.

Give me "Dawn of the Dead" over "Return of the Living Dead" any day. To me, zombie movies are thought provoking, dramatic fiction, on par with any Oscar worthy garbage that's rolled out year after year. Movies that make you question the fabric of our very society are what I like. And in GOOD zombie movies... you get that by the truckload.

With **THE WALKING DEAD,** I want to explore how people deal with extreme situations and how these events CHANGE them. I'm in this for the long haul. You guys are going to get to see Rick change and mature to the point that, when you look back on this book, you won't even recognize him. I hope you guys are looking forward to a sprawling epic, because that's the idea with this one.

Everything in this book is an attempt at showing the natural progression of events that I think would occur in these situations. This is a very character driven endeavor. How these characters get there is much more important than them getting there. I hope to show you reflections of your friends, your neighbors, your families, and yourselves, and what their reactions are to the extreme situations in this book.

So, if anything scares you... great, but this is not a horror book. And by that, I do not mean we think we're above that genre. Far from it, we're just setting out on a different path here. This book is more about watching Rick survive than it is about watching zombies pop around the corner and scare you. I hope that's what you guys are into.

All story commentary aside, at the very least, even if you hate the thing... you've got to admit... it at least looks good. I've been working with Tony Moore for as long as I can remember. I've SEEN Tony's work, I KNOW Tony's work, I know it better than anyone, and I've got to say... just in case you didn't notice... Tony really pulled out all the stops on this one. I can really tell that he shares my immense love for the subject matter. This book is really a thing of beauty. I couldn't be more pleased with how it turned out. I hope you all agree.

For me the worst part of every zombie movie is the end. I always want to know what happens next. Even when all the characters die at the end... I just want it to keep going.

More often than not, zombie movies feel like a slice of a person's life shown until whoever is in charge of the movie gets bored. So we get to know the character, they have an adventure and then, BOOM, as soon as things start getting good... those pesky credits start rolling.

The idea behind **THE WALKING DEAD** is to stay with the character, in this case, Rick Grimes for as long as is humanly possible. I want The Walking Dead to be a chronicle of years of Rick's life. We will NEVER wonder what happens to Rick next, we will see it. The Walking Dead will be the zombie movie that never ends.

Well... not for a good long time at least.

-Robert Kirkman

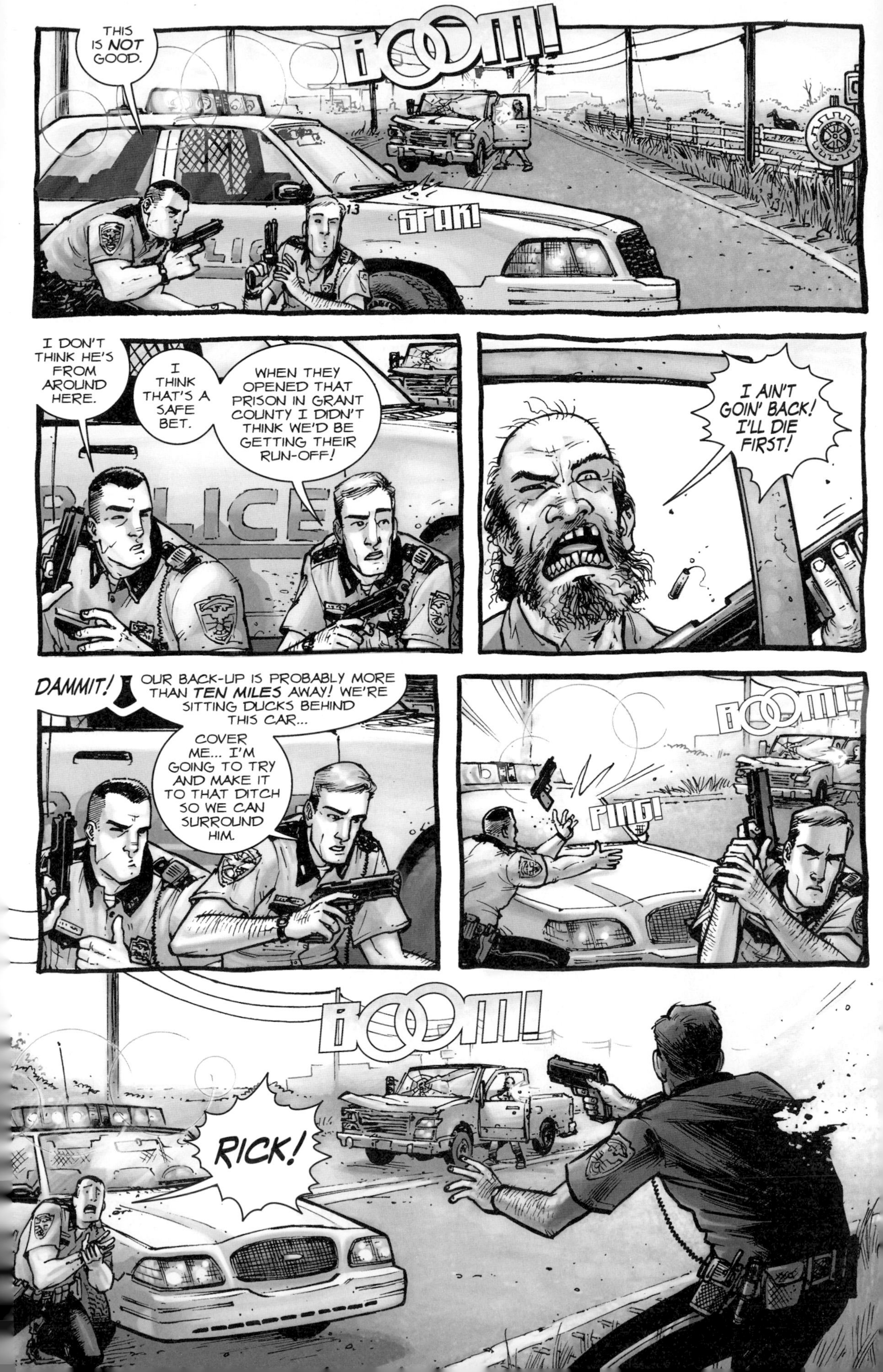
THIS IS NOT GOOD.
BOOM!
SPAK!
I DON'T THINK HE'S FROM AROUND HERE.
I THINK THAT'S A SAFE BET.
WHEN THEY OPENED THAT PRISON IN GRANT COUNTY I DIDN'T THINK WE'D BE GETTING THEIR RUN-OFF!
I AIN'T GOIN' BACK! I'LL DIE FIRST!
DAMMIT!
OUR BACK-UP IS PROBABLY MORE THAN TEN MILES AWAY! WE'RE SITTING DUCKS BEHIND THIS CAR...
COVER ME... I'M GOING TO TRY AND MAKE IT TO THAT DITCH SO WE CAN SURROUND HIM.
BOOM!
PING!
BOOM!
RICK!

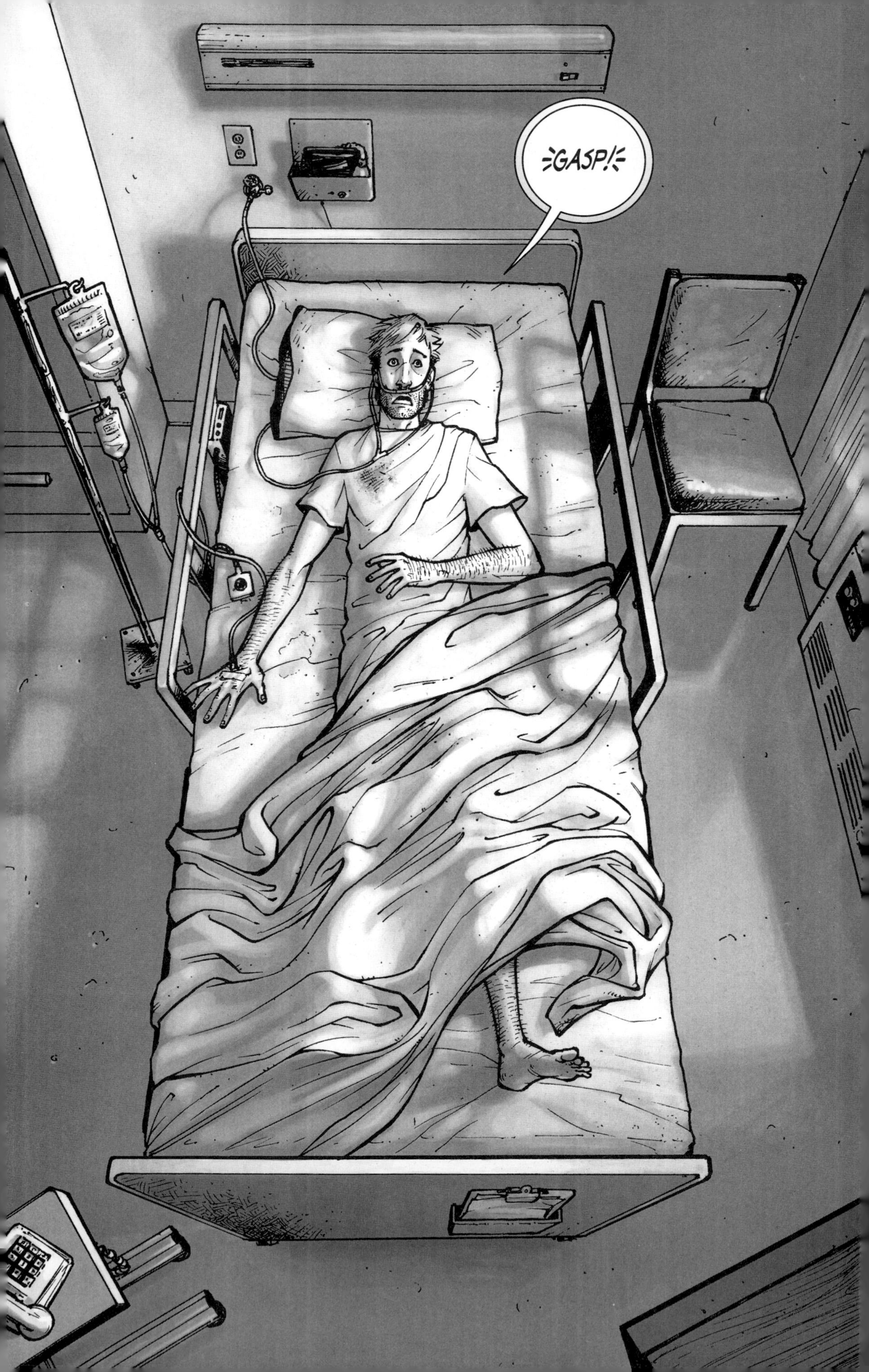
GASP!

NURSE!

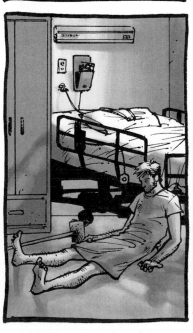
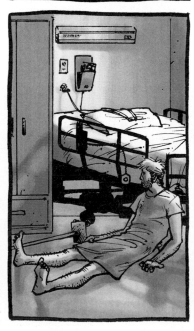

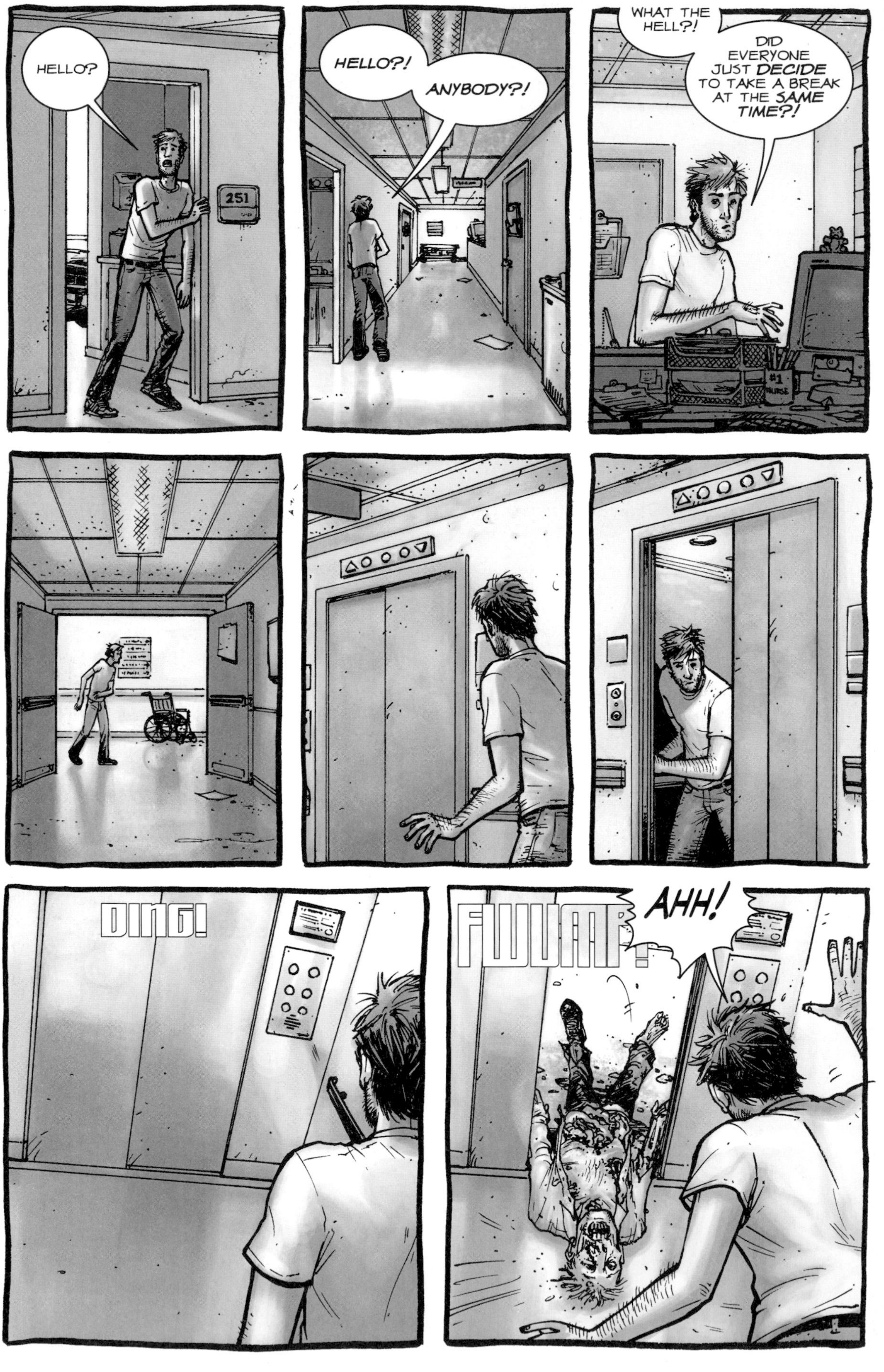
HELLO?
HELLO?!
ANYBODY?!
WHAT THE HELL?!
DID EVERYONE JUST DECIDE TO TAKE A BREAK AT THE SAME TIME?!
DING!
FWUMP!
AHH!

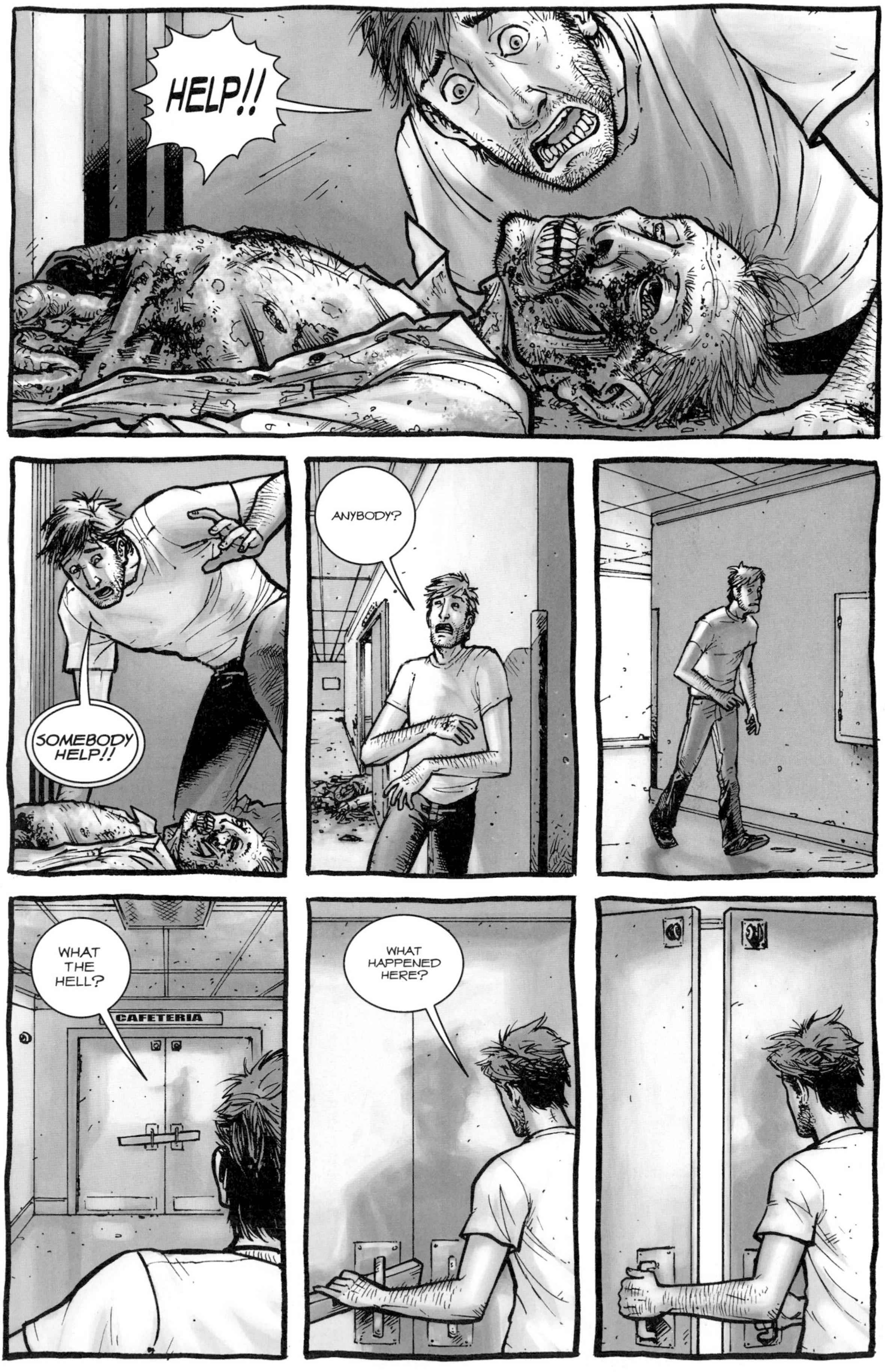
HELP!!
SOMEBODY HELP!!
ANYBODY?
WHAT THE HELL?
CAFETERIA
WHAT HAPPENED HERE?

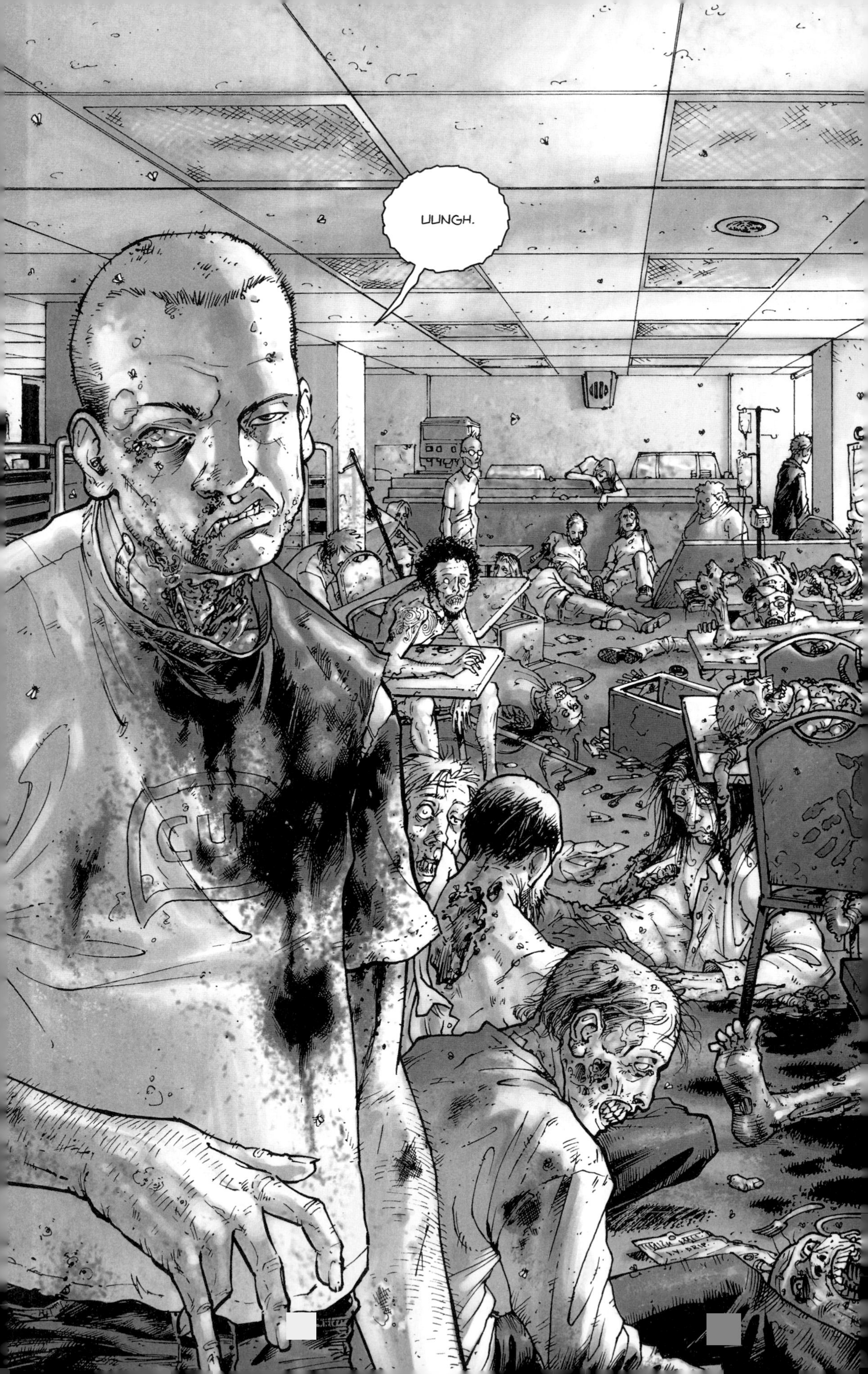
UUNGH.

UH.
UH.
UH.
UFF!
THAP!
STOP!
GET AWAY FROM ME!
CAN'T YOU UNDER-STAND?!
FWUMP!
PLEASE!
WHUMP!
SNAP!

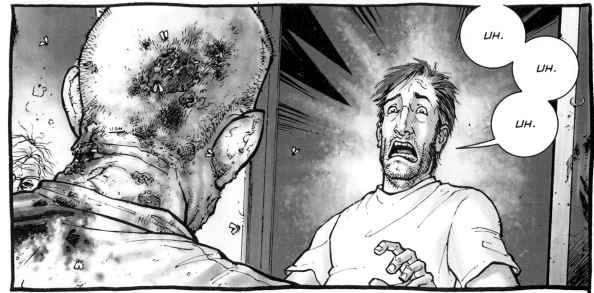

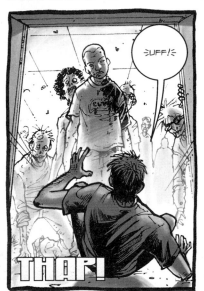

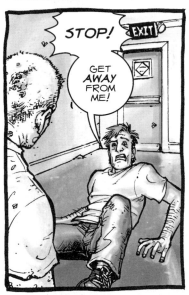

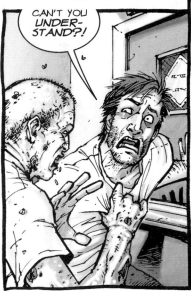

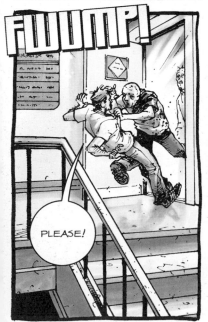

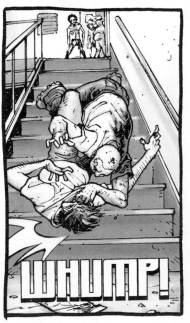

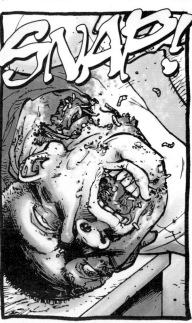

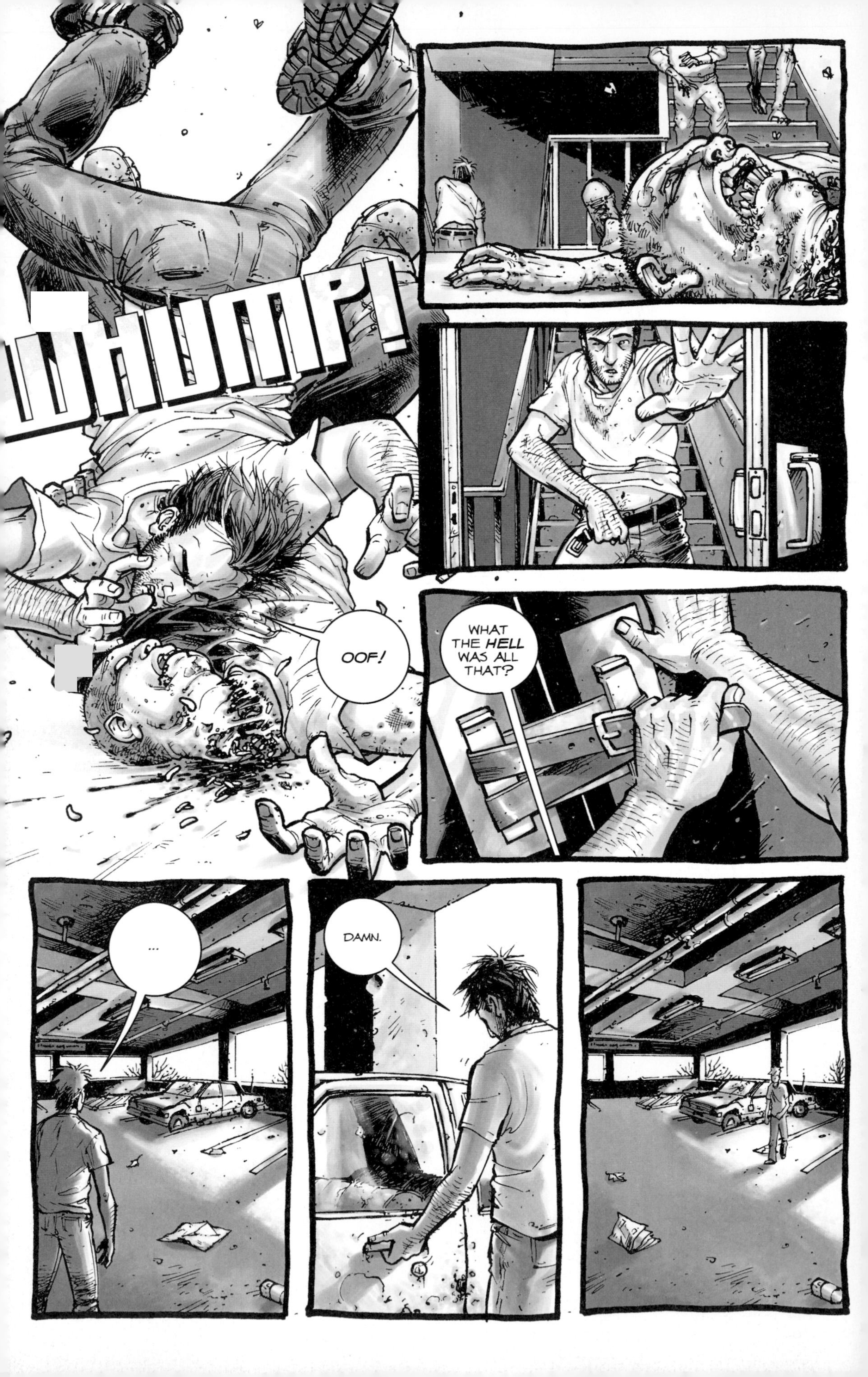
WHUMP!
OOF!
WHAT THE HELL WAS ALL THAT?
...
DAMN.

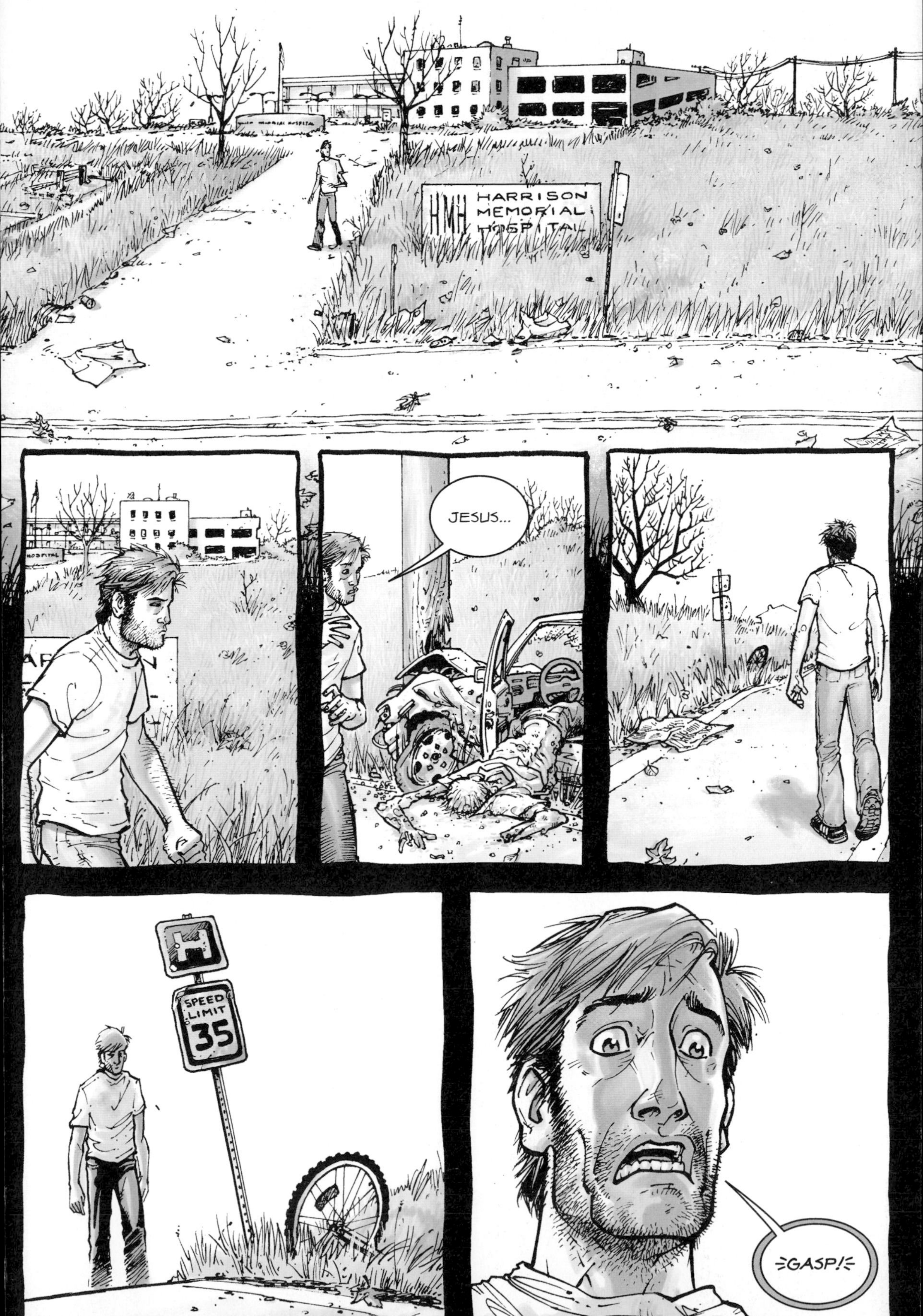
HMH
HARRISON
MEMORIAL
HOSPITAL
JESUS...
SPEED
LIMIT
35
GASP!

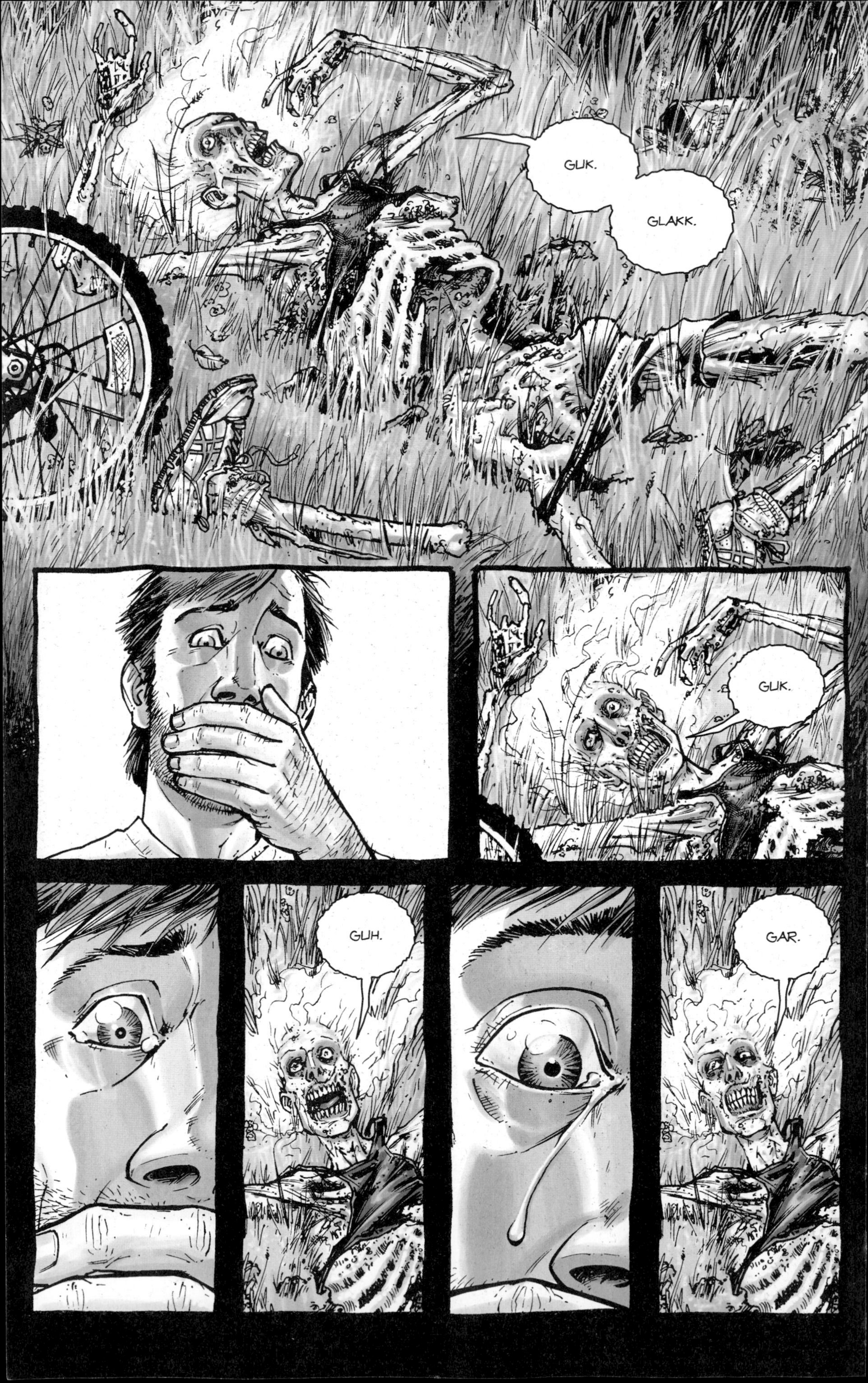
GUK.
GLAKK.
GUK.
GUH.
GAR.

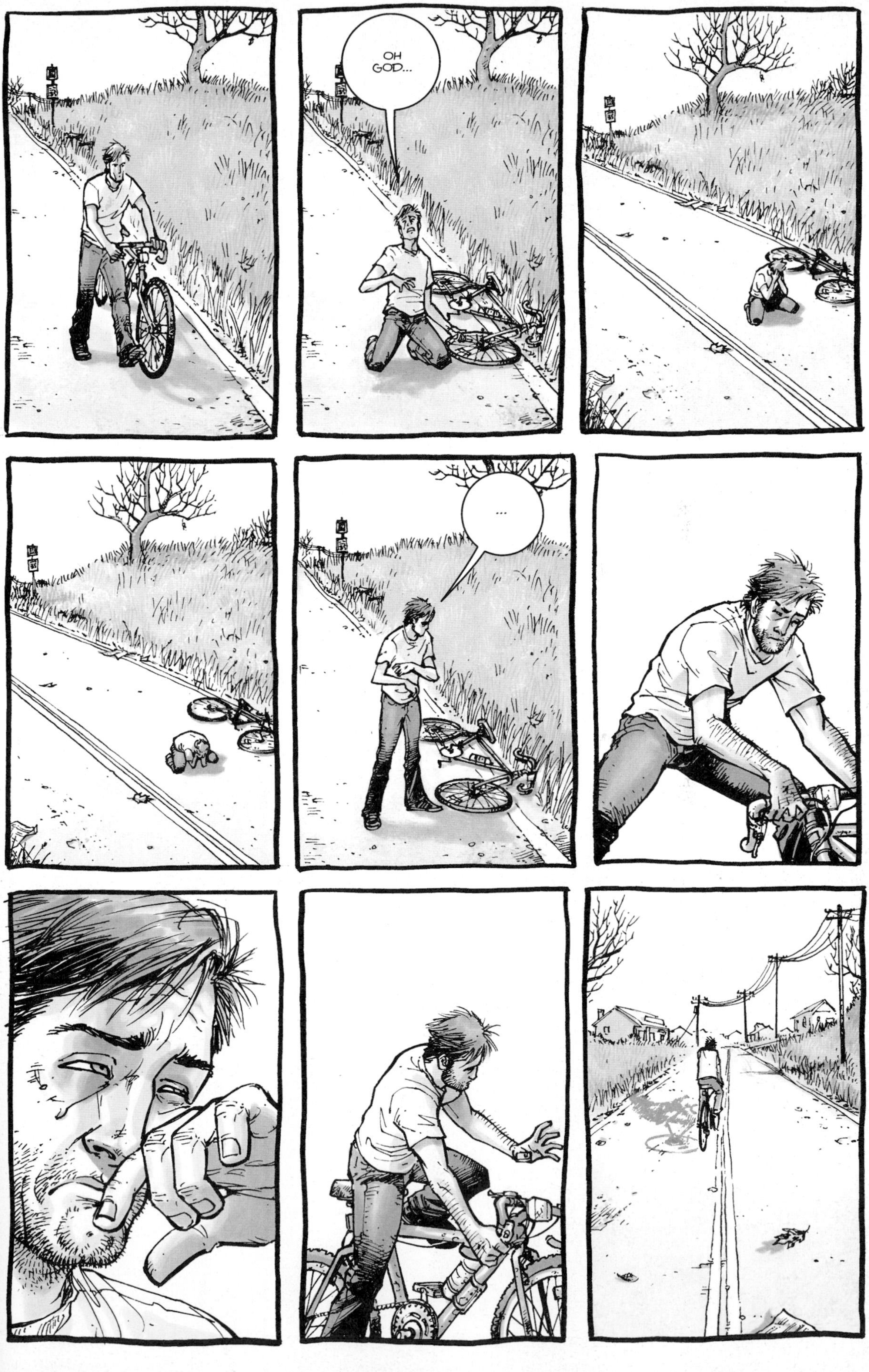

OH GOD...
...

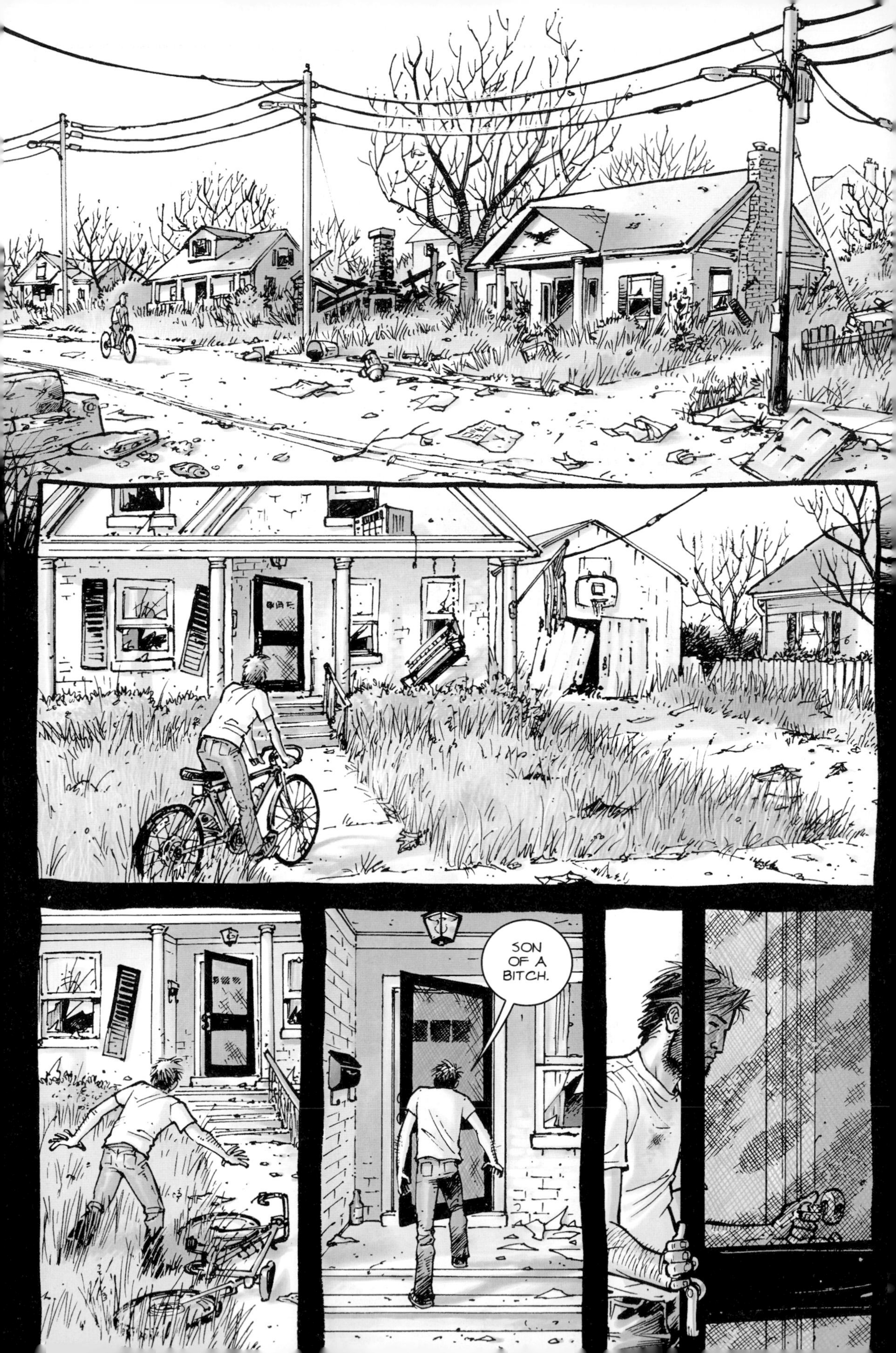
SON OF A BITCH.

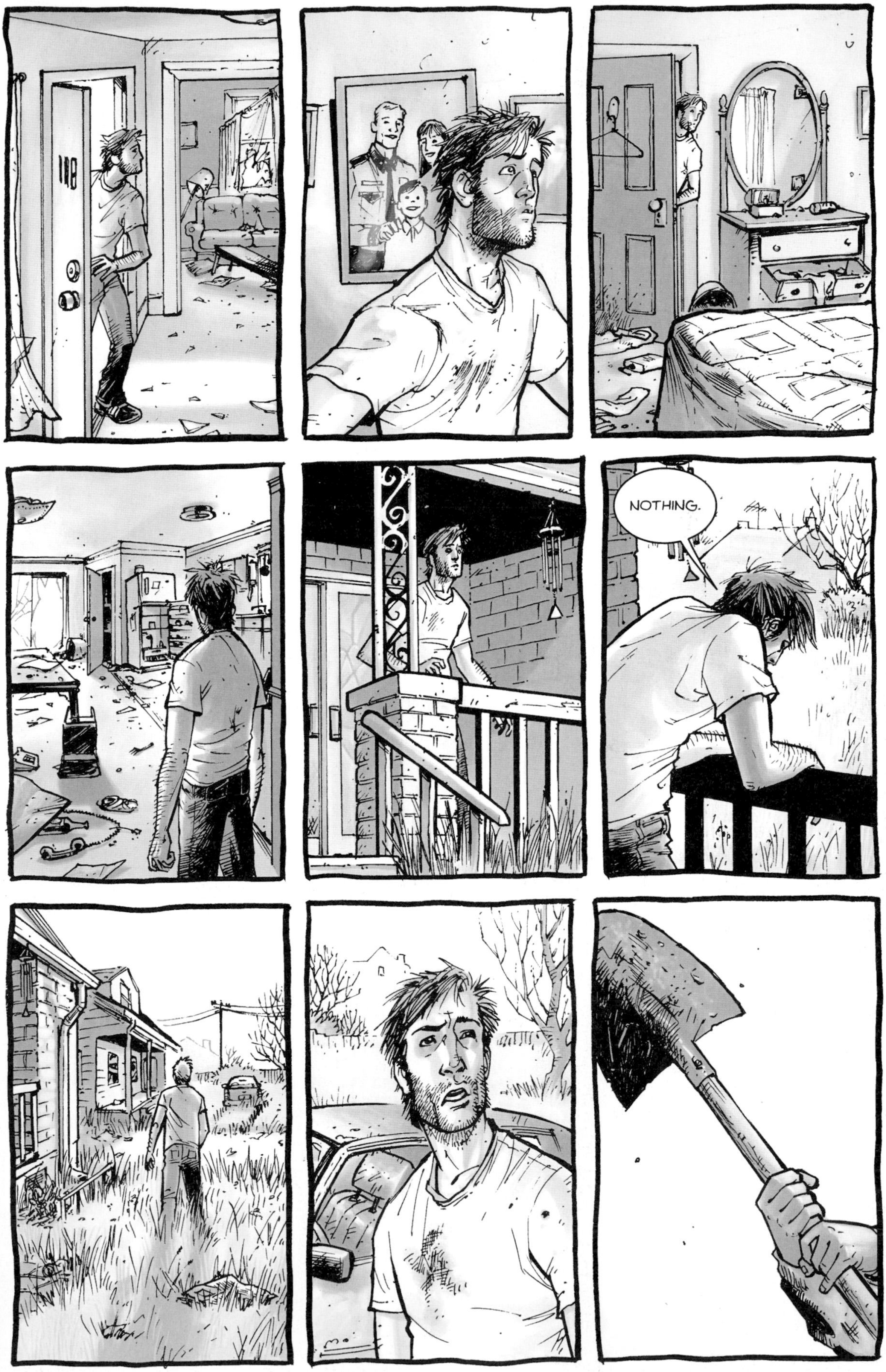
NOTHING.

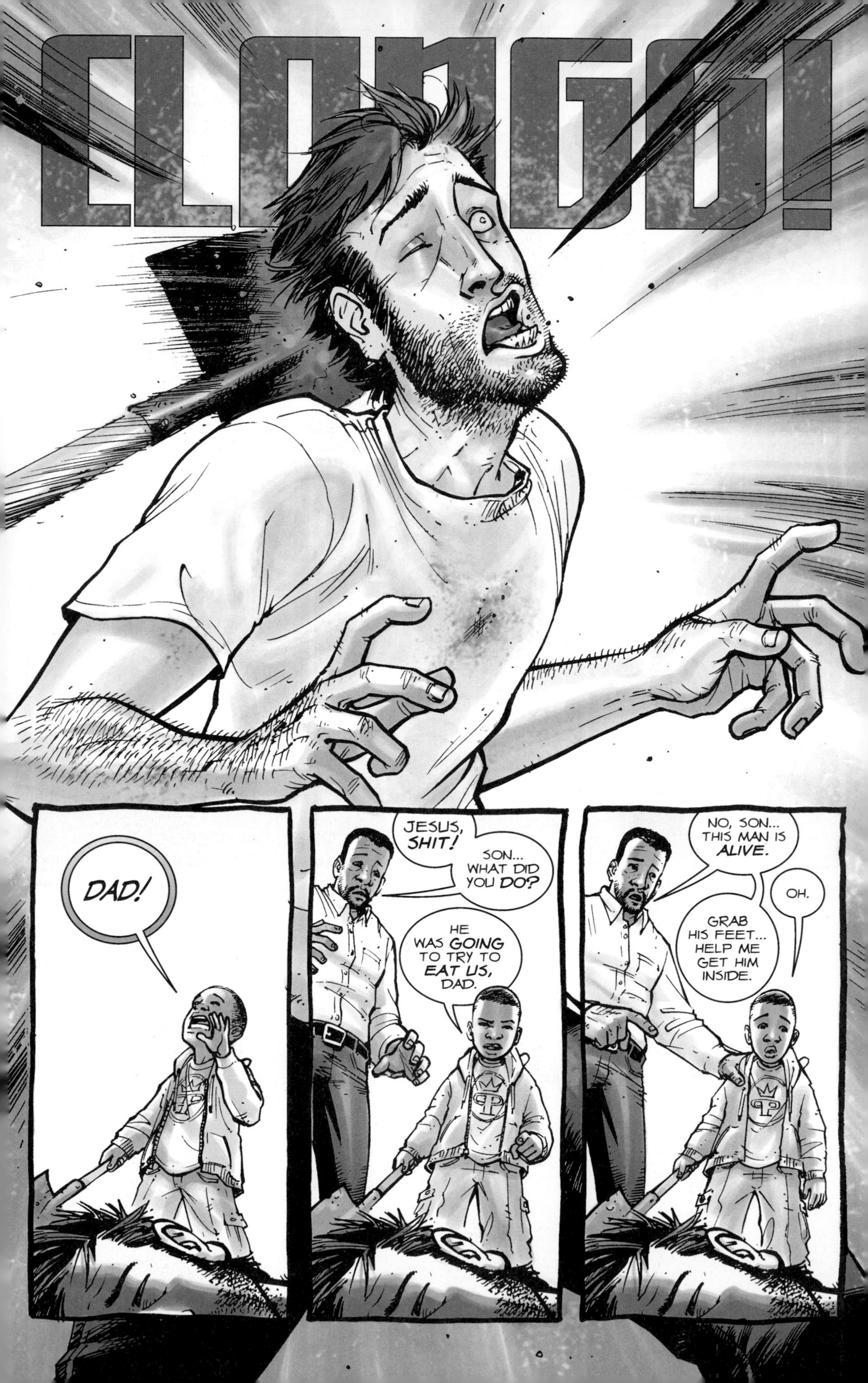
CLONGG!
DAD!
JESUS, SHIT!
SON... WHAT DID YOU DO?
HE WAS GOING TO TRY TO EAT US, DAD.
NO, SON... THIS MAN IS ALIVE.
OH.
GRAB HIS FEET... HELP ME GET HIM INSIDE.

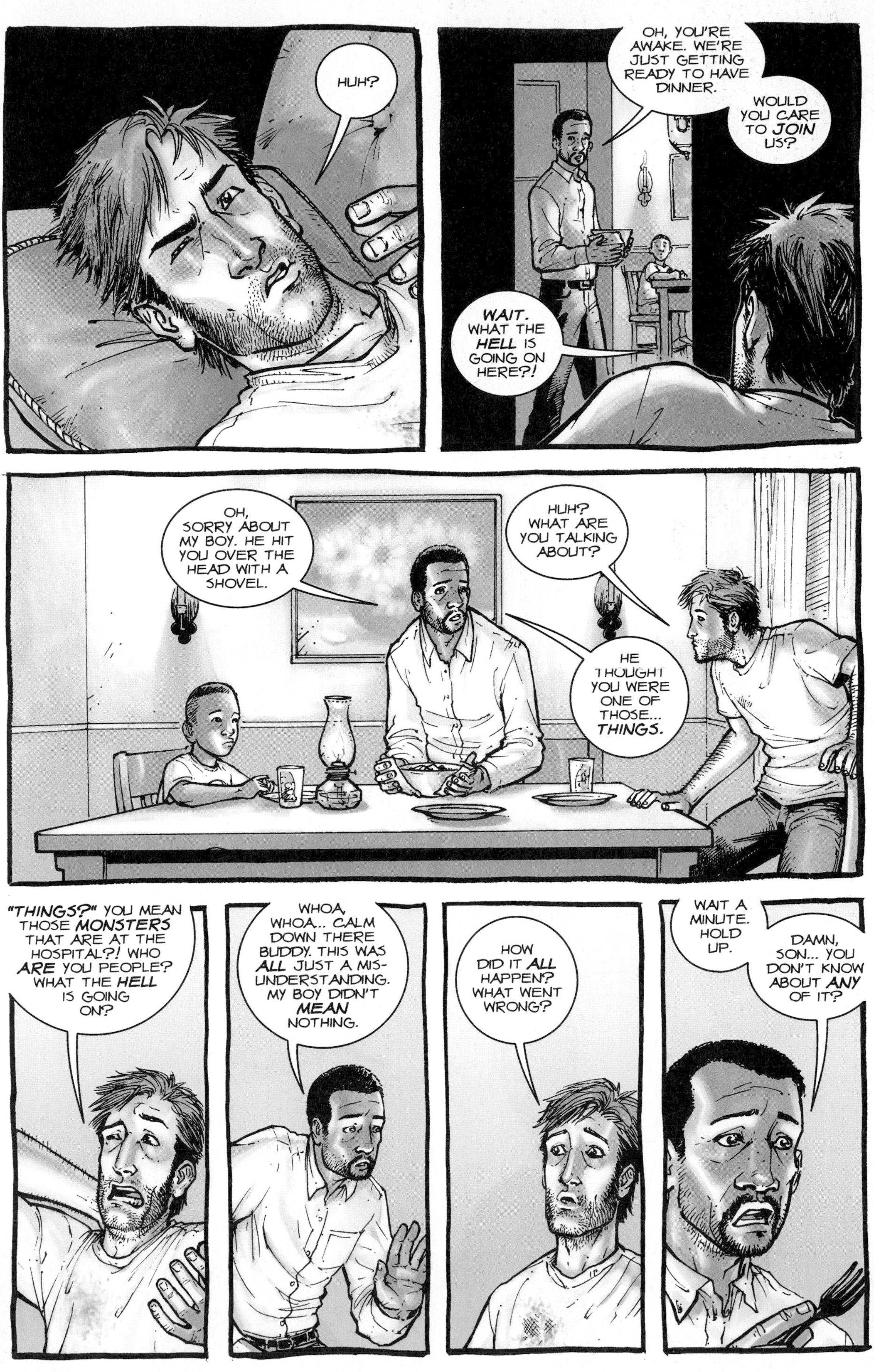
HUH?
OH, YOU'RE AWAKE. WE'RE JUST GETTING READY TO HAVE DINNER.
WOULD YOU CARE TO JOIN US?
WAIT. WHAT THE HELL IS GOING ON HERE?!
OH, SORRY ABOUT MY BOY. HE HIT YOU OVER THE HEAD WITH A SHOVEL.
HUH? WHAT ARE YOU TALKING ABOUT?
HE THOUGHT YOU WERE ONE OF THOSE... THINGS.
"THINGS?" YOU MEAN THOSE MONSTERS THAT ARE AT THE HOSPITAL?! WHO ARE YOU PEOPLE? WHAT THE HELL IS GOING ON?
WHOA, WHOA... CALM DOWN THERE BUDDY. THIS WAS ALL JUST A MIS-UNDERSTANDING. MY BOY DIDN'T MEAN NOTHING.
HOW DID IT ALL HAPPEN? WHAT WENT WRONG?
WAIT A MINUTE. HOLD UP.
DAMN, SON... YOU DON'T KNOW ABOUT ANY OF IT?

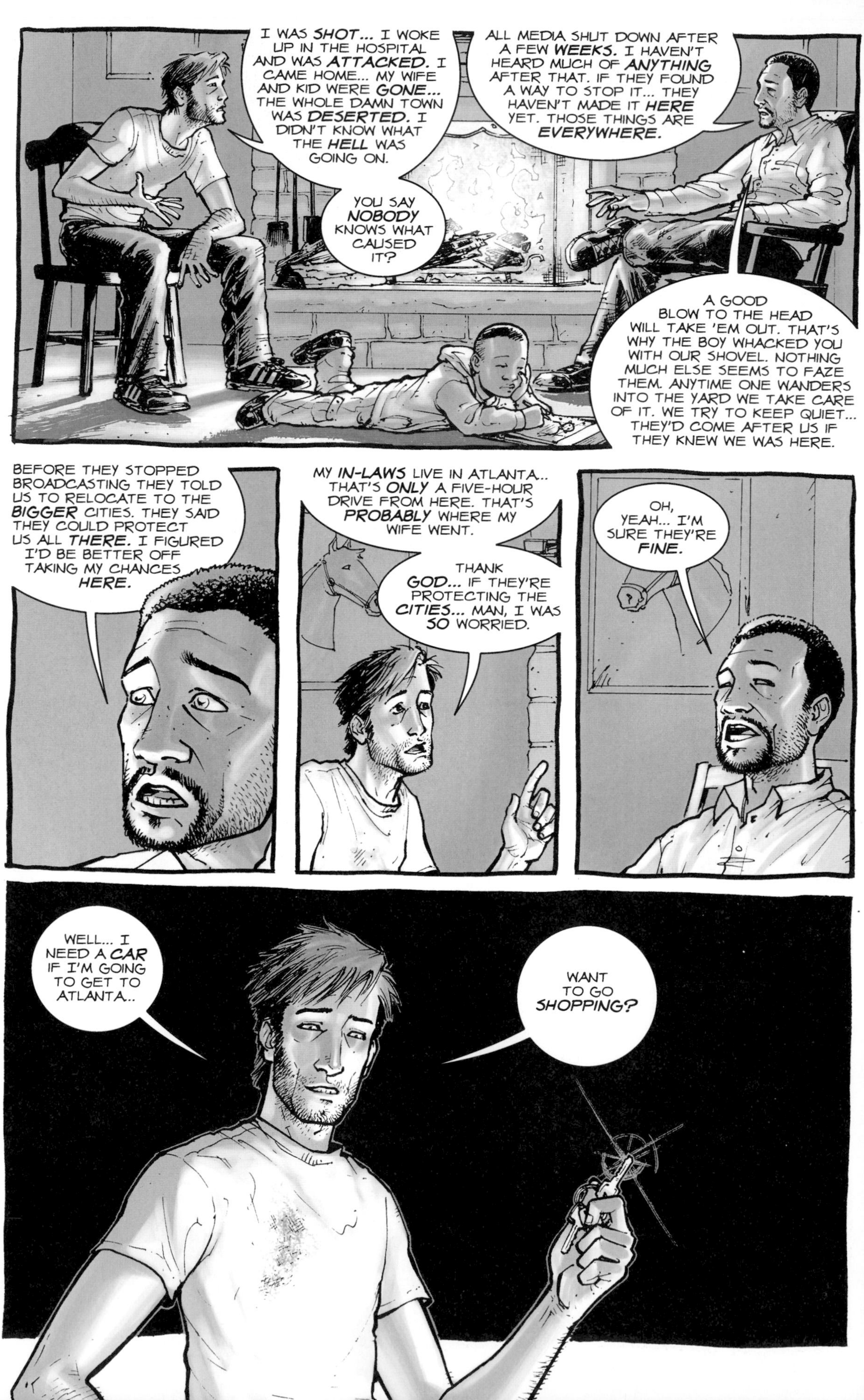
I WAS SHOT... I WOKE UP IN THE HOSPITAL AND WAS ATTACKED. I CAME HOME... MY WIFE AND KID WERE GONE... THE WHOLE DAMN TOWN WAS DESERTED. I DIDN'T KNOW WHAT THE HELL WAS GOING ON.
ALL MEDIA SHUT DOWN AFTER A FEW WEEKS. I HAVEN'T HEARD MUCH OF ANYTHING AFTER THAT. IF THEY FOUND A WAY TO STOP IT... THEY HAVEN'T MADE IT HERE YET. THOSE THINGS ARE EVERYWHERE.
YOU SAY NOBODY KNOWS WHAT CAUSED IT?
A GOOD BLOW TO THE HEAD WILL TAKE 'EM OUT. THAT'S WHY THE BOY WHACKED YOU WITH OUR SHOVEL. NOTHING MUCH ELSE SEEMS TO FAZE THEM. ANYTIME ONE WANDERS INTO THE YARD WE TAKE CARE OF IT. WE TRY TO KEEP QUIET... THEY'D COME AFTER US IF THEY KNEW WE WAS HERE.
BEFORE THEY STOPPED BROADCASTING THEY TOLD US TO RELOCATE TO THE BIGGER CITIES. THEY SAID THEY COULD PROTECT US ALL THERE. I FIGURED I'D BE BETTER OFF TAKING MY CHANCES HERE.
MY IN-LAWS LIVE IN ATLANTA.. THAT'S ONLY A FIVE-HOUR DRIVE FROM HERE. THAT'S PROBABLY WHERE MY WIFE WENT.
THANK GOD... IF THEY'RE PROTECTING THE CITIES... MAN, I WAS SO WORRIED.
OH, YEAH... I'M SURE THEY'RE FINE.
WELL... I NEED A CAR IF I'M GOING TO GET TO ATLANTA..
WANT TO GO SHOPPING?

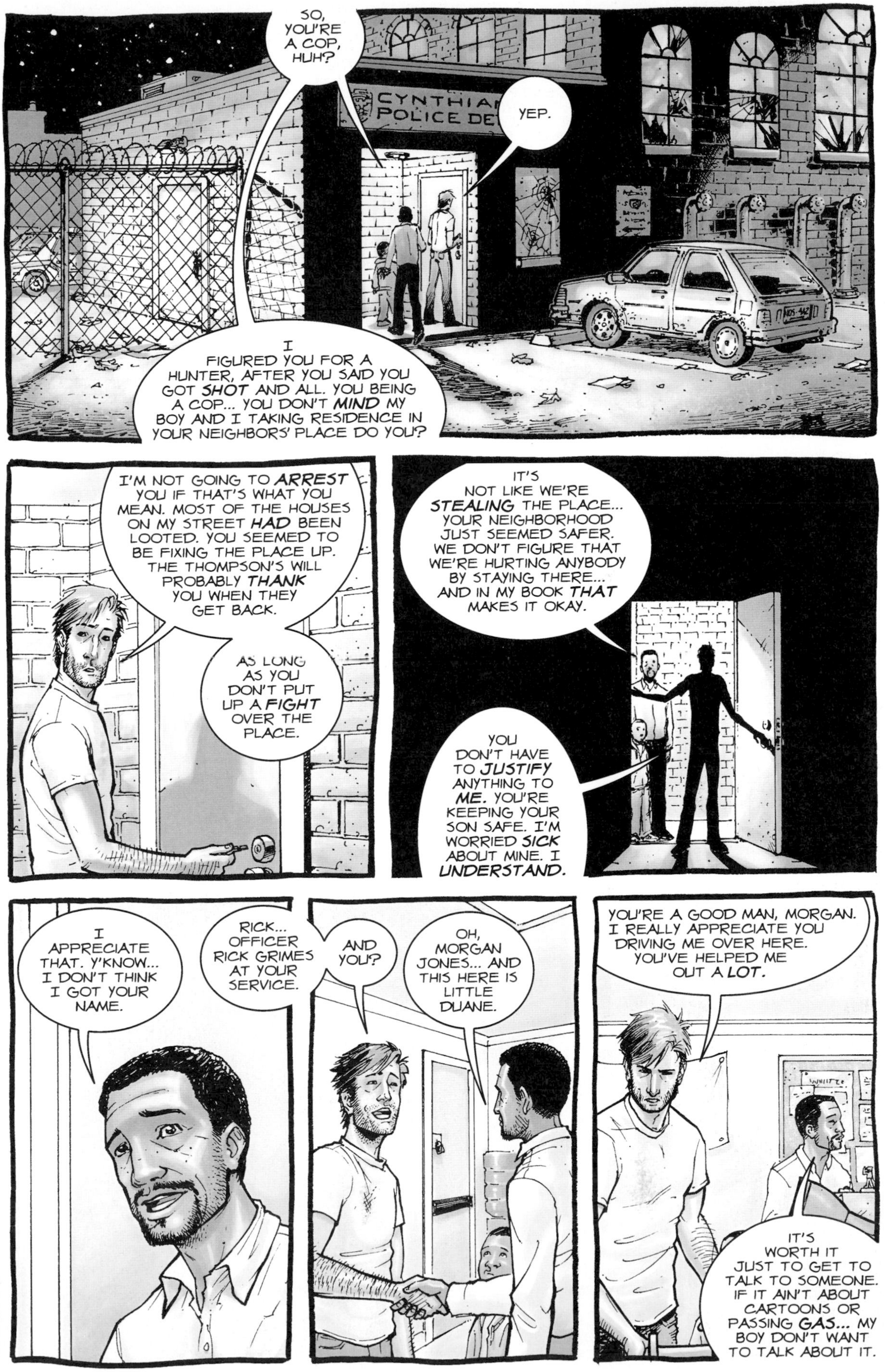
SO, YOU'RE A COP, HUH?
CYNTHIAN POLICE DE
YEP.
I FIGURED YOU FOR A HUNTER, AFTER YOU SAID YOU GOT SHOT AND ALL. YOU BEING A COP... YOU DON'T MIND MY BOY AND I TAKING RESIDENCE IN YOUR NEIGHBORS' PLACE DO YOU?
I'M NOT GOING TO ARREST YOU IF THAT'S WHAT YOU MEAN. MOST OF THE HOUSES ON MY STREET HAD BEEN LOOTED. YOU SEEMED TO BE FIXING THE PLACE UP. THE THOMPSON'S WILL PROBABLY THANK YOU WHEN THEY GET BACK.
AS LONG AS YOU DON'T PUT UP A FIGHT OVER THE PLACE.
IT'S NOT LIKE WE'RE STEALING THE PLACE... YOUR NEIGHBORHOOD JUST SEEMED SAFER. WE DON'T FIGURE THAT WE'RE HURTING ANYBODY BY STAYING THERE... AND IN MY BOOK THAT MAKES IT OKAY.
YOU DON'T HAVE TO JUSTIFY ANYTHING TO ME. YOU'RE KEEPING YOUR SON SAFE. I'M WORRIED SICK ABOUT MINE. I UNDERSTAND.
I APPRECIATE THAT. Y'KNOW... I DON'T THINK I GOT YOUR NAME.
RICK... OFFICER RICK GRIMES AT YOUR SERVICE.
AND YOU?
OH, MORGAN JONES... AND THIS HERE IS LITTLE DUANE.
YOU'RE A GOOD MAN, MORGAN. I REALLY APPRECIATE YOU DRIVING ME OVER HERE. YOU'VE HELPED ME OUT A LOT.
IT'S WORTH IT JUST TO GET TO TALK TO SOMEONE. IF IT AIN'T ABOUT CARTOONS OR PASSING GAS... MY BOY DON'T WANT TO TALK ABOUT IT.

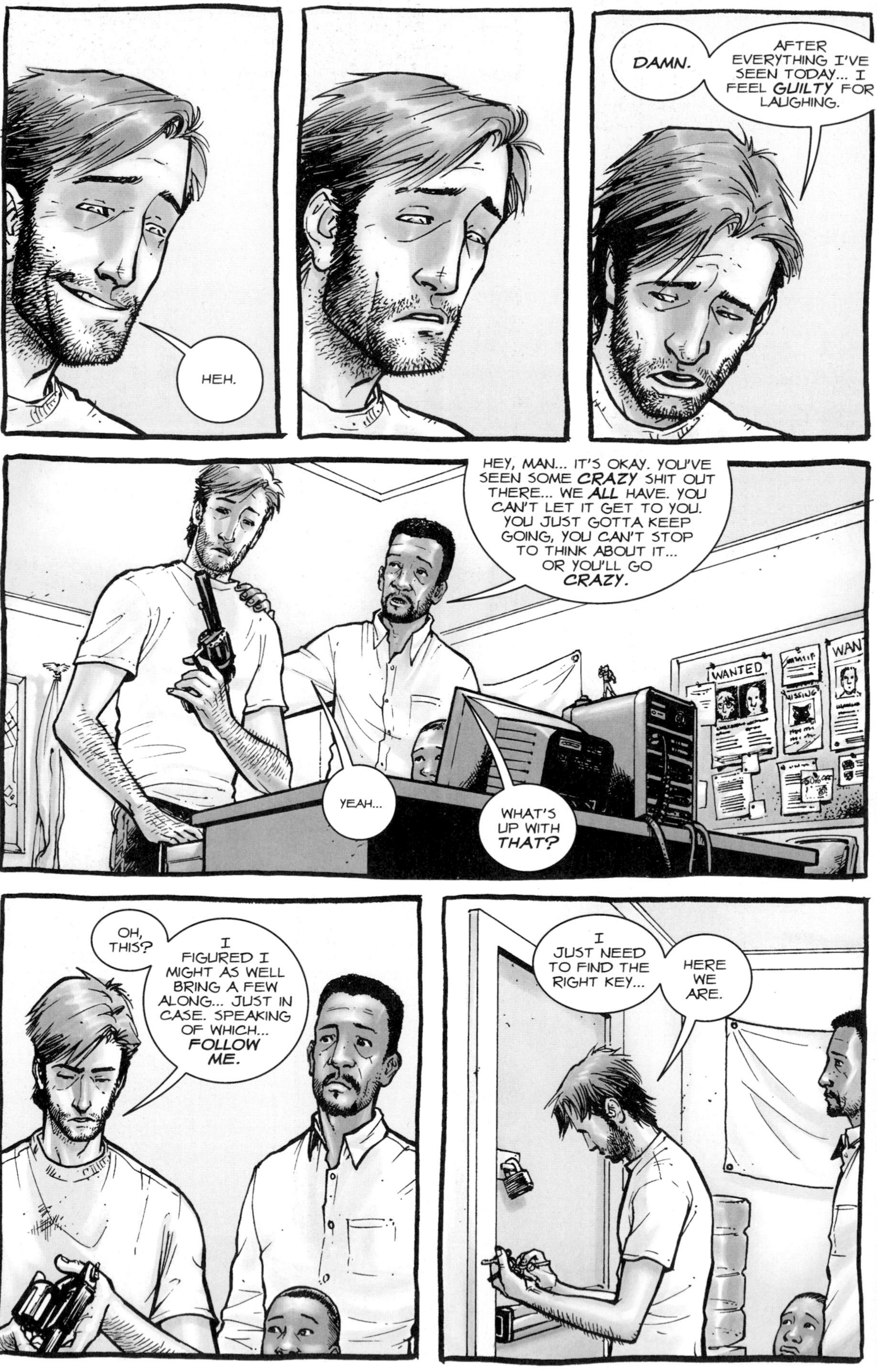
HEH.
DAMN.
AFTER EVERYTHING I'VE SEEN TODAY... I FEEL GUILTY FOR LAUGHING.
HEY, MAN... IT'S OKAY. YOU'VE SEEN SOME CRAZY SHIT OUT THERE... WE ALL HAVE. YOU CAN'T LET IT GET TO YOU. YOU JUST GOTTA KEEP GOING, YOU CAN'T STOP TO THINK ABOUT IT... OR YOU'LL GO CRAZY.
YEAH...
WHAT'S UP WITH THAT?
WANTED
OH, THIS?
I FIGURED I MIGHT AS WELL BRING A FEW ALONG... JUST IN CASE. SPEAKING OF WHICH... FOLLOW ME.
I JUST NEED TO FIND THE RIGHT KEY...
HERE WE ARE.

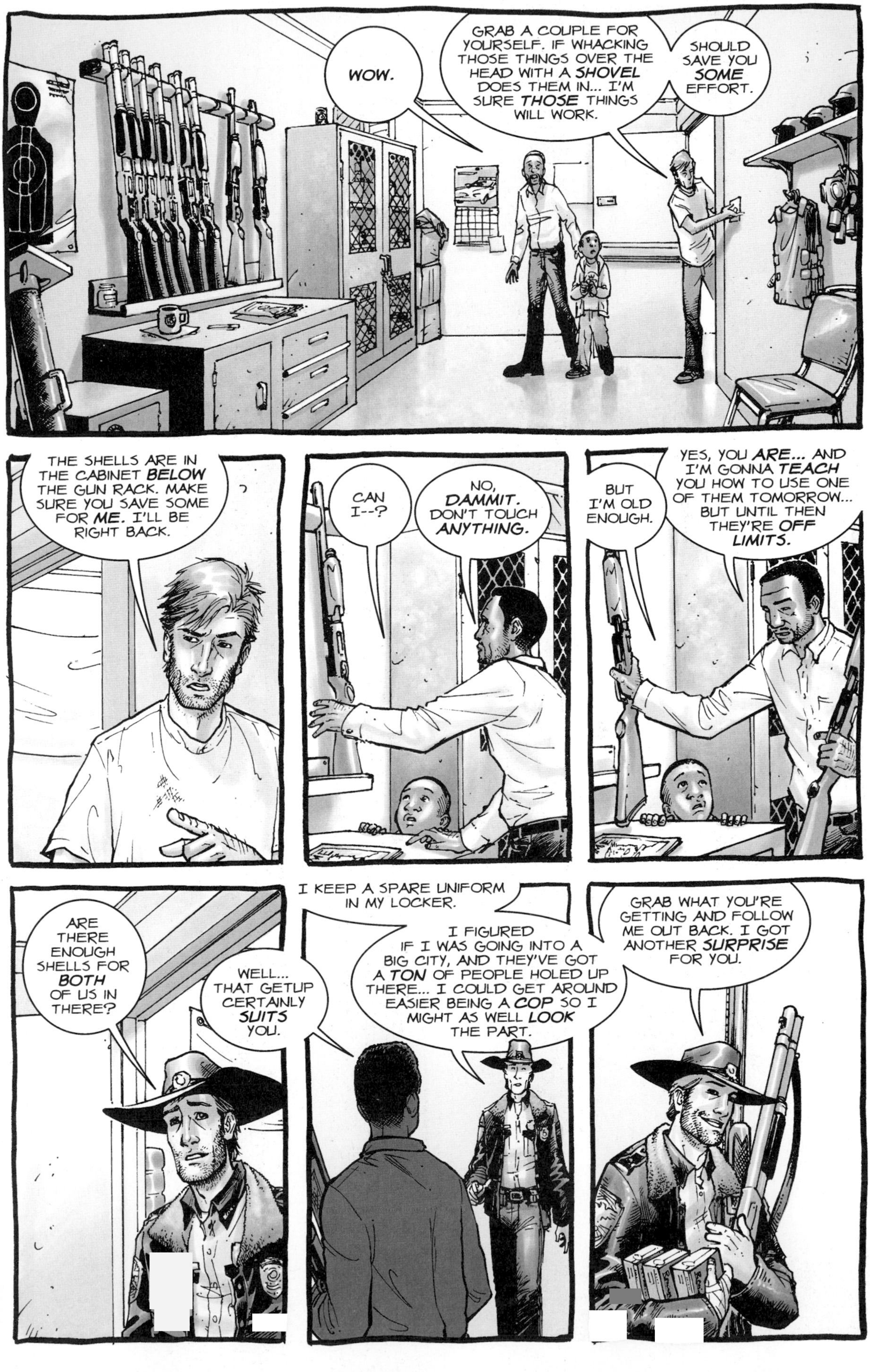
WOW.
GRAB A COUPLE FOR YOURSELF. IF WHACKING THOSE THINGS OVER THE HEAD WITH A SHOVEL DOES THEM IN... I'M SURE THOSE THINGS WILL WORK.
SHOULD SAVE YOU SOME EFFORT.
THE SHELLS ARE IN THE CABINET BELOW THE GUN RACK. MAKE SURE YOU SAVE SOME FOR ME. I'LL BE RIGHT BACK.
CAN I--?
NO, DAMMIT. DON'T TOUCH ANYTHING.
BUT I'M OLD ENOUGH.
YES, YOU ARE... AND I'M GONNA TEACH YOU HOW TO USE ONE OF THEM TOMORROW... BUT UNTIL THEN THEY'RE OFF LIMITS.
ARE THERE ENOUGH SHELLS FOR BOTH OF US IN THERE?
WELL... THAT GETUP CERTAINLY SUITS YOU.
I KEEP A SPARE UNIFORM IN MY LOCKER.
I FIGURED IF I WAS GOING INTO A BIG CITY, AND THEY'VE GOT A TON OF PEOPLE HOLED UP THERE... I COULD GET AROUND EASIER BEING A COP SO I MIGHT AS WELL LOOK THE PART.
GRAB WHAT YOU'RE GETTING AND FOLLOW ME OUT BACK. I GOT ANOTHER SURPRISE FOR YOU.

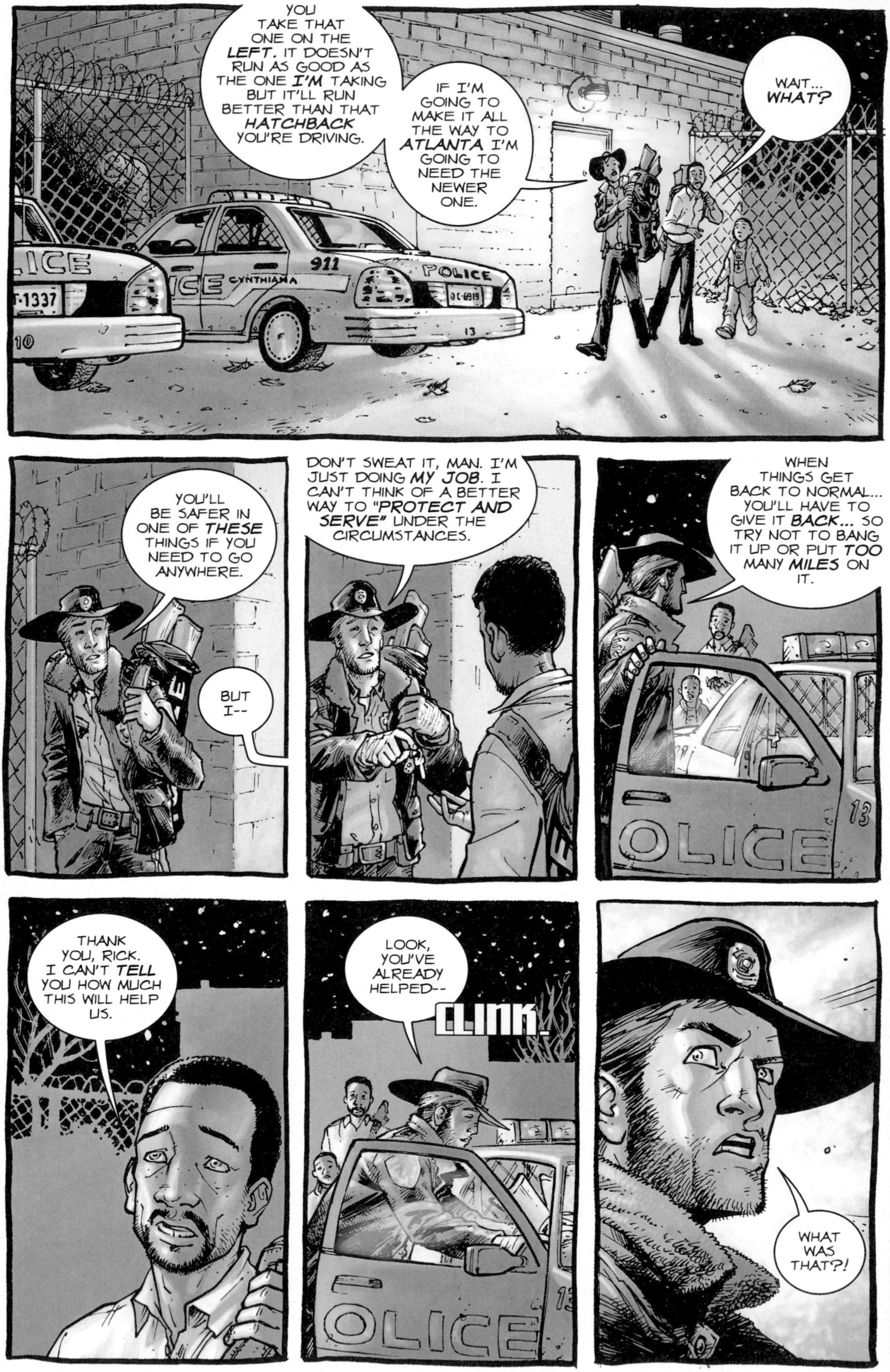
YOU TAKE THAT ONE ON THE LEFT. IT DOESN'T RUN AS GOOD AS THE ONE I'M TAKING BUT IT'LL RUN BETTER THAN THAT HATCHBACK YOU'RE DRIVING.
IF I'M GOING TO MAKE IT ALL THE WAY TO ATLANTA I'M GOING TO NEED THE NEWER ONE.
WAIT... WHAT?
POLICE
CYNTHIANA
911
YOU'LL BE SAFER IN ONE OF THESE THINGS IF YOU NEED TO GO ANYWHERE.
BUT I--
DON'T SWEAT IT, MAN. I'M JUST DOING MY JOB. I CAN'T THINK OF A BETTER WAY TO "PROTECT AND SERVE" UNDER THE CIRCUMSTANCES.
WHEN THINGS GET BACK TO NORMAL... YOU'LL HAVE TO GIVE IT BACK... SO TRY NOT TO BANG IT UP OR PUT TOO MANY MILES ON IT.
OLICE
THANK YOU, RICK. I CAN'T TELL YOU HOW MUCH THIS WILL HELP US.
LOOK, YOU'VE ALREADY HELPED--
CLINK.
OLICE
WHAT WAS THAT?!

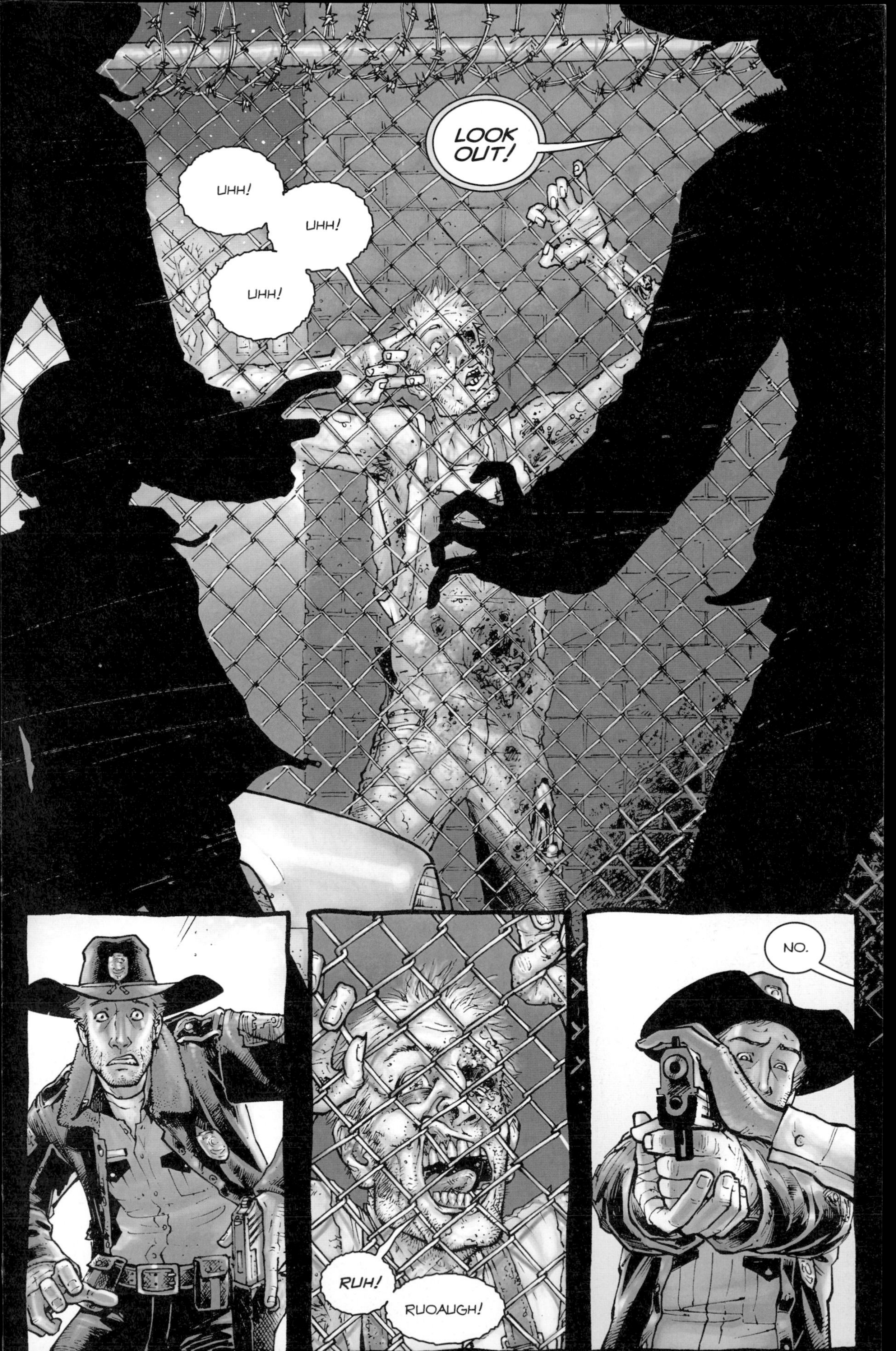

LOOK OUT!
UHH!
UHH!
UHH!
RUH!
RUOAUGH!
NO.

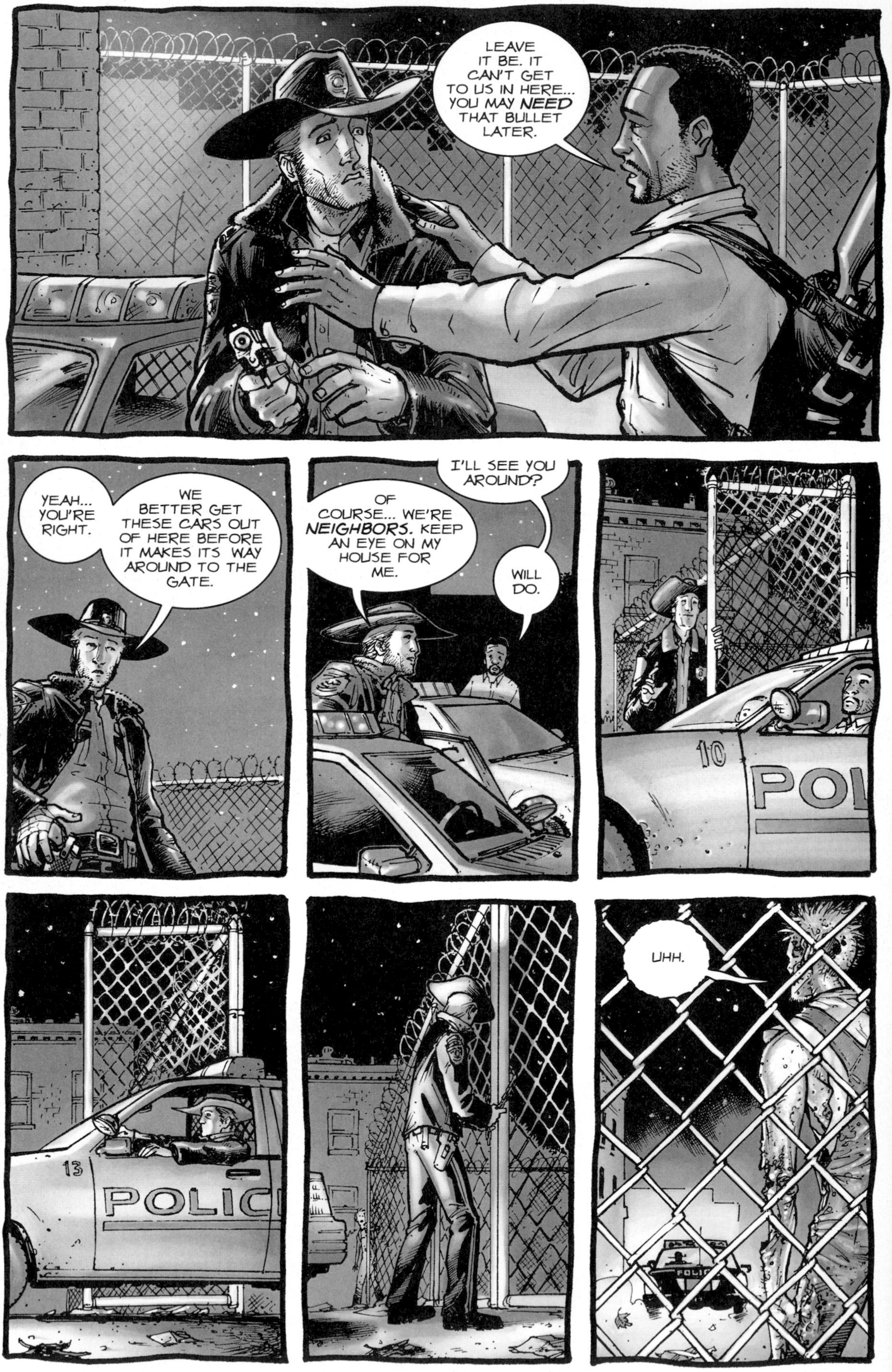

LEAVE IT BE. IT CAN'T GET TO US IN HERE... YOU MAY NEED THAT BULLET LATER.
YEAH... YOU'RE RIGHT.
WE BETTER GET THESE CARS OUT OF HERE BEFORE IT MAKES ITS WAY AROUND TO THE GATE.
OF COURSE... WE'RE NEIGHBORS. KEEP AN EYE ON MY HOUSE FOR ME.
I'LL SEE YOU AROUND?
WILL DO.
10
POLI
13
POLIC
POLIC
UHH.

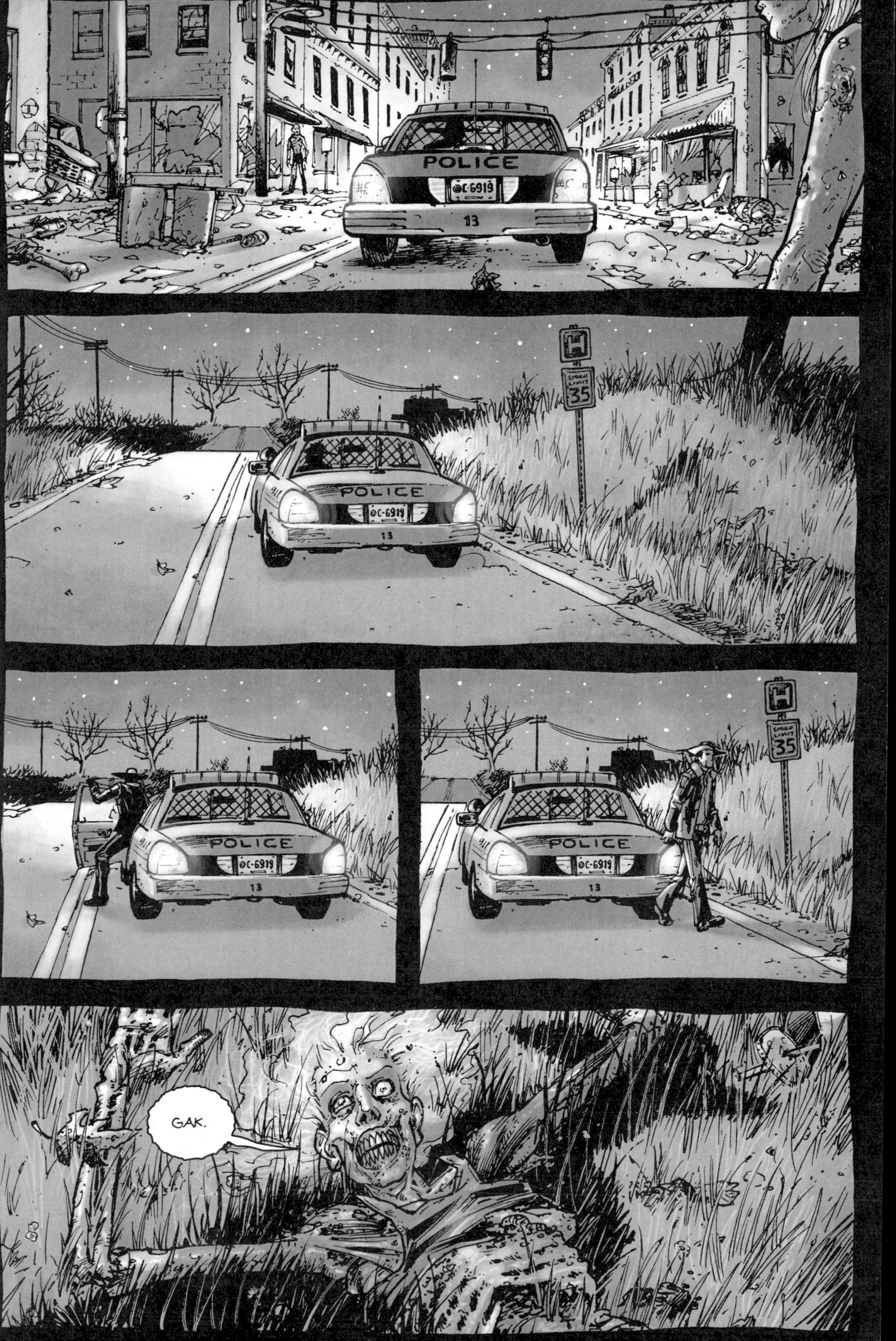
POLICE
C-6919
13
POLICE
C-6919
13
35
POLICE
C-6919
13
POLICE
C-6919
13
35
GAK.

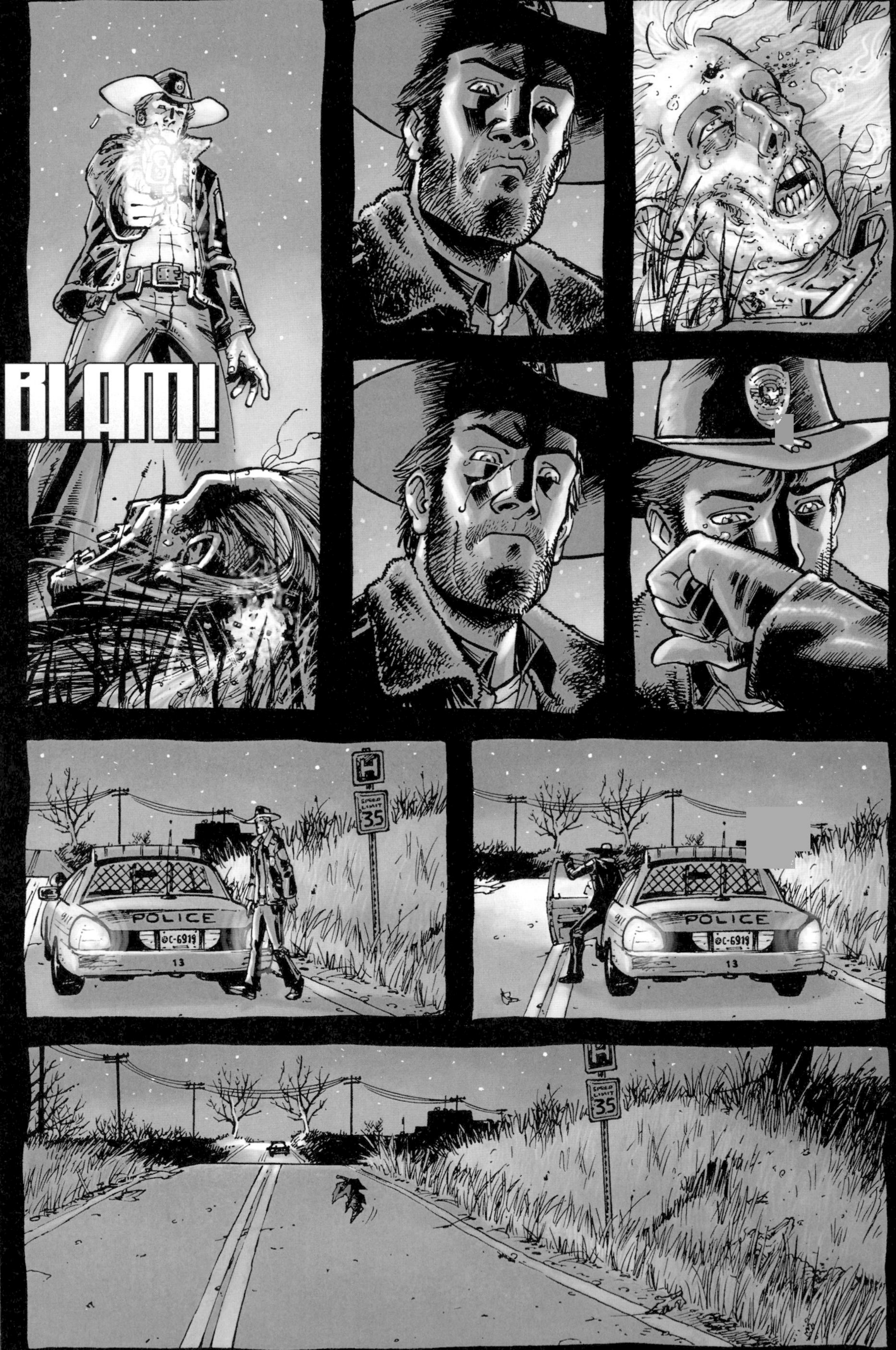
BLAM!
SPEED LIMIT 35
POLICE
C-6919
13
POLICE
C-6919
13
SPEED LIMIT 35

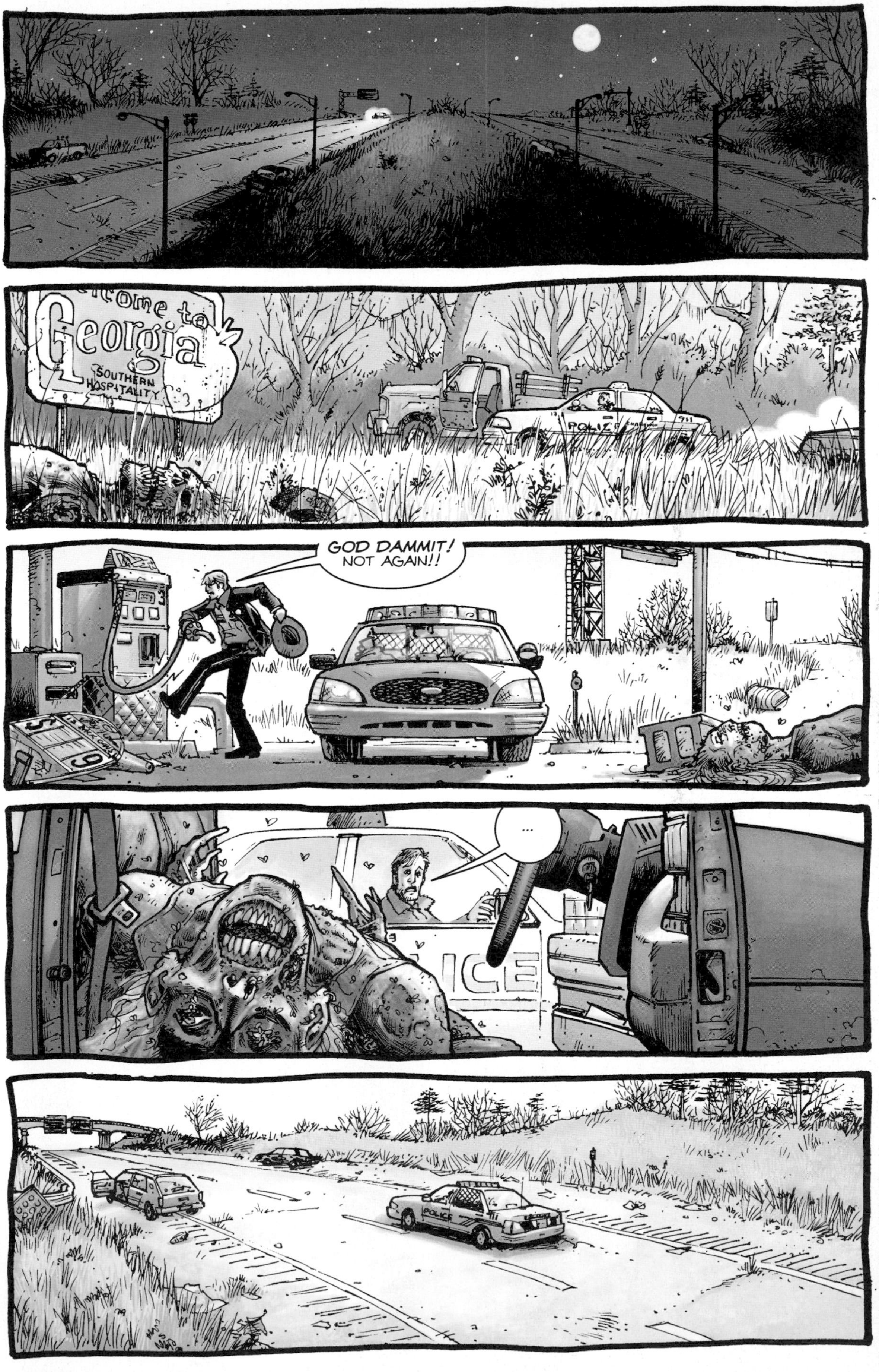
lcome to
Georgia
SOUTHERN
HOSPITALITY
GOD DAMMIT!
NOT AGAIN!!
...
POLICE

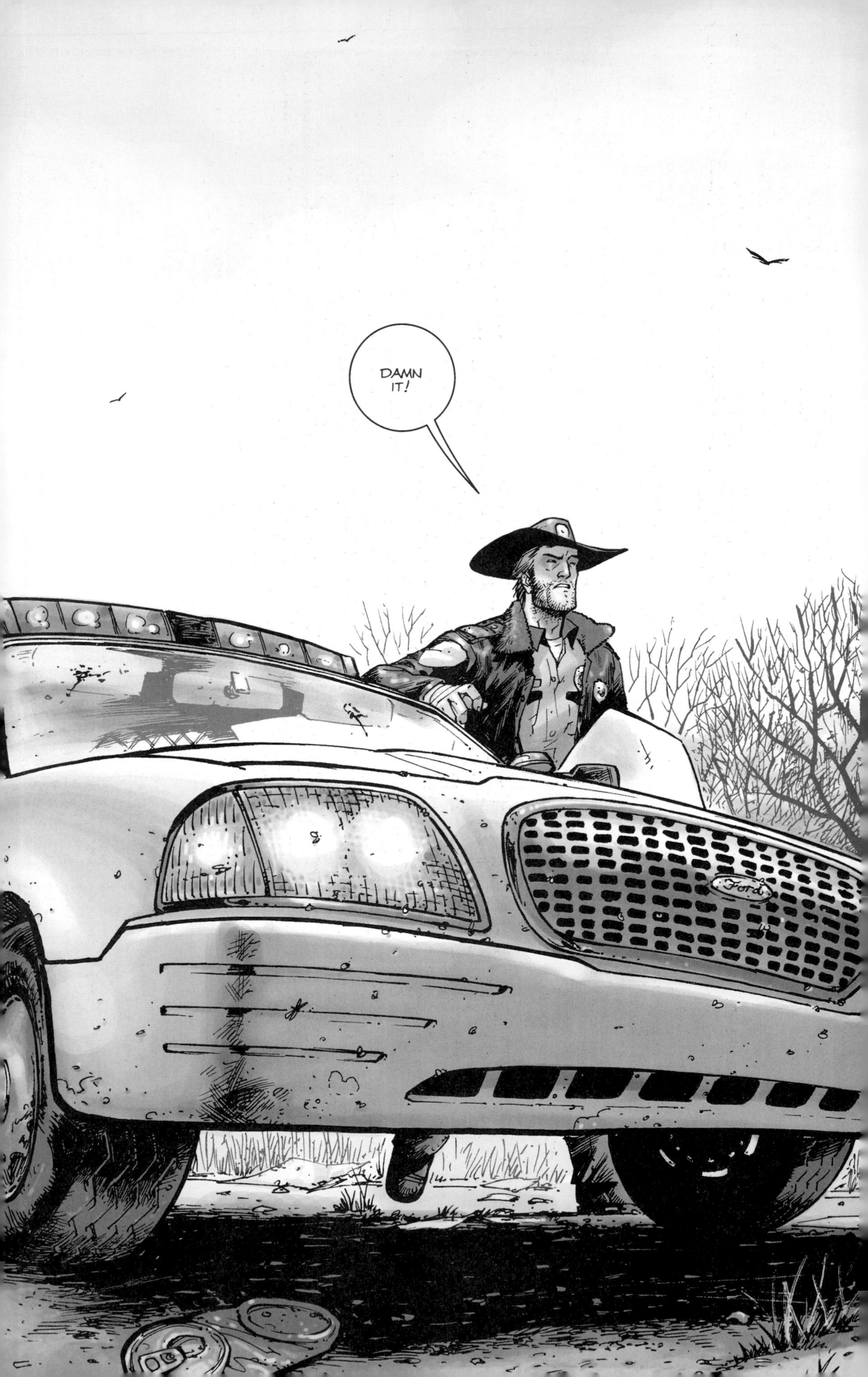
DAMN IT!

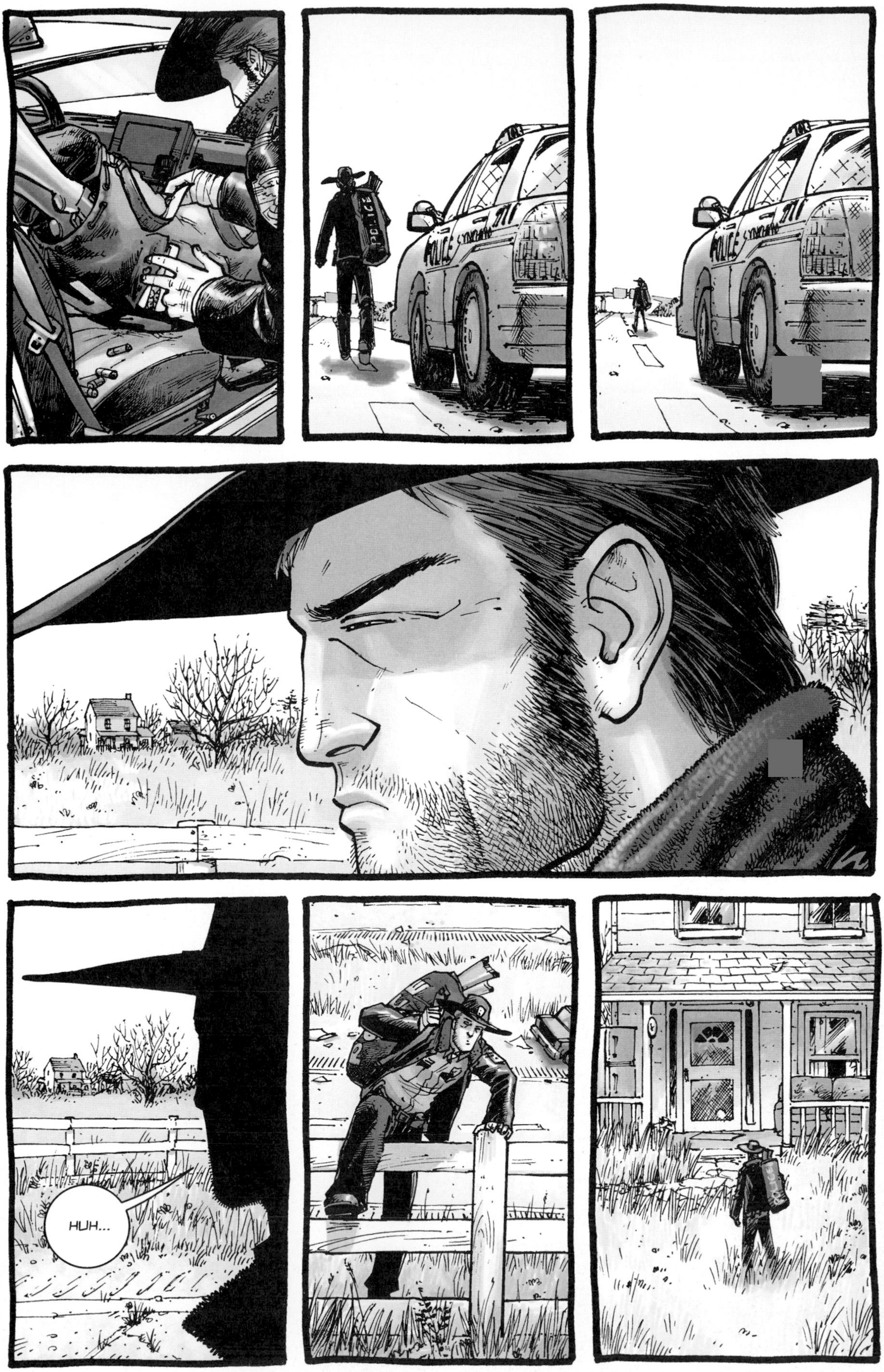

HUH...

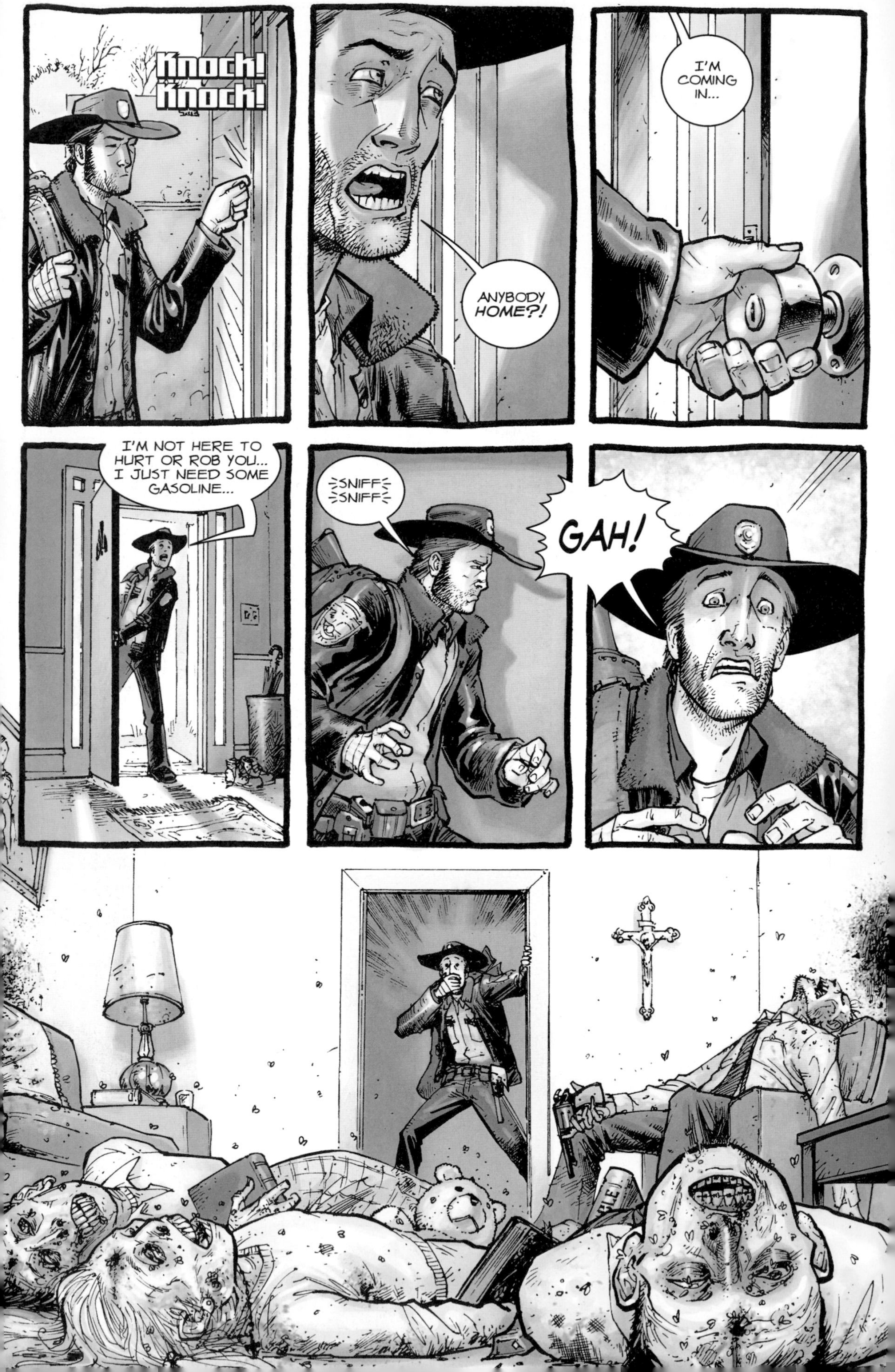
KNOCK! KNOCK!
ANYBODY HOME?!
I'M COMING IN...
I'M NOT HERE TO HURT OR ROB YOU... I JUST NEED SOME GASOLINE...
SNIFF SNIFF
GAH!

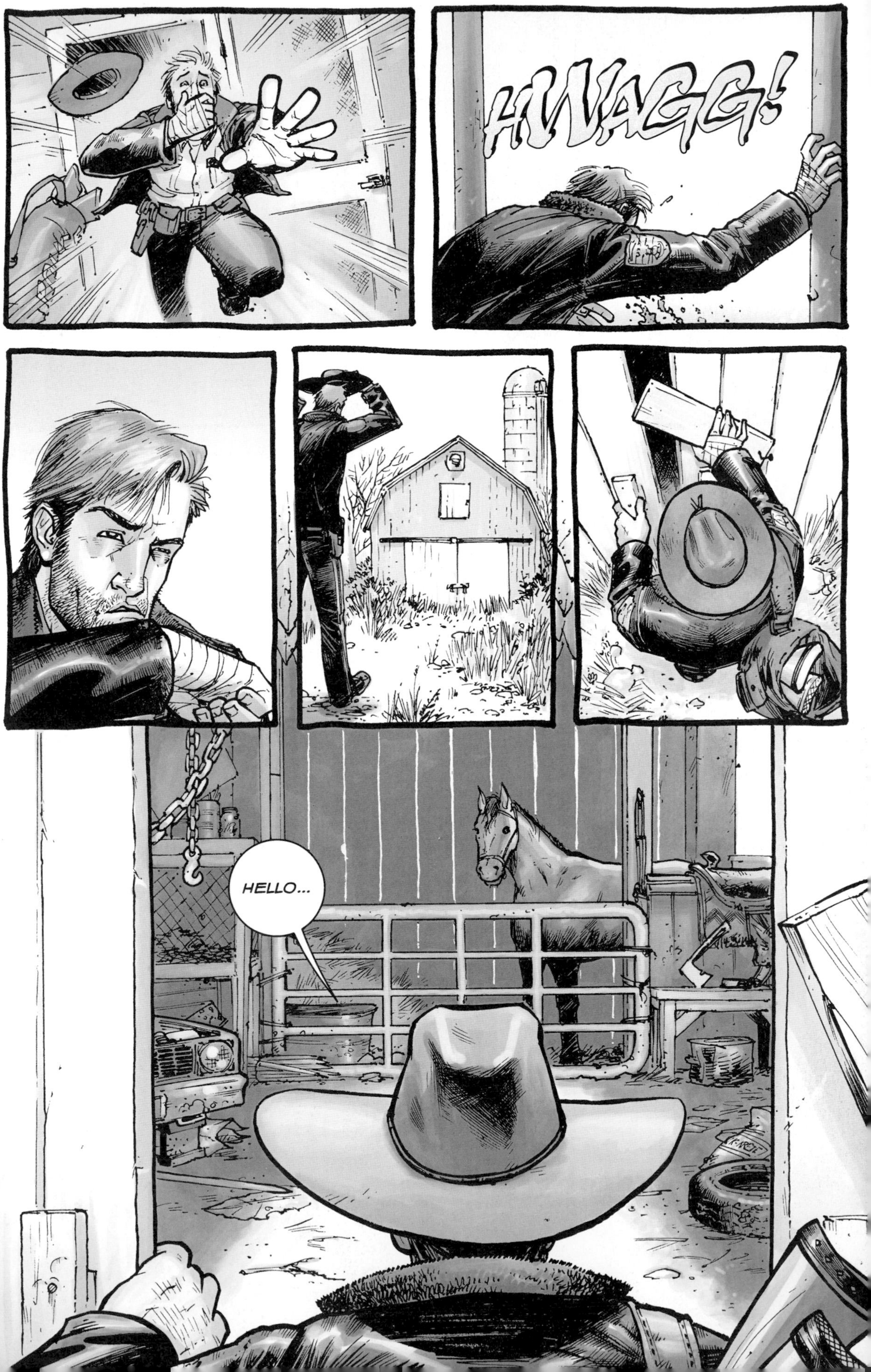
HWAGG!
HELLO...

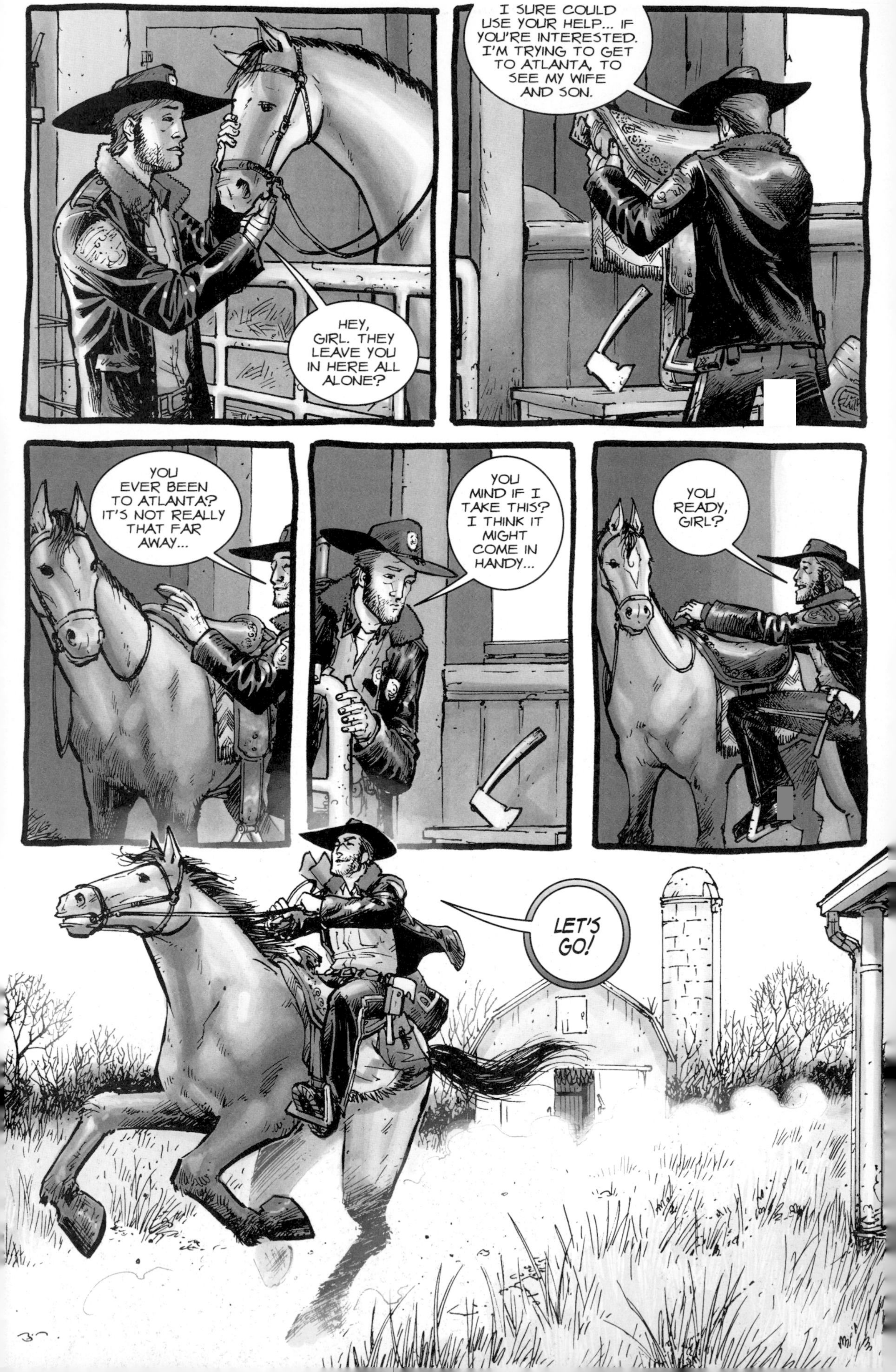
HEY, GIRL. THEY LEAVE YOU IN HERE ALL ALONE?
I SURE COULD USE YOUR HELP... IF YOU'RE INTERESTED. I'M TRYING TO GET TO ATLANTA, TO SEE MY WIFE AND SON.
YOU EVER BEEN TO ATLANTA? IT'S NOT REALLY THAT FAR AWAY...
YOU MIND IF I TAKE THIS? I THINK IT MIGHT COME IN HANDY...
YOU READY, GIRL?
LET'S GO!

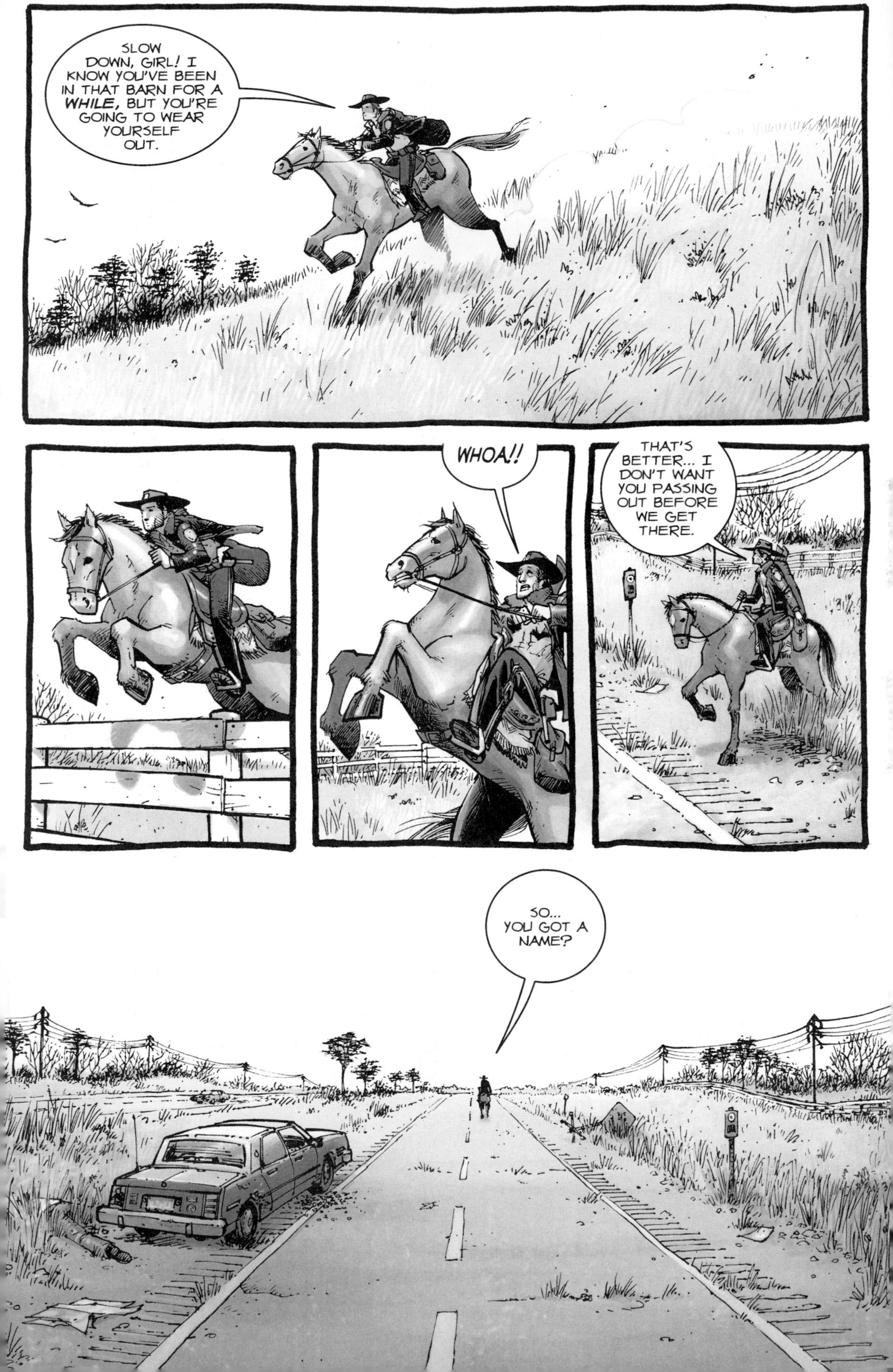
SLOW DOWN, GIRL! I KNOW YOU'VE BEEN IN THAT BARN FOR A WHILE, BUT YOU'RE GOING TO WEAR YOURSELF OUT.
WHOA!!
THAT'S BETTER... I DON'T WANT YOU PASSING OUT BEFORE WE GET THERE.
SO... YOU GOT A NAME?

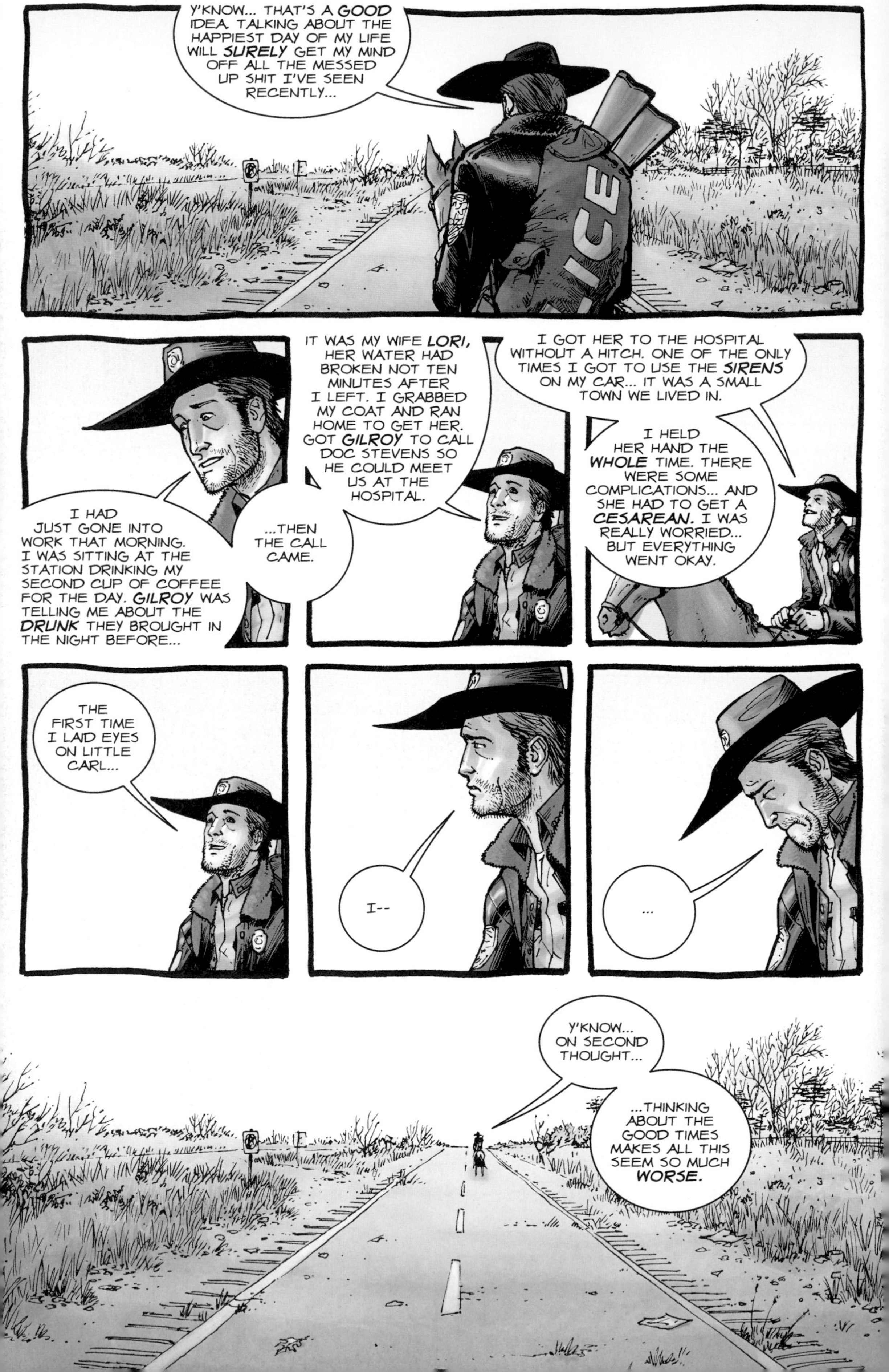
Y'KNOW... THAT'S A GOOD IDEA. TALKING ABOUT THE HAPPIEST DAY OF MY LIFE WILL SURELY GET MY MIND OFF ALL THE MESSED UP SHIT I'VE SEEN RECENTLY...
I HAD JUST GONE INTO WORK THAT MORNING. I WAS SITTING AT THE STATION DRINKING MY SECOND CUP OF COFFEE FOR THE DAY. GILROY WAS TELLING ME ABOUT THE DRUNK THEY BROUGHT IN THE NIGHT BEFORE...
...THEN THE CALL CAME.
IT WAS MY WIFE LORI, HER WATER HAD BROKEN NOT TEN MINUTES AFTER I LEFT. I GRABBED MY COAT AND RAN HOME TO GET HER. GOT GILROY TO CALL DOC STEVENS SO HE COULD MEET US AT THE HOSPITAL.
I GOT HER TO THE HOSPITAL WITHOUT A HITCH. ONE OF THE ONLY TIMES I GOT TO USE THE SIRENS ON MY CAR... IT WAS A SMALL TOWN WE LIVED IN.
I HELD HER HAND THE WHOLE TIME. THERE WERE SOME COMPLICATIONS... AND SHE HAD TO GET A CESAREAN. I WAS REALLY WORRIED... BUT EVERYTHING WENT OKAY.
THE FIRST TIME I LAID EYES ON LITTLE CARL...
I--
...
Y'KNOW... ON SECOND THOUGHT...
...THINKING ABOUT THE GOOD TIMES MAKES ALL THIS SEEM SO MUCH WORSE.

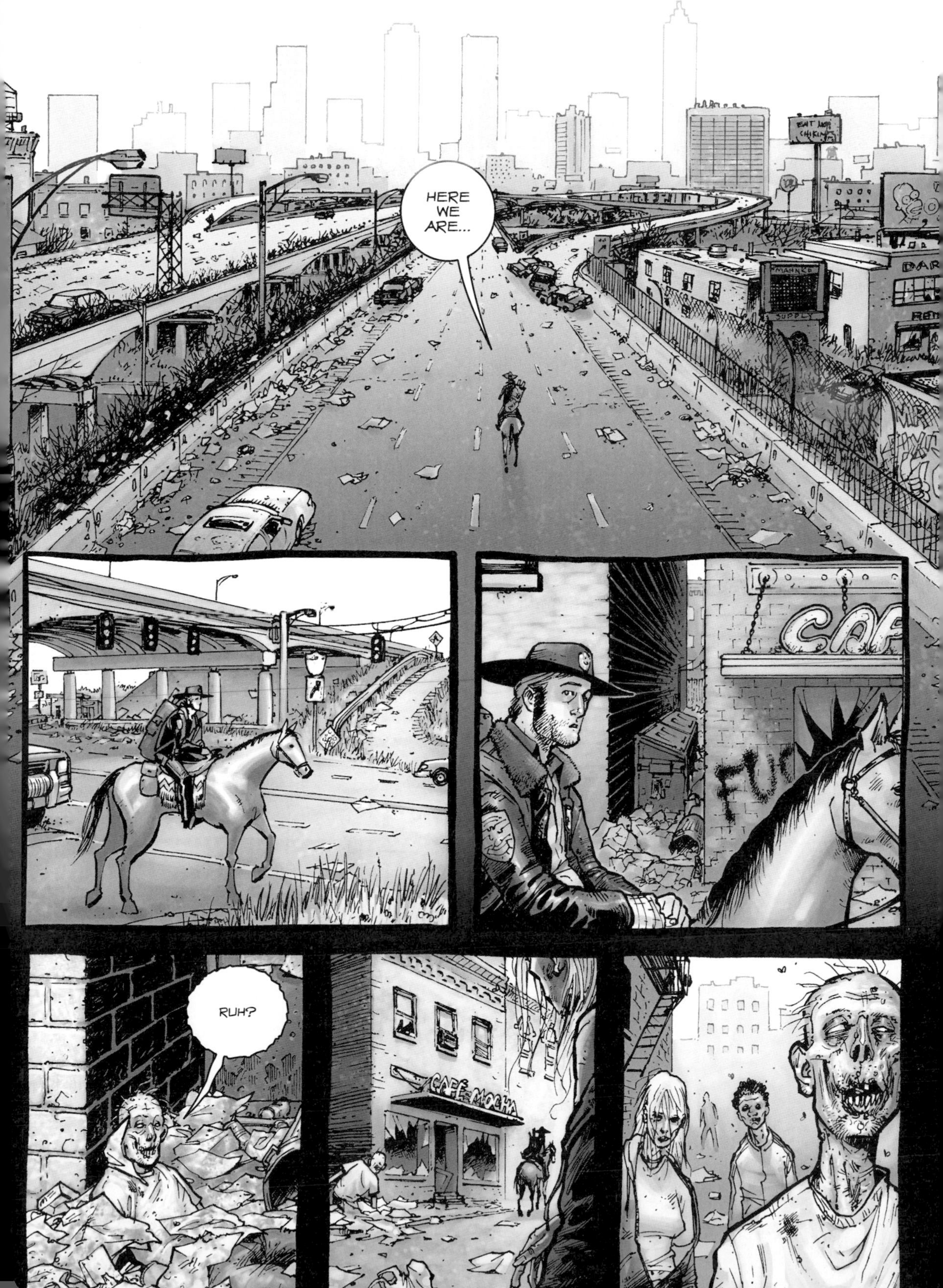
HERE WE ARE...
CAF
FUC
RUH?
CAFÉ MOCHA

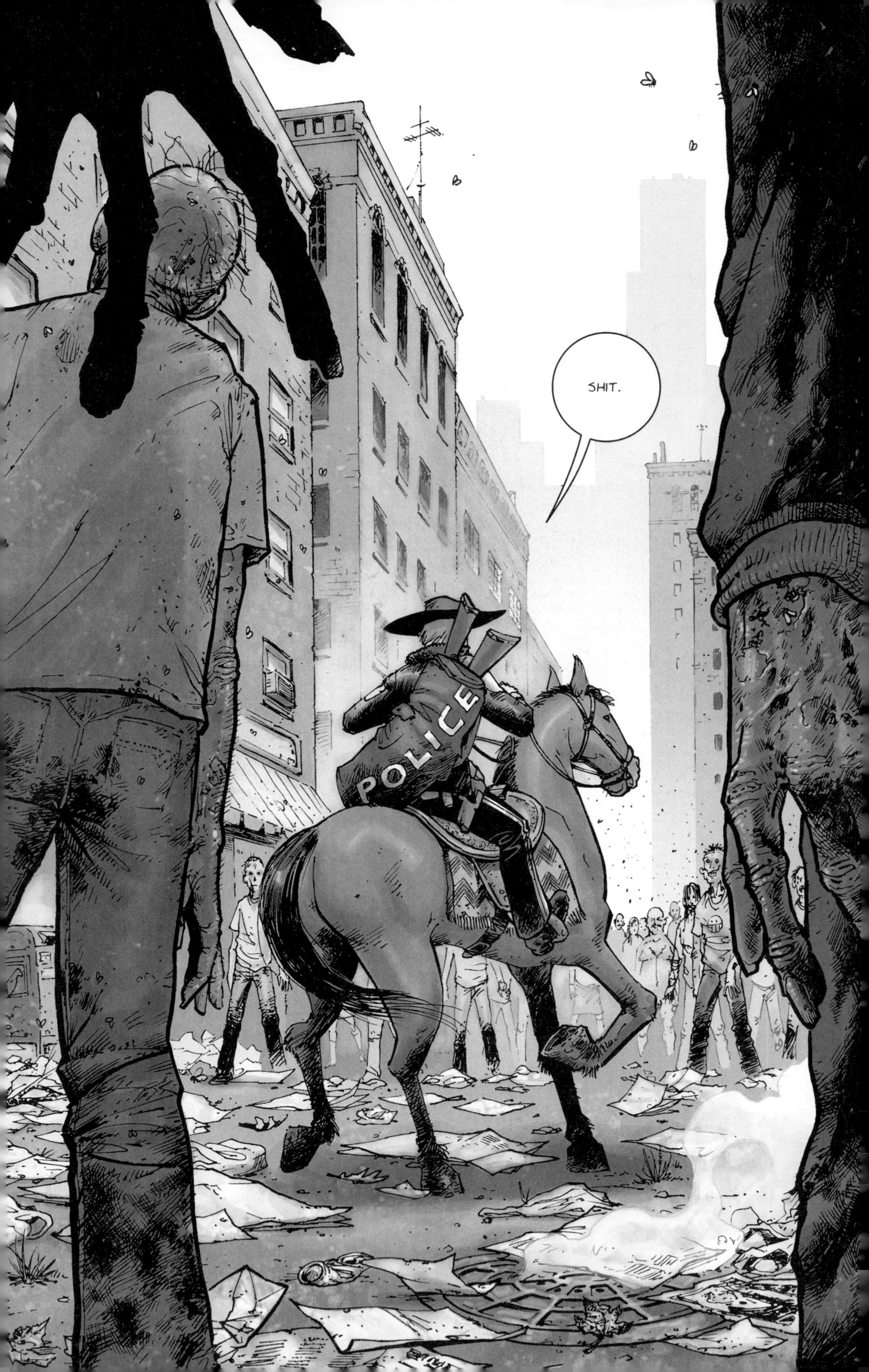
SHIT.
POLICE

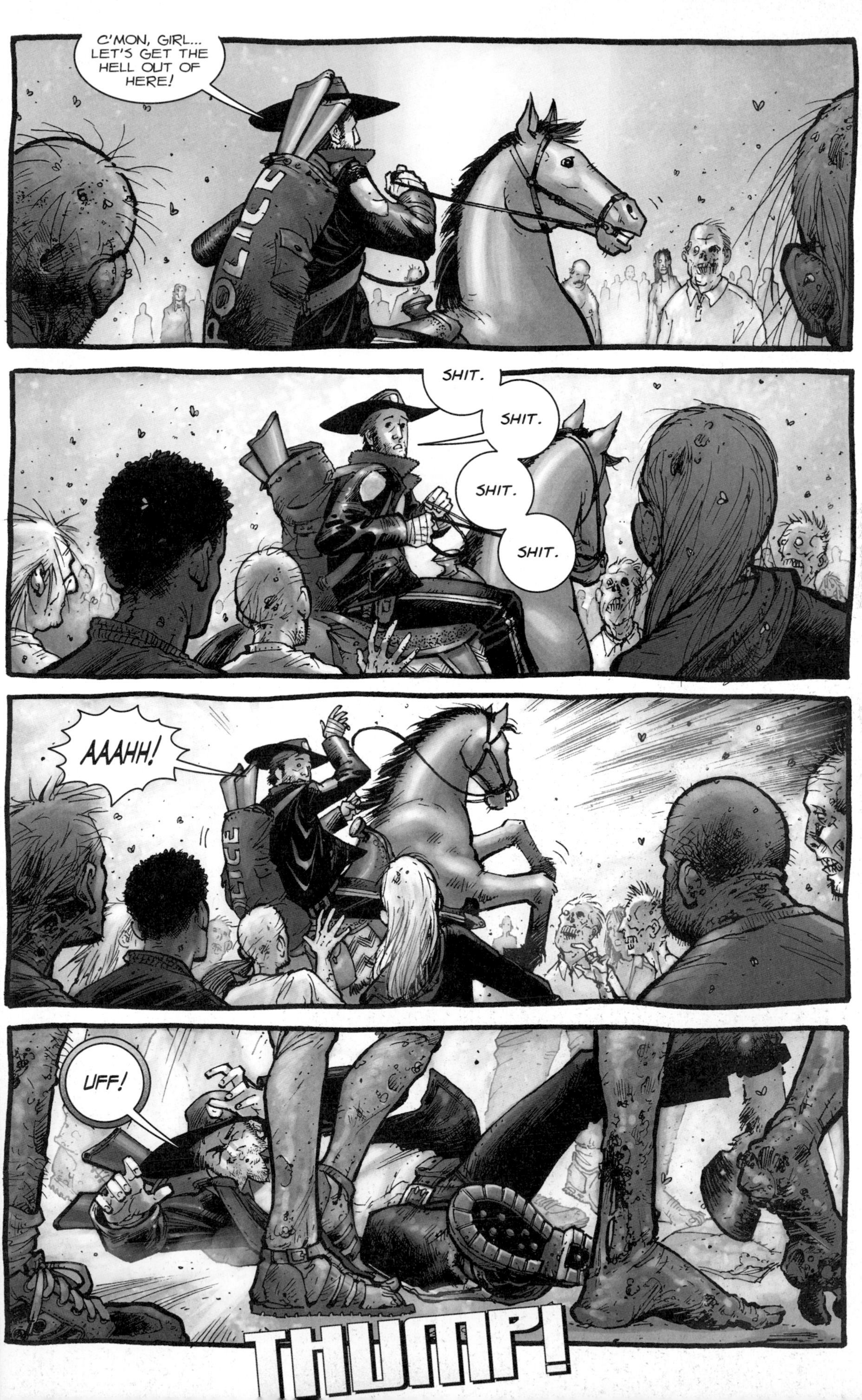

C'MON, GIRL... LET'S GET THE HELL OUT OF HERE!
SHIT.
SHIT.
SHIT.
SHIT.
AAAHH!
UFF!
THUMP!

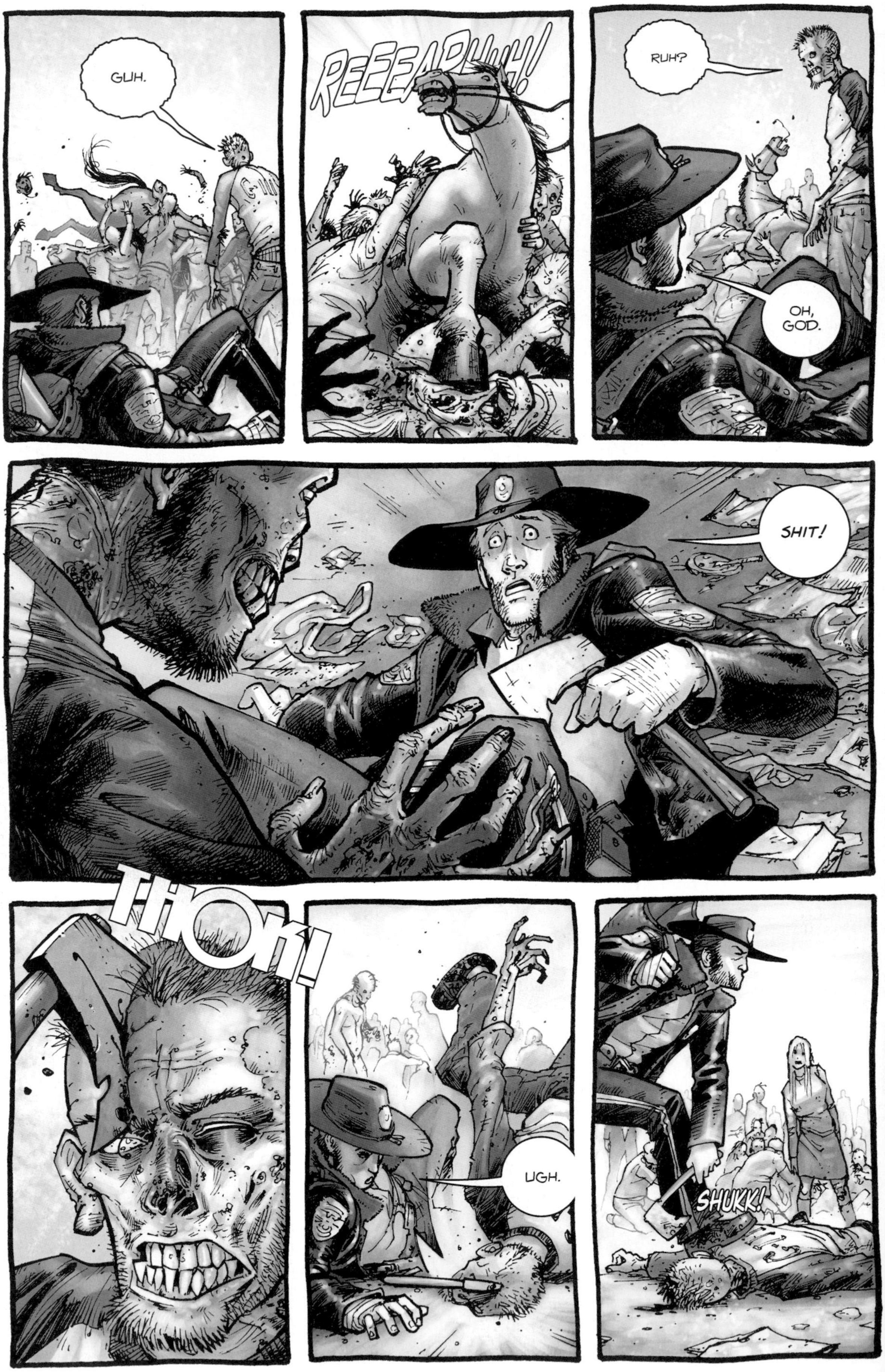
GUH.
REEEEARHHH!
RUH?
OH, GOD.
SHIT!
THOK!
UGH.
SHUKK!

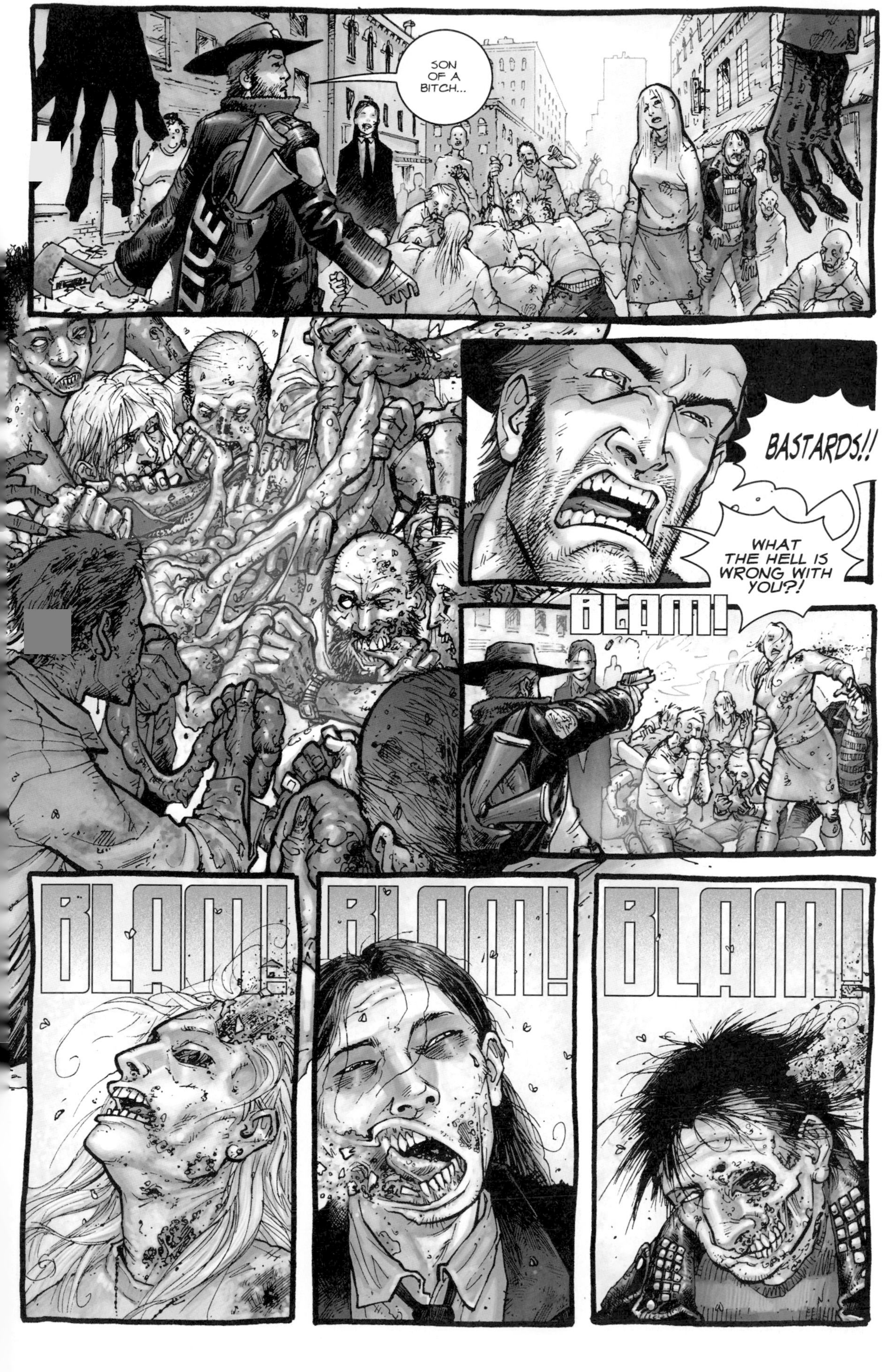

SON OF A BITCH...
BASTARDS!!
WHAT THE HELL IS WRONG WITH YOU?!
BLAM!
BLAM!
BLAM!
BLAM!

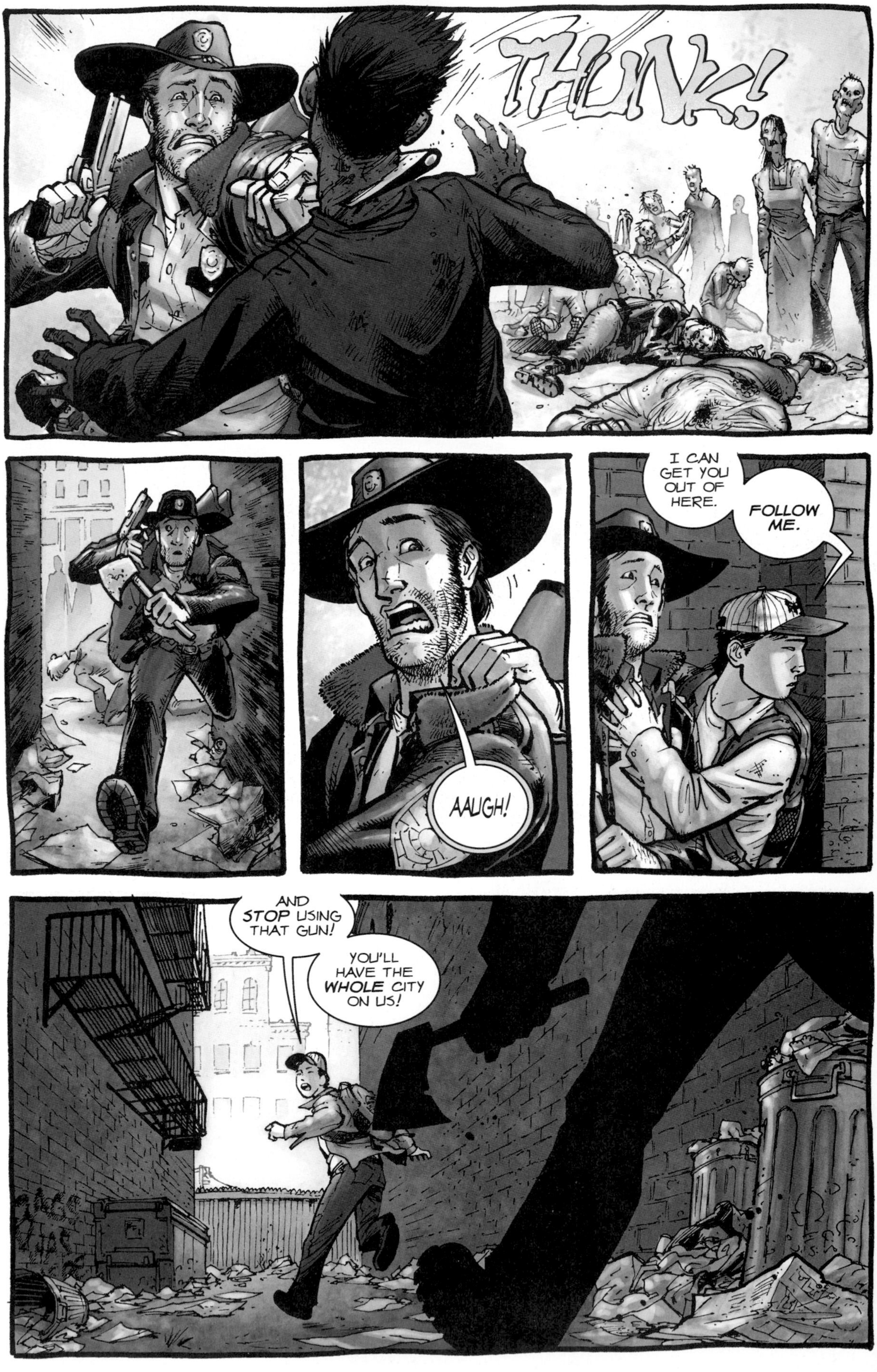
THUNK!
AAUGH!
I CAN GET YOU OUT OF HERE.
FOLLOW ME.
AND STOP USING THAT GUN!
YOU'LL HAVE THE WHOLE CITY ON US!

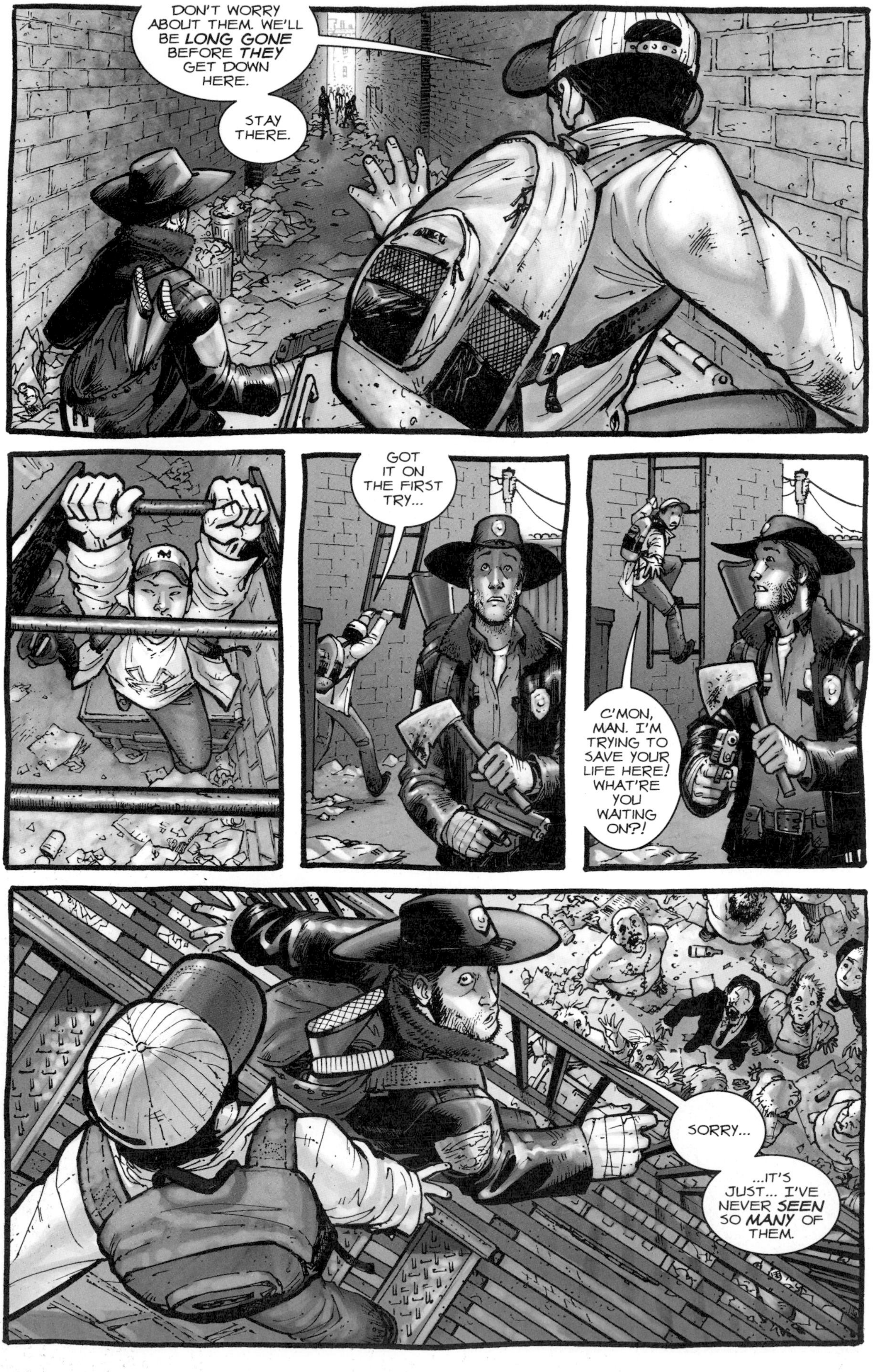
DON'T WORRY ABOUT THEM. WE'LL BE LONG GONE BEFORE THEY GET DOWN HERE.
STAY THERE.
GOT IT ON THE FIRST TRY...
C'MON, MAN. I'M TRYING TO SAVE YOUR LIFE HERE! WHAT'RE YOU WAITING ON?!
SORRY...
...IT'S JUST... I'VE NEVER SEEN SO MANY OF THEM.

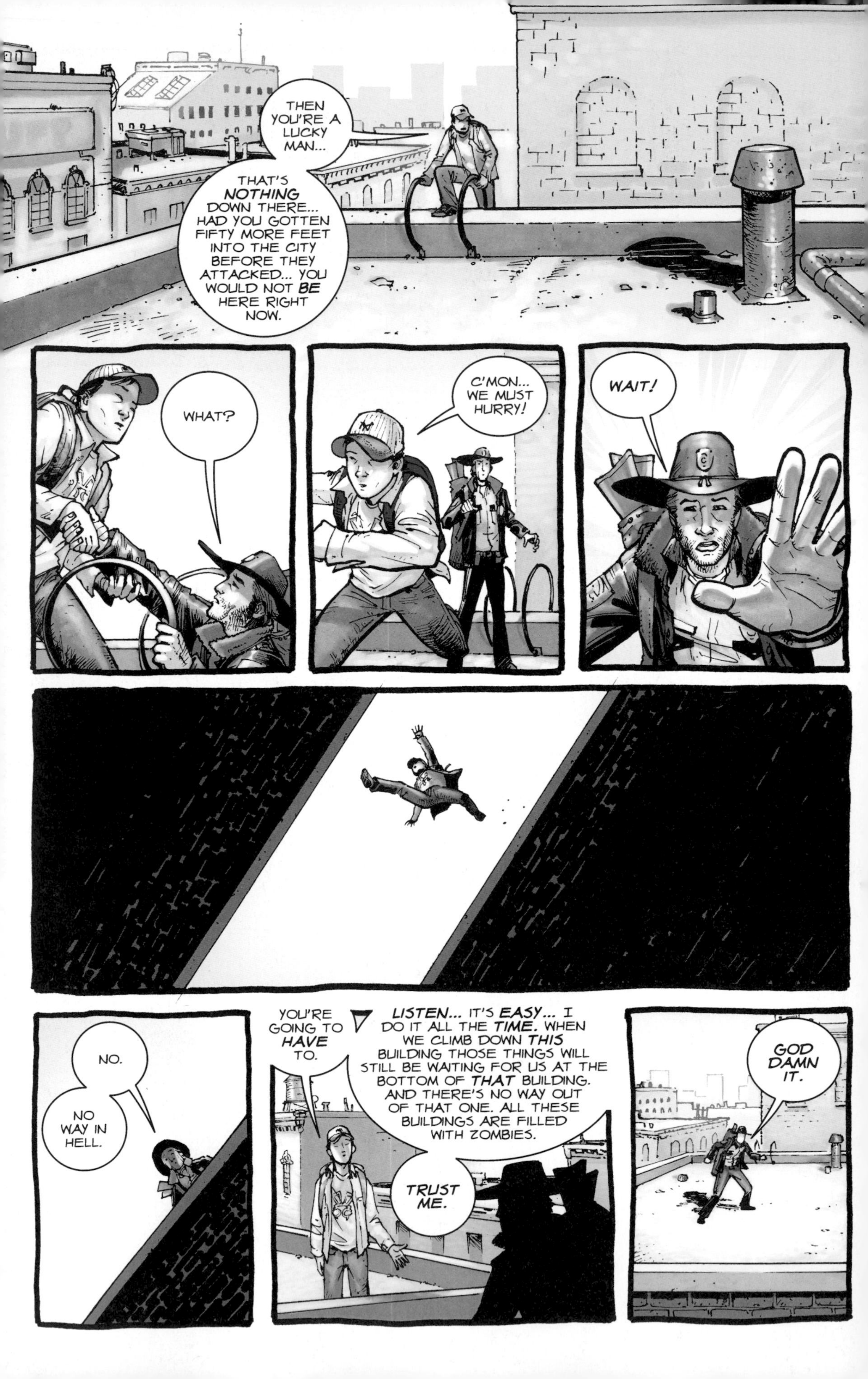
THEN YOU'RE A LUCKY MAN...
THAT'S NOTHING DOWN THERE... HAD YOU GOTTEN FIFTY MORE FEET INTO THE CITY BEFORE THEY ATTACKED... YOU WOULD NOT BE HERE RIGHT NOW.
WHAT?
C'MON... WE MUST HURRY!
WAIT!
NO.
NO WAY IN HELL.
YOU'RE GOING TO HAVE TO.
LISTEN... IT'S EASY... I DO IT ALL THE TIME. WHEN WE CLIMB DOWN THIS BUILDING THOSE THINGS WILL STILL BE WAITING FOR US AT THE BOTTOM OF THAT BUILDING. AND THERE'S NO WAY OUT OF THAT ONE. ALL THESE BUILDINGS ARE FILLED WITH ZOMBIES.
TRUST ME.
GOD DAMN IT.

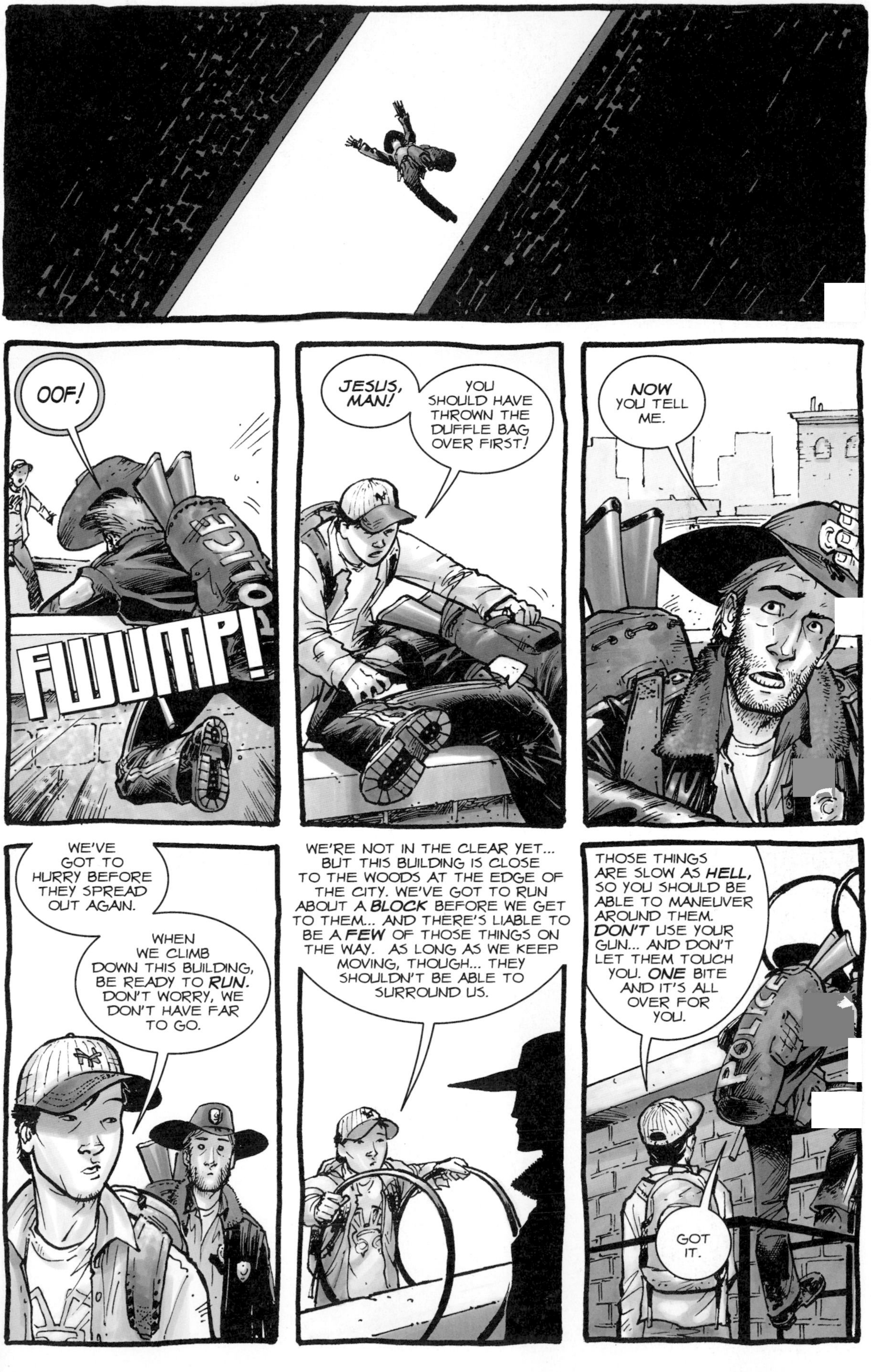
OOF!
FWUMP!
JESUS, MAN!
YOU SHOULD HAVE THROWN THE DUFFLE BAG OVER FIRST!
NOW YOU TELL ME.
WE'VE GOT TO HURRY BEFORE THEY SPREAD OUT AGAIN.
WHEN WE CLIMB DOWN THIS BUILDING, BE READY TO RUN. DON'T WORRY, WE DON'T HAVE FAR TO GO.
WE'RE NOT IN THE CLEAR YET... BUT THIS BUILDING IS CLOSE TO THE WOODS AT THE EDGE OF THE CITY. WE'VE GOT TO RUN ABOUT A BLOCK BEFORE WE GET TO THEM... AND THERE'S LIABLE TO BE A FEW OF THOSE THINGS ON THE WAY. AS LONG AS WE KEEP MOVING, THOUGH... THEY SHOULDN'T BE ABLE TO SURROUND US.
THOSE THINGS ARE SLOW AS HELL, SO YOU SHOULD BE ABLE TO MANEUVER AROUND THEM. DON'T USE YOUR GUN... AND DON'T LET THEM TOUCH YOU. ONE BITE AND IT'S ALL OVER FOR YOU.
GOT IT.

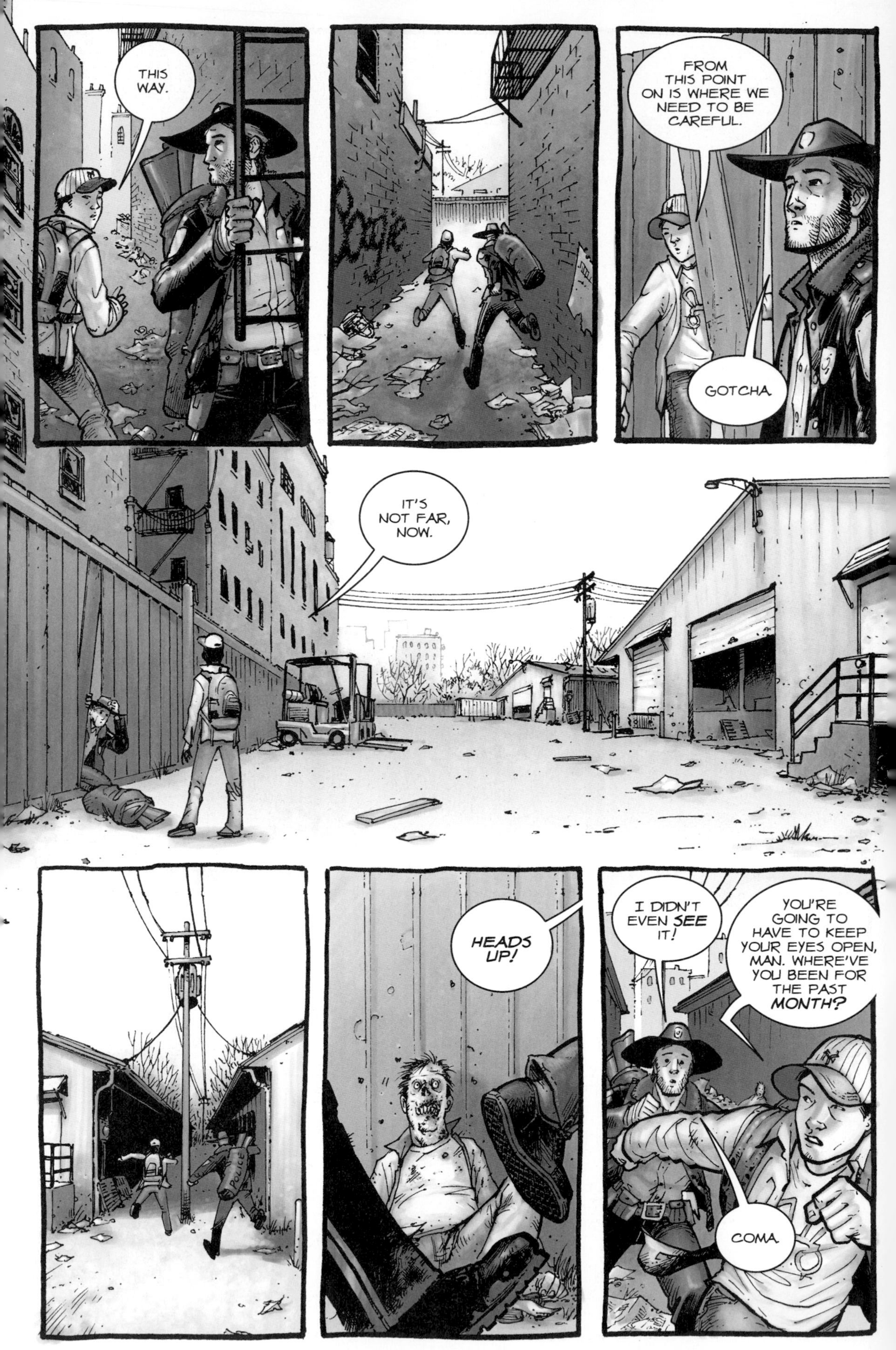
THIS WAY.
FROM THIS POINT ON IS WHERE WE NEED TO BE CAREFUL.
GOTCHA.
IT'S NOT FAR, NOW.
HEADS UP!
I DIDN'T EVEN SEE IT!
YOU'RE GOING TO HAVE TO KEEP YOUR EYES OPEN, MAN. WHERE'VE YOU BEEN FOR THE PAST MONTH?
COMA.

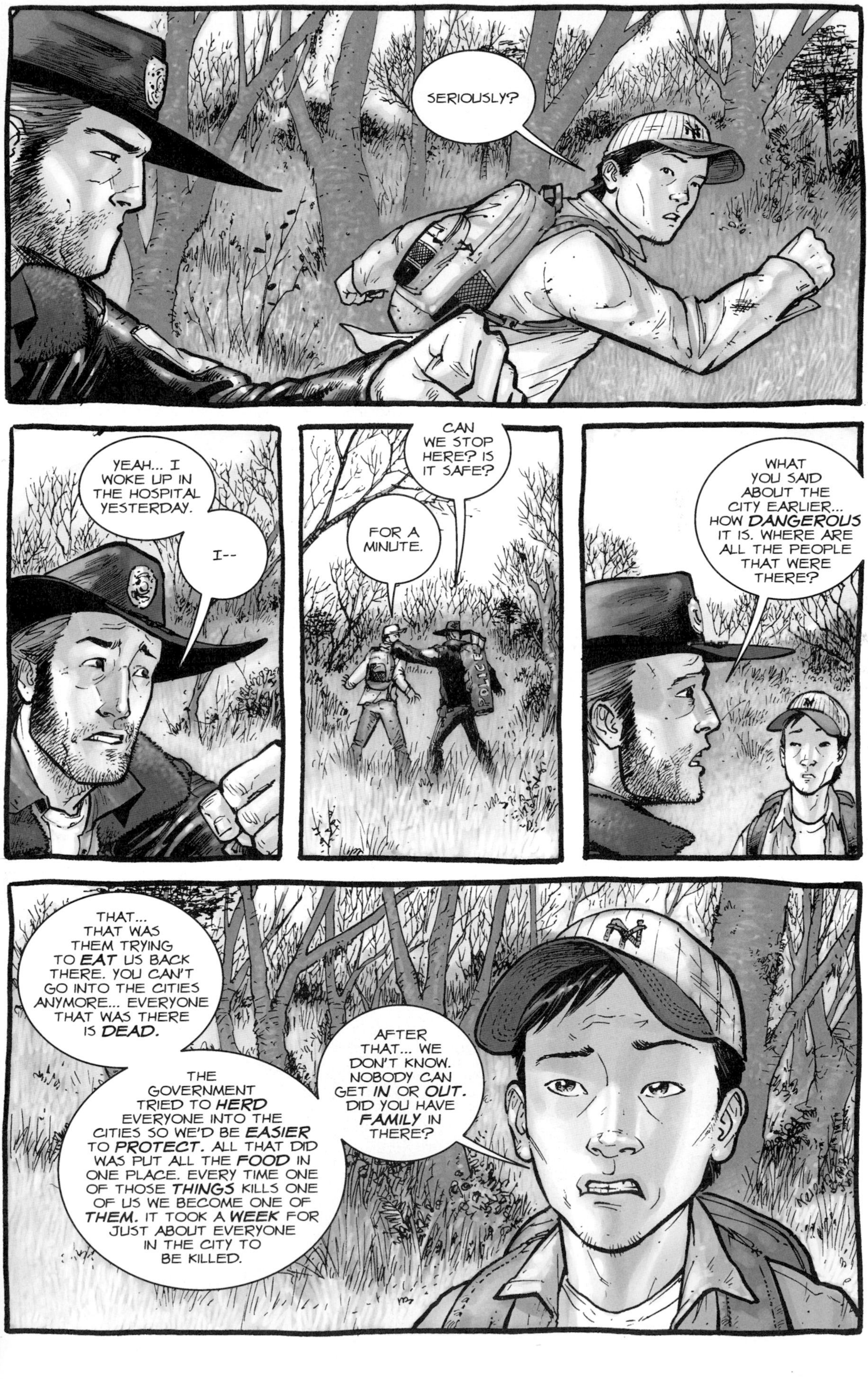
SERIOUSLY?
YEAH... I WOKE UP IN THE HOSPITAL YESTERDAY.
I--
CAN WE STOP HERE? IS IT SAFE?
FOR A MINUTE.
WHAT YOU SAID ABOUT THE CITY EARLIER... HOW DANGEROUS IT IS. WHERE ARE ALL THE PEOPLE THAT WERE THERE?
THAT... THAT WAS THEM TRYING TO EAT US BACK THERE. YOU CAN'T GO INTO THE CITIES ANYMORE... EVERYONE THAT WAS THERE IS DEAD.
THE GOVERNMENT TRIED TO HERD EVERYONE INTO THE CITIES SO WE'D BE EASIER TO PROTECT. ALL THAT DID WAS PUT ALL THE FOOD IN ONE PLACE. EVERY TIME ONE OF THOSE THINGS KILLS ONE OF US WE BECOME ONE OF THEM. IT TOOK A WEEK FOR JUST ABOUT EVERYONE IN THE CITY TO BE KILLED.
AFTER THAT... WE DON'T KNOW. NOBODY CAN GET IN OR OUT. DID YOU HAVE FAMILY IN THERE?

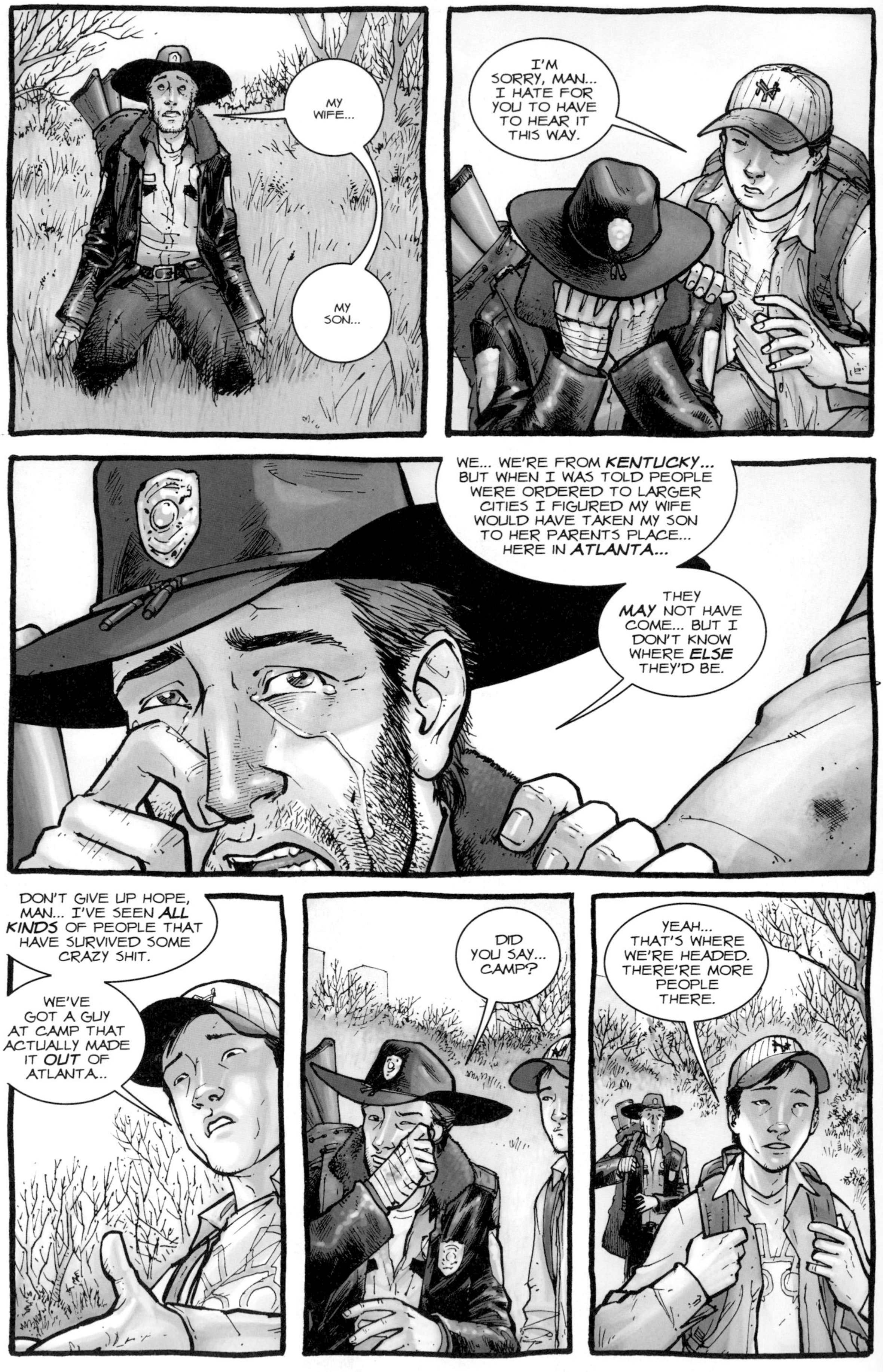
MY WIFE...
MY SON...
I'M SORRY, MAN... I HATE FOR YOU TO HAVE TO HEAR IT THIS WAY.
WE... WE'RE FROM KENTUCKY... BUT WHEN I WAS TOLD PEOPLE WERE ORDERED TO LARGER CITIES I FIGURED MY WIFE WOULD HAVE TAKEN MY SON TO HER PARENTS PLACE... HERE IN ATLANTA...
THEY MAY NOT HAVE COME... BUT I DON'T KNOW WHERE ELSE THEY'D BE.
DON'T GIVE UP HOPE, MAN... I'VE SEEN ALL KINDS OF PEOPLE THAT HAVE SURVIVED SOME CRAZY SHIT.
WE'VE GOT A GUY AT CAMP THAT ACTUALLY MADE IT OUT OF ATLANTA..
DID YOU SAY... CAMP?
YEAH... THAT'S WHERE WE'RE HEADED. THERE'RE MORE PEOPLE THERE.

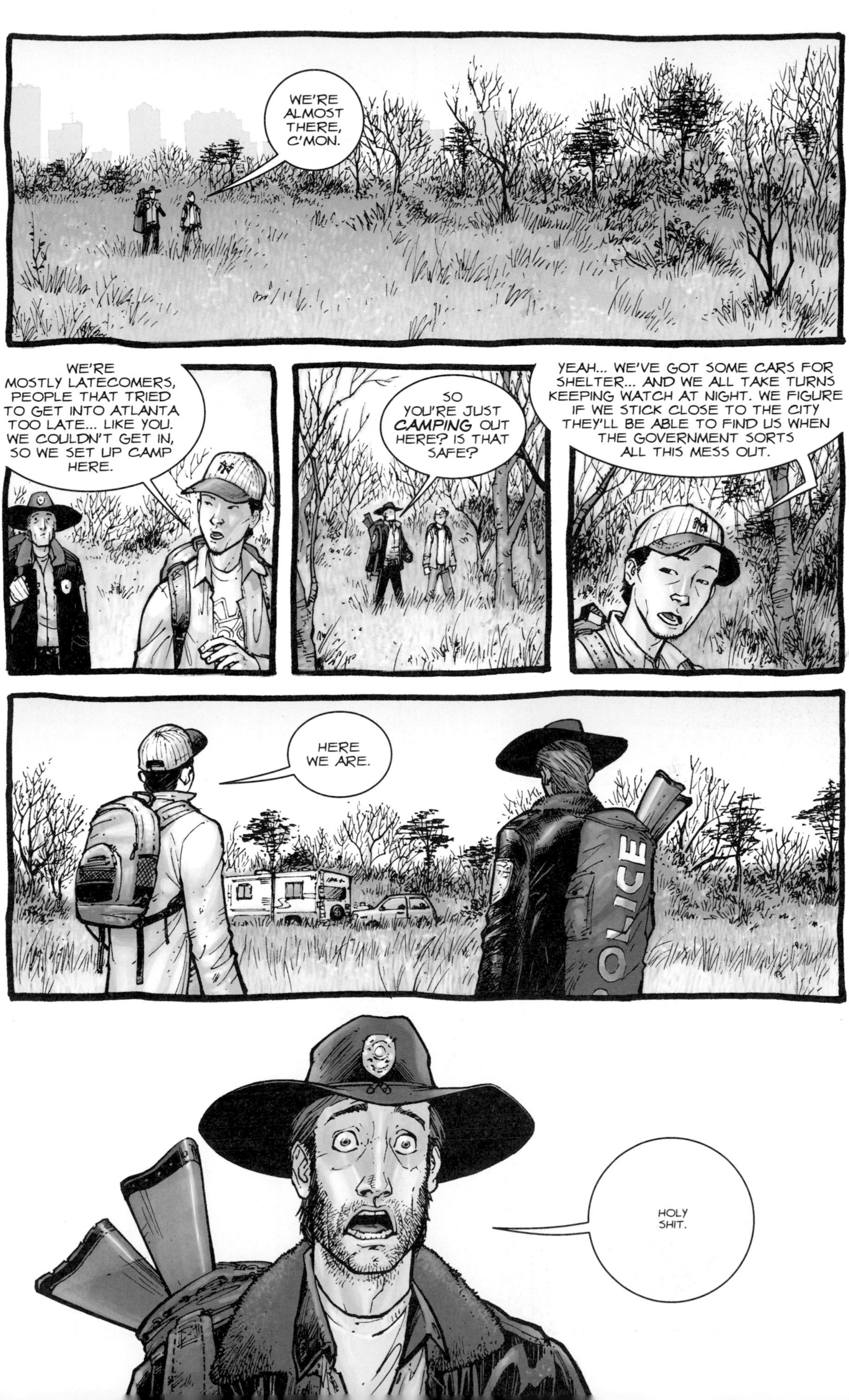
WE'RE ALMOST THERE, C'MON.
WE'RE MOSTLY LATECOMERS, PEOPLE THAT TRIED TO GET INTO ATLANTA TOO LATE... LIKE YOU. WE COULDN'T GET IN, SO WE SET UP CAMP HERE.
SO YOU'RE JUST CAMPING OUT HERE? IS THAT SAFE?
YEAH... WE'VE GOT SOME CARS FOR SHELTER... AND WE ALL TAKE TURNS KEEPING WATCH AT NIGHT. WE FIGURE IF WE STICK CLOSE TO THE CITY THEY'LL BE ABLE TO FIND US WHEN THE GOVERNMENT SORTS ALL THIS MESS OUT.
HERE WE ARE.
POLICE
HOLY SHIT.

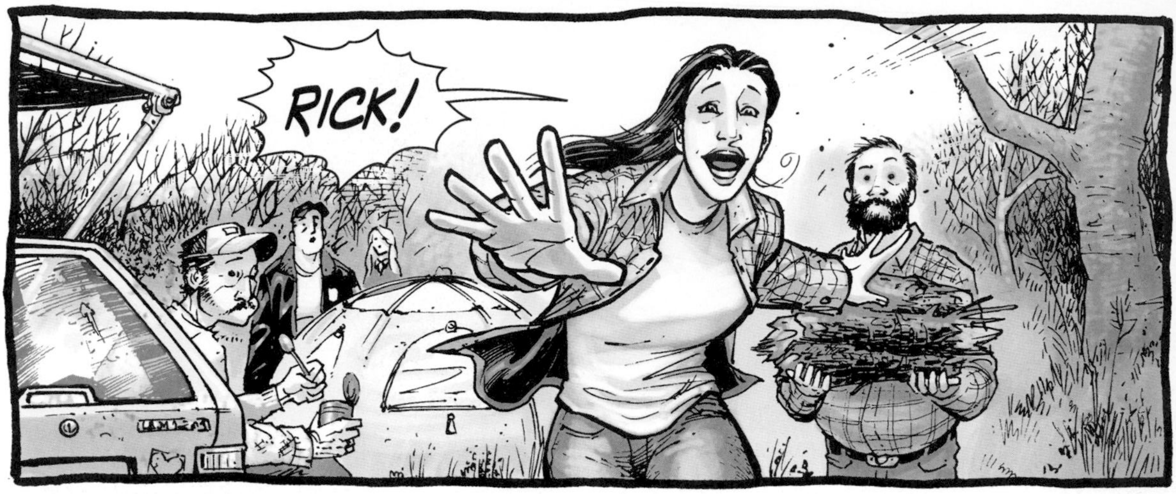
RICK!
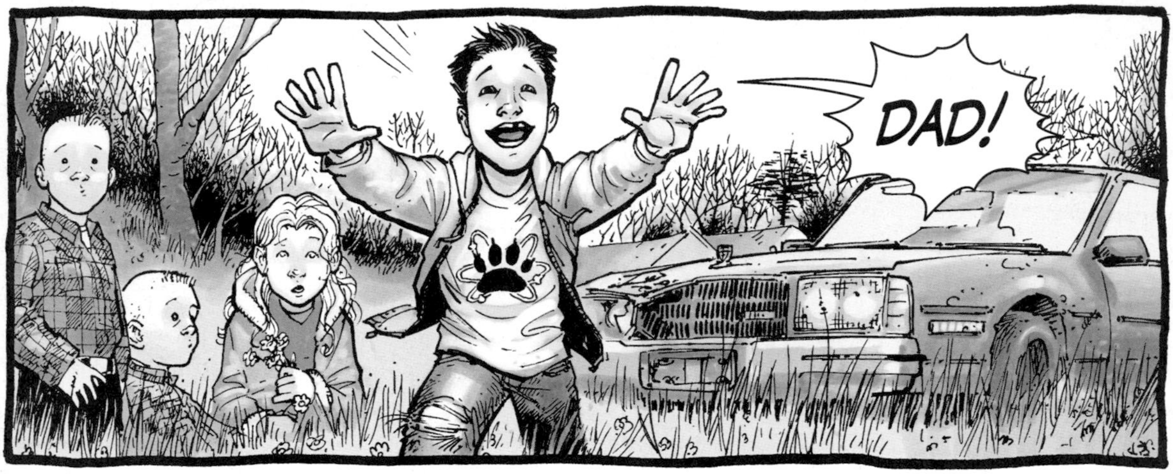
DAD!
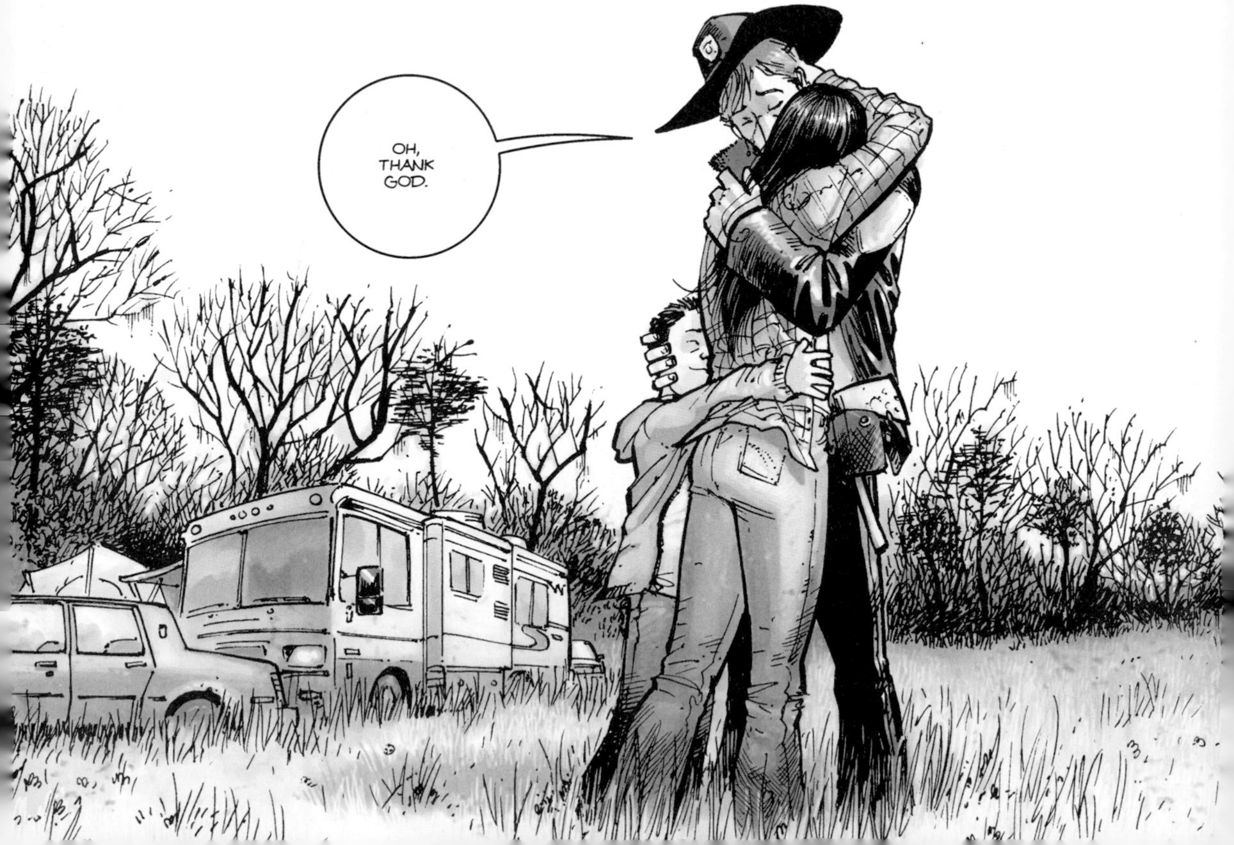
OH, THANK GOD.

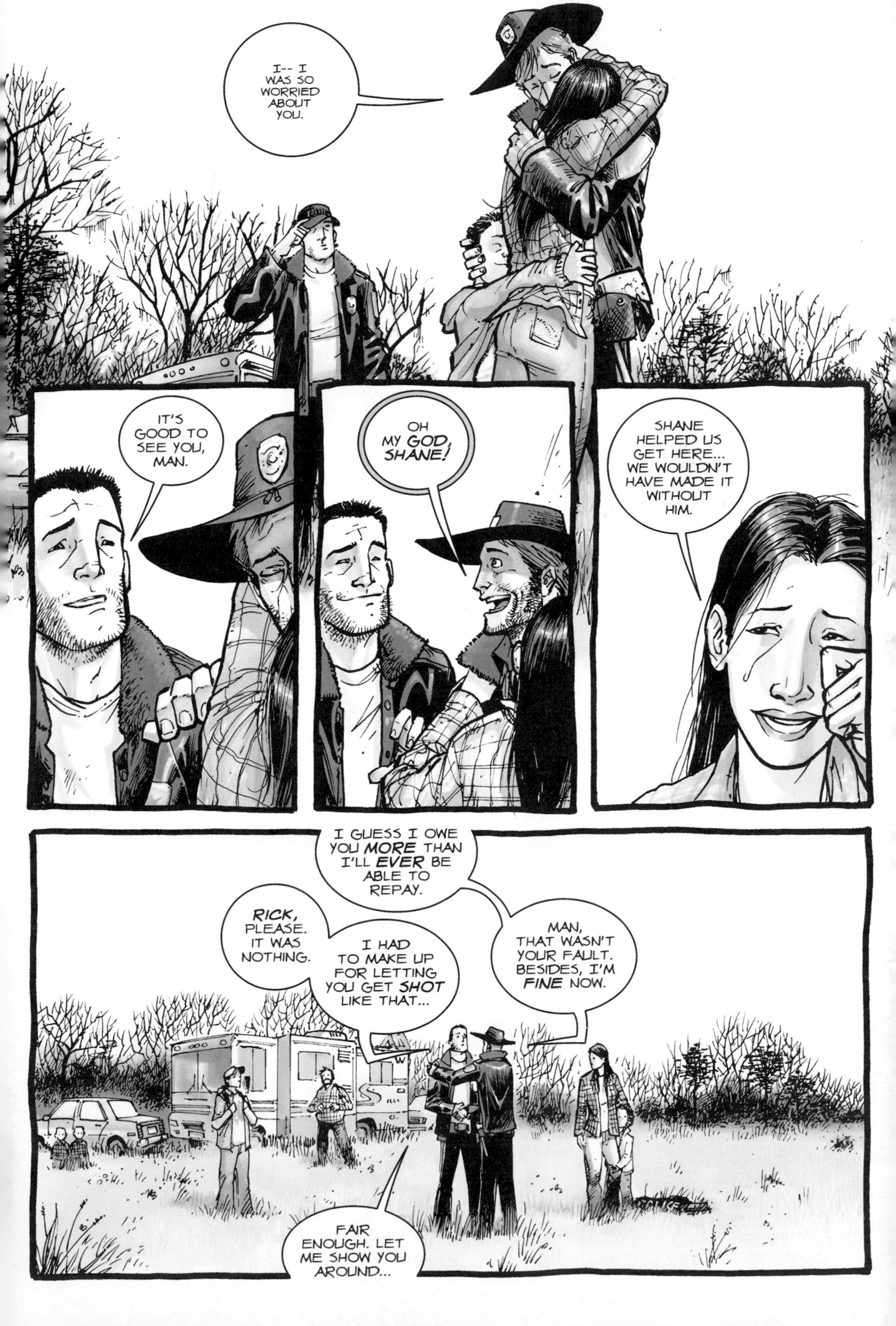
I-- I WAS SO WORRIED ABOUT YOU.
IT'S GOOD TO SEE YOU, MAN.
OH MY GOD, SHANE!
SHANE HELPED US GET HERE... WE WOULDN'T HAVE MADE IT WITHOUT HIM.
I GUESS I OWE YOU MORE THAN I'LL EVER BE ABLE TO REPAY.
RICK, PLEASE. IT WAS NOTHING.
I HAD TO MAKE UP FOR LETTING YOU GET SHOT LIKE THAT...
MAN, THAT WASN'T YOUR FAULT. BESIDES, I'M FINE NOW.
FAIR ENOUGH. LET ME SHOW YOU AROUND...

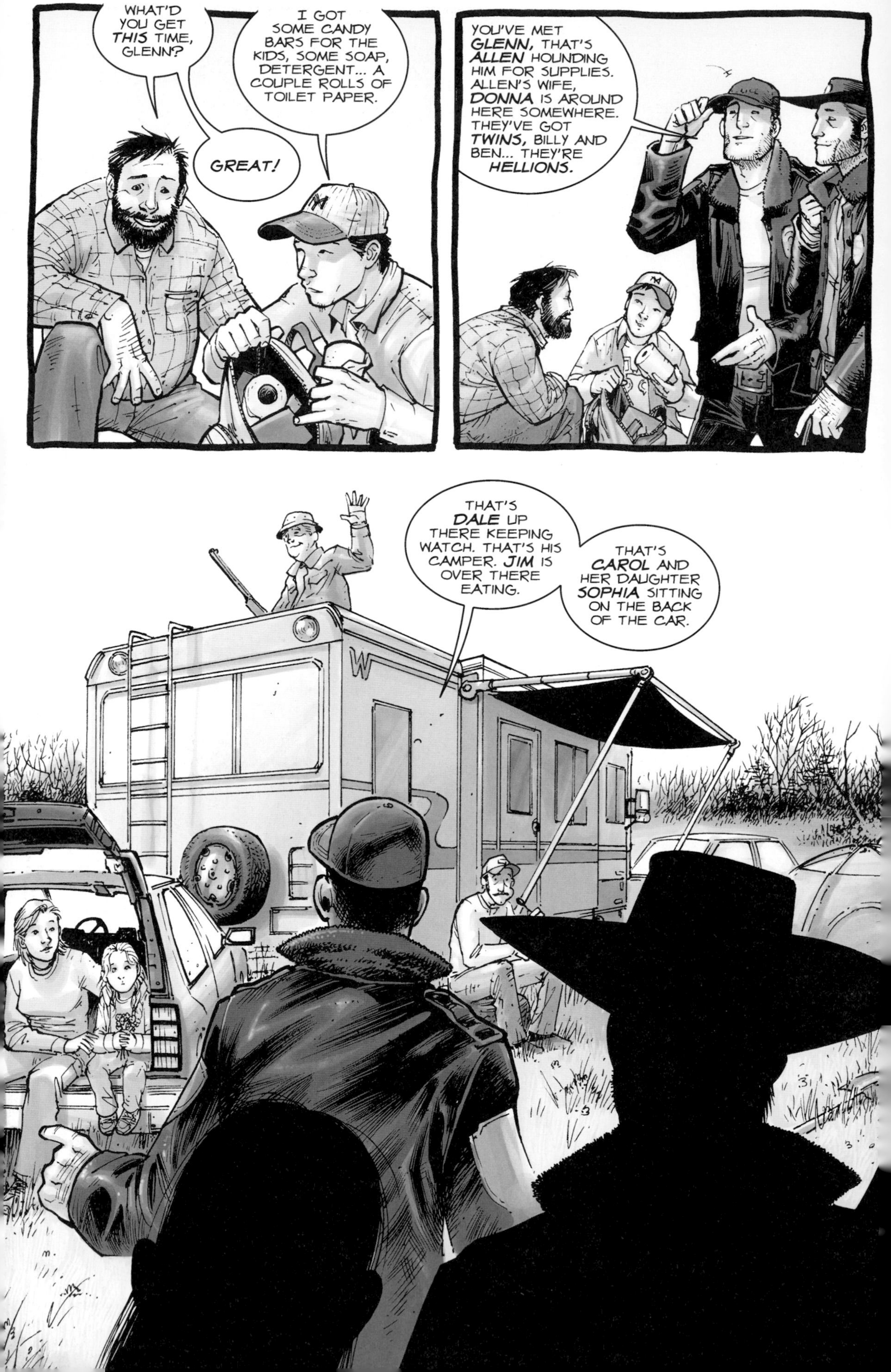
WHAT'D YOU GET THIS TIME, GLENN?
I GOT SOME CANDY BARS FOR THE KIDS, SOME SOAP, DETERGENT... A COUPLE ROLLS OF TOILET PAPER.
GREAT!
YOU'VE MET GLENN, THAT'S ALLEN HOUNDING HIM FOR SUPPLIES. ALLEN'S WIFE, DONNA IS AROUND HERE SOMEWHERE. THEY'VE GOT TWINS, BILLY AND BEN... THEY'RE HELLIONS.
THAT'S DALE UP THERE KEEPING WATCH. THAT'S HIS CAMPER. JIM IS OVER THERE EATING.
THAT'S CAROL AND HER DAUGHTER SOPHIA SITTING ON THE BACK OF THE CAR.

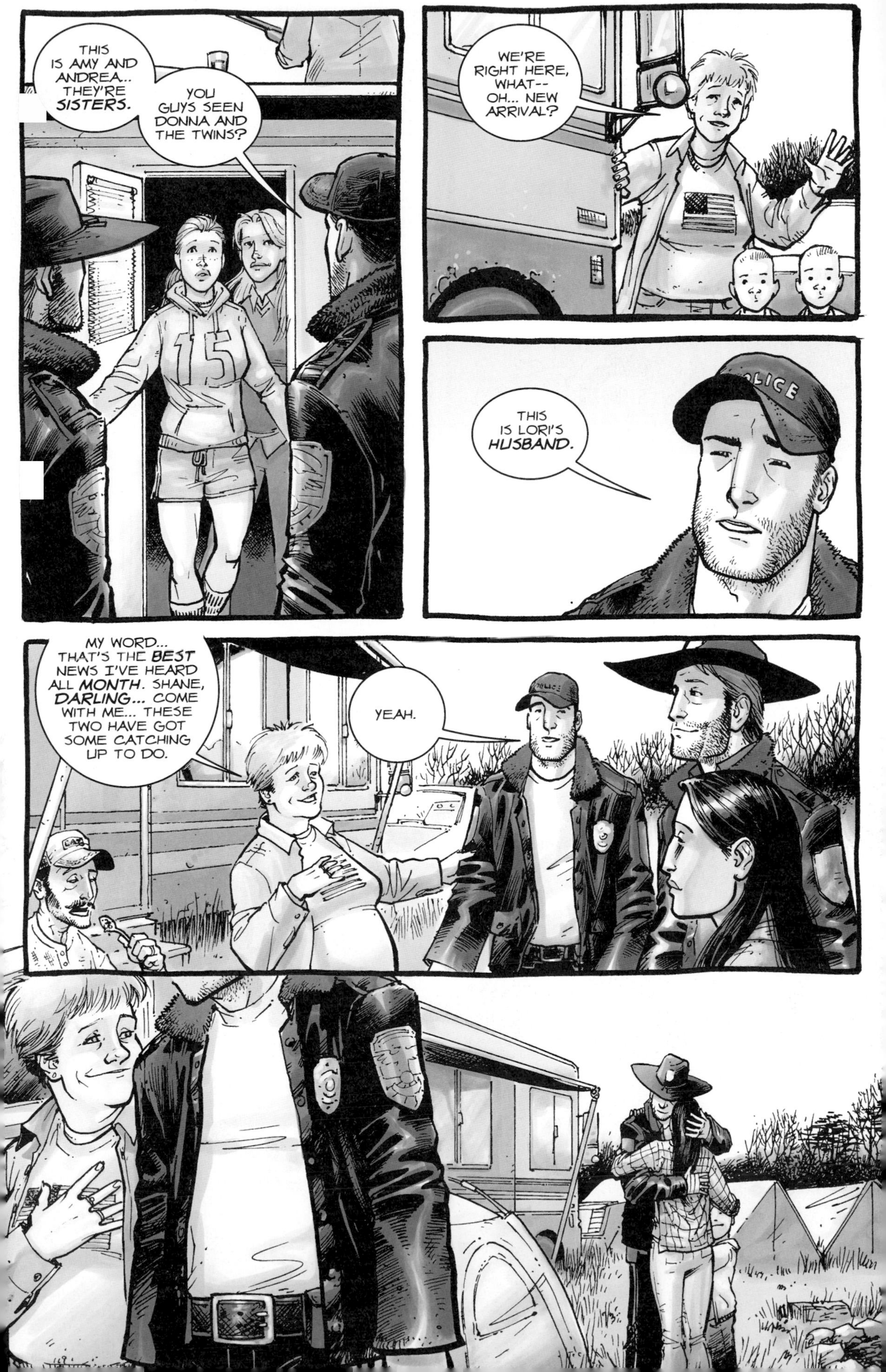
THIS IS AMY AND ANDREA... THEY'RE SISTERS.
YOU GUYS SEEN DONNA AND THE TWINS?
WE'RE RIGHT HERE, WHAT-- OH... NEW ARRIVAL?
POLICE
THIS IS LORI'S HUSBAND.
MY WORD... THAT'S THE BEST NEWS I'VE HEARD ALL MONTH. SHANE, DARLING... COME WITH ME... THESE TWO HAVE GOT SOME CATCHING UP TO DO.
YEAH.

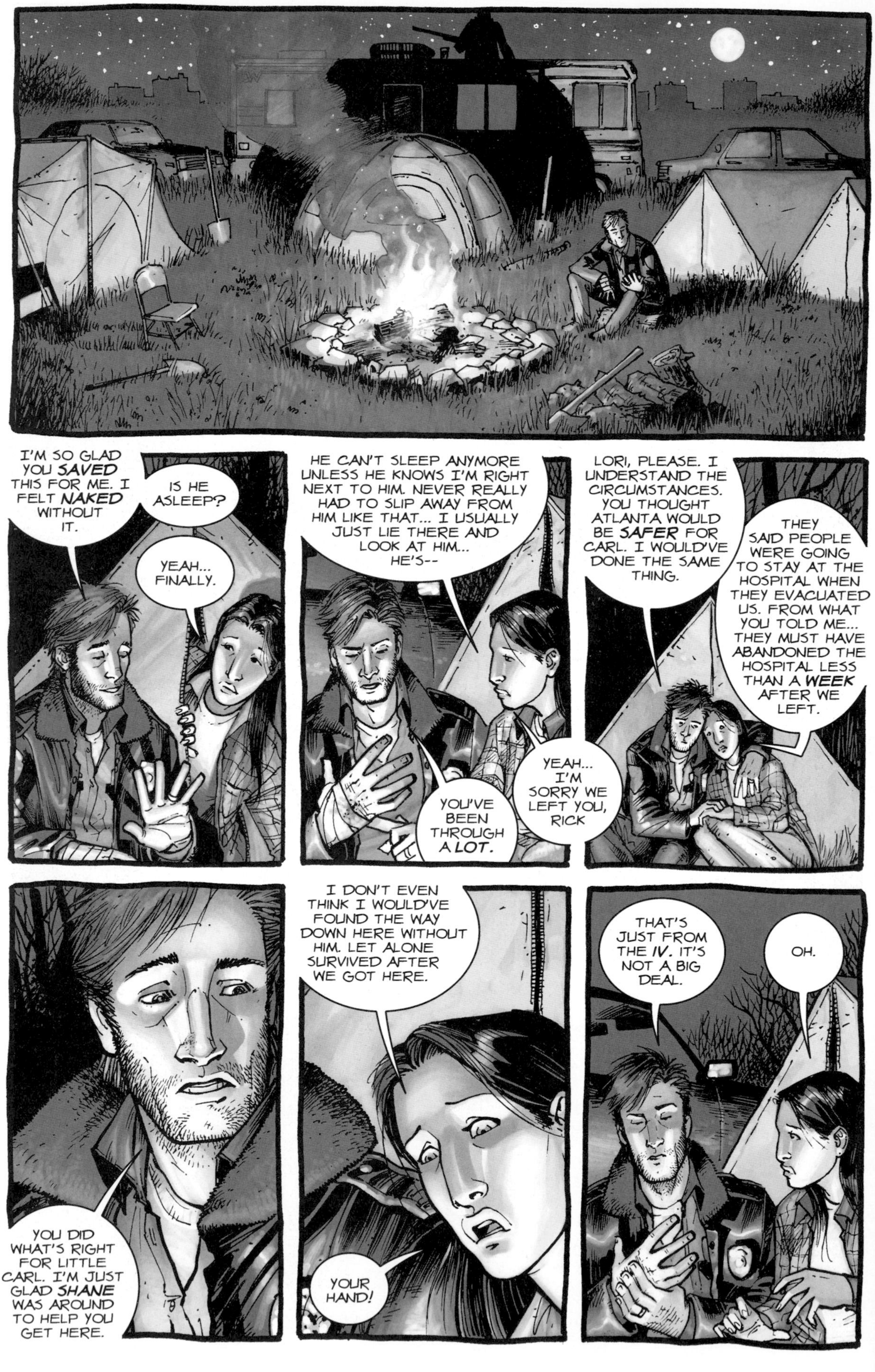
I'M SO GLAD YOU SAVED THIS FOR ME. I FELT NAKED WITHOUT IT.
IS HE ASLEEP?
YEAH... FINALLY.
HE CAN'T SLEEP ANYMORE UNLESS HE KNOWS I'M RIGHT NEXT TO HIM. NEVER REALLY HAD TO SLIP AWAY FROM HIM LIKE THAT... I USUALLY JUST LIE THERE AND LOOK AT HIM... HE'S--
YOU'VE BEEN THROUGH A LOT.
YEAH... I'M SORRY WE LEFT YOU, RICK
LORI, PLEASE. I UNDERSTAND THE CIRCUMSTANCES. YOU THOUGHT ATLANTA WOULD BE SAFER FOR CARL. I WOULD'VE DONE THE SAME THING.
THEY SAID PEOPLE WERE GOING TO STAY AT THE HOSPITAL WHEN THEY EVACUATED US. FROM WHAT YOU TOLD ME... THEY MUST HAVE ABANDONED THE HOSPITAL LESS THAN A WEEK AFTER WE LEFT.
YOU DID WHAT'S RIGHT FOR LITTLE CARL. I'M JUST GLAD SHANE WAS AROUND TO HELP YOU GET HERE.
I DON'T EVEN THINK I WOULD'VE FOUND THE WAY DOWN HERE WITHOUT HIM. LET ALONE SURVIVED AFTER WE GOT HERE.
YOUR HAND!
THAT'S JUST FROM THE IV. IT'S NOT A BIG DEAL.
OH.

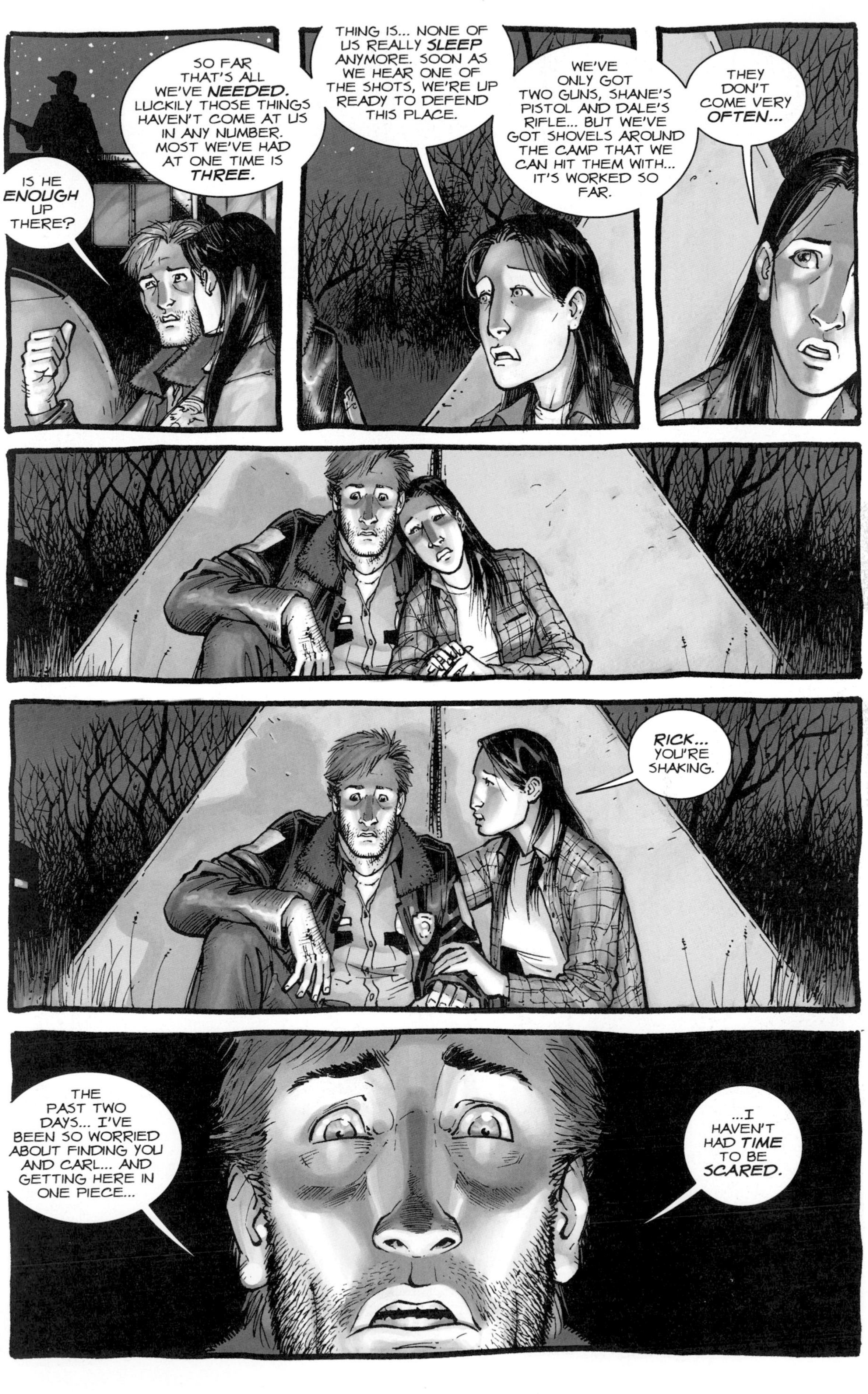
IS HE ENOUGH UP THERE?
SO FAR THAT'S ALL WE'VE NEEDED. LUCKILY THOSE THINGS HAVEN'T COME AT US IN ANY NUMBER. MOST WE'VE HAD AT ONE TIME IS THREE.
THING IS... NONE OF US REALLY SLEEP ANYMORE. SOON AS WE HEAR ONE OF THE SHOTS, WE'RE UP READY TO DEFEND THIS PLACE.
WE'VE ONLY GOT TWO GUNS, SHANE'S PISTOL AND DALE'S RIFLE... BUT WE'VE GOT SHOVELS AROUND THE CAMP THAT WE CAN HIT THEM WITH... IT'S WORKED SO FAR.
THEY DON'T COME VERY OFTEN...
RICK... YOU'RE SHAKING.
THE PAST TWO DAYS... I'VE BEEN SO WORRIED ABOUT FINDING YOU AND CARL... AND GETTING HERE IN ONE PIECE...
...I HAVEN'T HAD TIME TO BE SCARED.

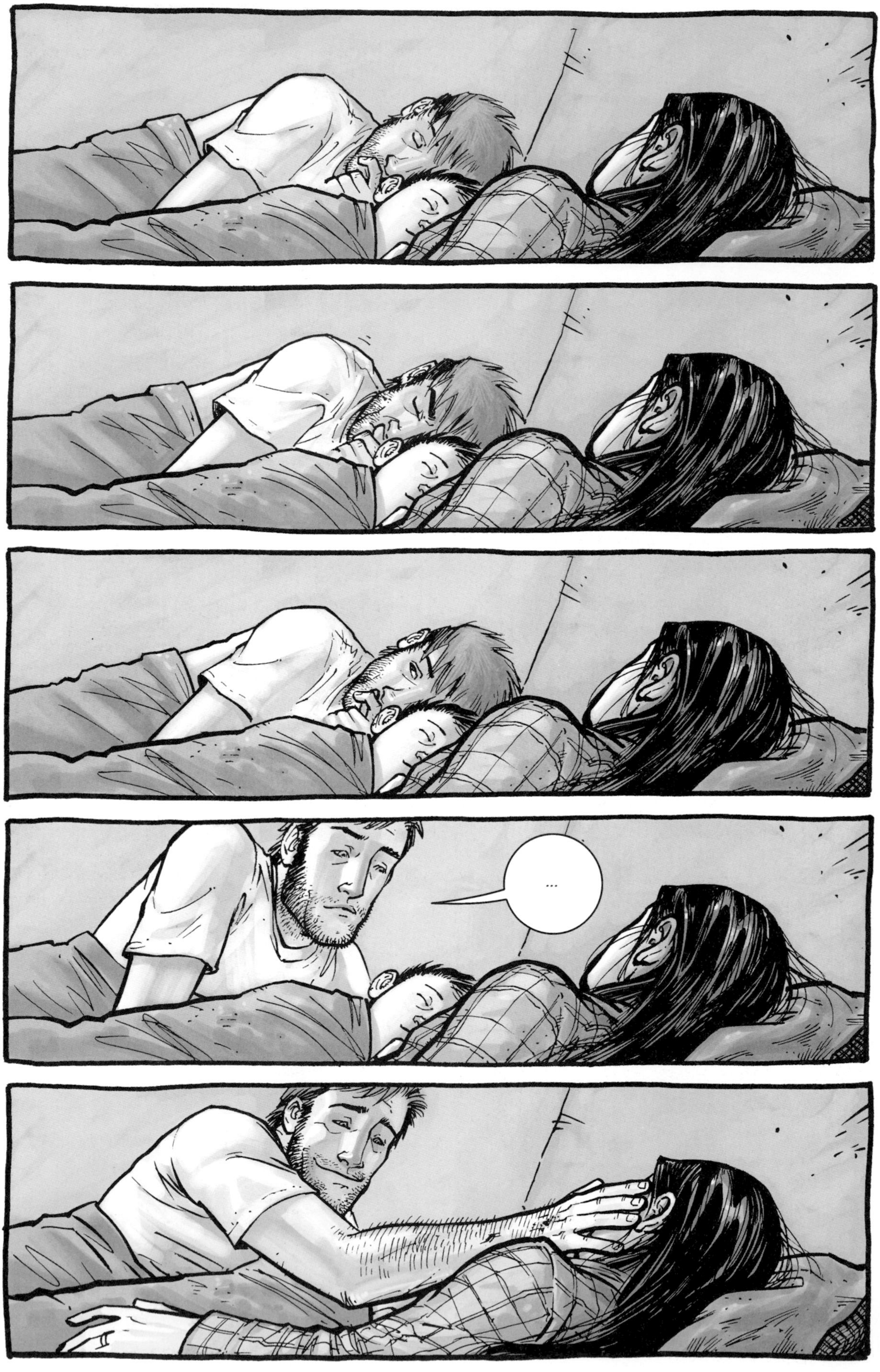
...

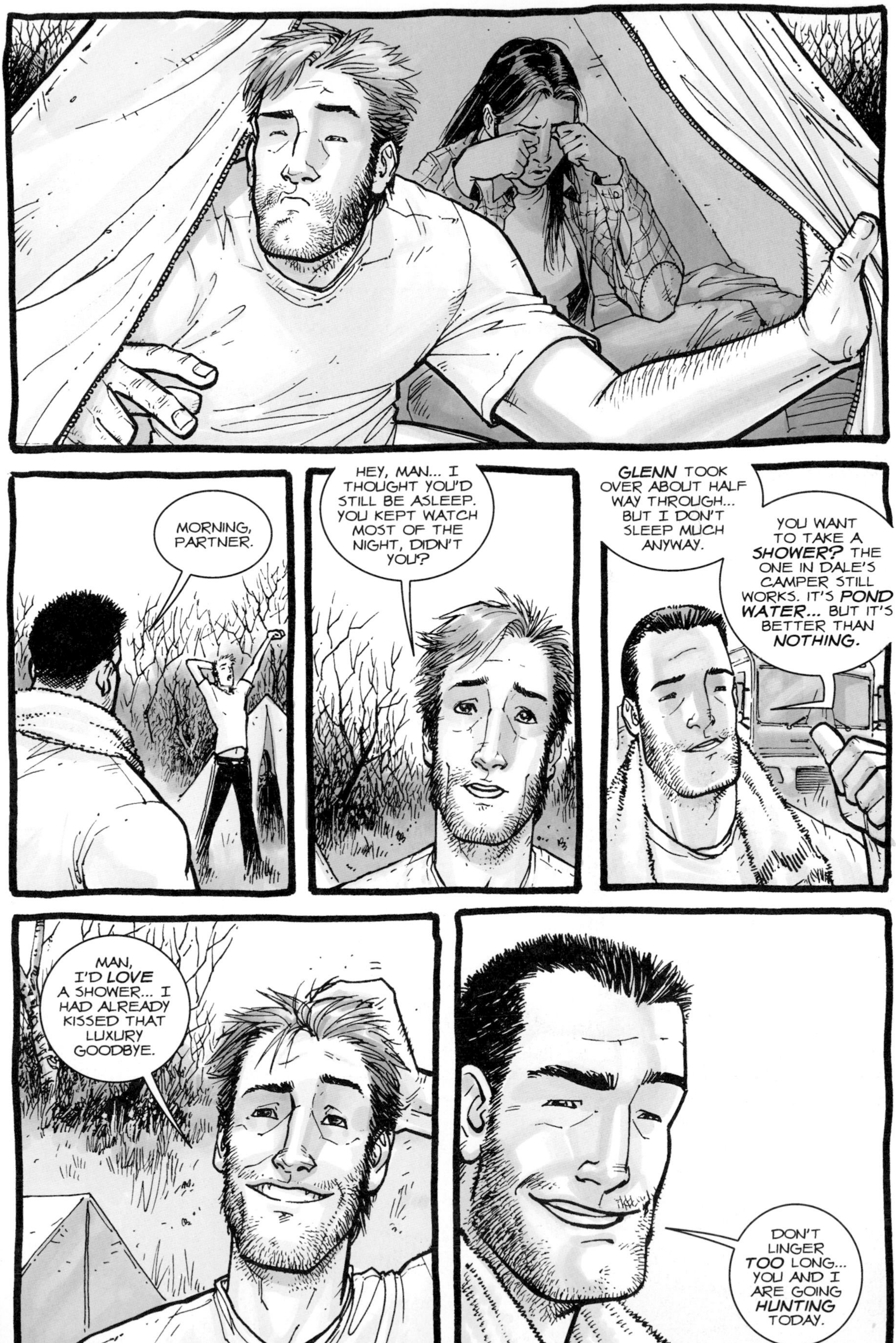
MORNING, PARTNER.
HEY, MAN... I THOUGHT YOU'D STILL BE ASLEEP. YOU KEPT WATCH MOST OF THE NIGHT, DIDN'T YOU?
GLENN TOOK OVER ABOUT HALF WAY THROUGH... BUT I DON'T SLEEP MUCH ANYWAY.
YOU WANT TO TAKE A SHOWER? THE ONE IN DALE'S CAMPER STILL WORKS. IT'S POND WATER... BUT IT'S BETTER THAN NOTHING.
MAN, I'D LOVE A SHOWER... I HAD ALREADY KISSED THAT LUXURY GOODBYE.
DON'T LINGER TOO LONG... YOU AND I ARE GOING HUNTING TODAY.

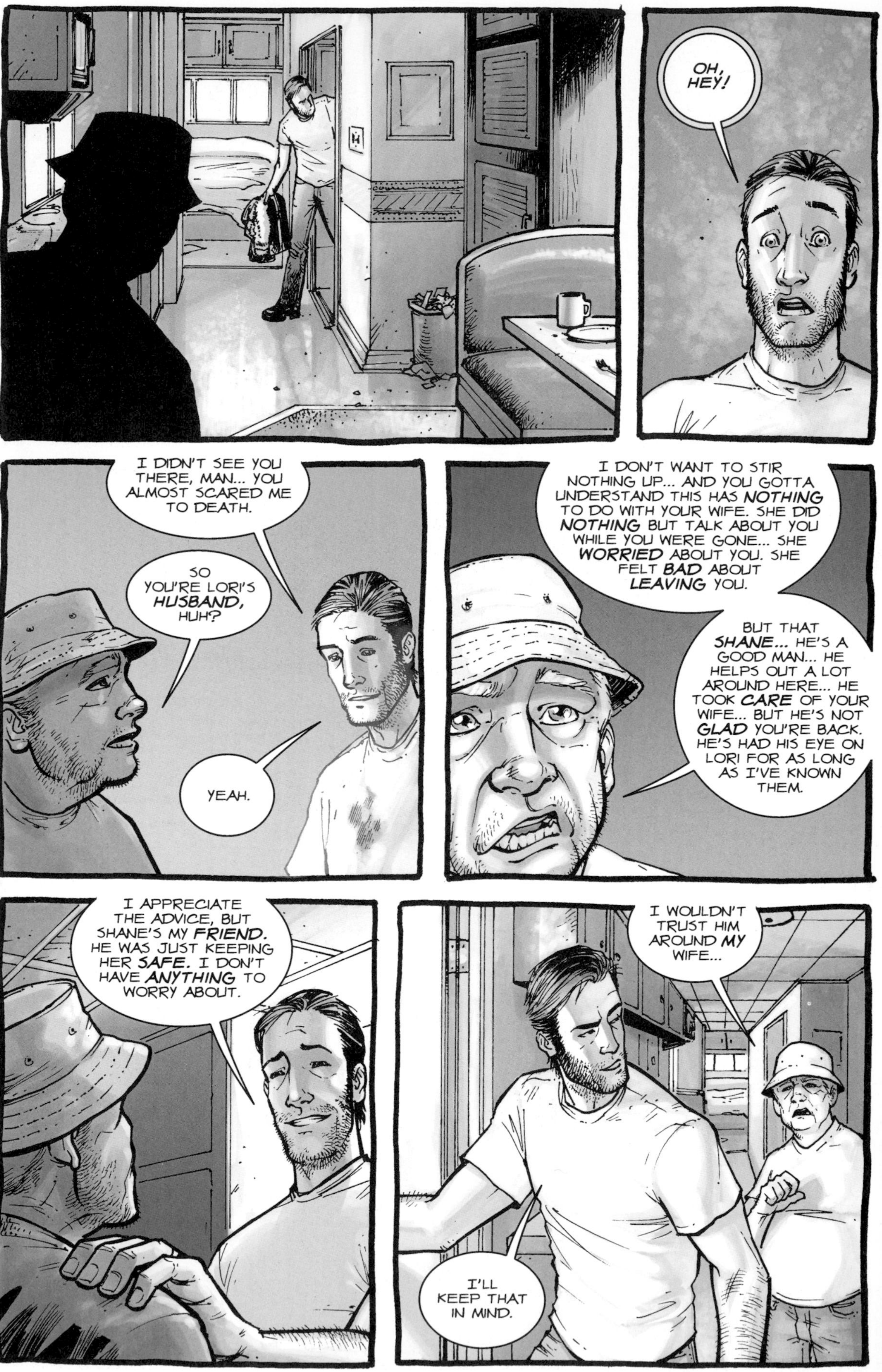
OH, HEY!
I DIDN'T SEE YOU THERE, MAN... YOU ALMOST SCARED ME TO DEATH.
SO YOU'RE LORI'S HUSBAND, HUH?
YEAH.
I DON'T WANT TO STIR NOTHING UP... AND YOU GOTTA UNDERSTAND THIS HAS NOTHING TO DO WITH YOUR WIFE. SHE DID NOTHING BUT TALK ABOUT YOU WHILE YOU WERE GONE... SHE WORRIED ABOUT YOU. SHE FELT BAD ABOUT LEAVING YOU.
BUT THAT SHANE... HE'S A GOOD MAN... HE HELPS OUT A LOT AROUND HERE... HE TOOK CARE OF YOUR WIFE... BUT HE'S NOT GLAD YOU'RE BACK. HE'S HAD HIS EYE ON LORI FOR AS LONG AS I'VE KNOWN THEM.
I APPRECIATE THE ADVICE, BUT SHANE'S MY FRIEND. HE WAS JUST KEEPING HER SAFE. I DON'T HAVE ANYTHING TO WORRY ABOUT.
I WOULDN'T TRUST HIM AROUND MY WIFE...
I'LL KEEP THAT IN MIND.

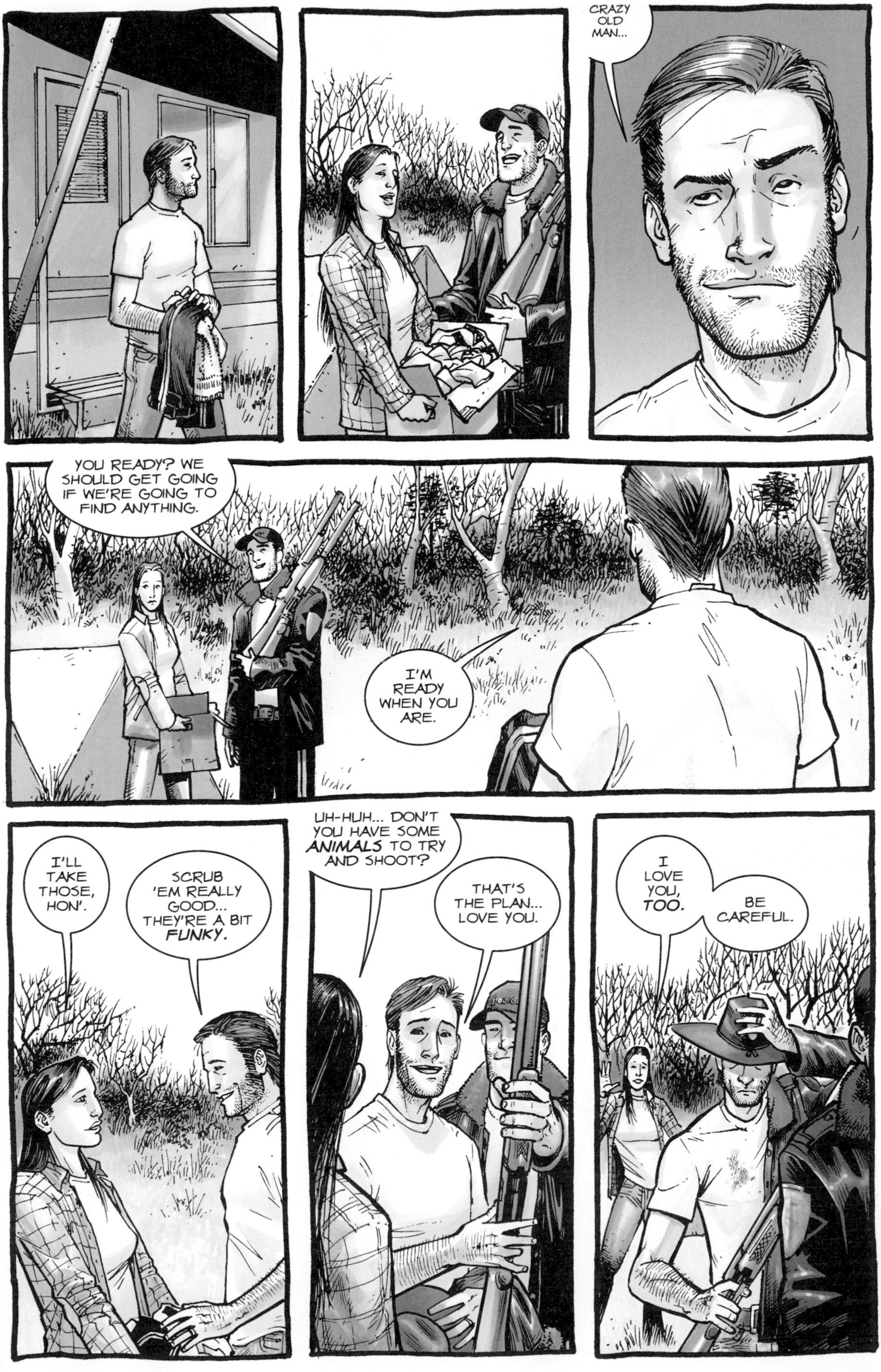
CRAZY OLD MAN...
YOU READY? WE SHOULD GET GOING IF WE'RE GOING TO FIND ANYTHING.
I'M READY WHEN YOU ARE.
I'LL TAKE THOSE, HON'.
SCRUB 'EM REALLY GOOD... THEY'RE A BIT FUNKY.
UH-HUH... DON'T YOU HAVE SOME ANIMALS TO TRY AND SHOOT?
THAT'S THE PLAN... LOVE YOU.
I LOVE YOU, TOO.
BE CAREFUL.

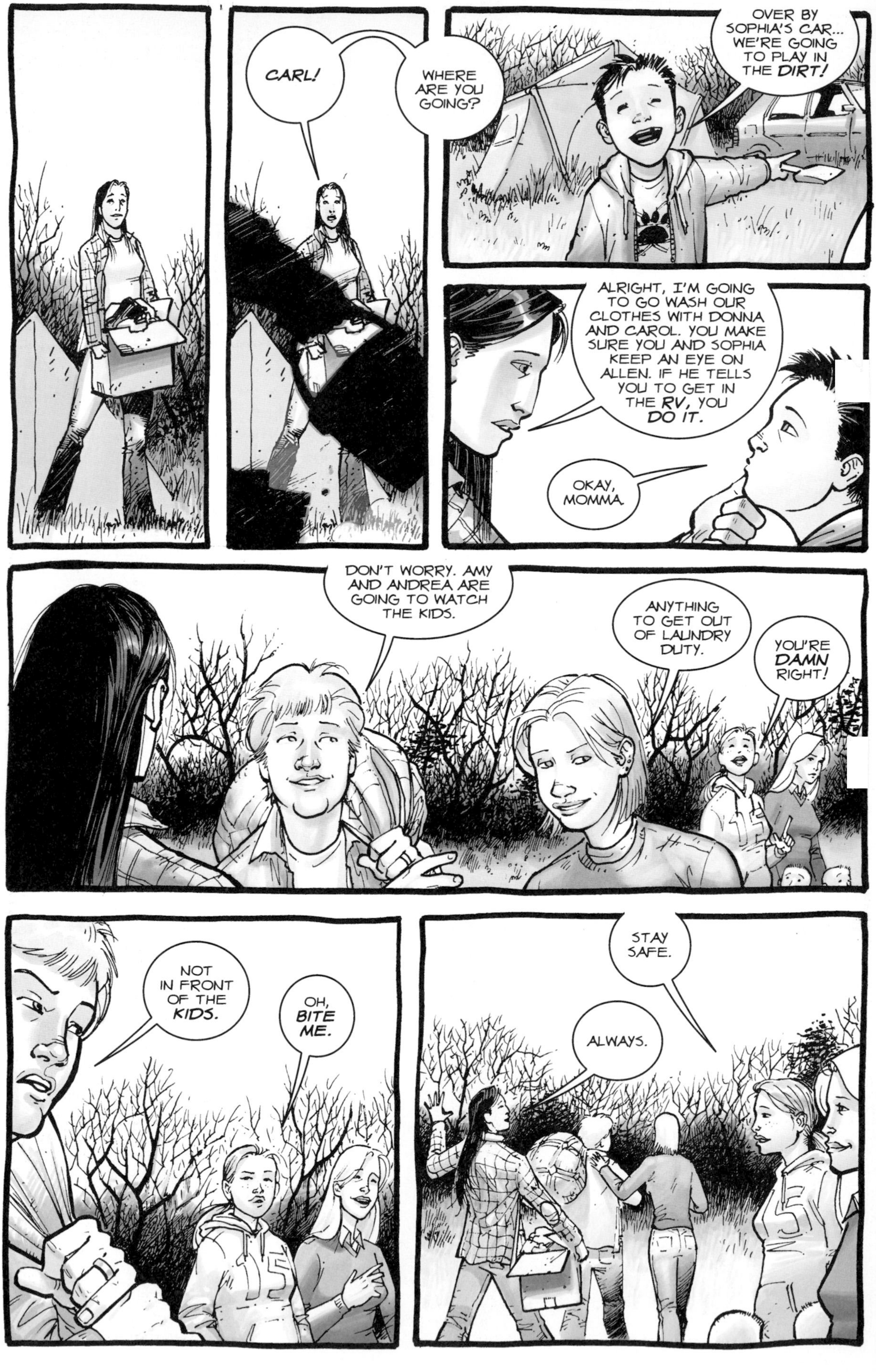
CARL!
WHERE ARE YOU GOING?
OVER BY SOPHIA'S CAR... WE'RE GOING TO PLAY IN THE DIRT!
ALRIGHT, I'M GOING TO GO WASH OUR CLOTHES WITH DONNA AND CAROL. YOU MAKE SURE YOU AND SOPHIA KEEP AN EYE ON ALLEN. IF HE TELLS YOU TO GET IN THE RV, YOU DO IT.
OKAY, MOMMA.
DON'T WORRY. AMY AND ANDREA ARE GOING TO WATCH THE KIDS.
ANYTHING TO GET OUT OF LAUNDRY DUTY.
YOU'RE DAMN RIGHT!
NOT IN FRONT OF THE KIDS.
OH, BITE ME.
STAY SAFE.
ALWAYS.

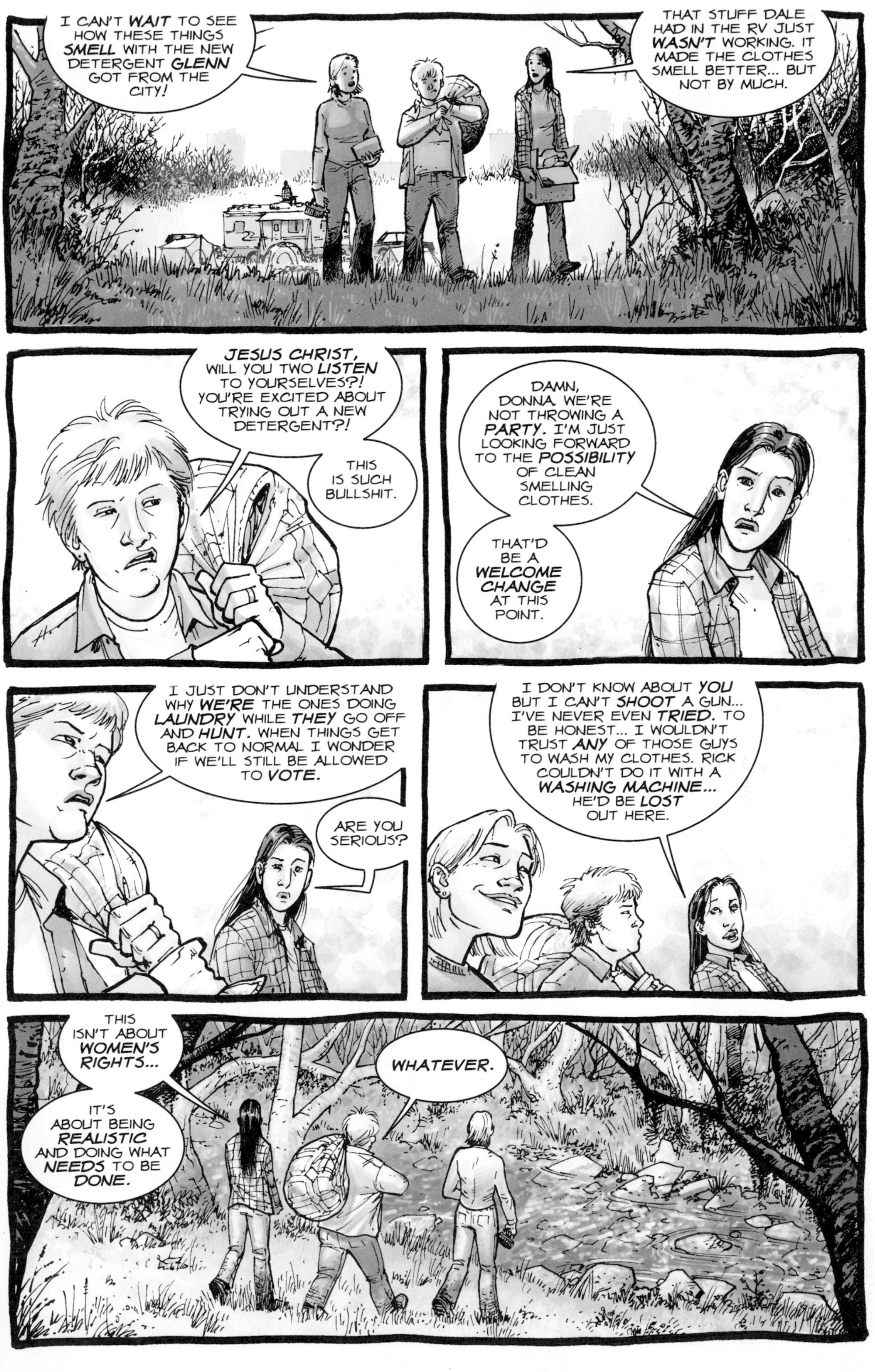
I CAN'T WAIT TO SEE HOW THESE THINGS SMELL WITH THE NEW DETERGENT GLENN GOT FROM THE CITY!
THAT STUFF DALE HAD IN THE RV JUST WASN'T WORKING. IT MADE THE CLOTHES SMELL BETTER... BUT NOT BY MUCH.
JESUS CHRIST, WILL YOU TWO LISTEN TO YOURSELVES?! YOU'RE EXCITED ABOUT TRYING OUT A NEW DETERGENT?!
THIS IS SUCH BULLSHIT.
DAMN, DONNA. WE'RE NOT THROWING A PARTY. I'M JUST LOOKING FORWARD TO THE POSSIBILITY OF CLEAN SMELLING CLOTHES.
THAT'D BE A WELCOME CHANGE AT THIS POINT.
I JUST DON'T UNDERSTAND WHY WE'RE THE ONES DOING LAUNDRY WHILE THEY GO OFF AND HUNT. WHEN THINGS GET BACK TO NORMAL I WONDER IF WE'LL STILL BE ALLOWED TO VOTE.
ARE YOU SERIOUS?
I DON'T KNOW ABOUT YOU BUT I CAN'T SHOOT A GUN... I'VE NEVER EVEN TRIED. TO BE HONEST... I WOULDN'T TRUST ANY OF THOSE GUYS TO WASH MY CLOTHES. RICK COULDN'T DO IT WITH A WASHING MACHINE... HE'D BE LOST OUT HERE.
THIS ISN'T ABOUT WOMEN'S RIGHTS...
IT'S ABOUT BEING REALISTIC AND DOING WHAT NEEDS TO BE DONE.
WHATEVER.

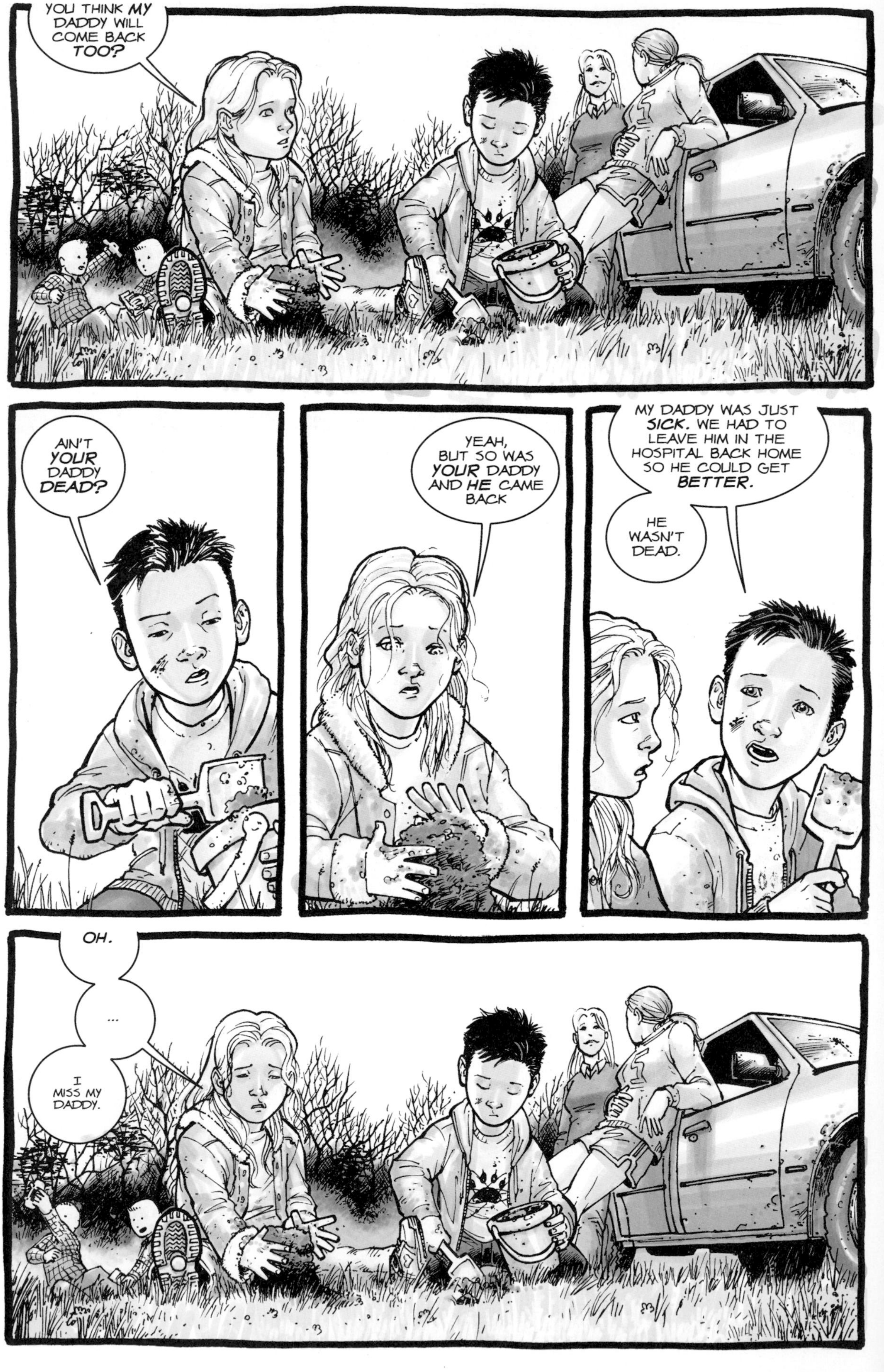

YOU THINK MY DADDY WILL COME BACK TOO?
AIN'T YOUR DADDY DEAD?
YEAH, BUT SO WAS YOUR DADDY AND HE CAME BACK
MY DADDY WAS JUST SICK. WE HAD TO LEAVE HIM IN THE HOSPITAL BACK HOME SO HE COULD GET BETTER.
HE WASN'T DEAD.
OH.
...
I MISS MY DADDY.

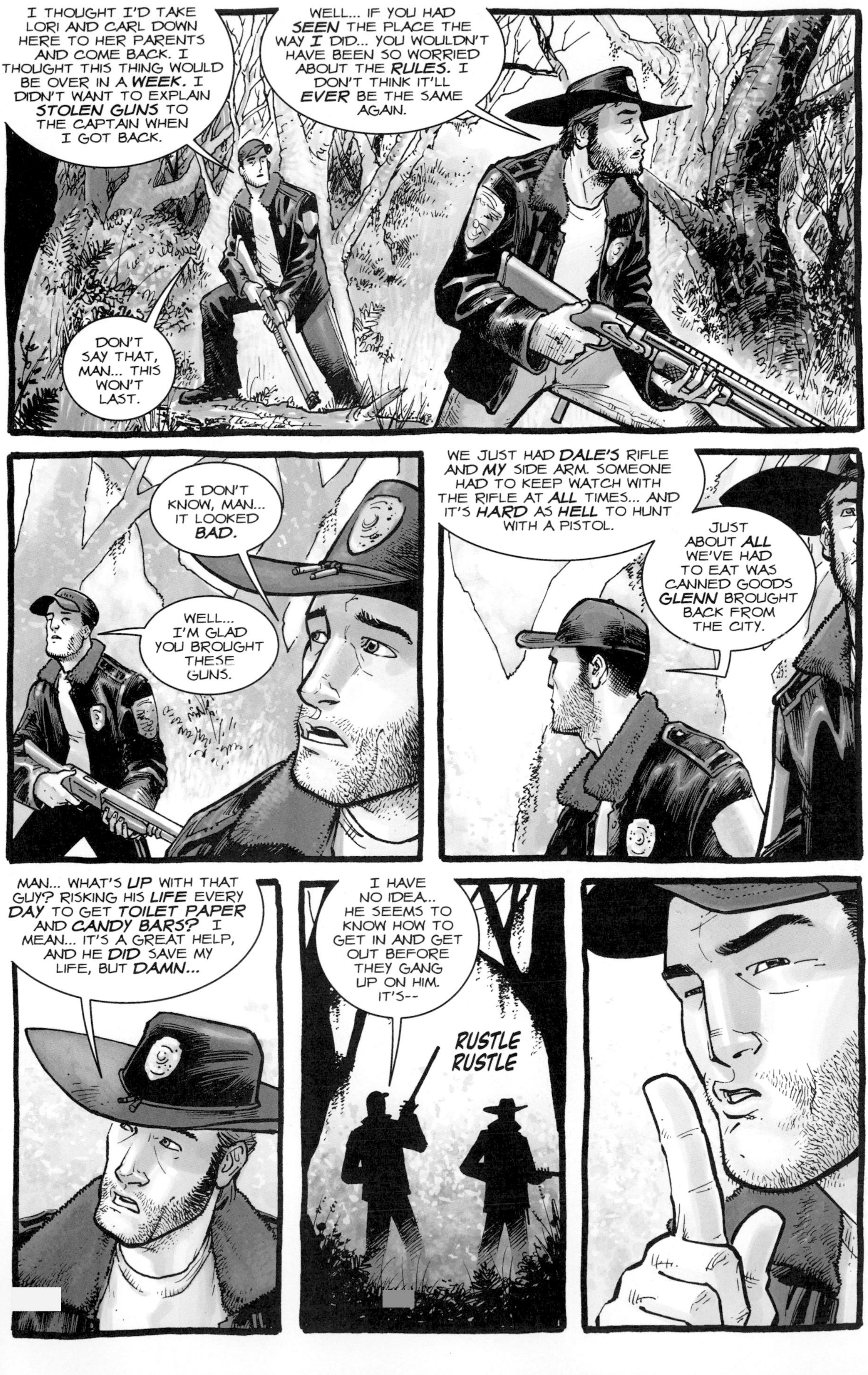
I THOUGHT I'D TAKE LORI AND CARL DOWN HERE TO HER PARENTS AND COME BACK. I THOUGHT THIS THING WOULD BE OVER IN A WEEK. I DIDN'T WANT TO EXPLAIN STOLEN GUNS TO THE CAPTAIN WHEN I GOT BACK.
WELL... IF YOU HAD SEEN THE PLACE THE WAY I DID... YOU WOULDN'T HAVE BEEN SO WORRIED ABOUT THE RULES. I DON'T THINK IT'LL EVER BE THE SAME AGAIN.
DON'T SAY THAT, MAN... THIS WON'T LAST.
I DON'T KNOW, MAN... IT LOOKED BAD.
WELL... I'M GLAD YOU BROUGHT THESE GUNS.
WE JUST HAD DALE'S RIFLE AND MY SIDE ARM. SOMEONE HAD TO KEEP WATCH WITH THE RIFLE AT ALL TIMES... AND IT'S HARD AS HELL TO HUNT WITH A PISTOL.
JUST ABOUT ALL WE'VE HAD TO EAT WAS CANNED GOODS GLENN BROUGHT BACK FROM THE CITY.
MAN... WHAT'S UP WITH THAT GUY? RISKING HIS LIFE EVERY DAY TO GET TOILET PAPER AND CANDY BARS? I MEAN... IT'S A GREAT HELP, AND HE DID SAVE MY LIFE, BUT DAMN...
I HAVE NO IDEA... HE SEEMS TO KNOW HOW TO GET IN AND GET OUT BEFORE THEY GANG UP ON HIM. IT'S--
RUSTLE RUSTLE

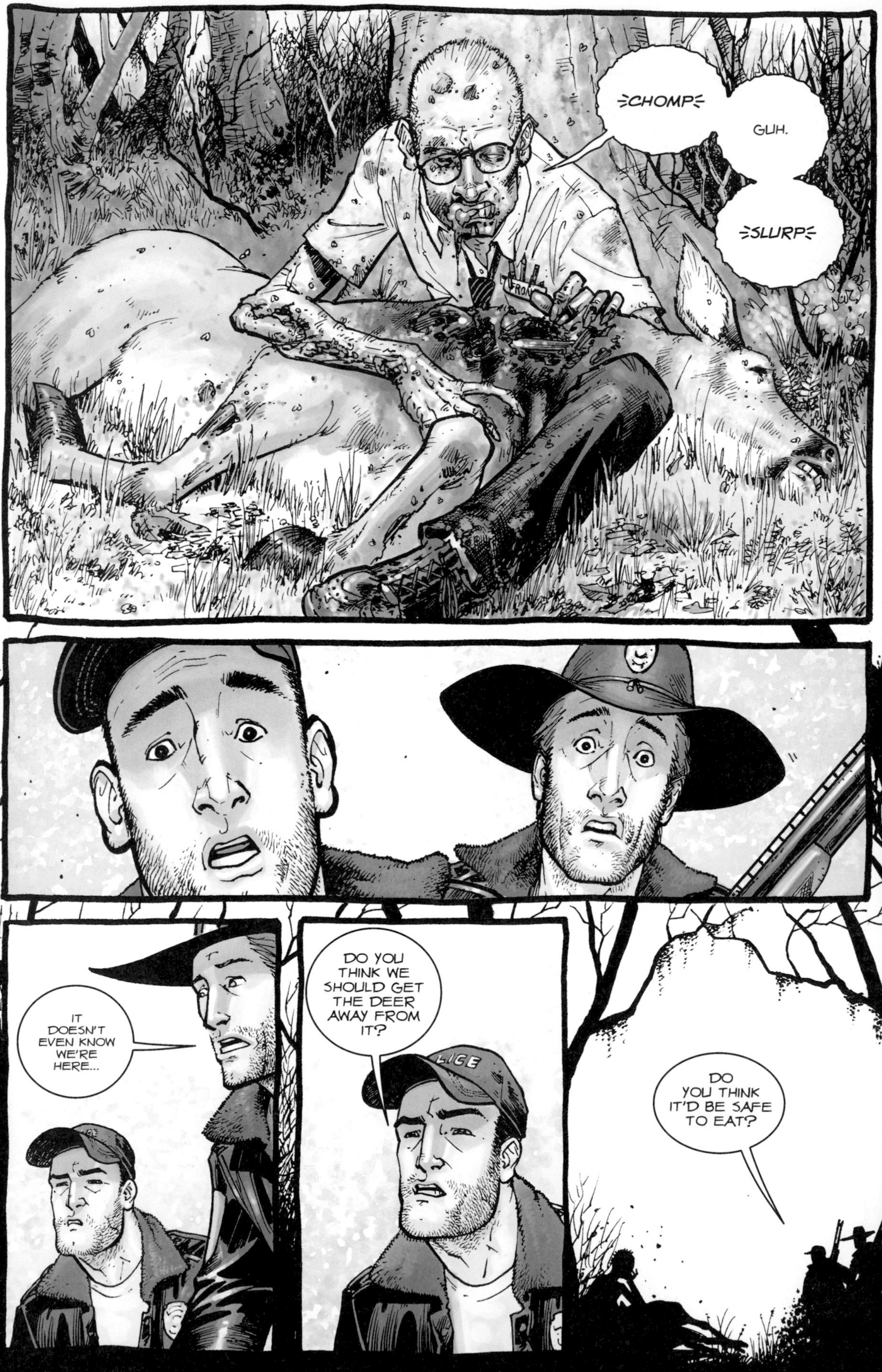
CHOMP
GUH.
SLURP
IT DOESN'T EVEN KNOW WE'RE HERE...
DO YOU THINK WE SHOULD GET THE DEER AWAY FROM IT?
DO YOU THINK IT'D BE SAFE TO EAT?

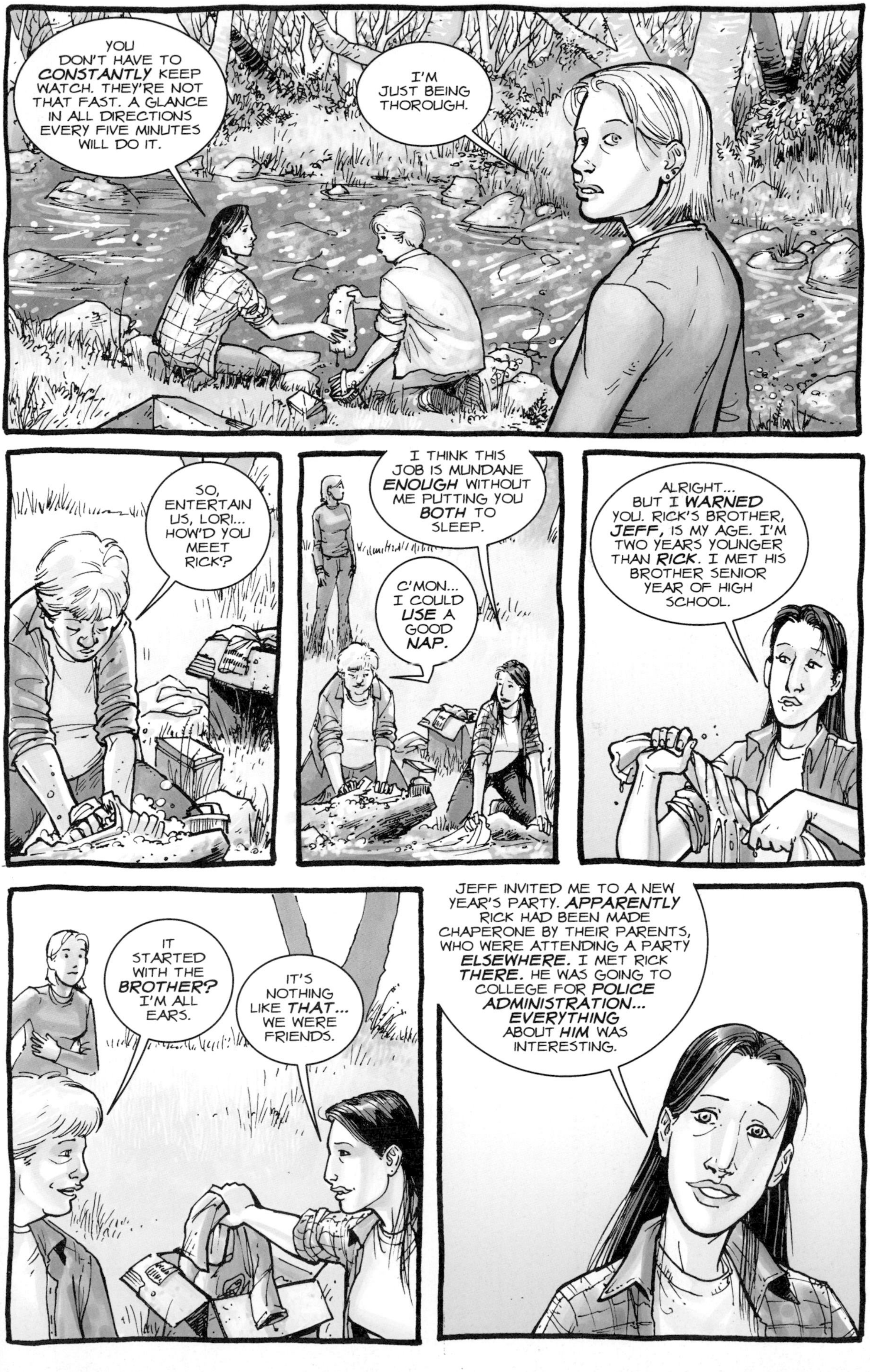
YOU DON'T HAVE TO CONSTANTLY KEEP WATCH. THEY'RE NOT THAT FAST. A GLANCE IN ALL DIRECTIONS EVERY FIVE MINUTES WILL DO IT.
I'M JUST BEING THOROUGH.
SO, ENTERTAIN US, LORI... HOW'D YOU MEET RICK?
I THINK THIS JOB IS MUNDANE ENOUGH WITHOUT ME PUTTING YOU BOTH TO SLEEP.
C'MON... I COULD USE A GOOD NAP.
ALRIGHT... BUT I WARNED YOU. RICK'S BROTHER, JEFF, IS MY AGE. I'M TWO YEARS YOUNGER THAN RICK. I MET HIS BROTHER SENIOR YEAR OF HIGH SCHOOL.
IT STARTED WITH THE BROTHER? I'M ALL EARS.
IT'S NOTHING LIKE THAT... WE WERE FRIENDS.
JEFF INVITED ME TO A NEW YEAR'S PARTY. APPARENTLY RICK HAD BEEN MADE CHAPERONE BY THEIR PARENTS, WHO WERE ATTENDING A PARTY ELSEWHERE. I MET RICK THERE. HE WAS GOING TO COLLEGE FOR POLICE ADMINISTRATION... EVERYTHING ABOUT HIM WAS INTERESTING.

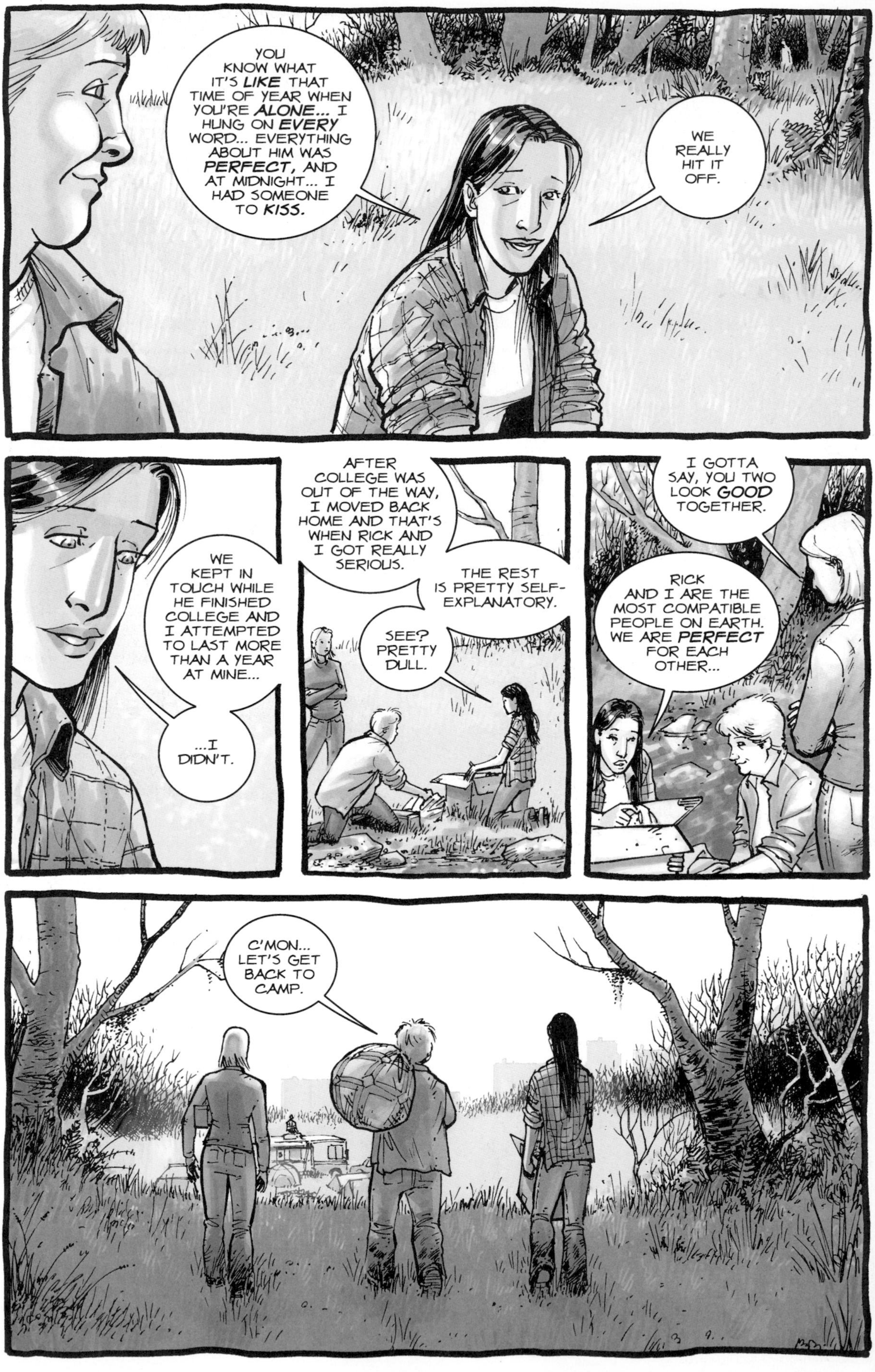
YOU KNOW WHAT IT'S LIKE THAT TIME OF YEAR WHEN YOU'RE ALONE... I HUNG ON EVERY WORD... EVERYTHING ABOUT HIM WAS PERFECT, AND AT MIDNIGHT... I HAD SOMEONE TO KISS.
WE REALLY HIT IT OFF.
WE KEPT IN TOUCH WHILE HE FINISHED COLLEGE AND I ATTEMPTED TO LAST MORE THAN A YEAR AT MINE...
...I DIDN'T.
AFTER COLLEGE WAS OUT OF THE WAY, I MOVED BACK HOME AND THAT'S WHEN RICK AND I GOT REALLY SERIOUS.
THE REST IS PRETTY SELF-EXPLANATORY.
SEE? PRETTY DULL.
I GOTTA SAY, YOU TWO LOOK GOOD TOGETHER.
RICK AND I ARE THE MOST COMPATIBLE PEOPLE ON EARTH. WE ARE PERFECT FOR EACH OTHER...
C'MON... LET'S GET BACK TO CAMP.

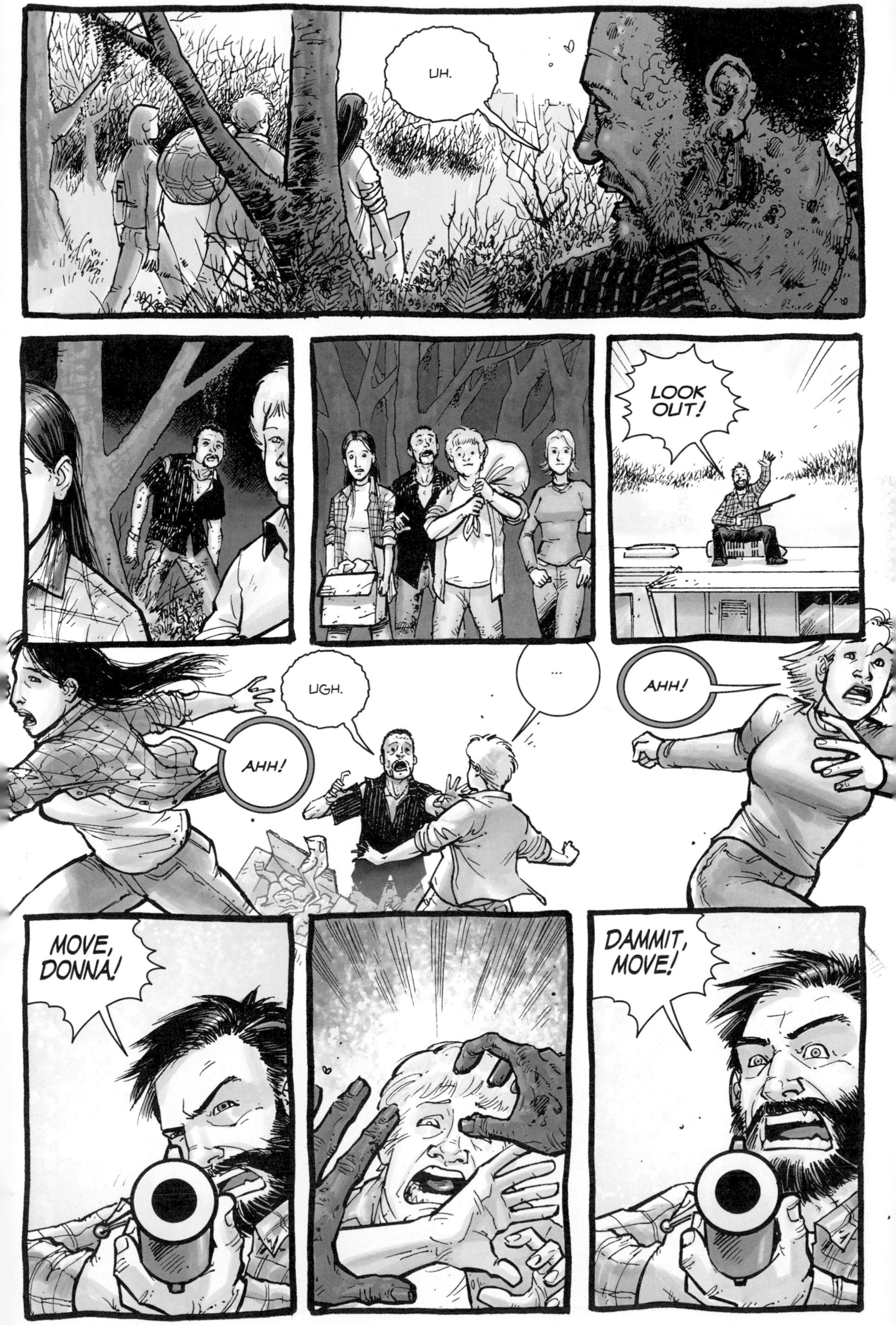
UH.
LOOK OUT!
AHH!
UGH.
...
AHH!
MOVE, DONNA!
DAMMIT, MOVE!

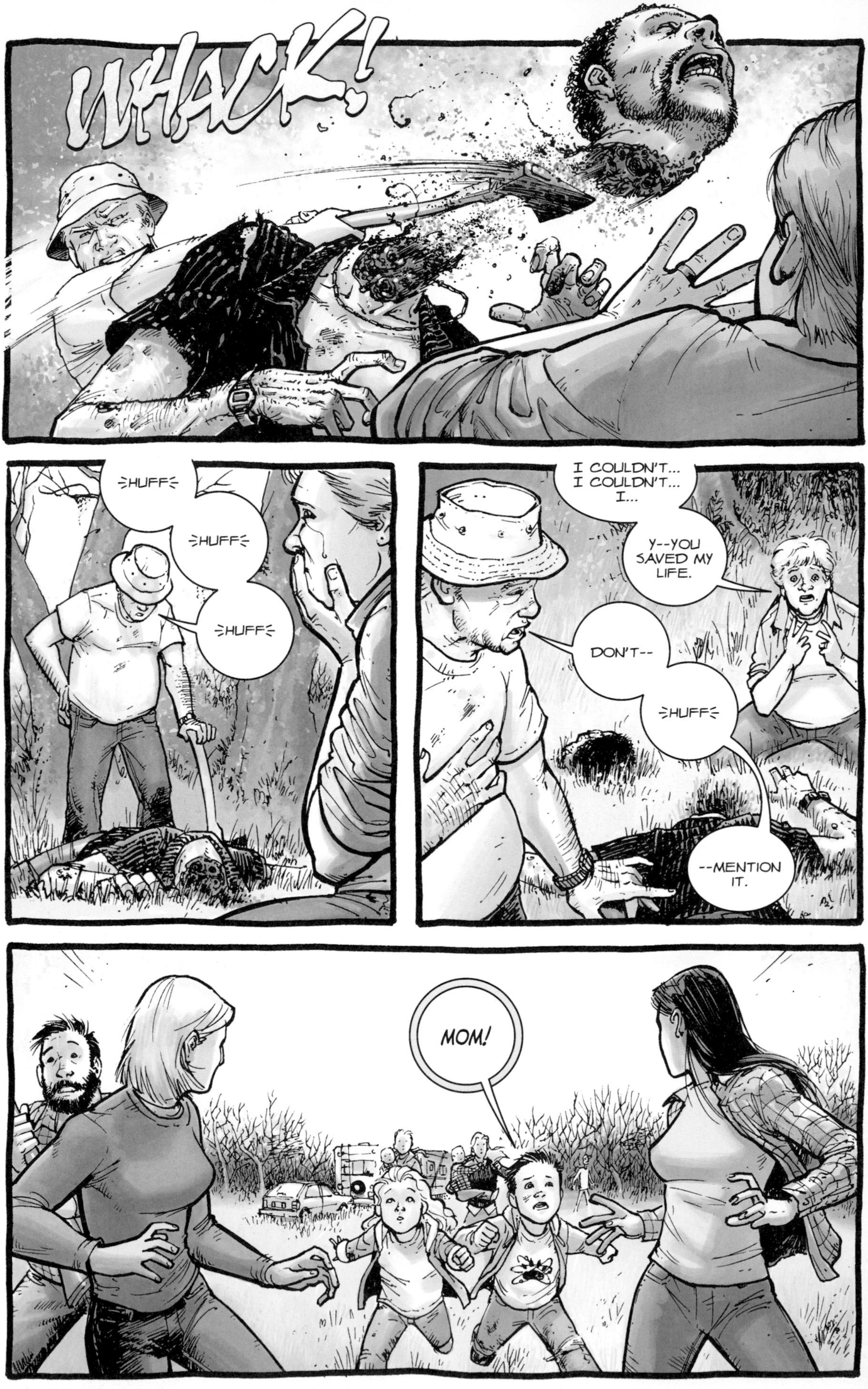
WHACK!
HUFF
HUFF
HUFF
I COULDN'T... I COULDN'T... I...
Y--YOU SAVED MY LIFE.
DON'T--
HUFF
--MENTION IT.
MOM!

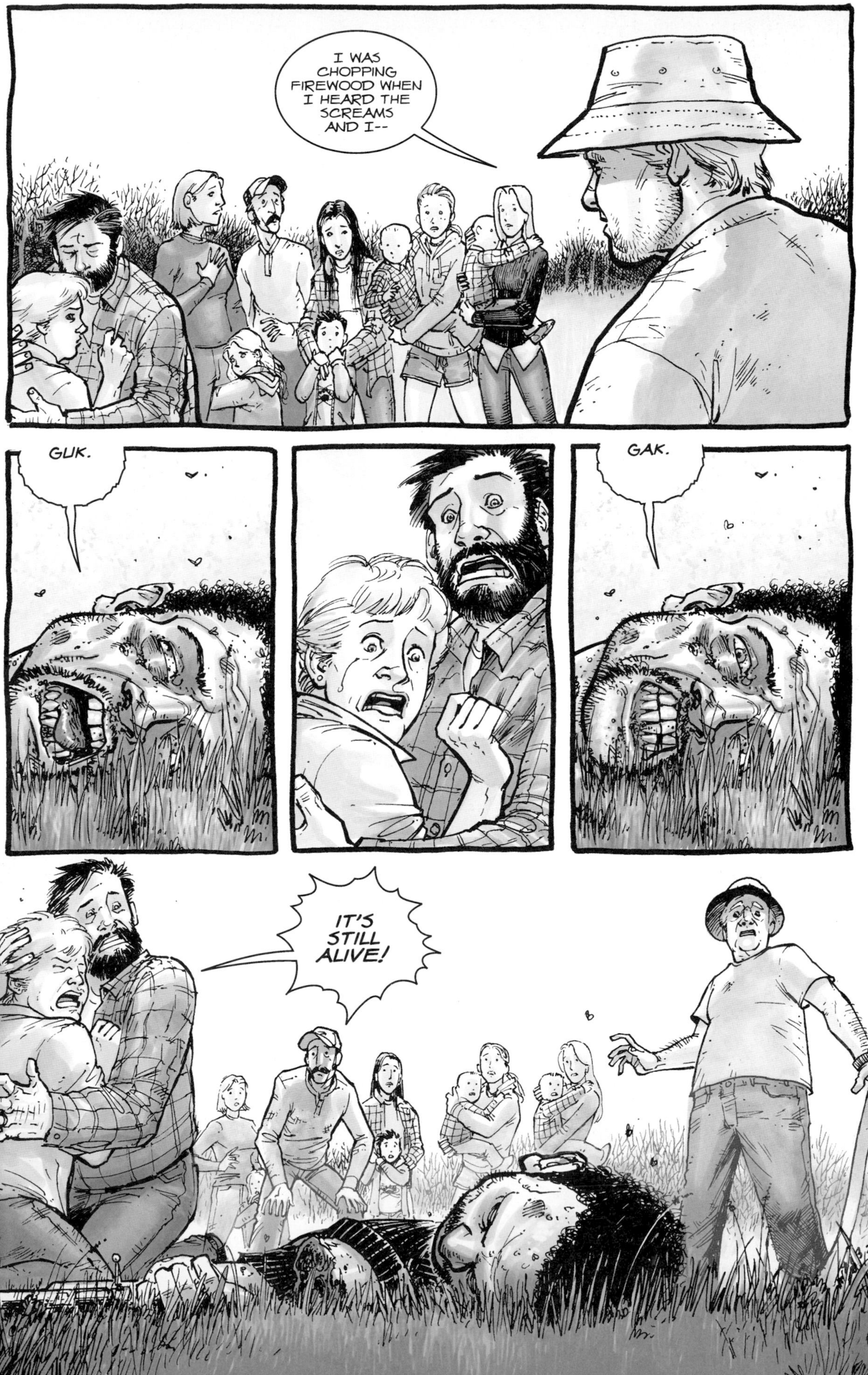
I WAS CHOPPING FIREWOOD WHEN I HEARD THE SCREAMS AND I--
GUK.
GAK.
IT'S STILL ALIVE!

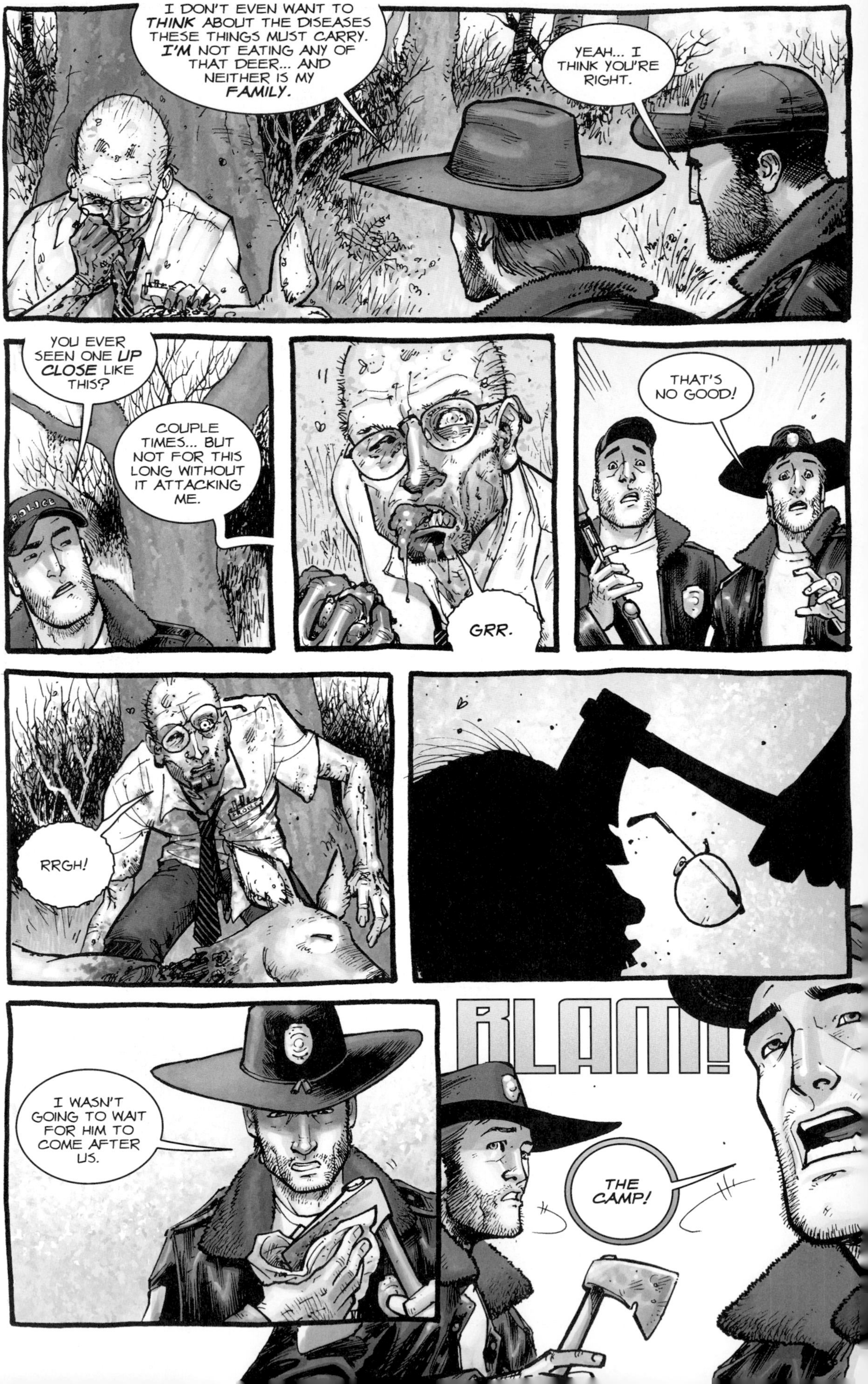
I DON'T EVEN WANT TO THINK ABOUT THE DISEASES THESE THINGS MUST CARRY. I'M NOT EATING ANY OF THAT DEER... AND NEITHER IS MY FAMILY.
YEAH... I THINK YOU'RE RIGHT.
YOU EVER SEEN ONE UP CLOSE LIKE THIS?
COUPLE TIMES... BUT NOT FOR THIS LONG WITHOUT IT ATTACKING ME.
GRR.
THAT'S NO GOOD!
RRGH!
BLAM!
I WASN'T GOING TO WAIT FOR HIM TO COME AFTER US.
THE CAMP!

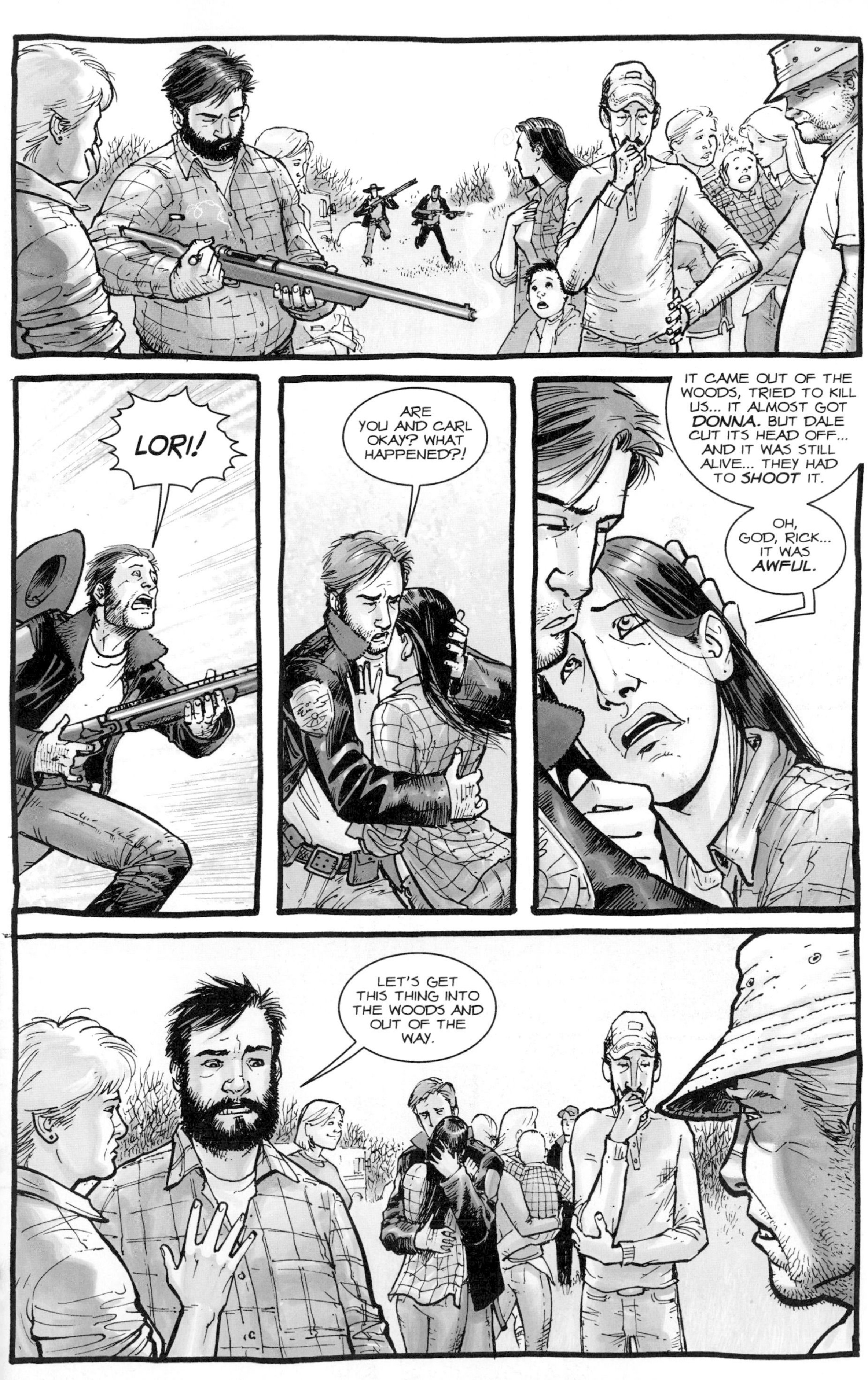
LORI!
ARE YOU AND CARL OKAY? WHAT HAPPENED?!
IT CAME OUT OF THE WOODS, TRIED TO KILL US... IT ALMOST GOT DONNA. BUT DALE CUT ITS HEAD OFF... AND IT WAS STILL ALIVE... THEY HAD TO SHOOT IT.
OH, GOD, RICK... IT WAS AWFUL.
LET'S GET THIS THING INTO THE WOODS AND OUT OF THE WAY.

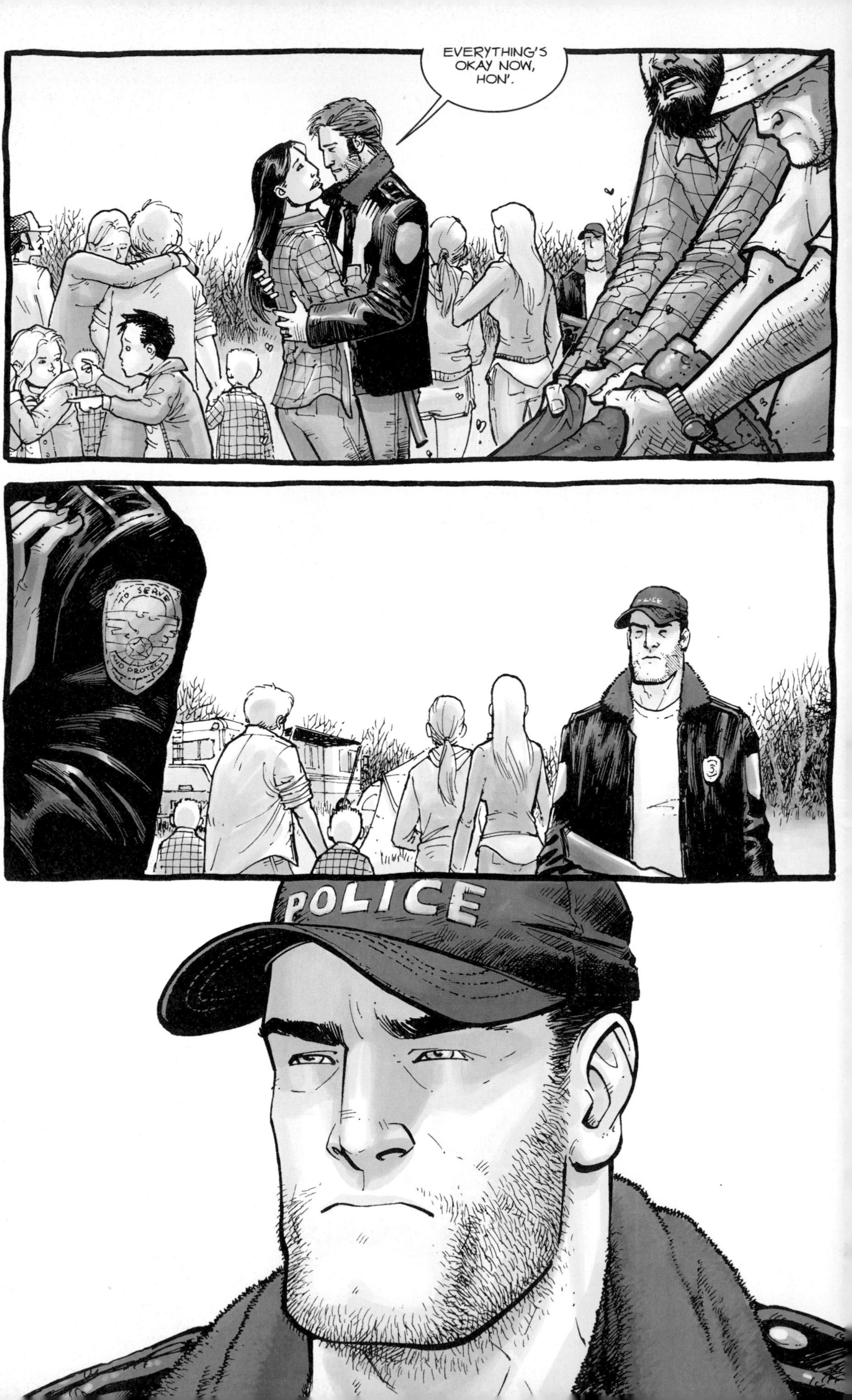
EVERYTHING'S OKAY NOW, HON'.
TO SERVE AND PROTECT
POLICE
POLICE

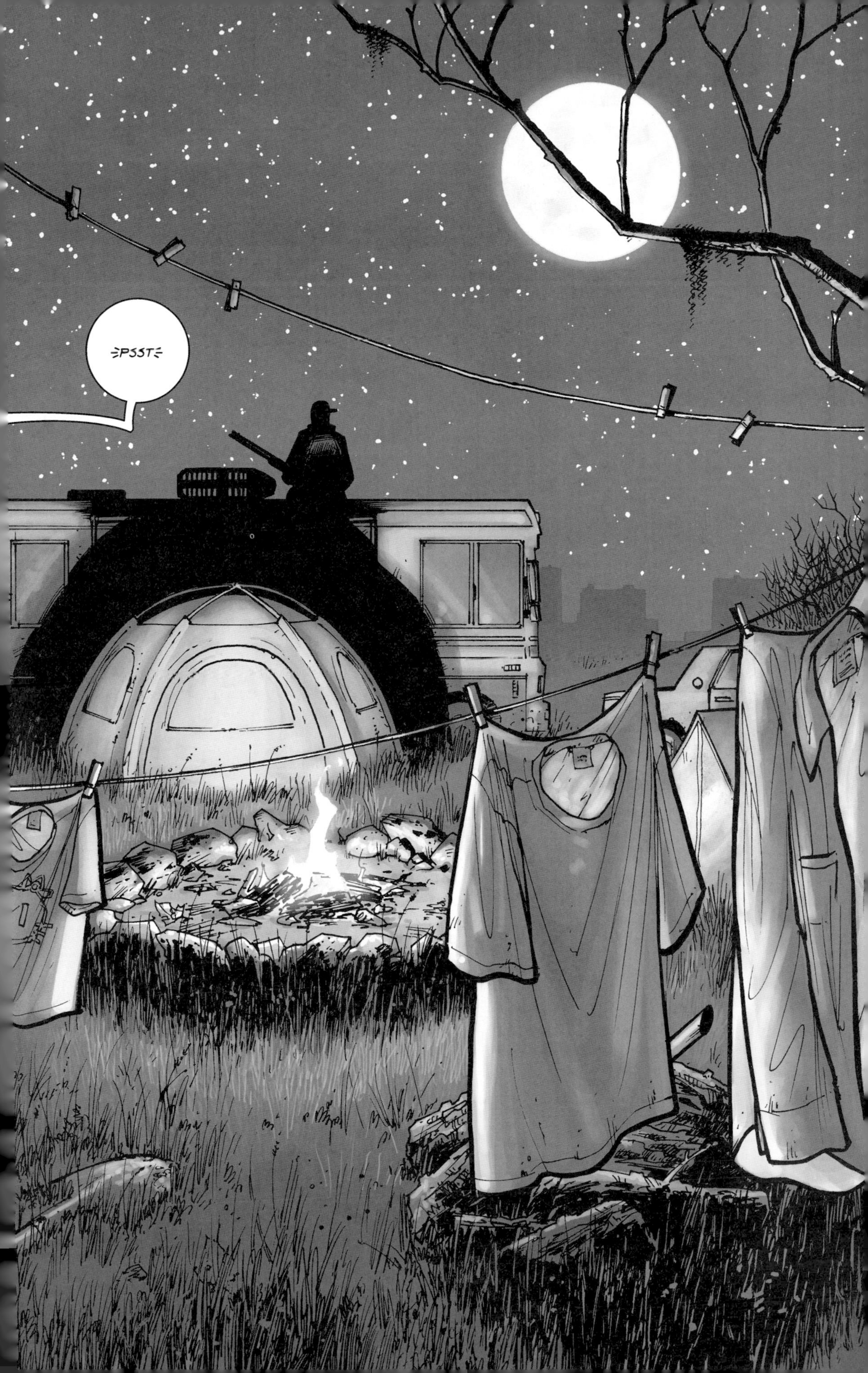
PSST

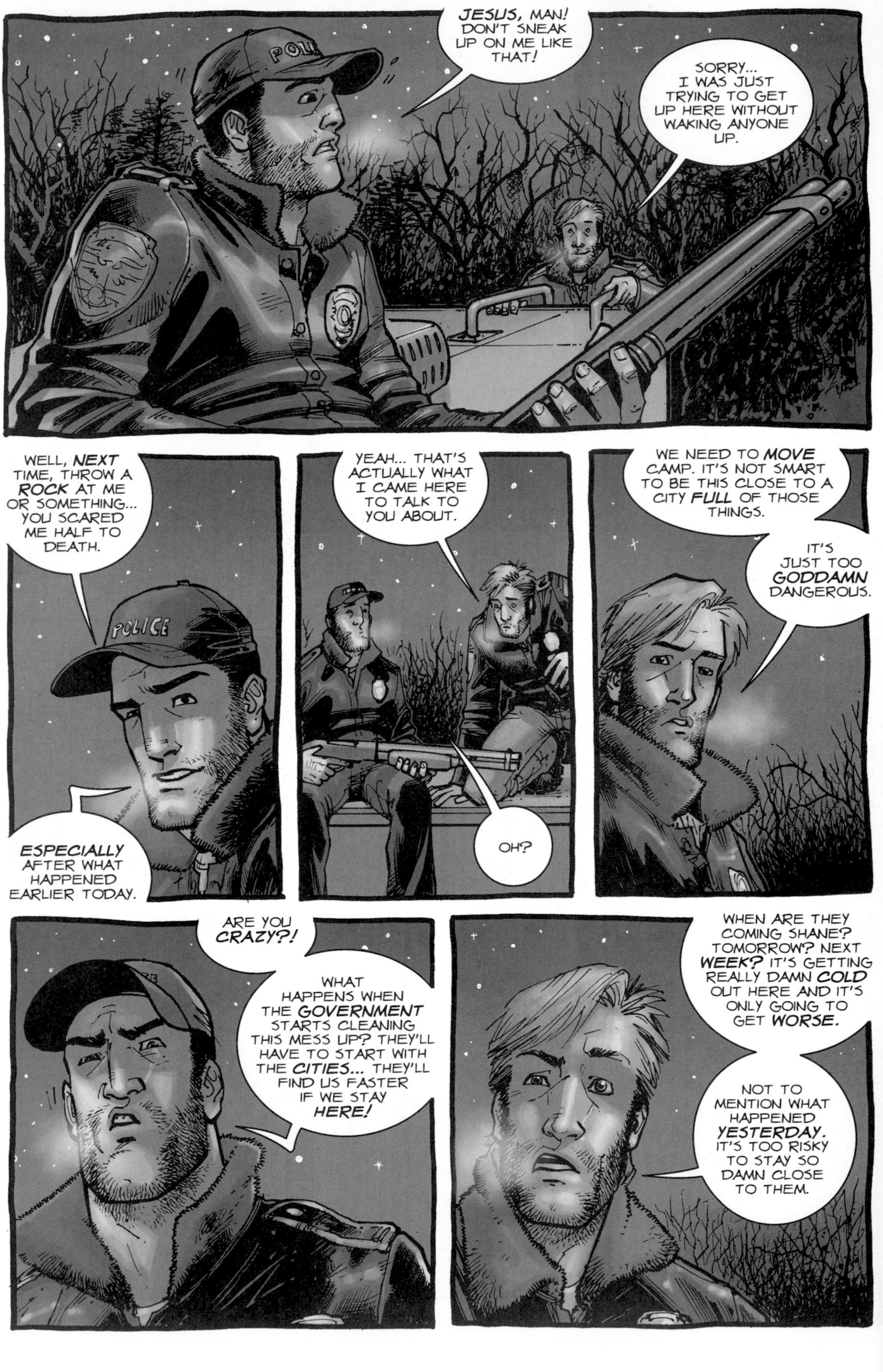
JESUS, MAN! DON'T SNEAK UP ON ME LIKE THAT!
SORRY... I WAS JUST TRYING TO GET UP HERE WITHOUT WAKING ANYONE UP.
WELL, NEXT TIME, THROW A ROCK AT ME OR SOMETHING... YOU SCARED ME HALF TO DEATH.
ESPECIALLY AFTER WHAT HAPPENED EARLIER TODAY.
YEAH... THAT'S ACTUALLY WHAT I CAME HERE TO TALK TO YOU ABOUT.
OH?
WE NEED TO MOVE CAMP. IT'S NOT SMART TO BE THIS CLOSE TO A CITY FULL OF THOSE THINGS.
IT'S JUST TOO GODDAMN DANGEROUS.
ARE YOU CRAZY?!
WHAT HAPPENS WHEN THE GOVERNMENT STARTS CLEANING THIS MESS UP? THEY'LL HAVE TO START WITH THE CITIES... THEY'LL FIND US FASTER IF WE STAY HERE!
WHEN ARE THEY COMING SHANE? TOMORROW? NEXT WEEK? IT'S GETTING REALLY DAMN COLD OUT HERE AND IT'S ONLY GOING TO GET WORSE.
NOT TO MENTION WHAT HAPPENED YESTERDAY. IT'S TOO RISKY TO STAY SO DAMN CLOSE TO THEM.

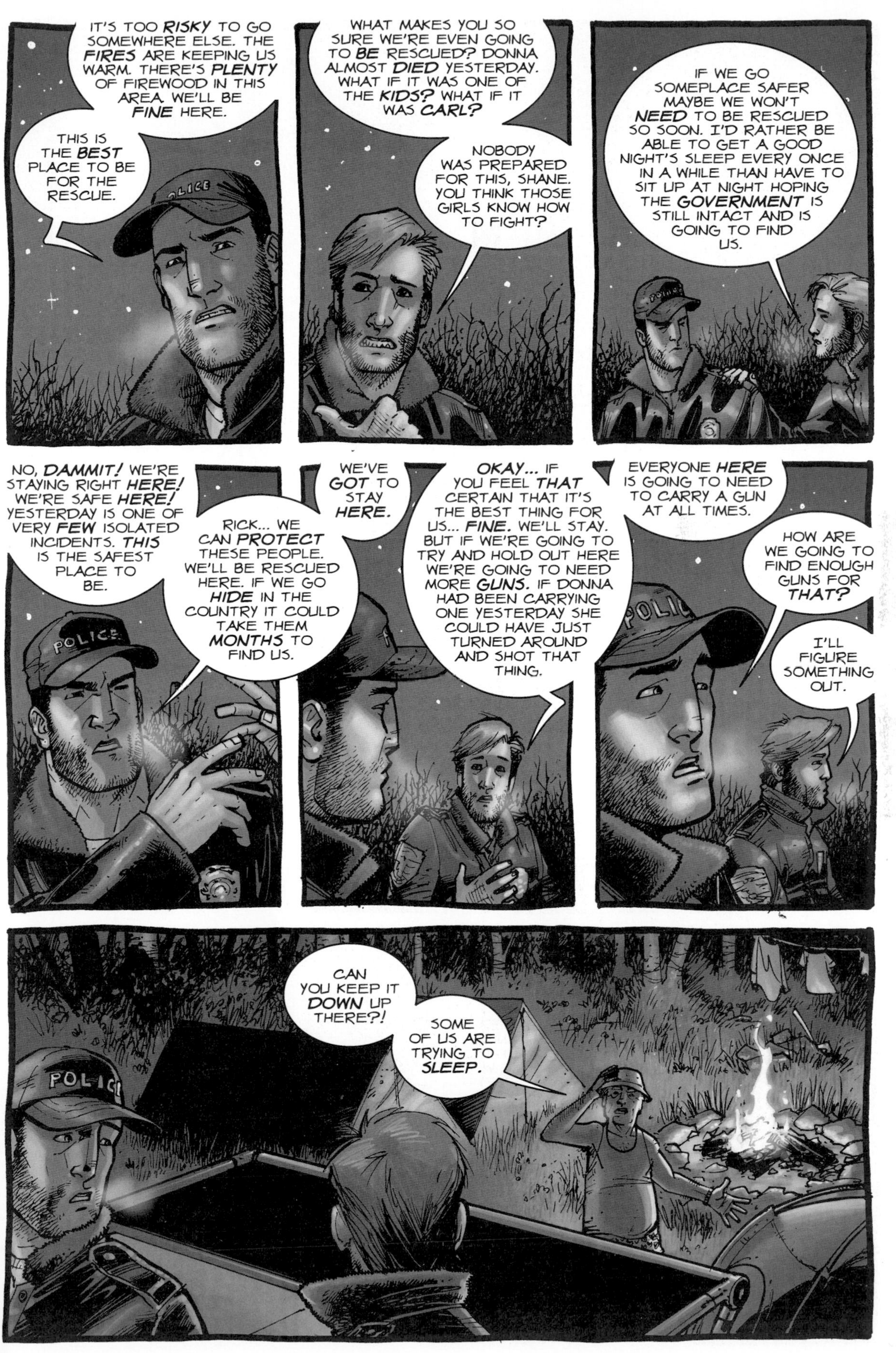
IT'S TOO RISKY TO GO SOMEWHERE ELSE. THE FIRES ARE KEEPING US WARM. THERE'S PLENTY OF FIREWOOD IN THIS AREA. WE'LL BE FINE HERE.
THIS IS THE BEST PLACE TO BE FOR THE RESCUE.
POLICE
WHAT MAKES YOU SO SURE WE'RE EVEN GOING TO BE RESCUED? DONNA ALMOST DIED YESTERDAY. WHAT IF IT WAS ONE OF THE KIDS? WHAT IF IT WAS CARL?
NOBODY WAS PREPARED FOR THIS, SHANE. YOU THINK THOSE GIRLS KNOW HOW TO FIGHT?
IF WE GO SOMEPLACE SAFER MAYBE WE WON'T NEED TO BE RESCUED SO SOON. I'D RATHER BE ABLE TO GET A GOOD NIGHT'S SLEEP EVERY ONCE IN A WHILE THAN HAVE TO SIT UP AT NIGHT HOPING THE GOVERNMENT IS STILL INTACT AND IS GOING TO FIND US.
NO, DAMMIT! WE'RE STAYING RIGHT HERE! WE'RE SAFE HERE! YESTERDAY IS ONE OF VERY FEW ISOLATED INCIDENTS. THIS IS THE SAFEST PLACE TO BE.
RICK... WE CAN PROTECT THESE PEOPLE. WE'LL BE RESCUED HERE. IF WE GO HIDE IN THE COUNTRY IT COULD TAKE THEM MONTHS TO FIND US.
POLICE
WE'VE GOT TO STAY HERE.
OKAY... IF YOU FEEL THAT CERTAIN THAT IT'S THE BEST THING FOR US... FINE. WE'LL STAY. BUT IF WE'RE GOING TO TRY AND HOLD OUT HERE WE'RE GOING TO NEED MORE GUNS. IF DONNA HAD BEEN CARRYING ONE YESTERDAY SHE COULD HAVE JUST TURNED AROUND AND SHOT THAT THING.
EVERYONE HERE IS GOING TO NEED TO CARRY A GUN AT ALL TIMES.
HOW ARE WE GOING TO FIND ENOUGH GUNS FOR THAT?
I'LL FIGURE SOMETHING OUT.
CAN YOU KEEP IT DOWN UP THERE?!
SOME OF US ARE TRYING TO SLEEP.
POLICE

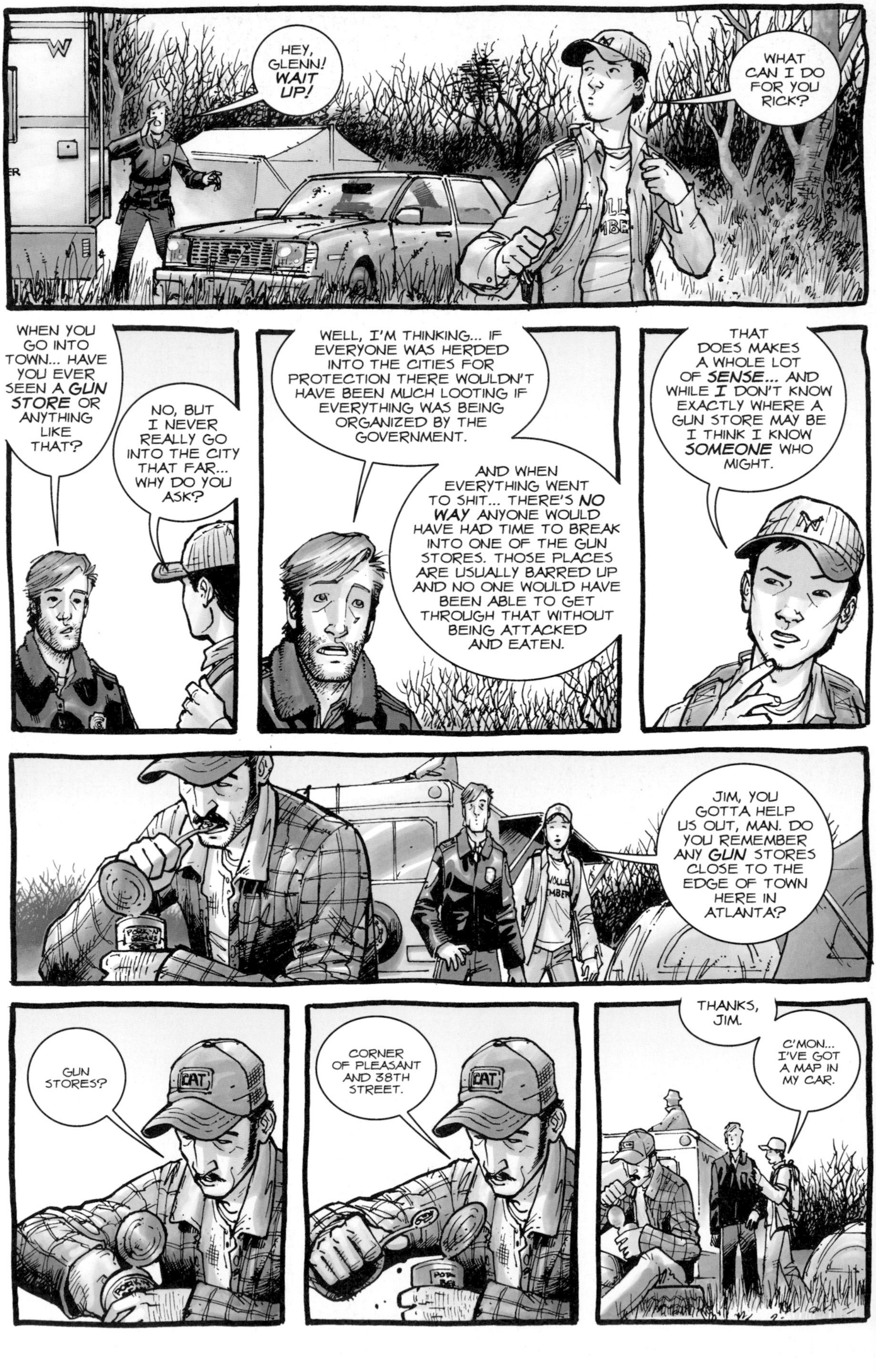

HEY, GLENN! WAIT UP!
WHAT CAN I DO FOR YOU RICK?
WHEN YOU GO INTO TOWN... HAVE YOU EVER SEEN A GUN STORE OR ANYTHING LIKE THAT?
NO, BUT I NEVER REALLY GO INTO THE CITY THAT FAR... WHY DO YOU ASK?
WELL, I'M THINKING... IF EVERYONE WAS HERDED INTO THE CITIES FOR PROTECTION THERE WOULDN'T HAVE BEEN MUCH LOOTING IF EVERYTHING WAS BEING ORGANIZED BY THE GOVERNMENT.
AND WHEN EVERYTHING WENT TO SHIT... THERE'S NO WAY ANYONE WOULD HAVE HAD TIME TO BREAK INTO ONE OF THE GUN STORES. THOSE PLACES ARE USUALLY BARRED UP AND NO ONE WOULD HAVE BEEN ABLE TO GET THROUGH THAT WITHOUT BEING ATTACKED AND EATEN.
THAT DOES MAKES A WHOLE LOT OF SENSE... AND WHILE I DON'T KNOW EXACTLY WHERE A GUN STORE MAY BE I THINK I KNOW SOMEONE WHO MIGHT.
JIM, YOU GOTTA HELP US OUT, MAN. DO YOU REMEMBER ANY GUN STORES CLOSE TO THE EDGE OF TOWN HERE IN ATLANTA?
GUN STORES?
CORNER OF PLEASANT AND 38TH STREET.
THANKS, JIM.
C'MON... I'VE GOT A MAP IN MY CAR.

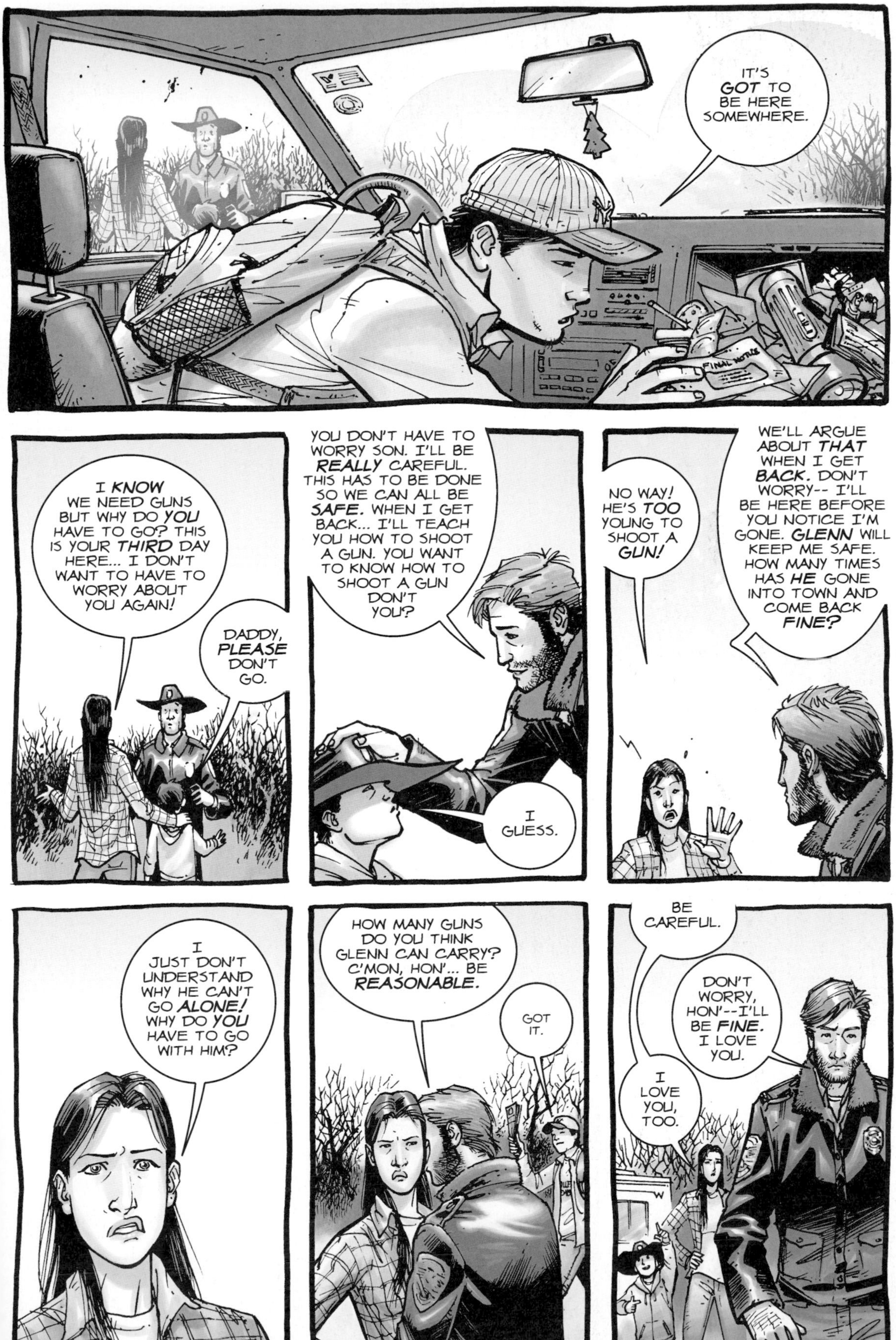
IT'S GOT TO BE HERE SOMEWHERE.
FINAL NOTICE
I KNOW WE NEED GUNS BUT WHY DO YOU HAVE TO GO? THIS IS YOUR THIRD DAY HERE... I DON'T WANT TO HAVE TO WORRY ABOUT YOU AGAIN!
DADDY, PLEASE DON'T GO.
YOU DON'T HAVE TO WORRY SON. I'LL BE REALLY CAREFUL. THIS HAS TO BE DONE SO WE CAN ALL BE SAFE. WHEN I GET BACK... I'LL TEACH YOU HOW TO SHOOT A GUN. YOU WANT TO KNOW HOW TO SHOOT A GUN DON'T YOU?
I GUESS.
NO WAY! HE'S TOO YOUNG TO SHOOT A GUN!
WE'LL ARGUE ABOUT THAT WHEN I GET BACK. DON'T WORRY-- I'LL BE HERE BEFORE YOU NOTICE I'M GONE. GLENN WILL KEEP ME SAFE. HOW MANY TIMES HAS HE GONE INTO TOWN AND COME BACK FINE?
I JUST DON'T UNDERSTAND WHY HE CAN'T GO ALONE! WHY DO YOU HAVE TO GO WITH HIM?
HOW MANY GUNS DO YOU THINK GLENN CAN CARRY? C'MON, HON'... BE REASONABLE.
GOT IT.
BE CAREFUL.
DON'T WORRY, HON'--I'LL BE FINE. I LOVE YOU.
I LOVE YOU, TOO.

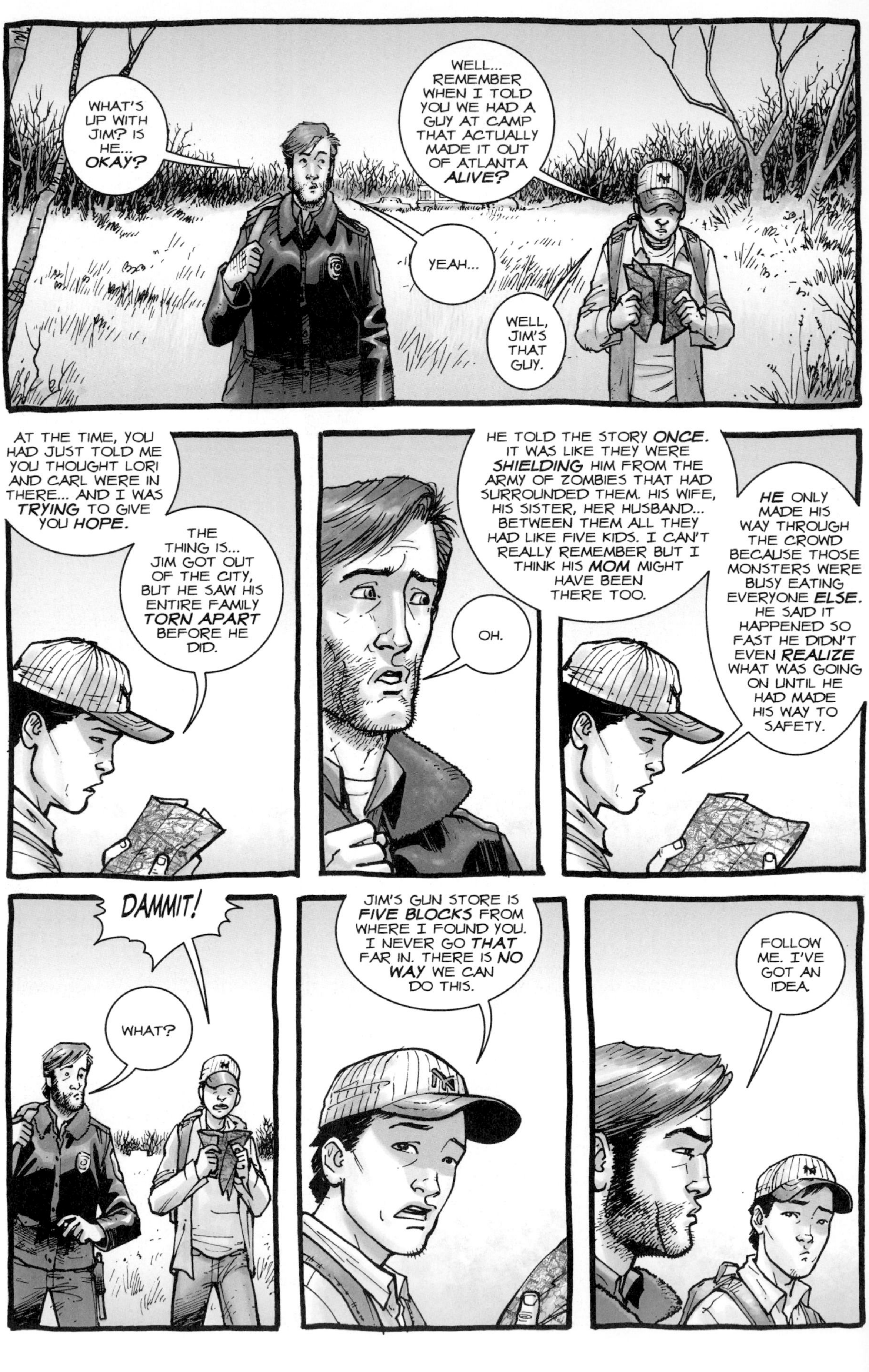
WHAT'S UP WITH JIM? IS HE... OKAY?
WELL... REMEMBER WHEN I TOLD YOU WE HAD A GUY AT CAMP THAT ACTUALLY MADE IT OUT OF ATLANTA ALIVE?
YEAH...
WELL, JIM'S THAT GUY.
AT THE TIME, YOU HAD JUST TOLD ME YOU THOUGHT LORI AND CARL WERE IN THERE... AND I WAS TRYING TO GIVE YOU HOPE.
THE THING IS... JIM GOT OUT OF THE CITY, BUT HE SAW HIS ENTIRE FAMILY TORN APART BEFORE HE DID.
HE TOLD THE STORY ONCE. IT WAS LIKE THEY WERE SHIELDING HIM FROM THE ARMY OF ZOMBIES THAT HAD SURROUNDED THEM. HIS WIFE, HIS SISTER, HER HUSBAND... BETWEEN THEM ALL THEY HAD LIKE FIVE KIDS. I CAN'T REALLY REMEMBER BUT I THINK HIS MOM MIGHT HAVE BEEN THERE TOO.
OH.
HE ONLY MADE HIS WAY THROUGH THE CROWD BECAUSE THOSE MONSTERS WERE BUSY EATING EVERYONE ELSE. HE SAID IT HAPPENED SO FAST HE DIDN'T EVEN REALIZE WHAT WAS GOING ON UNTIL HE HAD MADE HIS WAY TO SAFETY.
DAMMIT!
WHAT?
JIM'S GUN STORE IS FIVE BLOCKS FROM WHERE I FOUND YOU. I NEVER GO THAT FAR IN. THERE IS NO WAY WE CAN DO THIS.
FOLLOW ME. I'VE GOT AN IDEA.

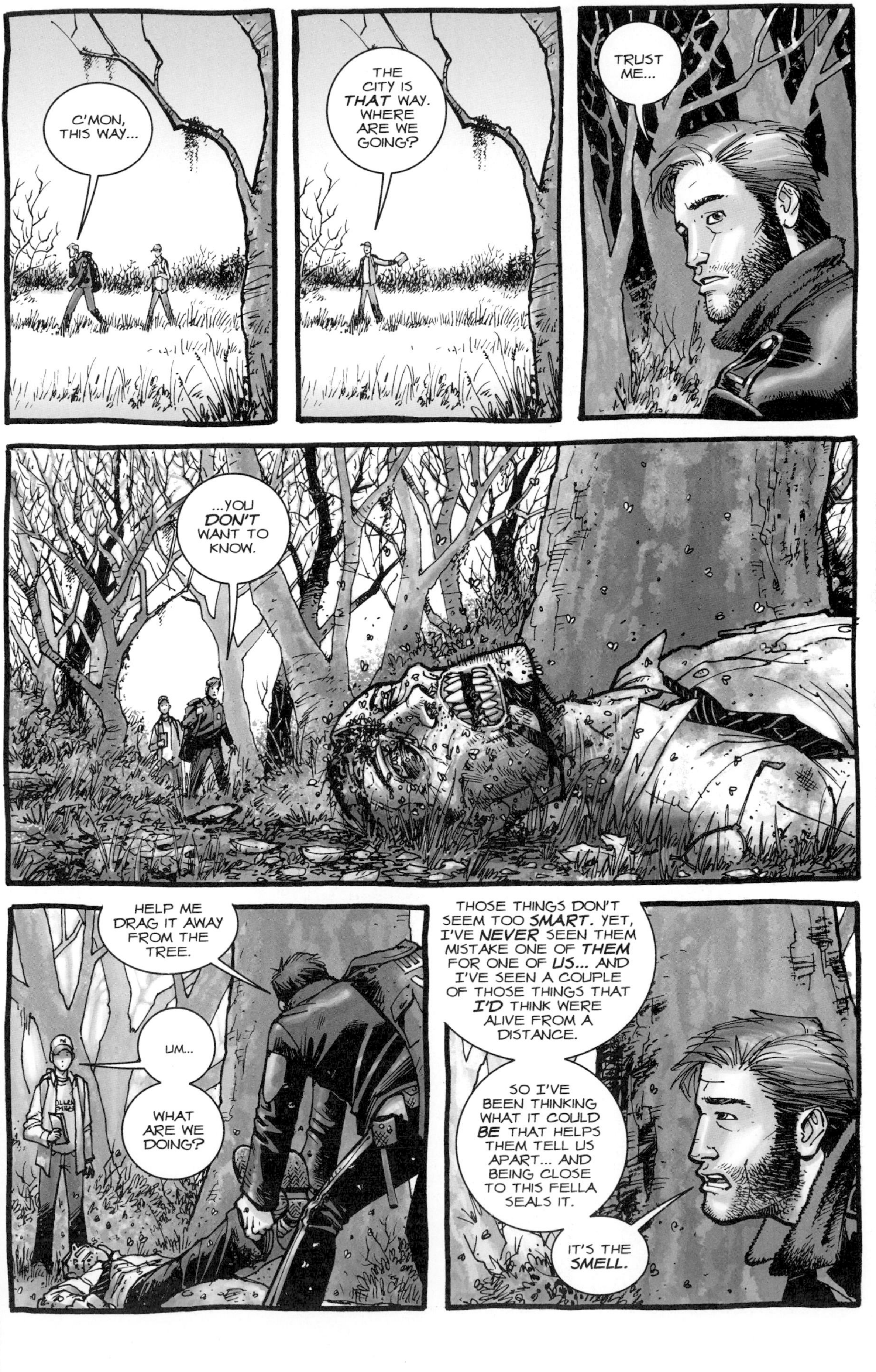
C'MON, THIS WAY...
THE CITY IS THAT WAY. WHERE ARE WE GOING?
TRUST ME...
...YOU DON'T WANT TO KNOW.
HELP ME DRAG IT AWAY FROM THE TREE.
UM...
WHAT ARE WE DOING?
THOSE THINGS DON'T SEEM TOO SMART. YET, I'VE NEVER SEEN THEM MISTAKE ONE OF THEM FOR ONE OF US... AND I'VE SEEN A COUPLE OF THOSE THINGS THAT I'D THINK WERE ALIVE FROM A DISTANCE.
SO I'VE BEEN THINKING WHAT IT COULD BE THAT HELPS THEM TELL US APART... AND BEING CLOSE TO THIS FELLA SEALS IT.
IT'S THE SMELL.

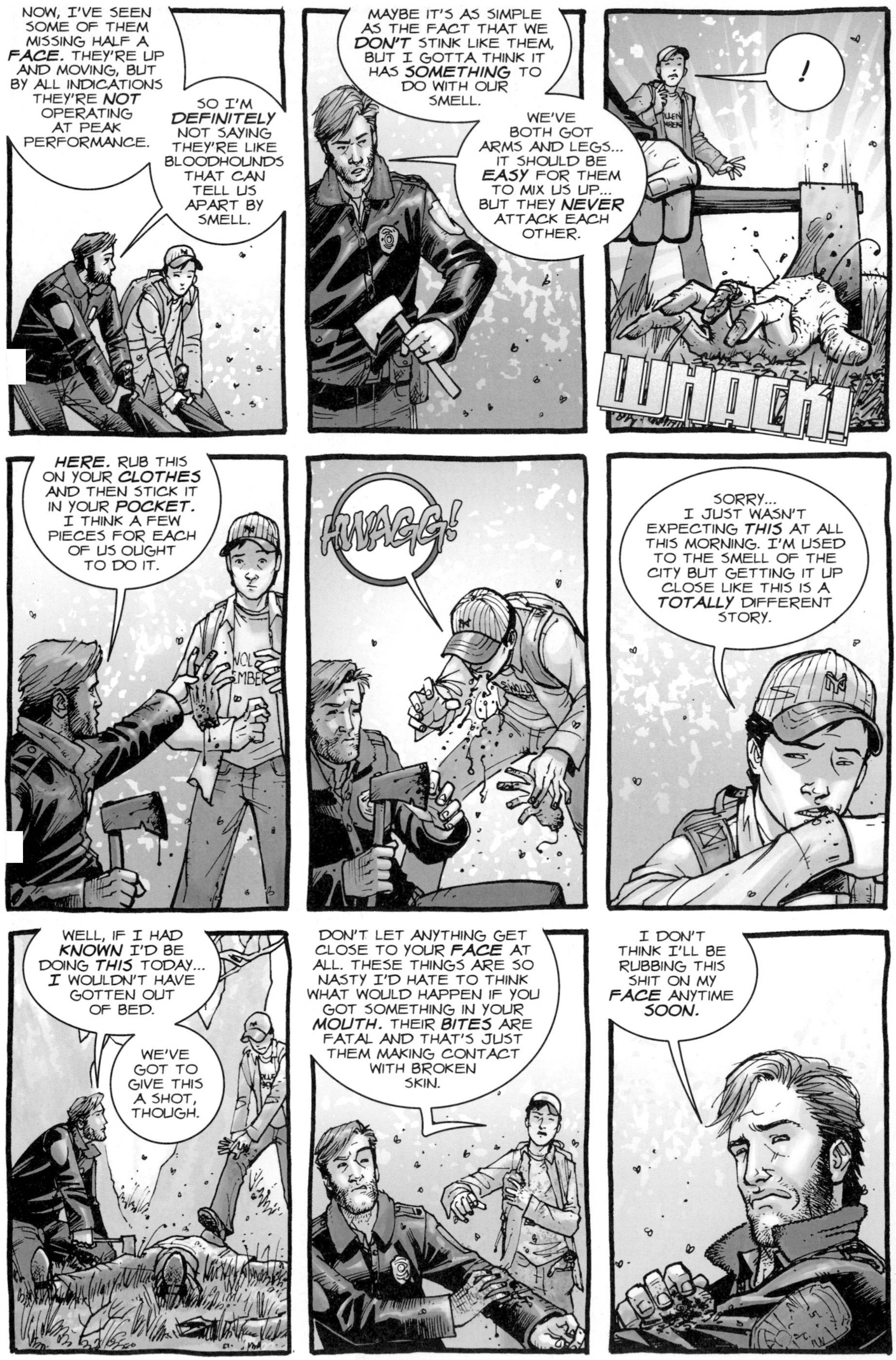
NOW, I'VE SEEN SOME OF THEM MISSING HALF A FACE. THEY'RE UP AND MOVING, BUT BY ALL INDICATIONS THEY'RE NOT OPERATING AT PEAK PERFORMANCE.
SO I'M DEFINITELY NOT SAYING THEY'RE LIKE BLOODHOUNDS THAT CAN TELL US APART BY SMELL.
MAYBE IT'S AS SIMPLE AS THE FACT THAT WE DON'T STINK LIKE THEM, BUT I GOTTA THINK IT HAS SOMETHING TO DO WITH OUR SMELL.
WE'VE BOTH GOT ARMS AND LEGS... IT SHOULD BE EASY FOR THEM TO MIX US UP... BUT THEY NEVER ATTACK EACH OTHER.
!
WHACK!
HERE. RUB THIS ON YOUR CLOTHES AND THEN STICK IT IN YOUR POCKET. I THINK A FEW PIECES FOR EACH OF US OUGHT TO DO IT.
HWAGG!
SORRY... I JUST WASN'T EXPECTING THIS AT ALL THIS MORNING. I'M USED TO THE SMELL OF THE CITY BUT GETTING IT UP CLOSE LIKE THIS IS A TOTALLY DIFFERENT STORY.
WELL, IF I HAD KNOWN I'D BE DOING THIS TODAY... I WOULDN'T HAVE GOTTEN OUT OF BED.
WE'VE GOT TO GIVE THIS A SHOT, THOUGH.
DON'T LET ANYTHING GET CLOSE TO YOUR FACE AT ALL. THESE THINGS ARE SO NASTY I'D HATE TO THINK WHAT WOULD HAPPEN IF YOU GOT SOMETHING IN YOUR MOUTH. THEIR BITES ARE FATAL AND THAT'S JUST THEM MAKING CONTACT WITH BROKEN SKIN.
I DON'T THINK I'LL BE RUBBING THIS SHIT ON MY FACE ANYTIME SOON.

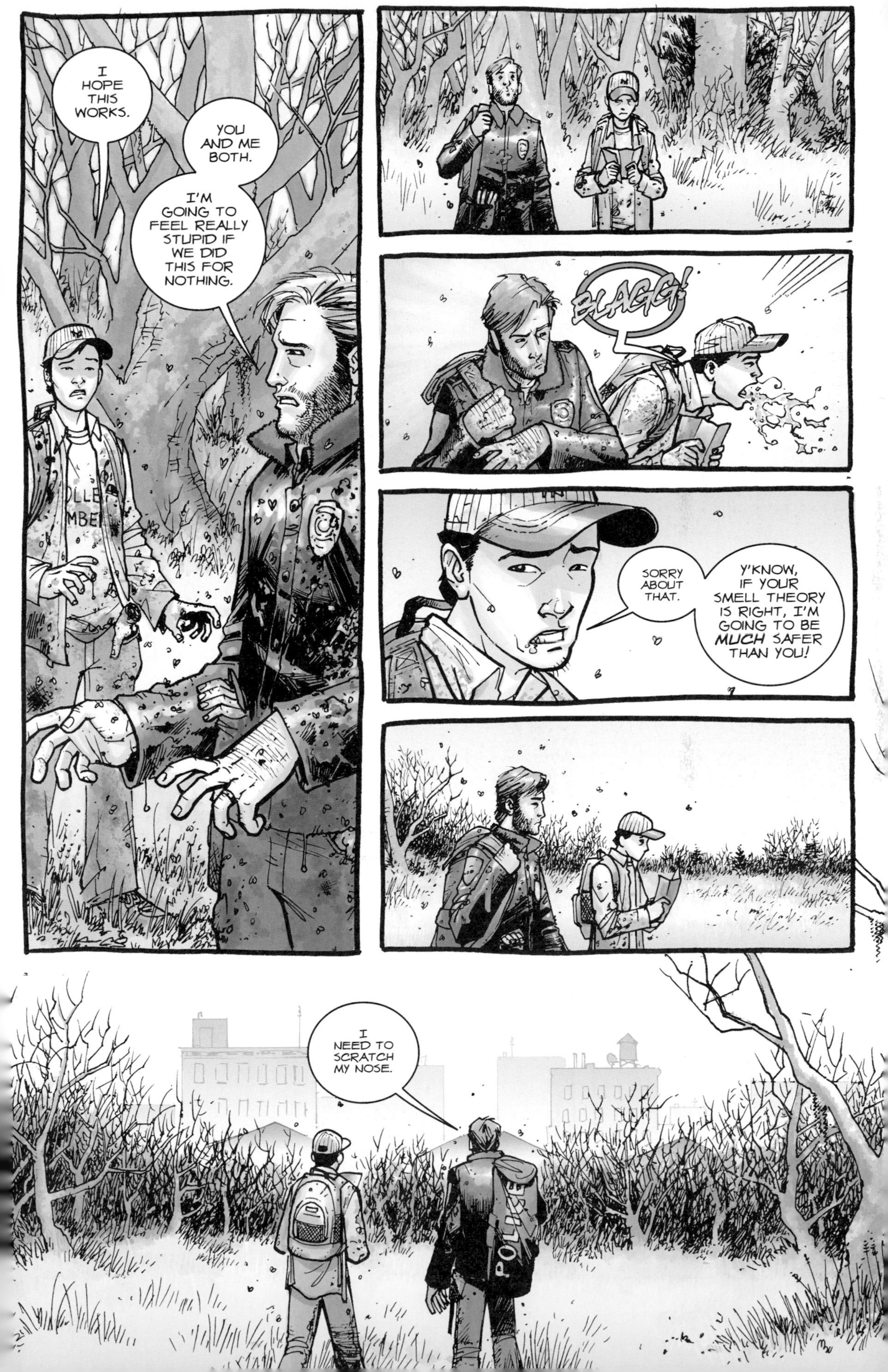
I HOPE THIS WORKS.
YOU AND ME BOTH.
I'M GOING TO FEEL REALLY STUPID IF WE DID THIS FOR NOTHING.
BLAGG!
SORRY ABOUT THAT.
Y'KNOW, IF YOUR SMELL THEORY IS RIGHT, I'M GOING TO BE MUCH SAFER THAN YOU!
I NEED TO SCRATCH MY NOSE.

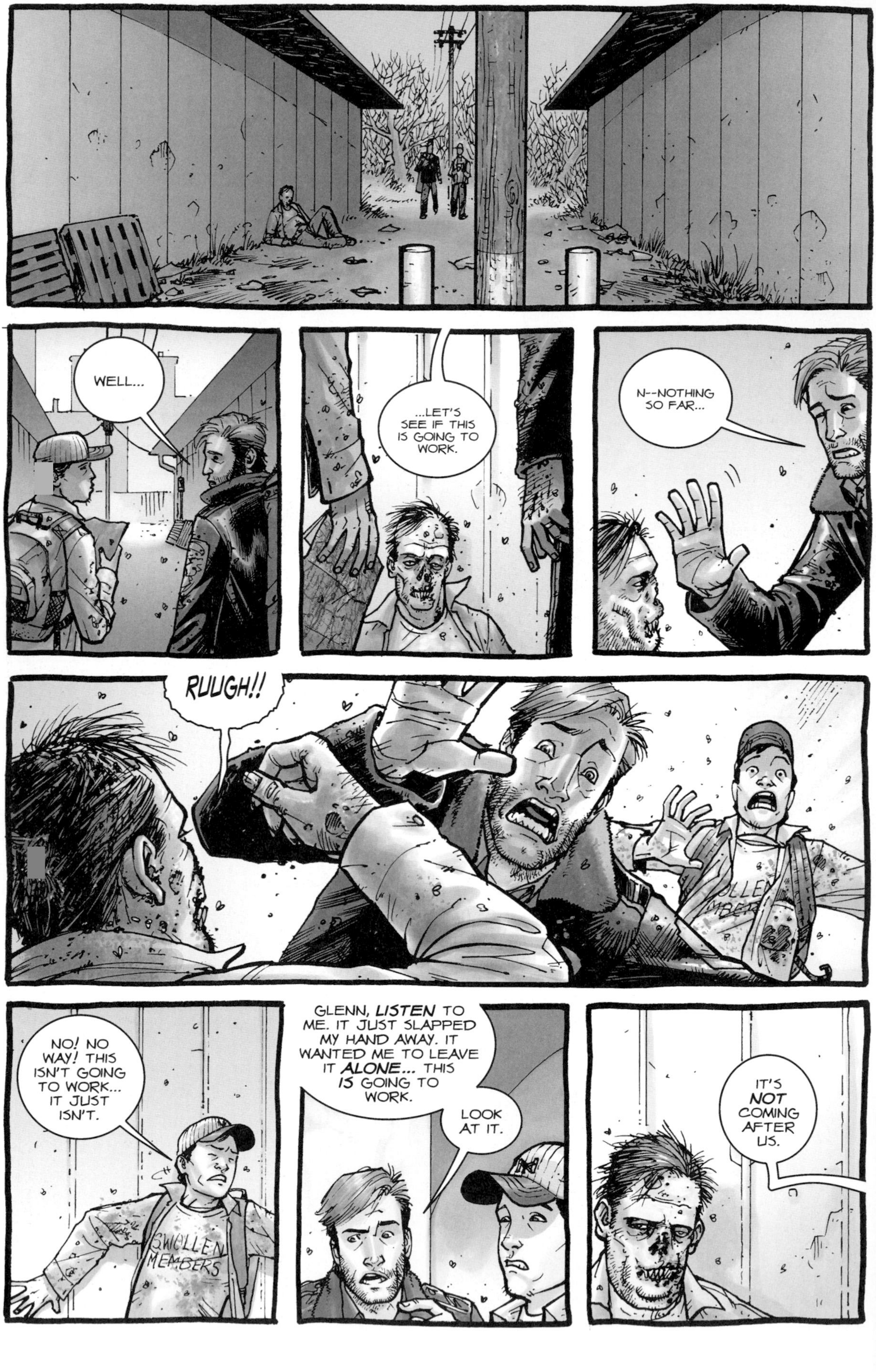
WELL...
...LET'S SEE IF THIS IS GOING TO WORK.
N--NOTHING SO FAR...
RUUGH!!
SWOLLEN MEMBERS
NO! NO WAY! THIS ISN'T GOING TO WORK... IT JUST ISN'T.
SWOLLEN MEMBERS
GLENN, LISTEN TO ME. IT JUST SLAPPED MY HAND AWAY. IT WANTED ME TO LEAVE IT ALONE... THIS IS GOING TO WORK.
LOOK AT IT.
IT'S NOT COMING AFTER US.

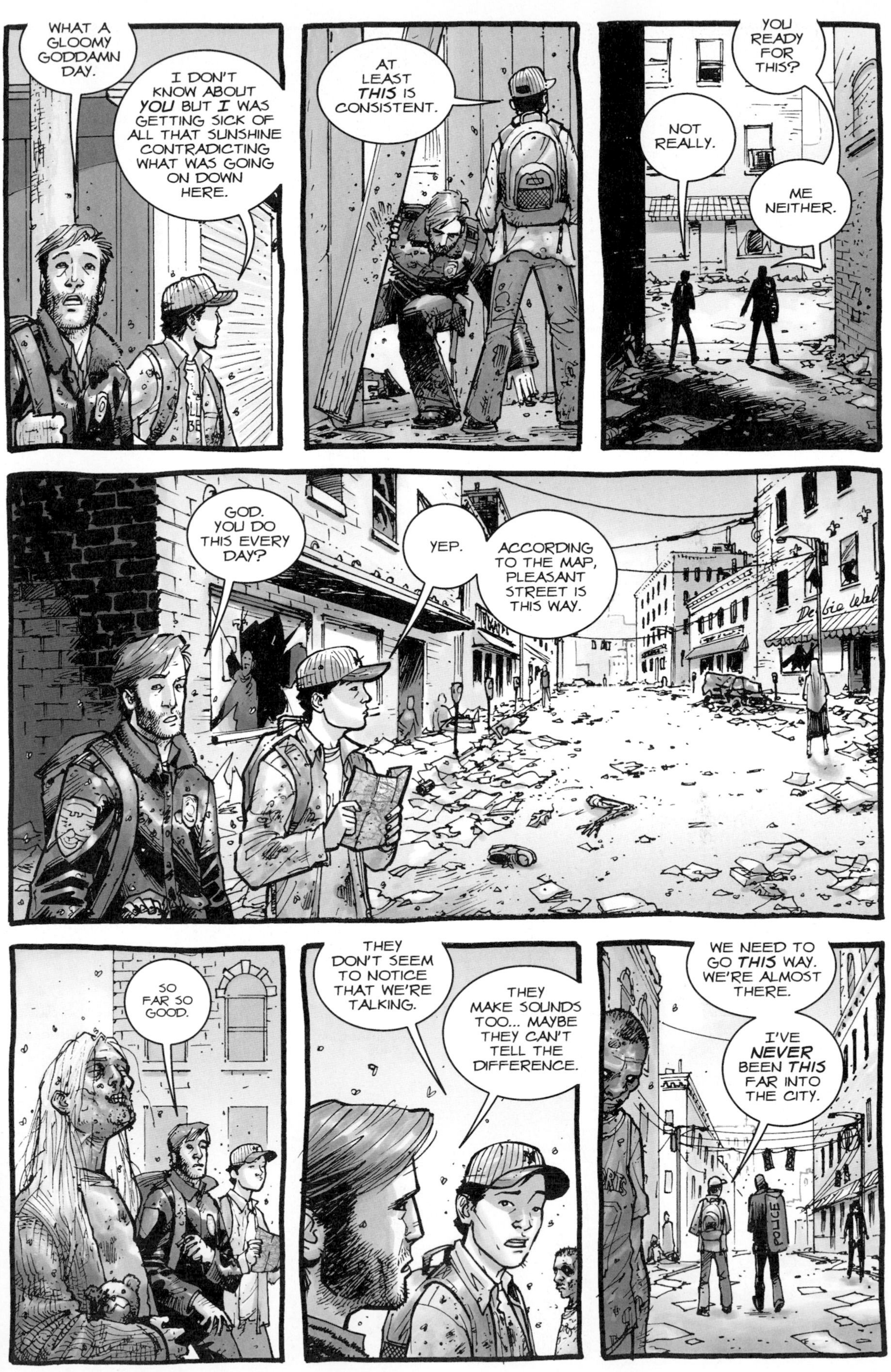
WHAT A GLOOMY GODDAMN DAY.
I DON'T KNOW ABOUT *YOU* BUT *I* WAS GETTING SICK OF ALL THAT SUNSHINE CONTRADICTING WHAT WAS GOING ON DOWN HERE.
AT LEAST *THIS* IS CONSISTENT.
YOU READY FOR THIS?
NOT REALLY.
ME NEITHER.
GOD. YOU DO THIS EVERY DAY?
YEP.
ACCORDING TO THE MAP, PLEASANT STREET IS THIS WAY.
SO FAR SO GOOD.
THEY DON'T SEEM TO NOTICE THAT WE'RE TALKING.
THEY MAKE SOUNDS TOO... MAYBE THEY CAN'T TELL THE DIFFERENCE.
WE NEED TO GO *THIS* WAY. WE'RE ALMOST THERE.
I'VE *NEVER* BEEN *THIS* FAR INTO THE CITY.

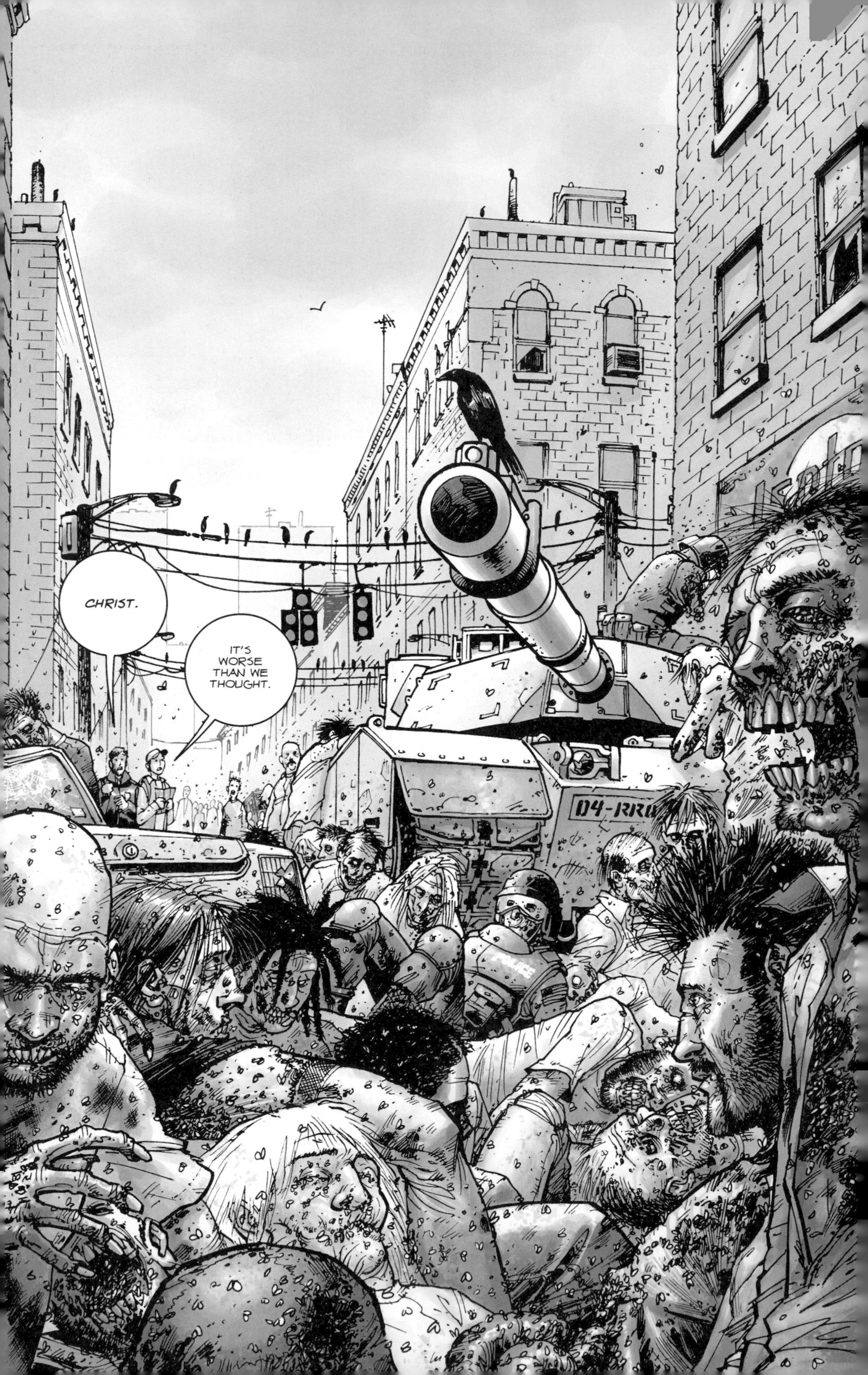
CHRIST.
IT'S WORSE THAN WE THOUGHT.

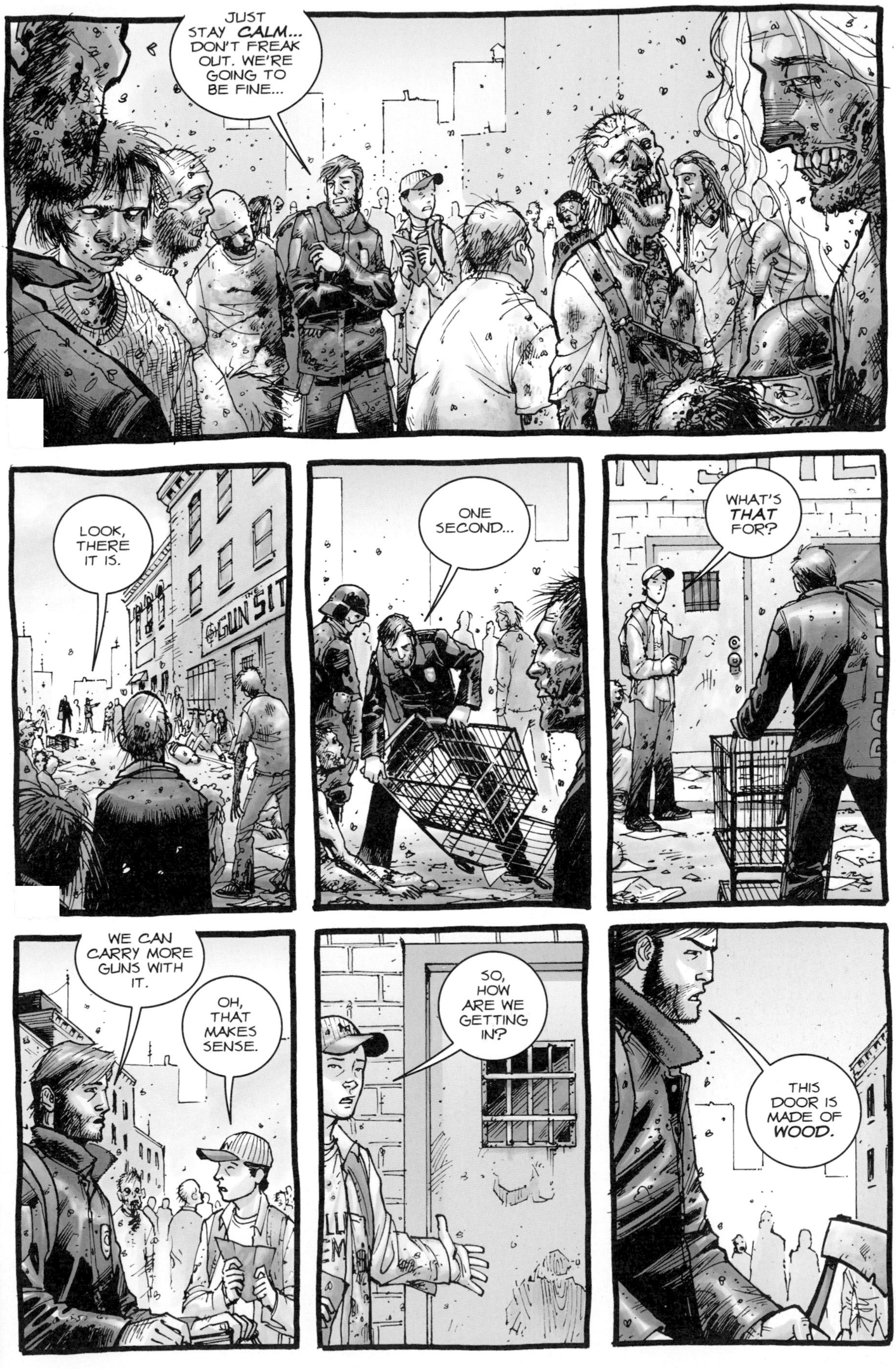
JUST STAY **CALM...** DON'T FREAK OUT. WE'RE GOING TO BE FINE...
LOOK, THERE IT IS.
GUN SIT
ONE SECOND...
WHAT'S *THAT* FOR?
WE CAN CARRY MORE GUNS WITH IT.
OH, THAT MAKES SENSE.
SO, HOW ARE WE GETTING IN?
THIS DOOR IS MADE OF **WOOD.**

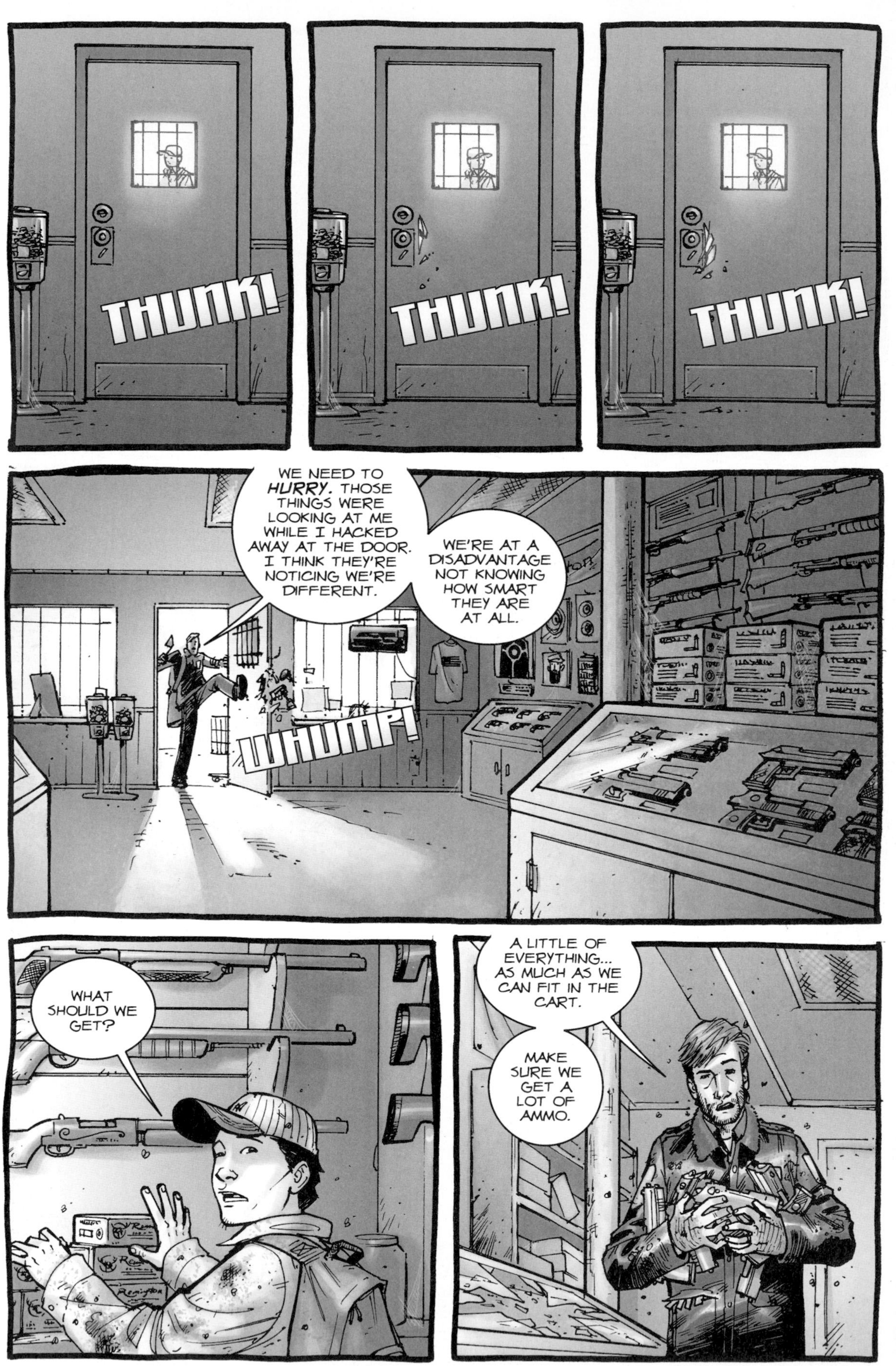
THUNK!
THUNK!
THUNK!
WE NEED TO HURRY. THOSE THINGS WERE LOOKING AT ME WHILE I HACKED AWAY AT THE DOOR. I THINK THEY'RE NOTICING WE'RE DIFFERENT.
WE'RE AT A DISADVANTAGE NOT KNOWING HOW SMART THEY ARE AT ALL.
WHUMP!
WHAT SHOULD WE GET?
A LITTLE OF EVERYTHING... AS MUCH AS WE CAN FIT IN THE CART.
MAKE SURE WE GET A LOT OF AMMO.

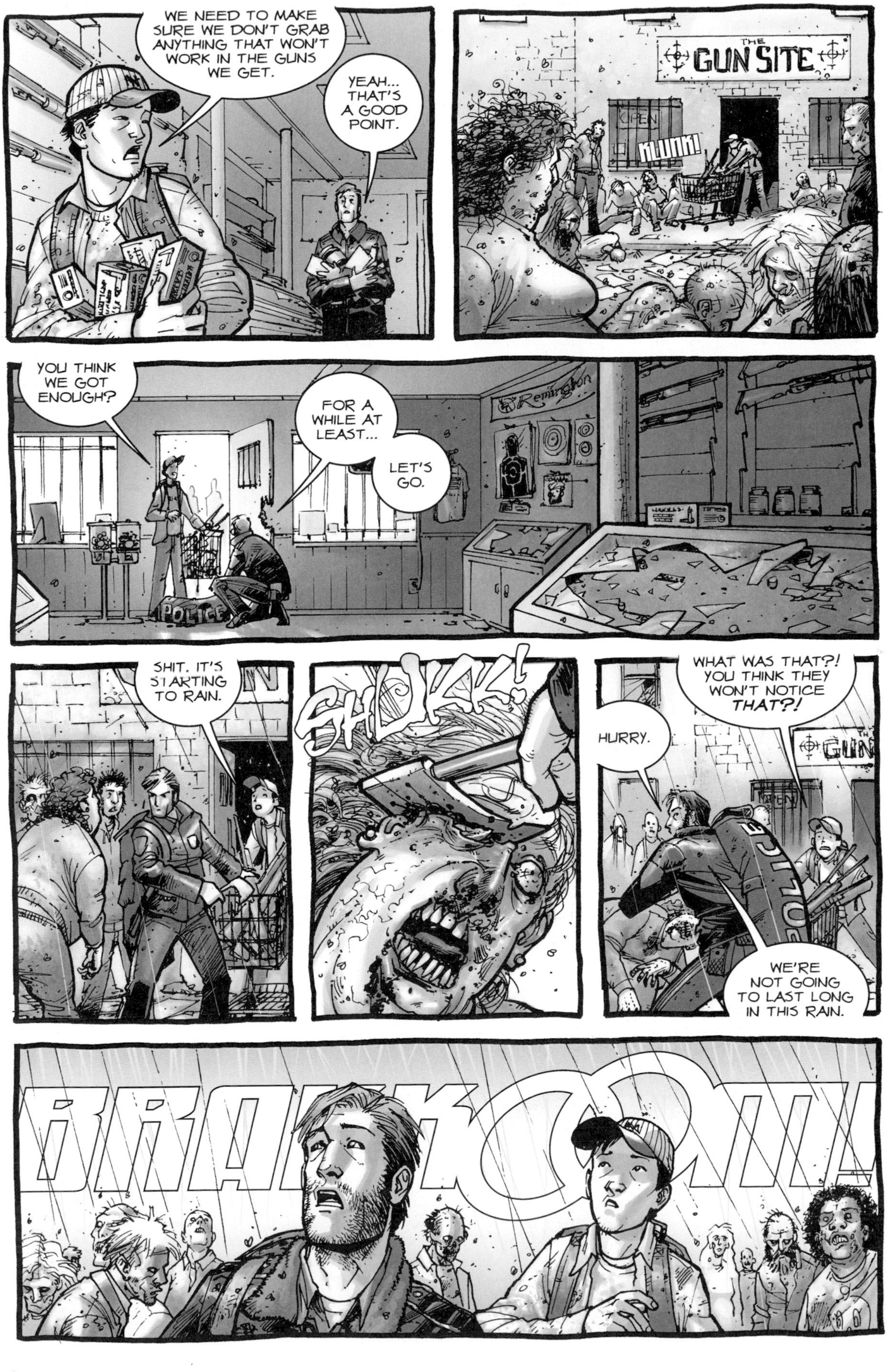
WE NEED TO MAKE SURE WE DON'T GRAB ANYTHING THAT WON'T WORK IN THE GUNS WE GET.
YEAH... THAT'S A GOOD POINT.
THE GUN SITE
OPEN
KLUNK!
YOU THINK WE GOT ENOUGH?
FOR A WHILE AT LEAST...
LET'S GO.
Remington
POLICE
SHIT. IT'S STARTING TO RAIN.
SHUKK!
WHAT WAS THAT?! YOU THINK THEY WON'T NOTICE *THAT?!*
HURRY.
WE'RE NOT GOING TO LAST LONG IN THIS RAIN.

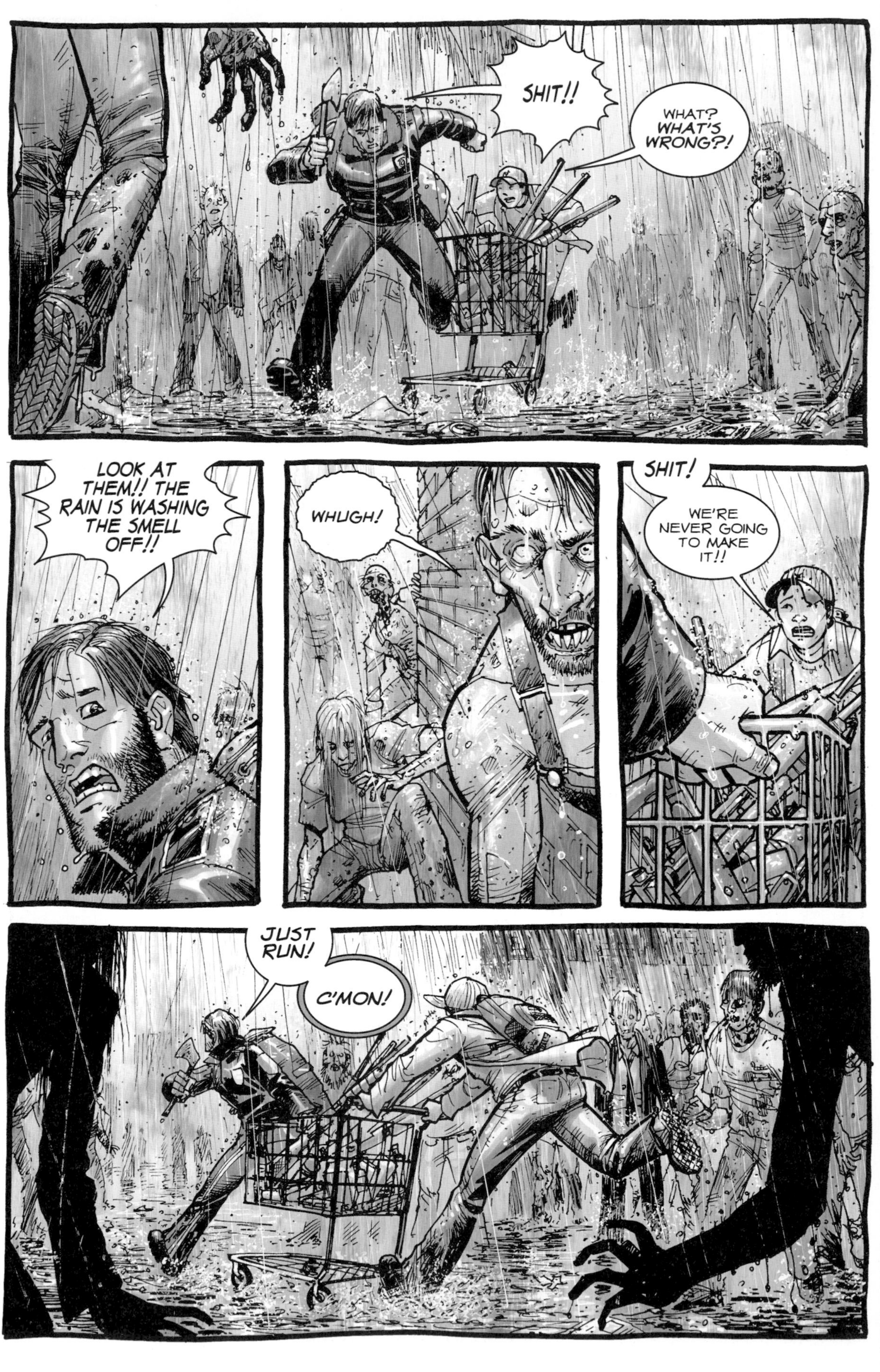

SHIT!!
WHAT? WHAT'S WRONG?!
LOOK AT THEM!! THE RAIN IS WASHING THE SMELL OFF!!
WHUGH!
SHIT!
WE'RE NEVER GOING TO MAKE IT!!
JUST RUN!
C'MON!

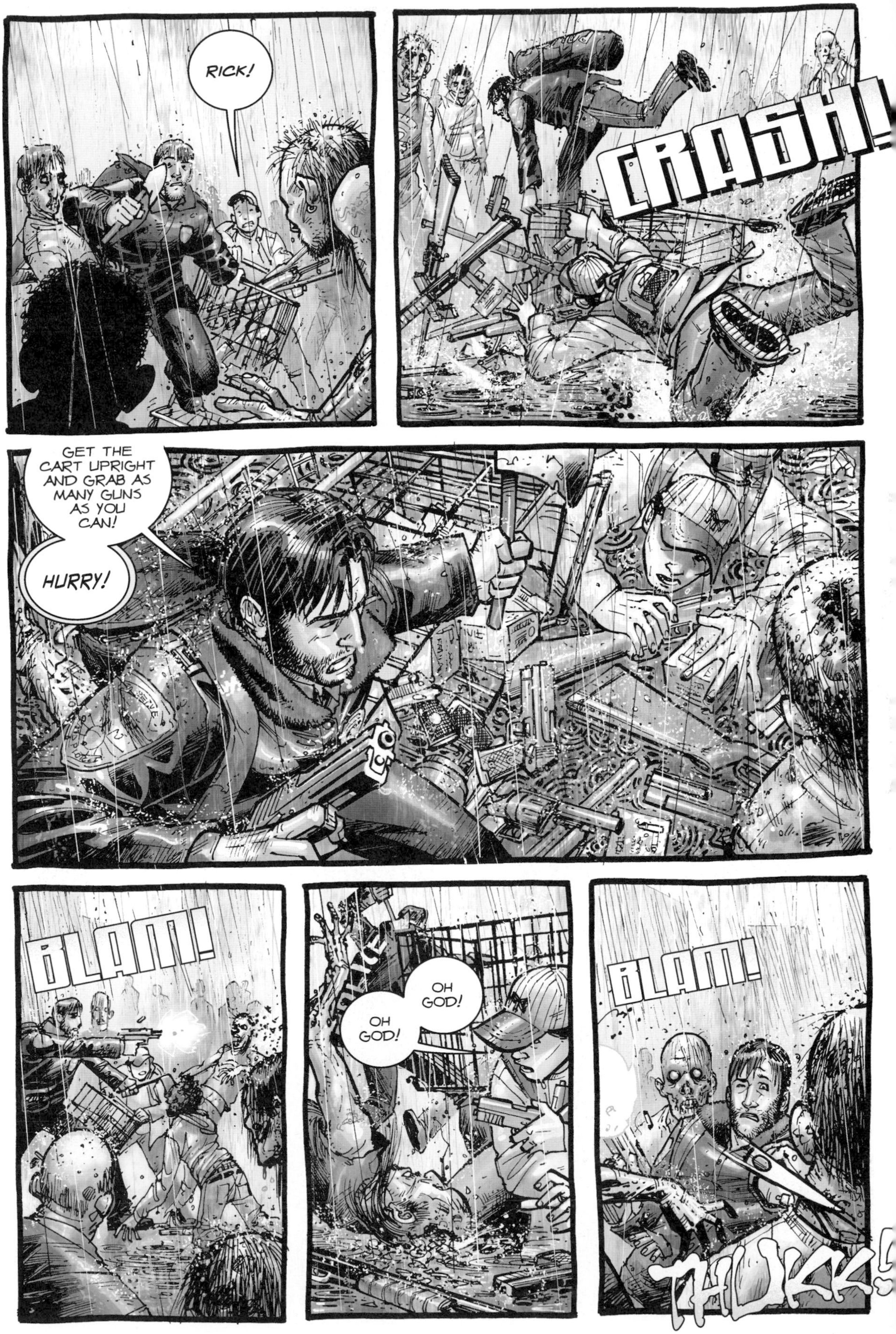
RICK!
CRASH!
GET THE CART UPRIGHT AND GRAB AS MANY GUNS AS YOU CAN!
HURRY!
BLAM!
OH GOD!
OH GOD!
BLAM!
THUKK!

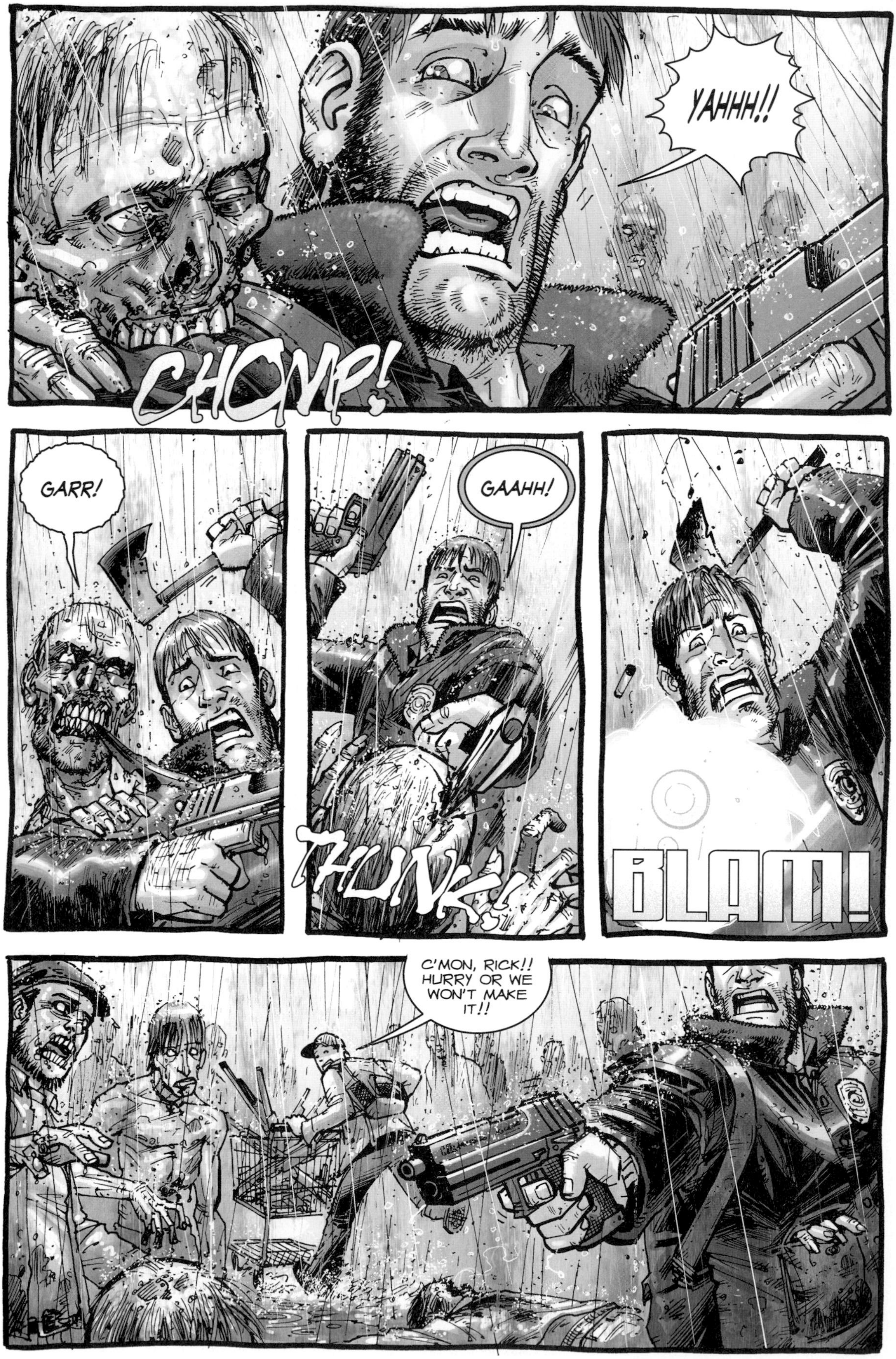
YAHHH!!
CHOMP!
GARR!
GAAHH!
THUNK!
BLAM!
C'MON, RICK!! HURRY OR WE WON'T MAKE IT!!

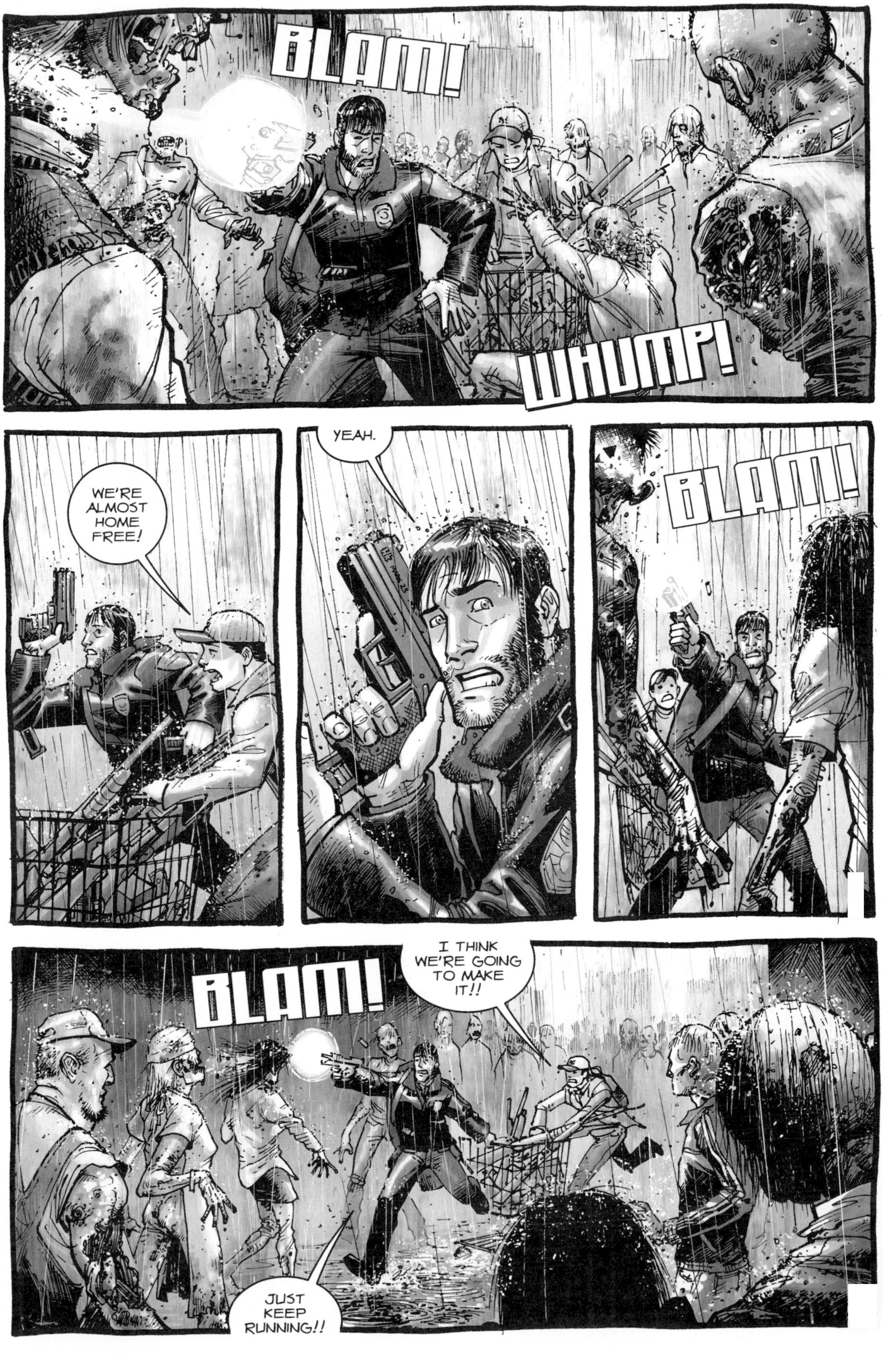
BLAM!
WHUMP!
WE'RE ALMOST HOME FREE!
YEAH.
BLAM!
BLAM!
I THINK WE'RE GOING TO MAKE IT!!
JUST KEEP RUNNING!!

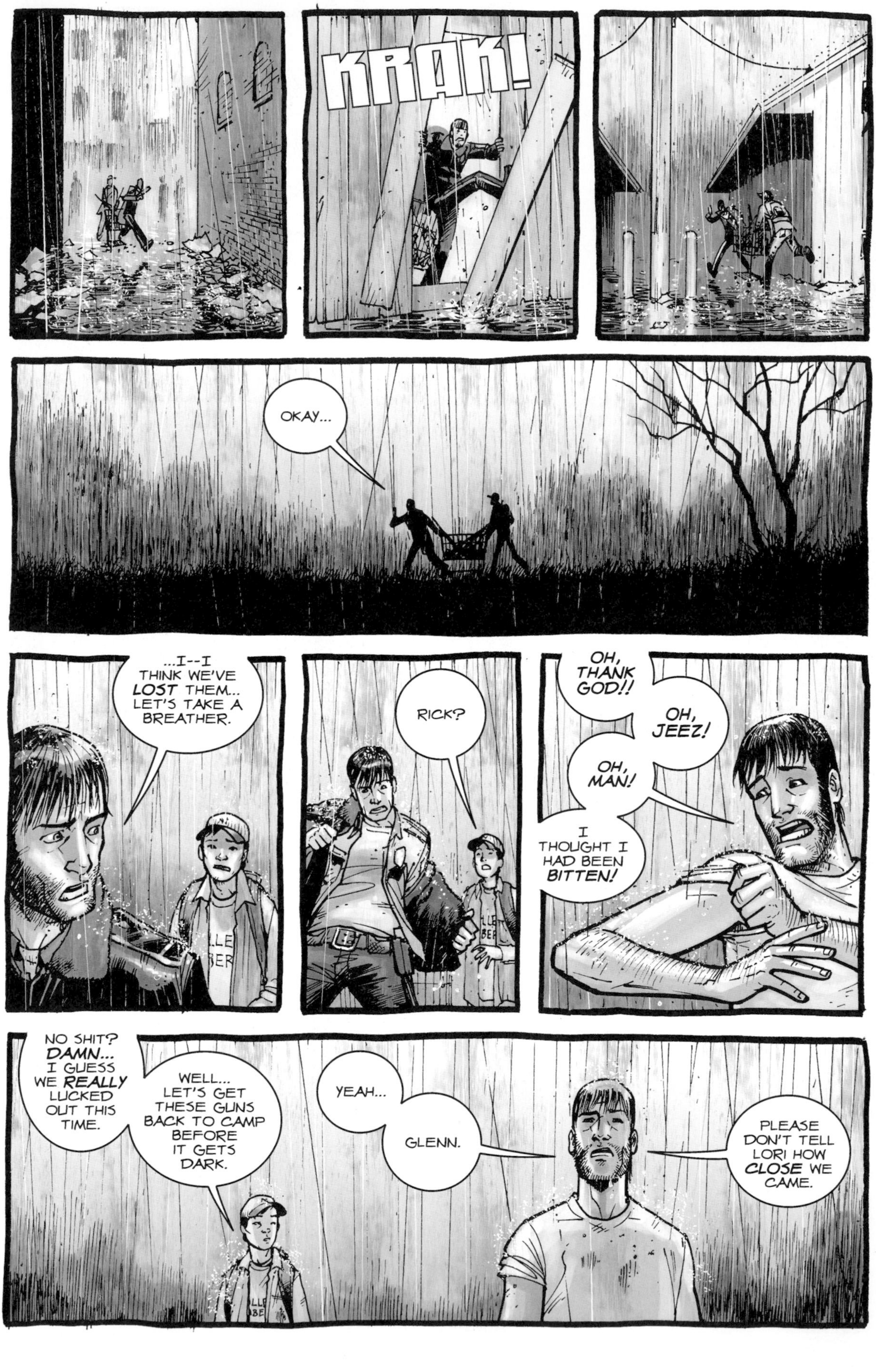

KRAK!
OKAY...
...I--I THINK WE'VE LOST THEM... LET'S TAKE A BREATHER.
RICK?
OH, THANK GOD!!
OH, JEEZ!
OH, MAN!
I THOUGHT I HAD BEEN BITTEN!
NO SHIT? DAMN... I GUESS WE REALLY LUCKED OUT THIS TIME.
WELL... LET'S GET THESE GUNS BACK TO CAMP BEFORE IT GETS DARK.
YEAH...
GLENN.
PLEASE DON'T TELL LORI HOW CLOSE WE CAME.

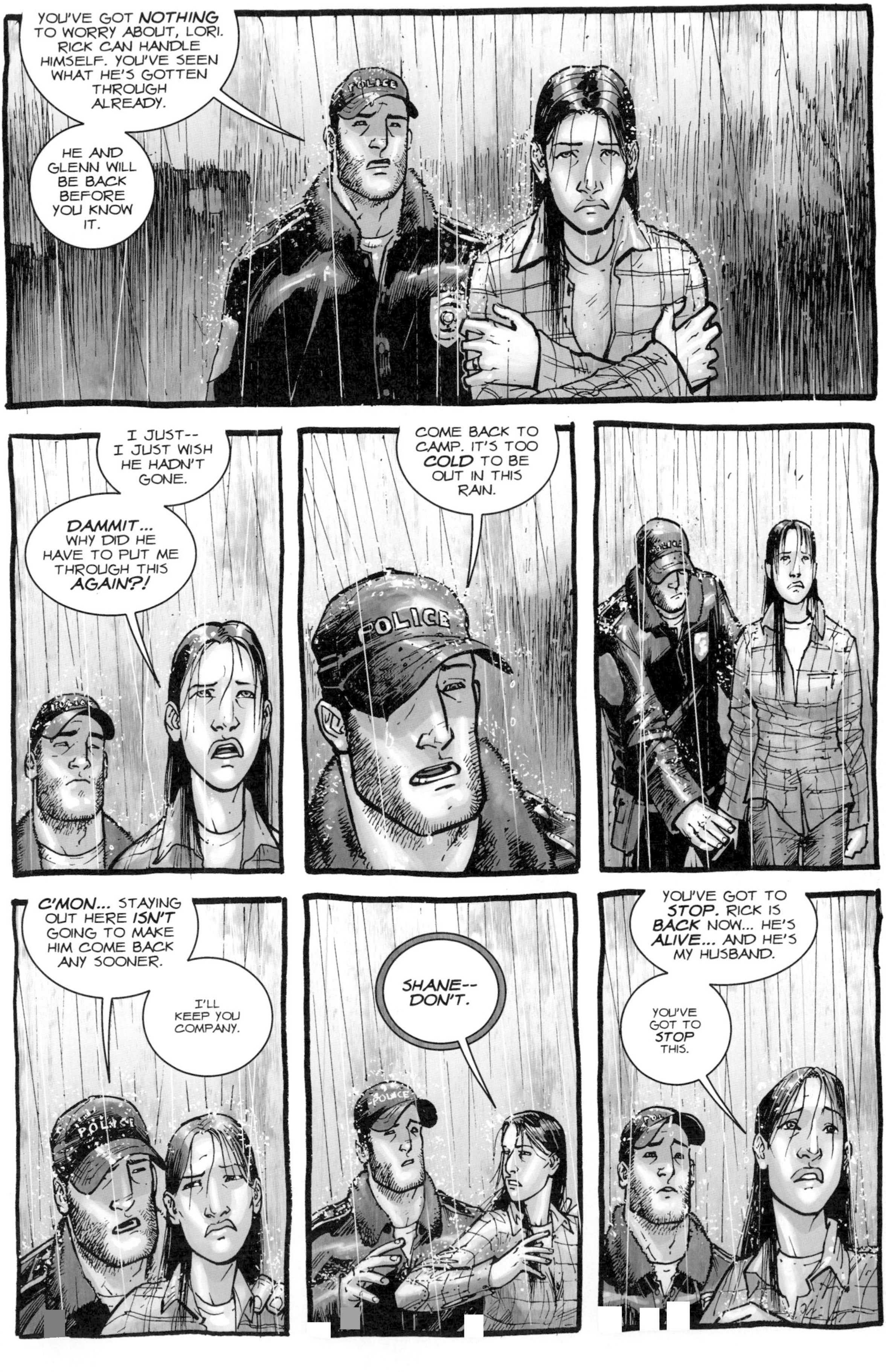
YOU'VE GOT NOTHING TO WORRY ABOUT, LORI. RICK CAN HANDLE HIMSELF. YOU'VE SEEN WHAT HE'S GOTTEN THROUGH ALREADY.
HE AND GLENN WILL BE BACK BEFORE YOU KNOW IT.
POLICE
I JUST-- I JUST WISH HE HADN'T GONE.
DAMMIT... WHY DID HE HAVE TO PUT ME THROUGH THIS AGAIN?!
COME BACK TO CAMP. IT'S TOO COLD TO BE OUT IN THIS RAIN.
POLICE
C'MON... STAYING OUT HERE ISN'T GOING TO MAKE HIM COME BACK ANY SOONER.
I'LL KEEP YOU COMPANY.
SHANE-- DON'T.
YOU'VE GOT TO STOP. RICK IS BACK NOW... HE'S ALIVE... AND HE'S MY HUSBAND.
YOU'VE GOT TO STOP THIS.

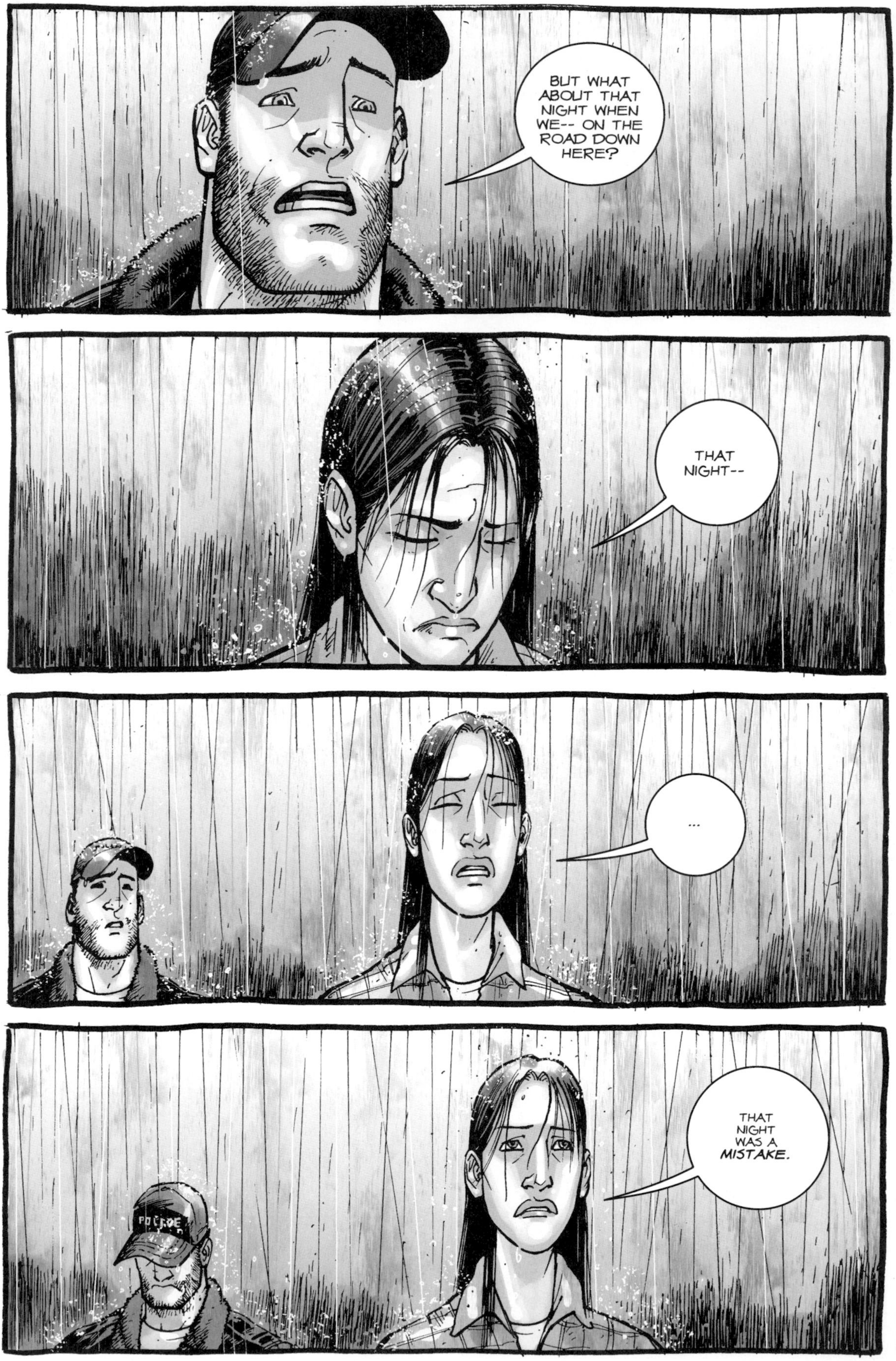
BUT WHAT ABOUT THAT NIGHT WHEN WE-- ON THE ROAD DOWN HERE?
THAT NIGHT--
...
THAT NIGHT WAS A *MISTAKE.*

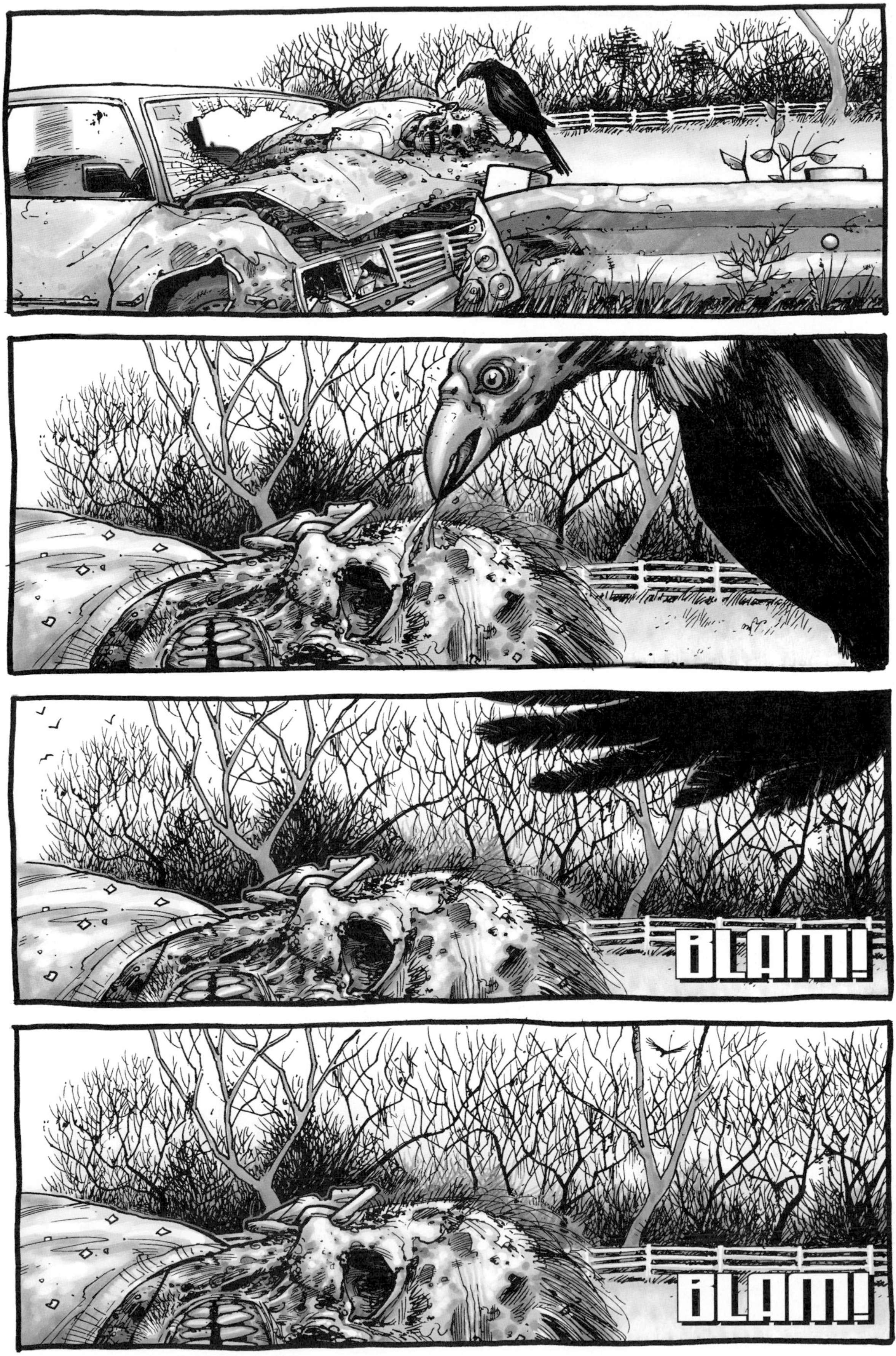
BLAM!
BLAM!

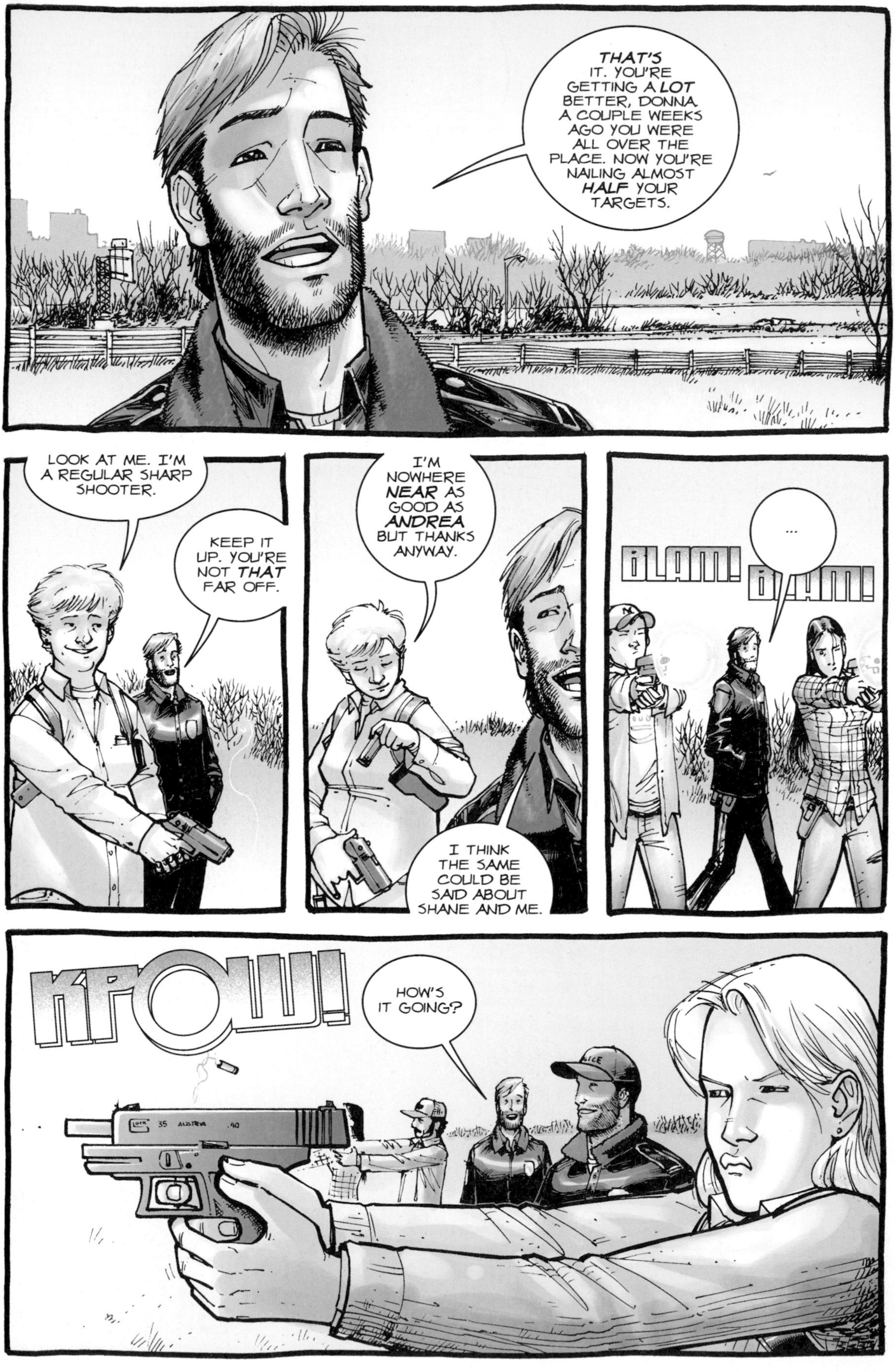
THAT'S IT. YOU'RE GETTING A LOT BETTER, DONNA. A COUPLE WEEKS AGO YOU WERE ALL OVER THE PLACE. NOW YOU'RE NAILING ALMOST HALF YOUR TARGETS.
LOOK AT ME. I'M A REGULAR SHARP SHOOTER.
KEEP IT UP. YOU'RE NOT THAT FAR OFF.
I'M NOWHERE NEAR AS GOOD AS ANDREA BUT THANKS ANYWAY.
I THINK THE SAME COULD BE SAID ABOUT SHANE AND ME.
BLAM!
BLAM!
...
KPOW!
HOW'S IT GOING?

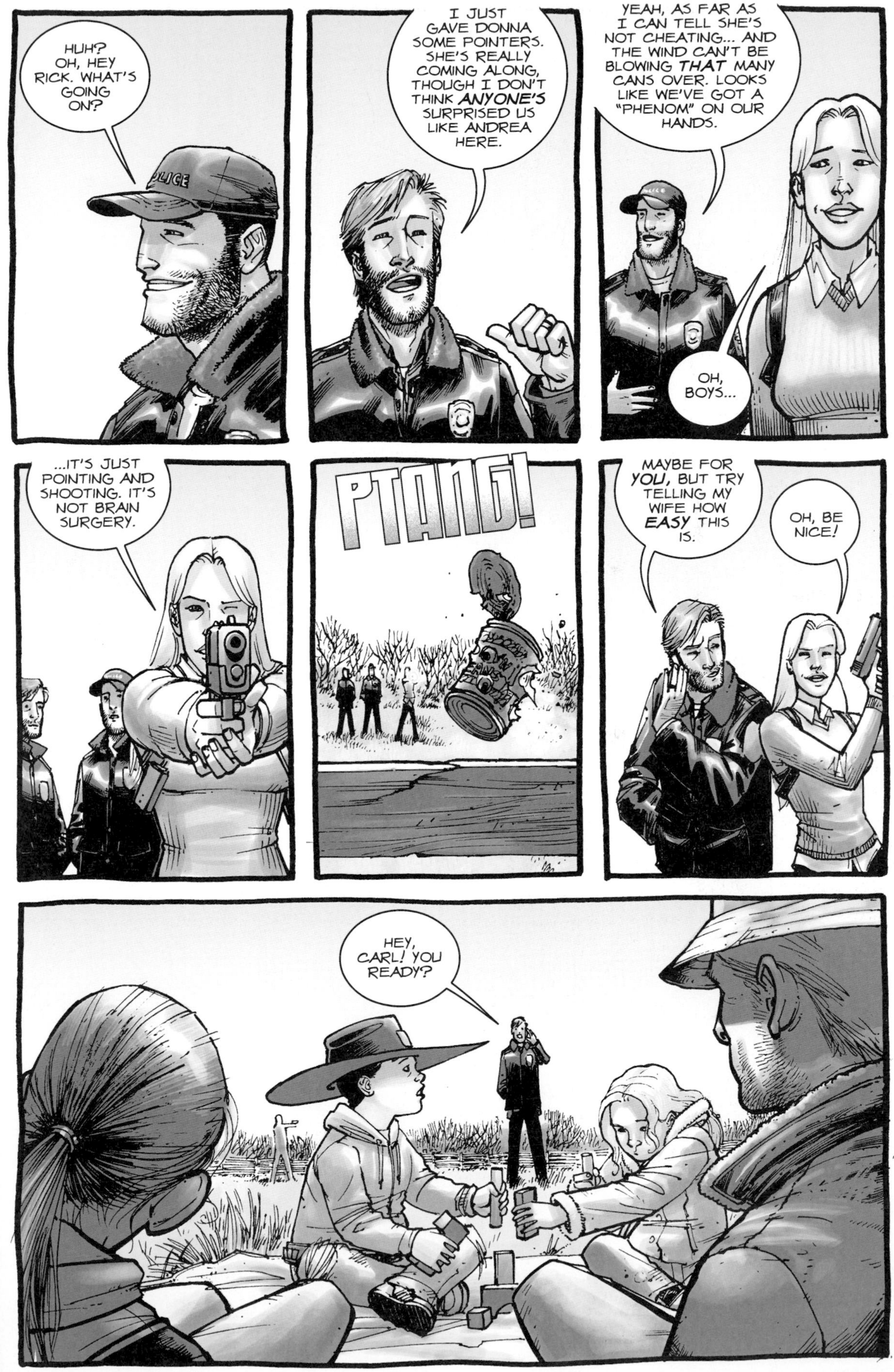
HUH? OH, HEY RICK. WHAT'S GOING ON?
I JUST GAVE DONNA SOME POINTERS. SHE'S REALLY COMING ALONG, THOUGH I DON'T THINK ANYONE'S SURPRISED US LIKE ANDREA HERE.
YEAH, AS FAR AS I CAN TELL SHE'S NOT CHEATING... AND THE WIND CAN'T BE BLOWING THAT MANY CANS OVER. LOOKS LIKE WE'VE GOT A "PHENOM" ON OUR HANDS.
OH, BOYS...
...IT'S JUST POINTING AND SHOOTING. IT'S NOT BRAIN SURGERY.
PTANG!
MAYBE FOR YOU, BUT TRY TELLING MY WIFE HOW EASY THIS IS.
OH, BE NICE!
HEY, CARL! YOU READY?

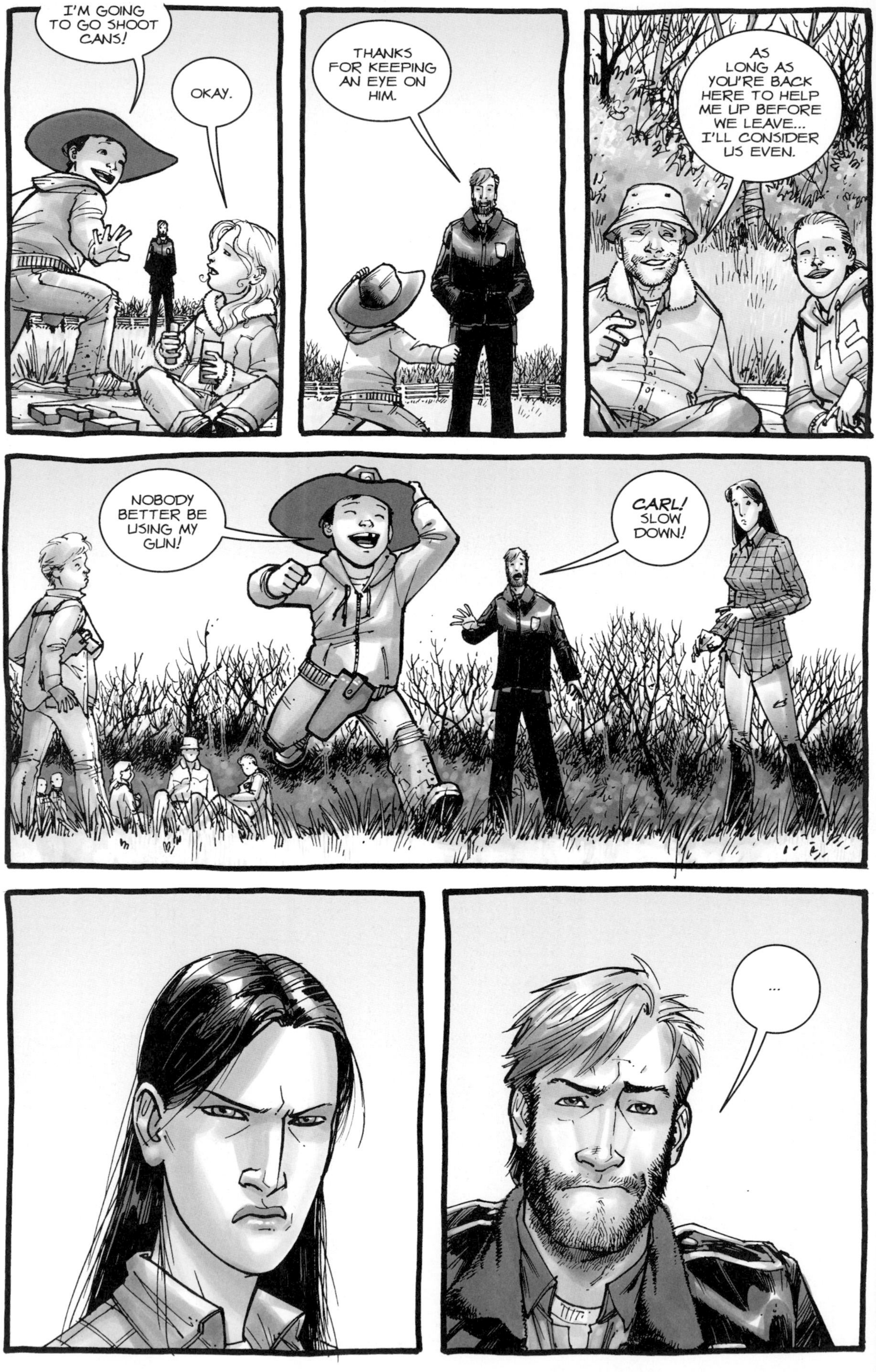
I'M GOING TO GO SHOOT CANS!
OKAY.
THANKS FOR KEEPING AN EYE ON HIM.
AS LONG AS YOU'RE BACK HERE TO HELP ME UP BEFORE WE LEAVE... I'LL CONSIDER US EVEN.
NOBODY BETTER BE USING MY GUN!
CARL! SLOW DOWN!
...

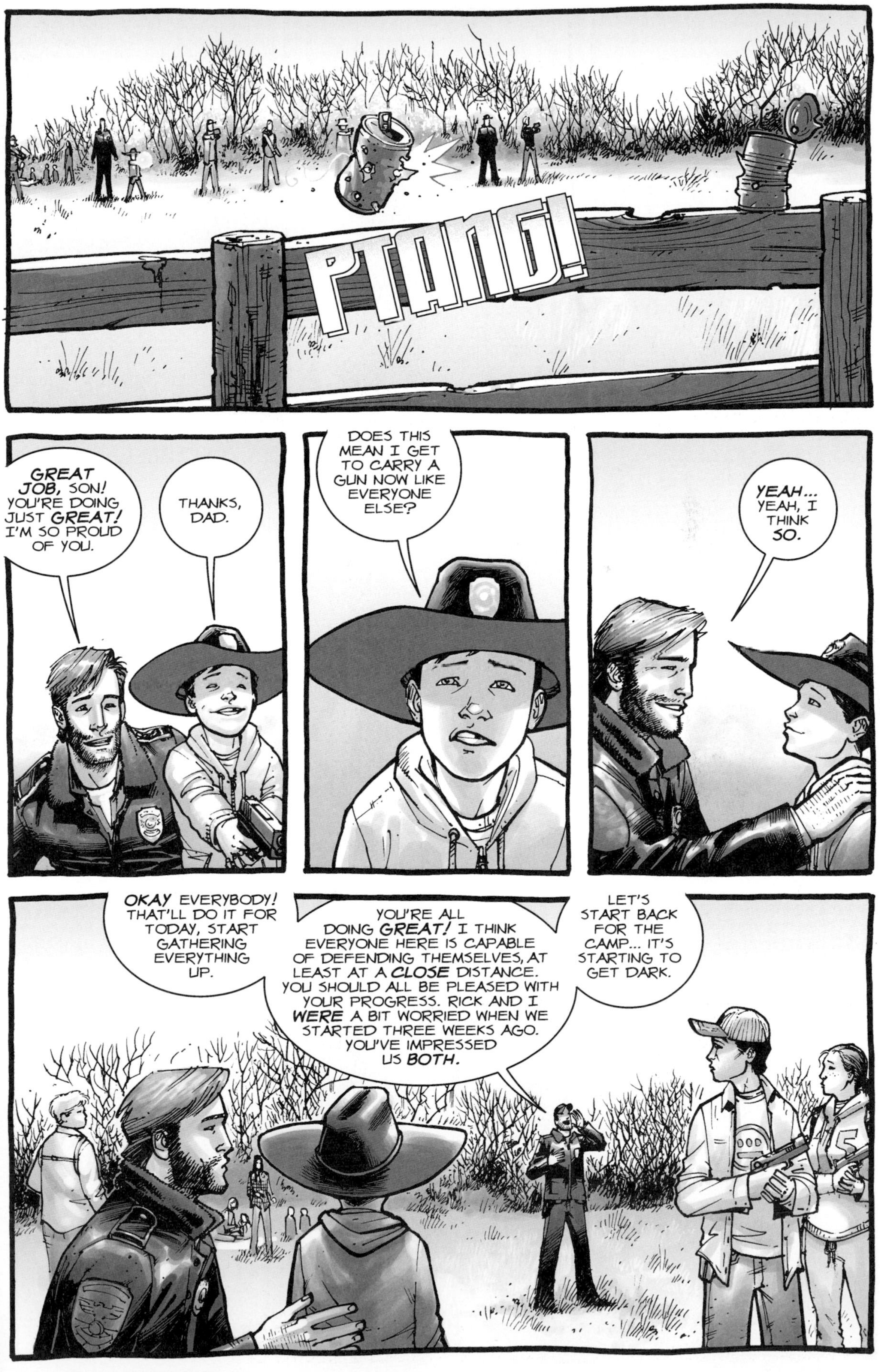
PTANG!
GREAT JOB, SON! YOU'RE DOING JUST GREAT! I'M SO PROUD OF YOU.
THANKS, DAD.
DOES THIS MEAN I GET TO CARRY A GUN NOW LIKE EVERYONE ELSE?
YEAH... YEAH, I THINK SO.
OKAY EVERYBODY! THAT'LL DO IT FOR TODAY, START GATHERING EVERYTHING UP.
YOU'RE ALL DOING GREAT! I THINK EVERYONE HERE IS CAPABLE OF DEFENDING THEMSELVES, AT LEAST AT A CLOSE DISTANCE. YOU SHOULD ALL BE PLEASED WITH YOUR PROGRESS. RICK AND I WERE A BIT WORRIED WHEN WE STARTED THREE WEEKS AGO. YOU'VE IMPRESSED US BOTH.
LET'S START BACK FOR THE CAMP... IT'S STARTING TO GET DARK.

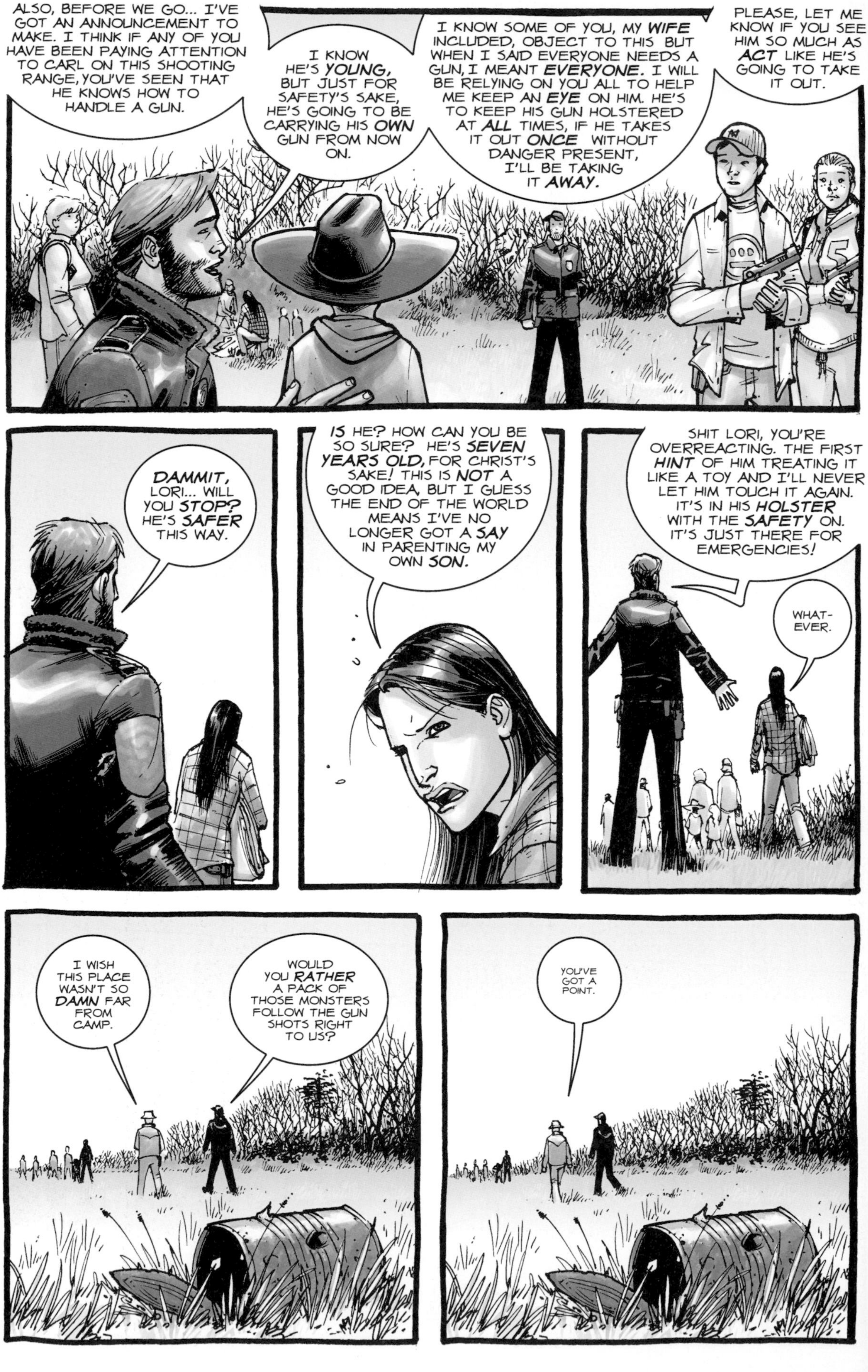

ALSO, BEFORE WE GO... I'VE GOT AN ANNOUNCEMENT TO MAKE. I THINK IF ANY OF YOU HAVE BEEN PAYING ATTENTION TO CARL ON THIS SHOOTING RANGE, YOU'VE SEEN THAT HE KNOWS HOW TO HANDLE A GUN.
I KNOW HE'S YOUNG, BUT JUST FOR SAFETY'S SAKE, HE'S GOING TO BE CARRYING HIS OWN GUN FROM NOW ON.
I KNOW SOME OF YOU, MY WIFE INCLUDED, OBJECT TO THIS BUT WHEN I SAID EVERYONE NEEDS A GUN, I MEANT EVERYONE. I WILL BE RELYING ON YOU ALL TO HELP ME KEEP AN EYE ON HIM. HE'S TO KEEP HIS GUN HOLSTERED AT ALL TIMES, IF HE TAKES IT OUT ONCE WITHOUT DANGER PRESENT, I'LL BE TAKING IT AWAY.
PLEASE, LET ME KNOW IF YOU SEE HIM SO MUCH AS ACT LIKE HE'S GOING TO TAKE IT OUT.
DAMMIT, LORI... WILL YOU STOP? HE'S SAFER THIS WAY.
IS HE? HOW CAN YOU BE SO SURE? HE'S SEVEN YEARS OLD, FOR CHRIST'S SAKE! THIS IS NOT A GOOD IDEA, BUT I GUESS THE END OF THE WORLD MEANS I'VE NO LONGER GOT A SAY IN PARENTING MY OWN SON.
SHIT LORI, YOU'RE OVERREACTING. THE FIRST HINT OF HIM TREATING IT LIKE A TOY AND I'LL NEVER LET HIM TOUCH IT AGAIN. IT'S IN HIS HOLSTER WITH THE SAFETY ON. IT'S JUST THERE FOR EMERGENCIES!
WHAT-EVER.
I WISH THIS PLACE WASN'T SO DAMN FAR FROM CAMP.
WOULD YOU RATHER A PACK OF THOSE MONSTERS FOLLOW THE GUN SHOTS RIGHT TO US?
YOU'VE GOT A POINT.

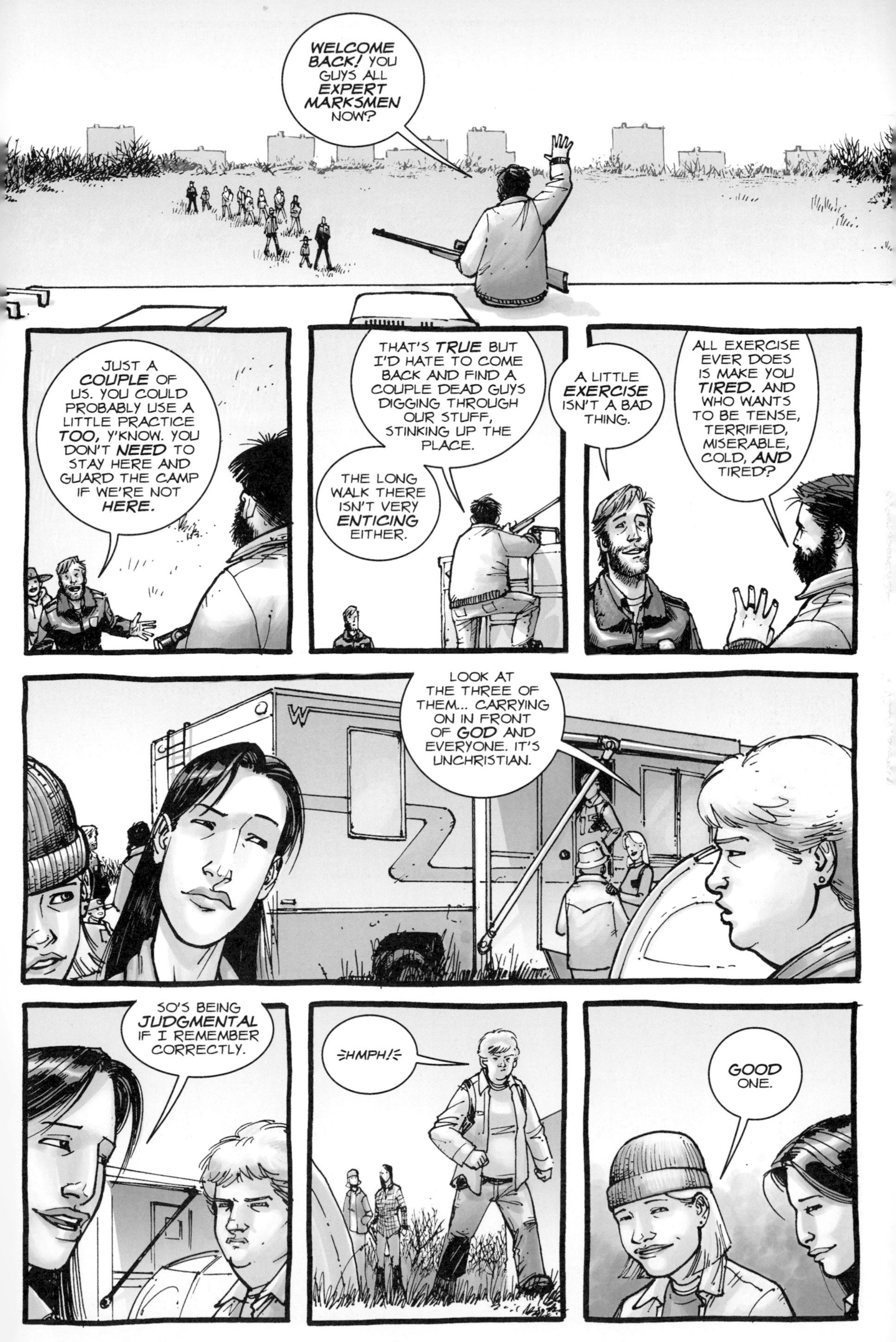
WELCOME BACK! YOU GUYS ALL EXPERT MARKSMEN NOW?
JUST A COUPLE OF US. YOU COULD PROBABLY USE A LITTLE PRACTICE TOO, Y'KNOW. YOU DON'T NEED TO STAY HERE AND GUARD THE CAMP IF WE'RE NOT HERE.
THAT'S TRUE BUT I'D HATE TO COME BACK AND FIND A COUPLE DEAD GUYS DIGGING THROUGH OUR STUFF, STINKING UP THE PLACE.
THE LONG WALK THERE ISN'T VERY ENTICING EITHER.
A LITTLE EXERCISE ISN'T A BAD THING.
ALL EXERCISE EVER DOES IS MAKE YOU TIRED. AND WHO WANTS TO BE TENSE, TERRIFIED, MISERABLE, COLD, AND TIRED?
LOOK AT THE THREE OF THEM... CARRYING ON IN FRONT OF GOD AND EVERYONE. IT'S UNCHRISTIAN.
SO'S BEING JUDGMENTAL IF I REMEMBER CORRECTLY.
HMPH!
GOOD ONE.

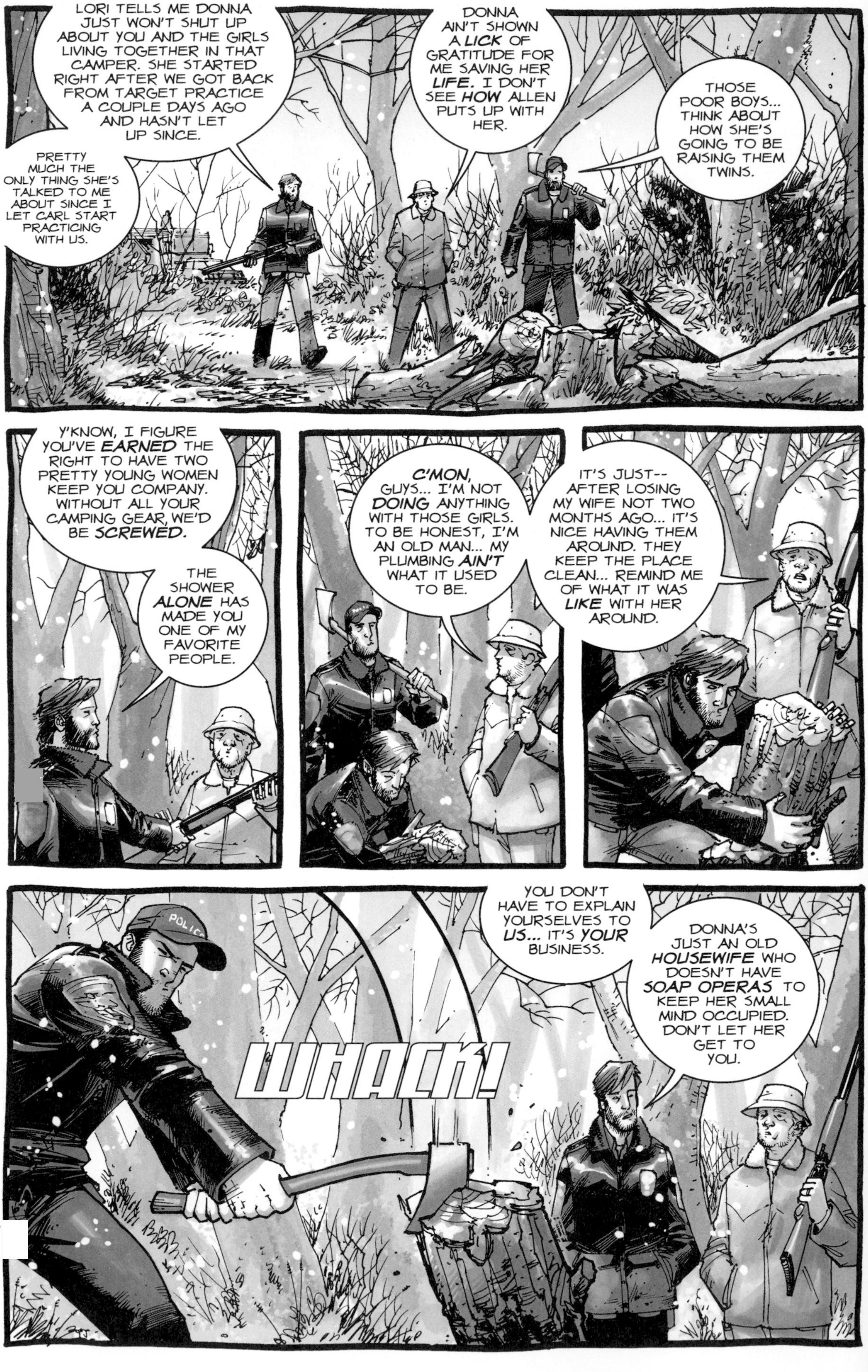
LORI TELLS ME DONNA JUST WON'T SHUT UP ABOUT YOU AND THE GIRLS LIVING TOGETHER IN THAT CAMPER. SHE STARTED RIGHT AFTER WE GOT BACK FROM TARGET PRACTICE A COUPLE DAYS AGO AND HASN'T LET UP SINCE.
PRETTY MUCH THE ONLY THING SHE'S TALKED TO ME ABOUT SINCE I LET CARL START PRACTICING WITH US.
DONNA AIN'T SHOWN A LICK OF GRATITUDE FOR ME SAVING HER LIFE. I DON'T SEE HOW ALLEN PUTS UP WITH HER.
THOSE POOR BOYS... THINK ABOUT HOW SHE'S GOING TO BE RAISING THEM TWINS.
Y'KNOW, I FIGURE YOU'VE EARNED THE RIGHT TO HAVE TWO PRETTY YOUNG WOMEN KEEP YOU COMPANY. WITHOUT ALL YOUR CAMPING GEAR, WE'D BE SCREWED.
THE SHOWER ALONE HAS MADE YOU ONE OF MY FAVORITE PEOPLE.
C'MON, GUYS... I'M NOT DOING ANYTHING WITH THOSE GIRLS. TO BE HONEST, I'M AN OLD MAN... MY PLUMBING AIN'T WHAT IT USED TO BE.
IT'S JUST-- AFTER LOSING MY WIFE NOT TWO MONTHS AGO... IT'S NICE HAVING THEM AROUND. THEY KEEP THE PLACE CLEAN... REMIND ME OF WHAT IT WAS LIKE WITH HER AROUND.
WHACK!
YOU DON'T HAVE TO EXPLAIN YOURSELVES TO US... IT'S YOUR BUSINESS.
DONNA'S JUST AN OLD HOUSEWIFE WHO DOESN'T HAVE SOAP OPERAS TO KEEP HER SMALL MIND OCCUPIED. DON'T LET HER GET TO YOU.

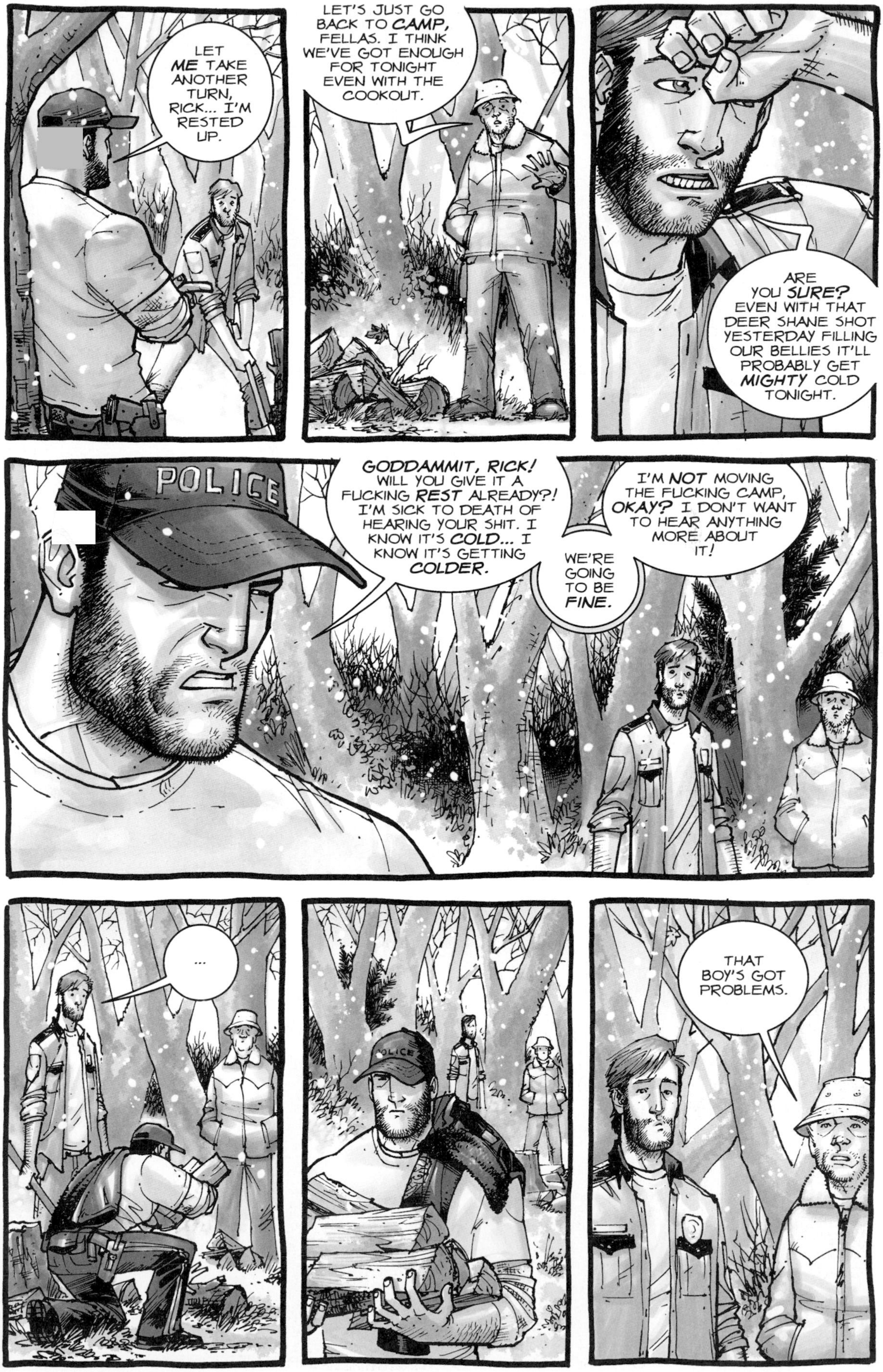
LET ME TAKE ANOTHER TURN, RICK... I'M RESTED UP.
LET'S JUST GO BACK TO CAMP, FELLAS. I THINK WE'VE GOT ENOUGH FOR TONIGHT EVEN WITH THE COOKOUT.
ARE YOU SURE? EVEN WITH THAT DEER SHANE SHOT YESTERDAY FILLING OUR BELLIES IT'LL PROBABLY GET MIGHTY COLD TONIGHT.
GODDAMMIT, RICK! WILL YOU GIVE IT A FUCKING REST ALREADY?! I'M SICK TO DEATH OF HEARING YOUR SHIT. I KNOW IT'S COLD... I KNOW IT'S GETTING COLDER.
WE'RE GOING TO BE FINE.
I'M NOT MOVING THE FUCKING CAMP, OKAY? I DON'T WANT TO HEAR ANYTHING MORE ABOUT IT!
POLICE
...
POLICE
THAT BOY'S GOT PROBLEMS.

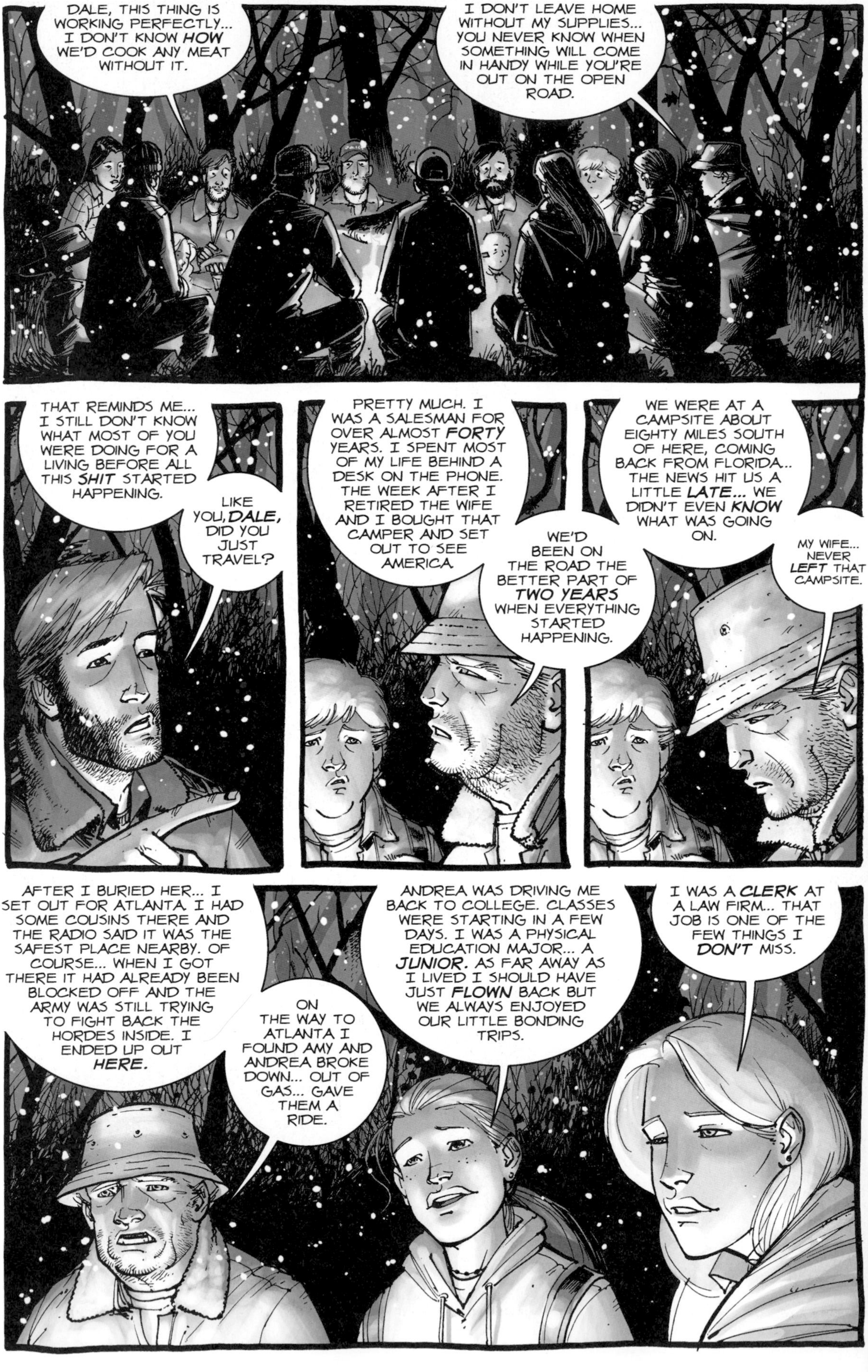
DALE, THIS THING IS WORKING PERFECTLY... I DON'T KNOW **HOW** WE'D COOK ANY MEAT WITHOUT IT.
I DON'T LEAVE HOME WITHOUT MY SUPPLIES... YOU NEVER KNOW WHEN SOMETHING WILL COME IN HANDY WHILE YOU'RE OUT ON THE OPEN ROAD.
THAT REMINDS ME... I STILL DON'T KNOW WHAT MOST OF YOU WERE DOING FOR A LIVING BEFORE ALL THIS **SHIT** STARTED HAPPENING.
LIKE YOU, **DALE,** DID YOU JUST TRAVEL?
PRETTY MUCH. I WAS A SALESMAN FOR OVER ALMOST **FORTY** YEARS. I SPENT MOST OF MY LIFE BEHIND A DESK ON THE PHONE. THE WEEK AFTER I RETIRED THE WIFE AND I BOUGHT THAT CAMPER AND SET OUT TO SEE AMERICA.
WE'D BEEN ON THE ROAD THE BETTER PART OF **TWO YEARS** WHEN EVERYTHING STARTED HAPPENING.
WE WERE AT A CAMPSITE ABOUT EIGHTY MILES SOUTH OF HERE, COMING BACK FROM FLORIDA.. THE NEWS HIT US A LITTLE **LATE...** WE DIDN'T EVEN **KNOW** WHAT WAS GOING ON.
MY WIFE... NEVER **LEFT** THAT CAMPSITE.
AFTER I BURIED HER... I SET OUT FOR ATLANTA. I HAD SOME COUSINS THERE AND THE RADIO SAID IT WAS THE SAFEST PLACE NEARBY. OF COURSE... WHEN I GOT THERE IT HAD ALREADY BEEN BLOCKED OFF AND THE ARMY WAS STILL TRYING TO FIGHT BACK THE HORDES INSIDE. I ENDED UP OUT **HERE.**
ON THE WAY TO ATLANTA I FOUND AMY AND ANDREA BROKE DOWN... OUT OF GAS... GAVE THEM A RIDE.
ANDREA WAS DRIVING ME BACK TO COLLEGE. CLASSES WERE STARTING IN A FEW DAYS. I WAS A PHYSICAL EDUCATION MAJOR... A **JUNIOR.** AS FAR AWAY AS I LIVED I SHOULD HAVE JUST **FLOWN** BACK BUT WE ALWAYS ENJOYED OUR LITTLE BONDING TRIPS.
I WAS A **CLERK** AT A LAW FIRM... THAT JOB IS ONE OF THE FEW THINGS I **DON'T** MISS.

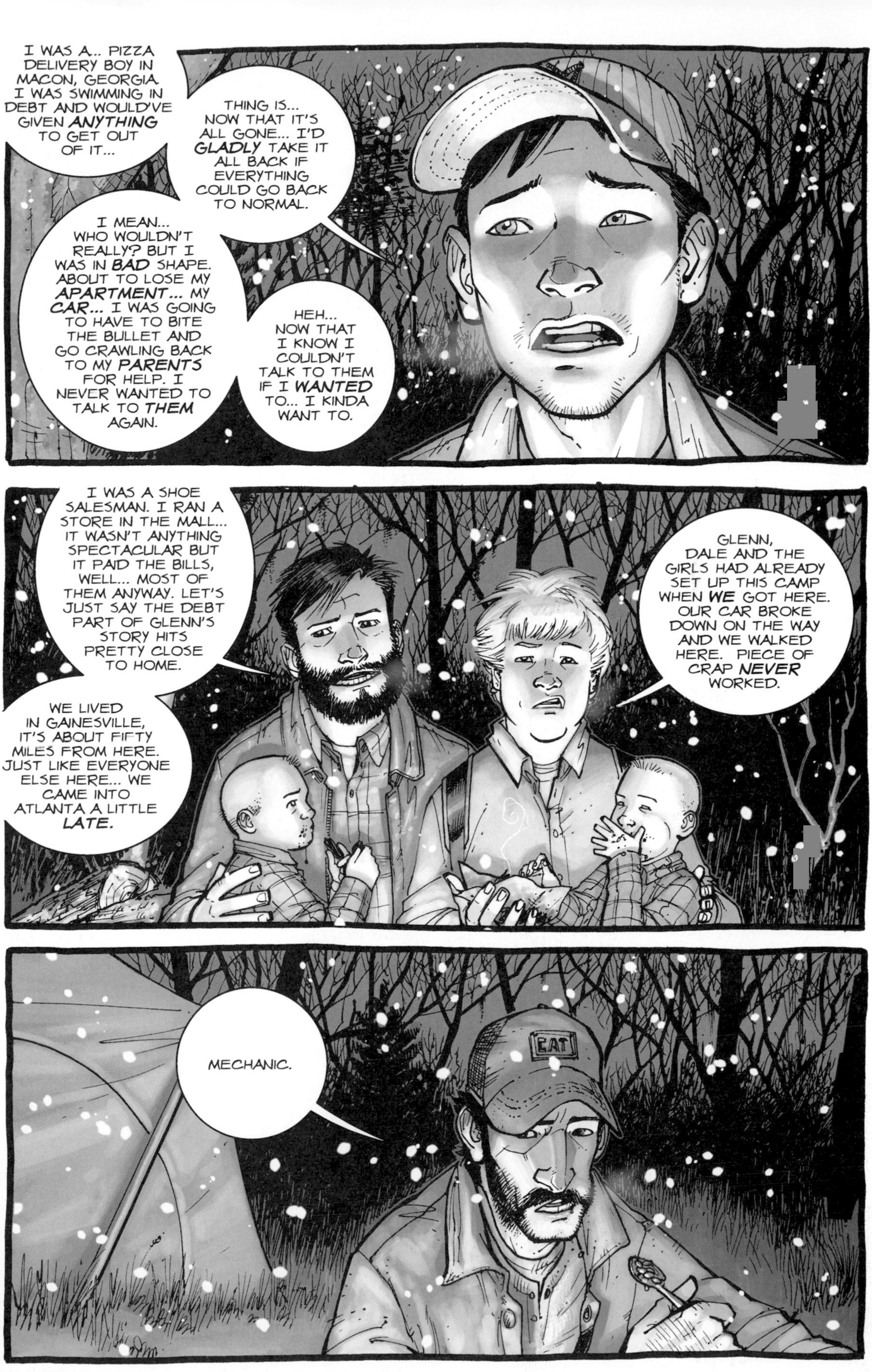
I WAS A... PIZZA DELIVERY BOY IN MACON, GEORGIA. I WAS SWIMMING IN DEBT AND WOULD'VE GIVEN ANYTHING TO GET OUT OF IT...
THING IS... NOW THAT IT'S ALL GONE... I'D GLADLY TAKE IT ALL BACK IF EVERYTHING COULD GO BACK TO NORMAL.
I MEAN... WHO WOULDN'T REALLY? BUT I WAS IN BAD SHAPE. ABOUT TO LOSE MY APARTMENT... MY CAR... I WAS GOING TO HAVE TO BITE THE BULLET AND GO CRAWLING BACK TO MY PARENTS FOR HELP. I NEVER WANTED TO TALK TO THEM AGAIN.
HEH... NOW THAT I KNOW I COULDN'T TALK TO THEM IF I WANTED TO... I KINDA WANT TO.
I WAS A SHOE SALESMAN. I RAN A STORE IN THE MALL... IT WASN'T ANYTHING SPECTACULAR BUT IT PAID THE BILLS, WELL... MOST OF THEM ANYWAY. LET'S JUST SAY THE DEBT PART OF GLENN'S STORY HITS PRETTY CLOSE TO HOME.
WE LIVED IN GAINESVILLE, IT'S ABOUT FIFTY MILES FROM HERE. JUST LIKE EVERYONE ELSE HERE... WE CAME INTO ATLANTA A LITTLE LATE.
GLENN, DALE AND THE GIRLS HAD ALREADY SET UP THIS CAMP WHEN WE GOT HERE. OUR CAR BROKE DOWN ON THE WAY AND WE WALKED HERE. PIECE OF CRAP NEVER WORKED.
MECHANIC.

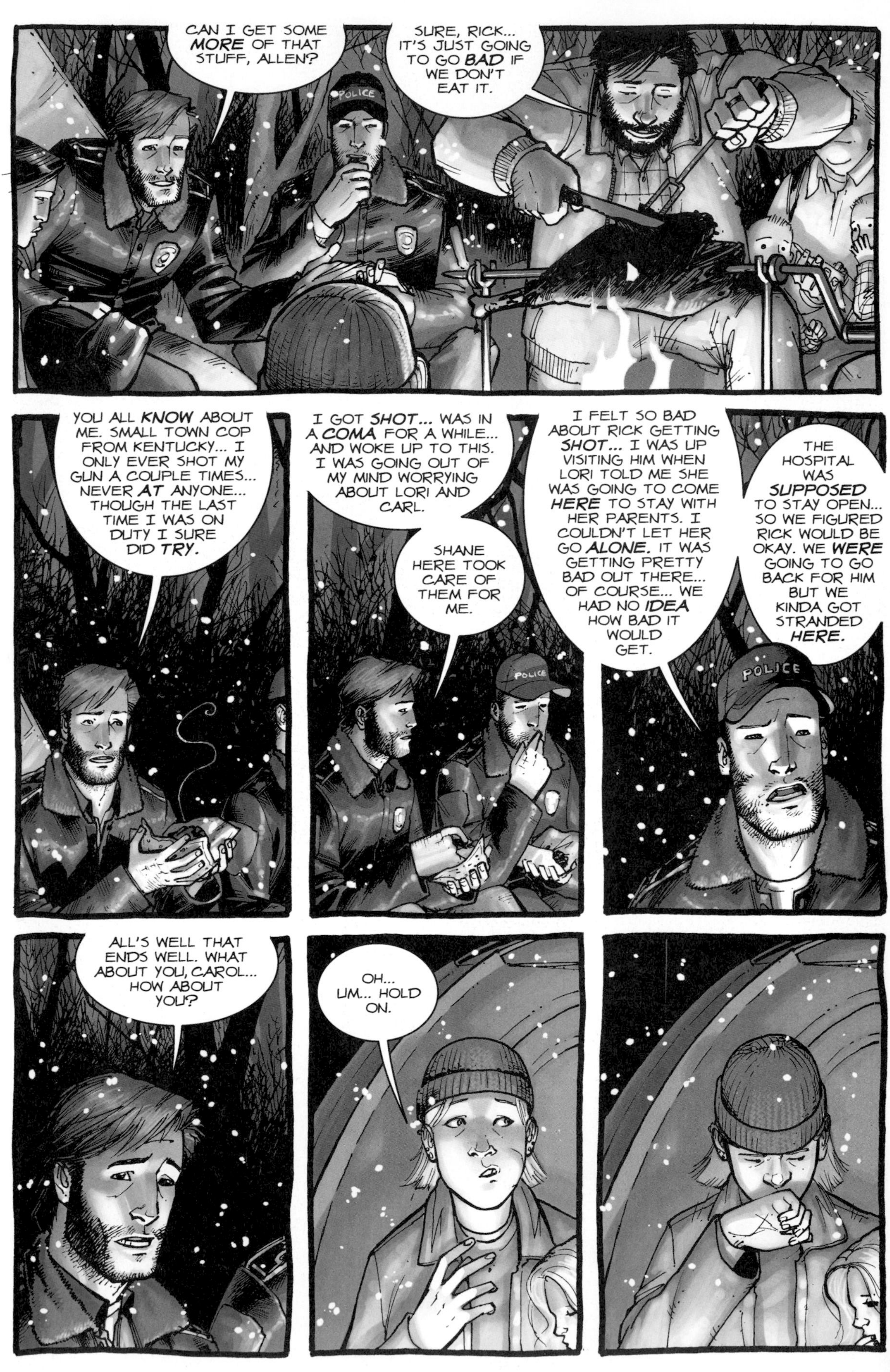
CAN I GET SOME MORE OF THAT STUFF, ALLEN?
SURE, RICK... IT'S JUST GOING TO GO BAD IF WE DON'T EAT IT.
POLICE
YOU ALL KNOW ABOUT ME. SMALL TOWN COP FROM KENTUCKY... I ONLY EVER SHOT MY GUN A COUPLE TIMES... NEVER AT ANYONE... THOUGH THE LAST TIME I WAS ON DUTY I SURE DID TRY.
I GOT SHOT... WAS IN A COMA FOR A WHILE... AND WOKE UP TO THIS. I WAS GOING OUT OF MY MIND WORRYING ABOUT LORI AND CARL.
SHANE HERE TOOK CARE OF THEM FOR ME.
POLICE
I FELT SO BAD ABOUT RICK GETTING SHOT... I WAS UP VISITING HIM WHEN LORI TOLD ME SHE WAS GOING TO COME HERE TO STAY WITH HER PARENTS. I COULDN'T LET HER GO ALONE. IT WAS GETTING PRETTY BAD OUT THERE... OF COURSE... WE HAD NO IDEA HOW BAD IT WOULD GET.
THE HOSPITAL WAS SUPPOSED TO STAY OPEN... SO WE FIGURED RICK WOULD BE OKAY. WE WERE GOING TO GO BACK FOR HIM BUT WE KINDA GOT STRANDED HERE.
POLICE
ALL'S WELL THAT ENDS WELL. WHAT ABOUT YOU, CAROL... HOW ABOUT YOU?
OH... UM... HOLD ON.

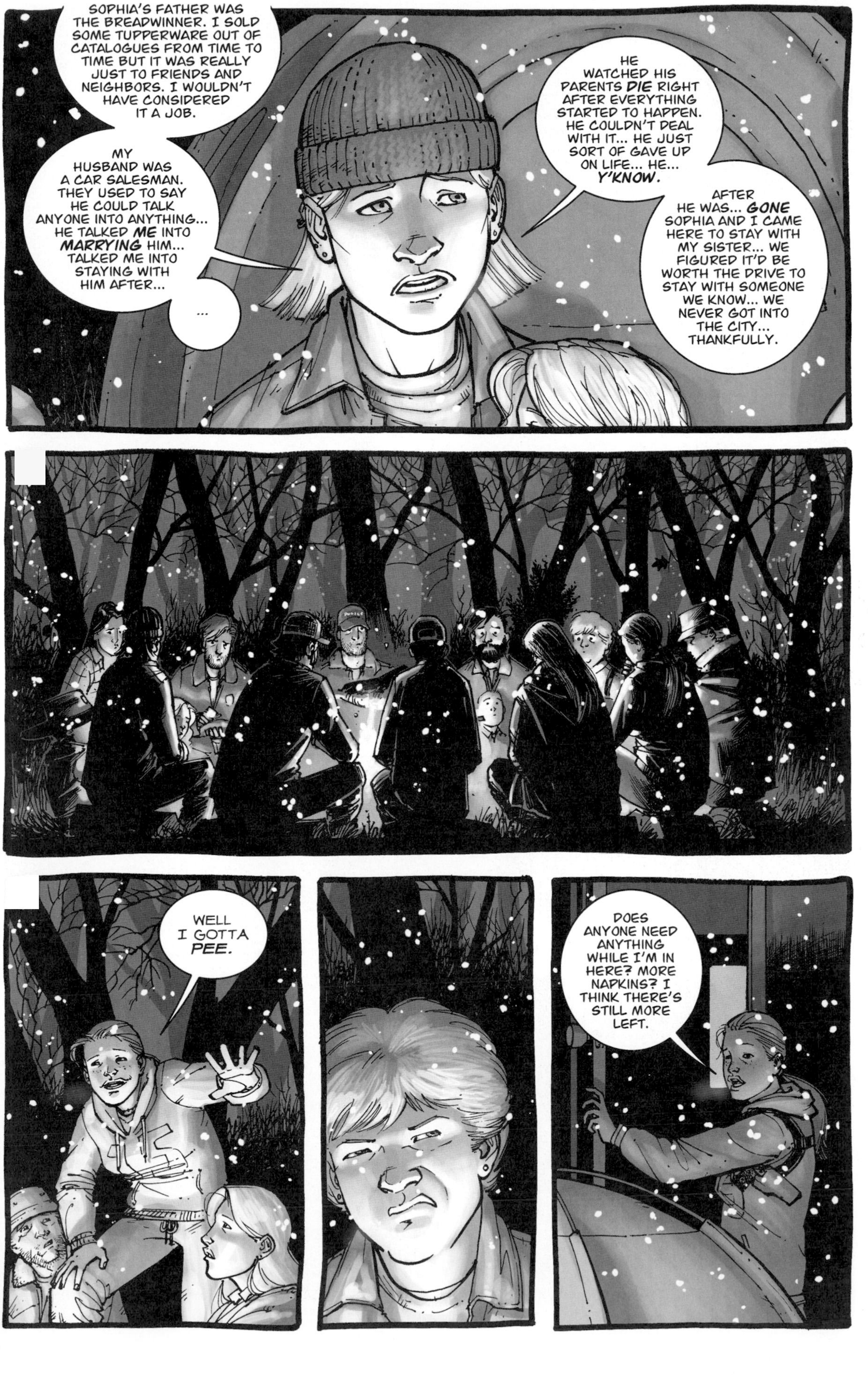

SOPHIA'S FATHER WAS THE BREADWINNER. I SOLD SOME TUPPERWARE OUT OF CATALOGUES FROM TIME TO TIME BUT IT WAS REALLY JUST TO FRIENDS AND NEIGHBORS. I WOULDN'T HAVE CONSIDERED IT A JOB.
MY HUSBAND WAS A CAR SALESMAN. THEY USED TO SAY HE COULD TALK ANYONE INTO ANYTHING... HE TALKED *ME* INTO *MARRYING* HIM... TALKED ME INTO STAYING WITH HIM AFTER...
...
HE WATCHED HIS PARENTS *DIE* RIGHT AFTER EVERYTHING STARTED TO HAPPEN. HE COULDN'T DEAL WITH IT... HE JUST SORT OF GAVE UP ON LIFE... HE... *Y'KNOW*.
AFTER HE WAS... *GONE* SOPHIA AND I CAME HERE TO STAY WITH MY SISTER... WE FIGURED IT'D BE WORTH THE DRIVE TO STAY WITH SOMEONE WE KNOW... WE NEVER GOT INTO THE CITY... THANKFULLY.
WELL I GOTTA *PEE*.
DOES ANYONE NEED ANYTHING WHILE I'M IN HERE? MORE NAPKINS? I THINK THERE'S STILL MORE LEFT.

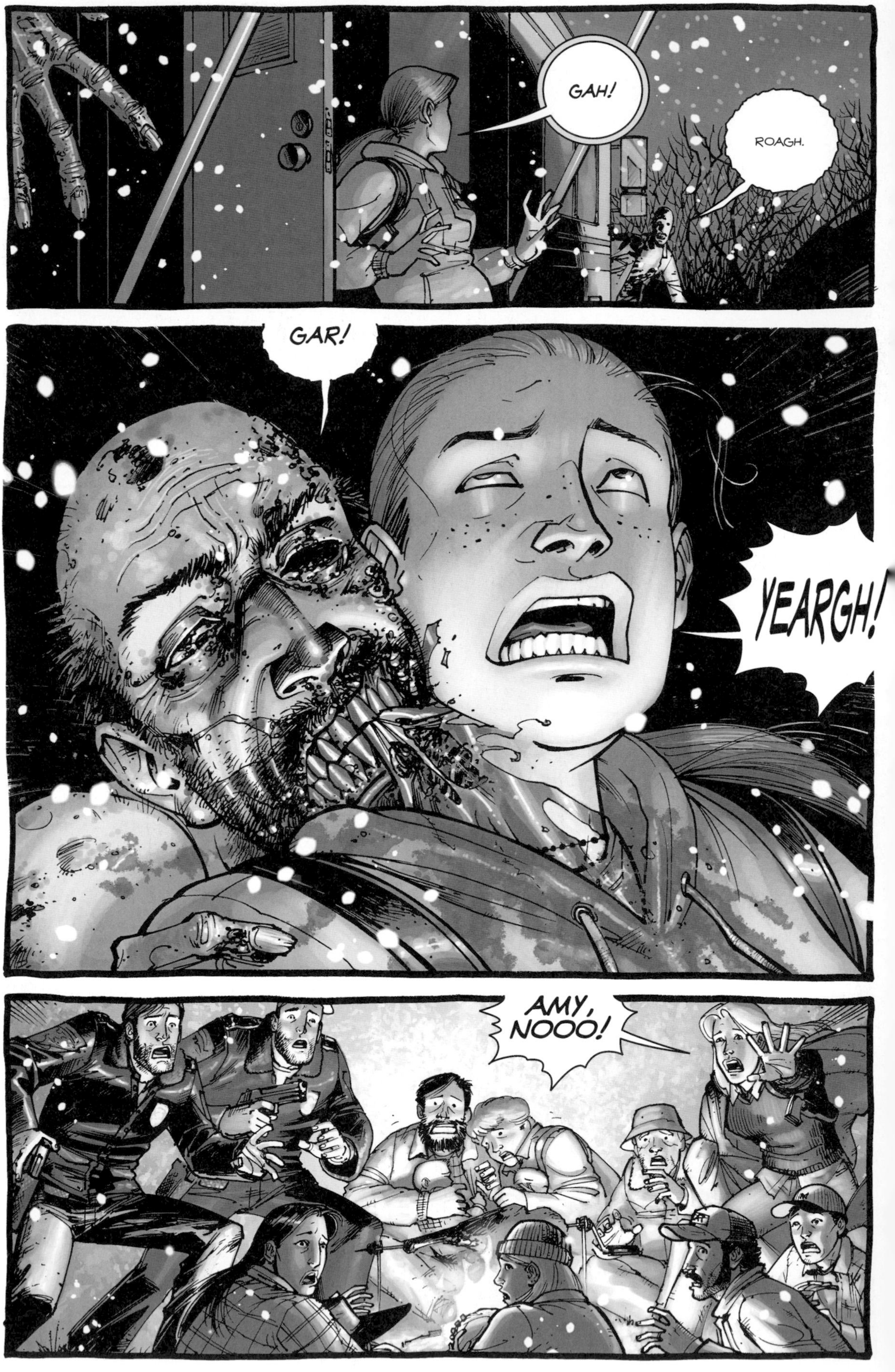
GAH!
ROAGH.
GAR!
YEARGH!
AMY, NOOO!

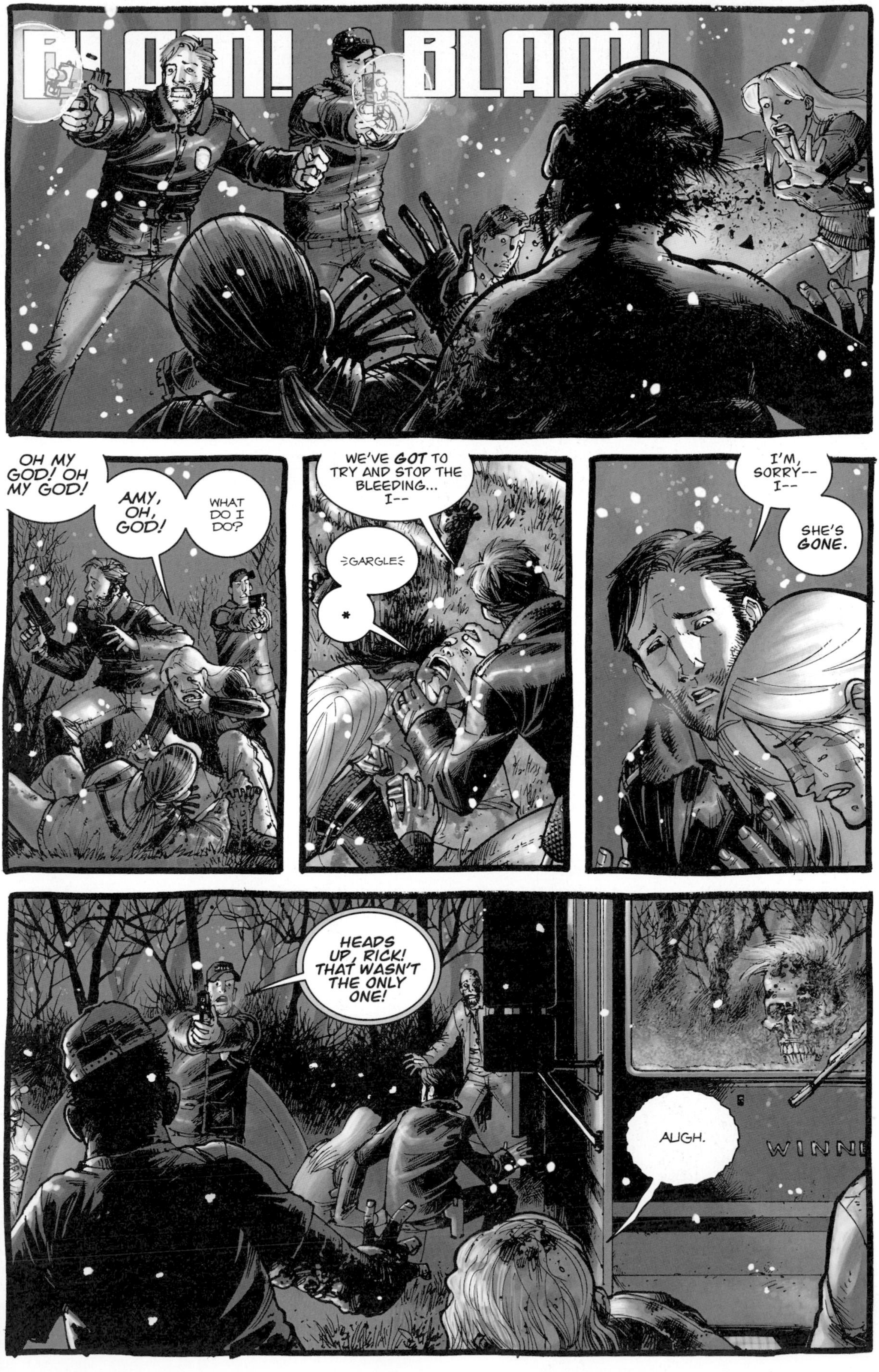
BLAM! BLAM!
OH MY GOD! OH MY GOD!
AMY, OH, GOD!
WHAT DO I DO?
WE'VE GOT TO TRY AND STOP THE BLEEDING... I--
GARGLE
*
I'M, SORRY-- I--
SHE'S GONE.
HEADS UP, RICK! THAT WASN'T THE ONLY ONE!
WINNE
AUGH.

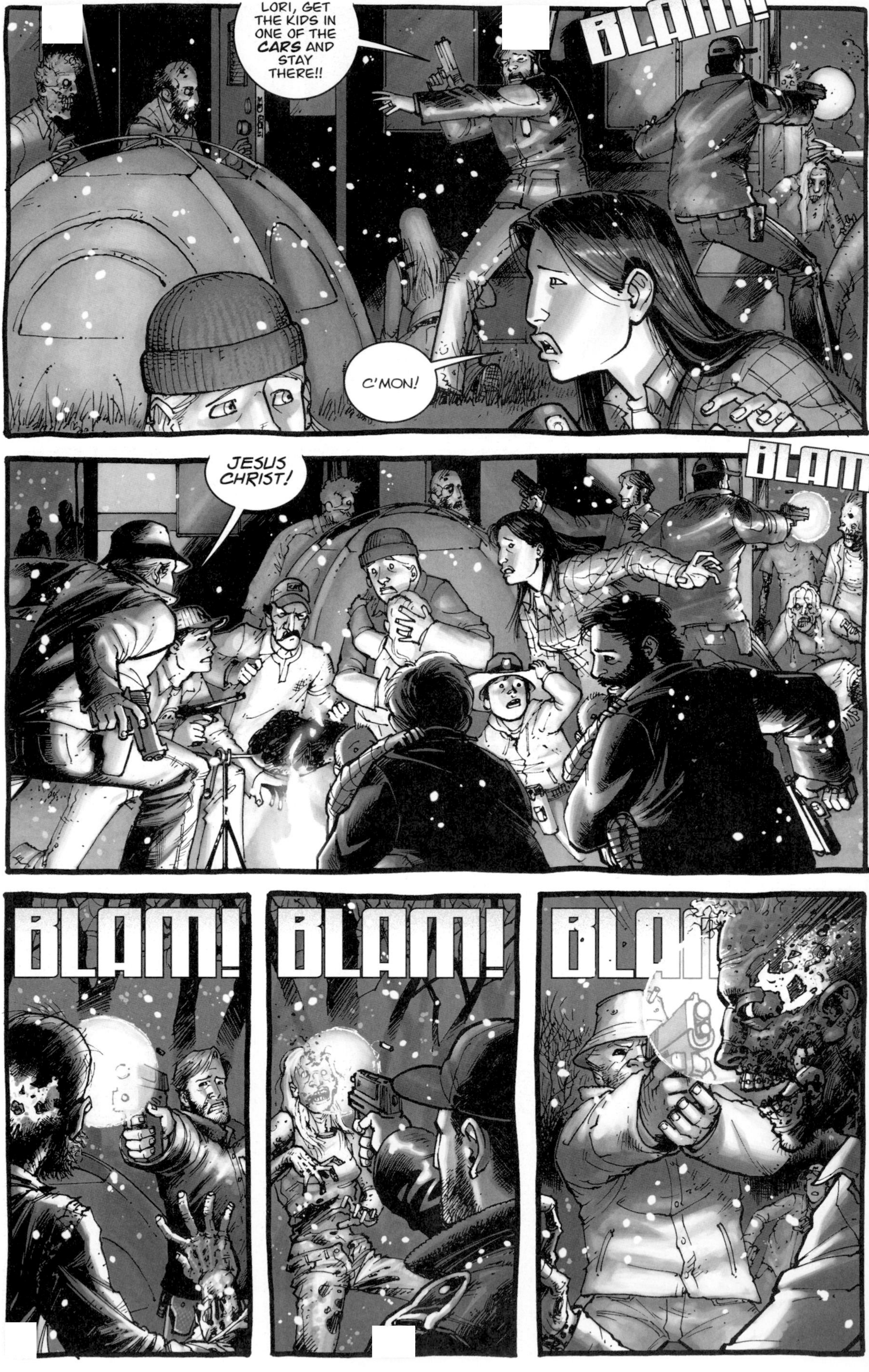

LORI, GET THE KIDS IN ONE OF THE CARS AND STAY THERE!!
BLAM!
C'MON!
JESUS CHRIST!
BLAM!
BLAM!
BLAM!

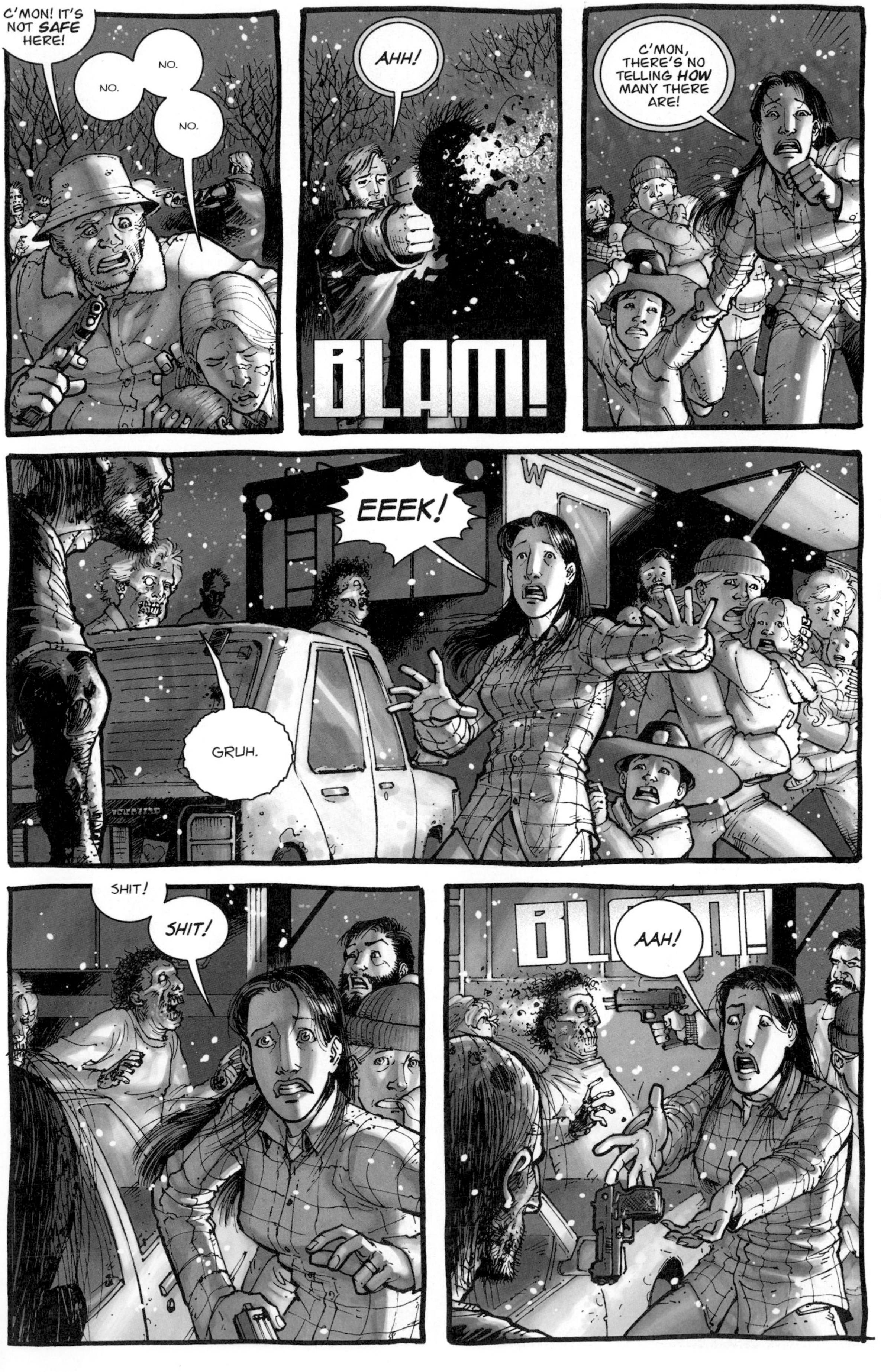
C'MON! IT'S NOT SAFE HERE!
NO.
NO.
NO.
AHH!
BLAM!
C'MON, THERE'S NO TELLING HOW MANY THERE ARE!
EEEK!
GRUH.
SHIT!
SHIT!
BLAM!
AAH!

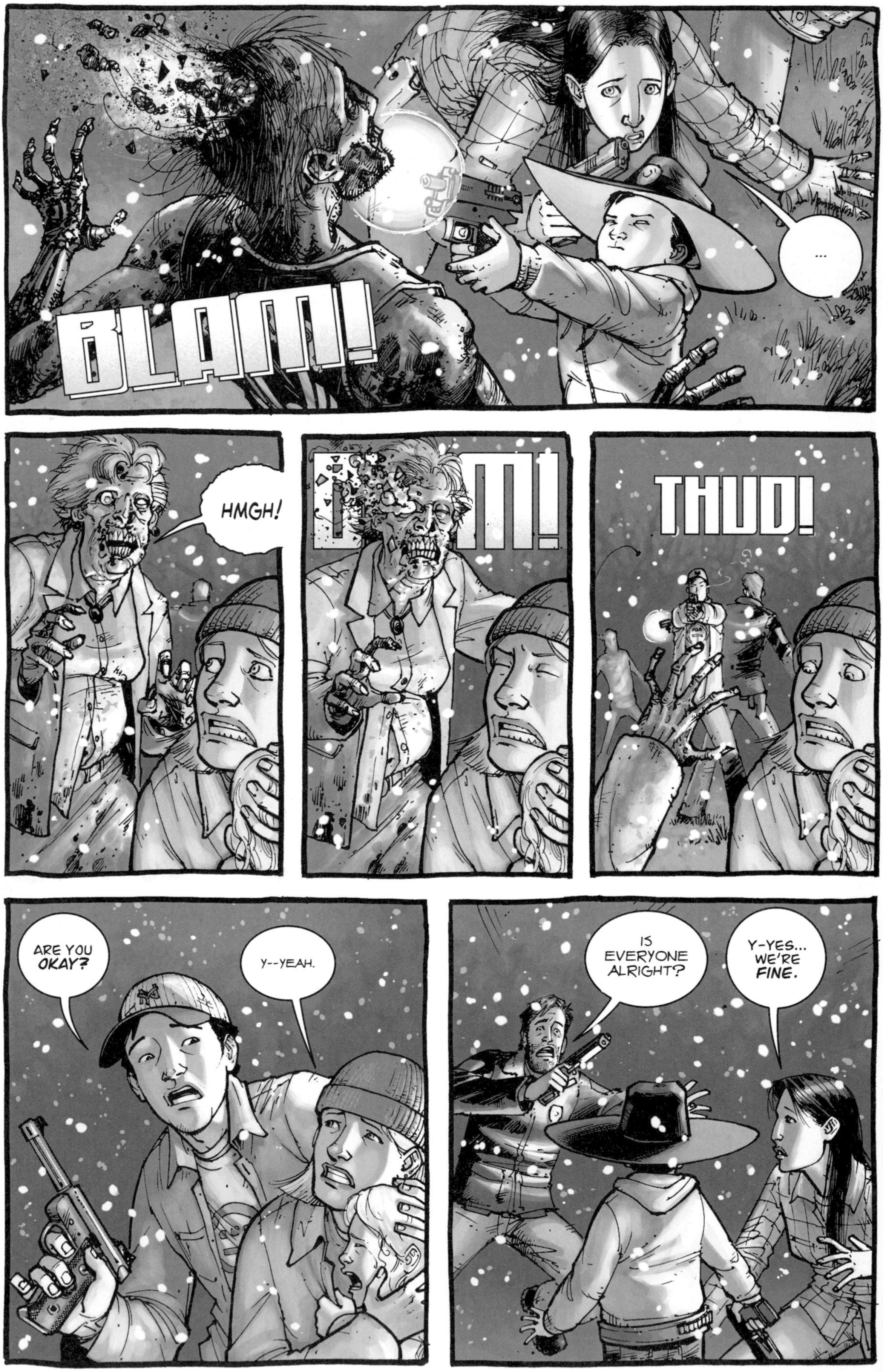

BLAM!
...
HMGH!
BLAM!
THUD!
ARE YOU OKAY?
Y--YEAH.
IS EVERYONE ALRIGHT?
Y-YES... WE'RE FINE.

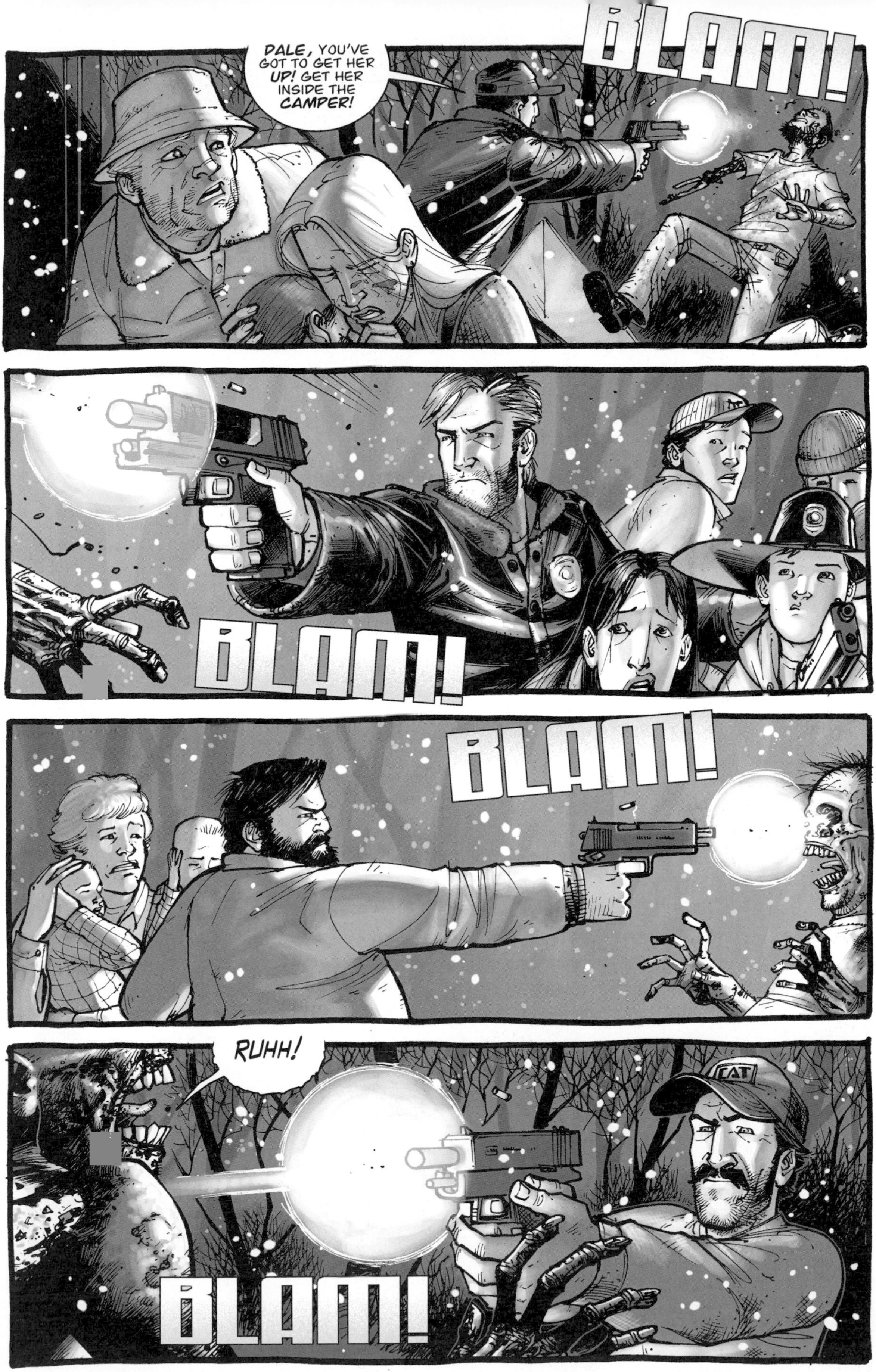
DALE, YOU'VE GOT TO GET HER UP! GET HER INSIDE THE CAMPER!
BLAM!
BLAM!
BLAM!
RUHH!
BLAM!

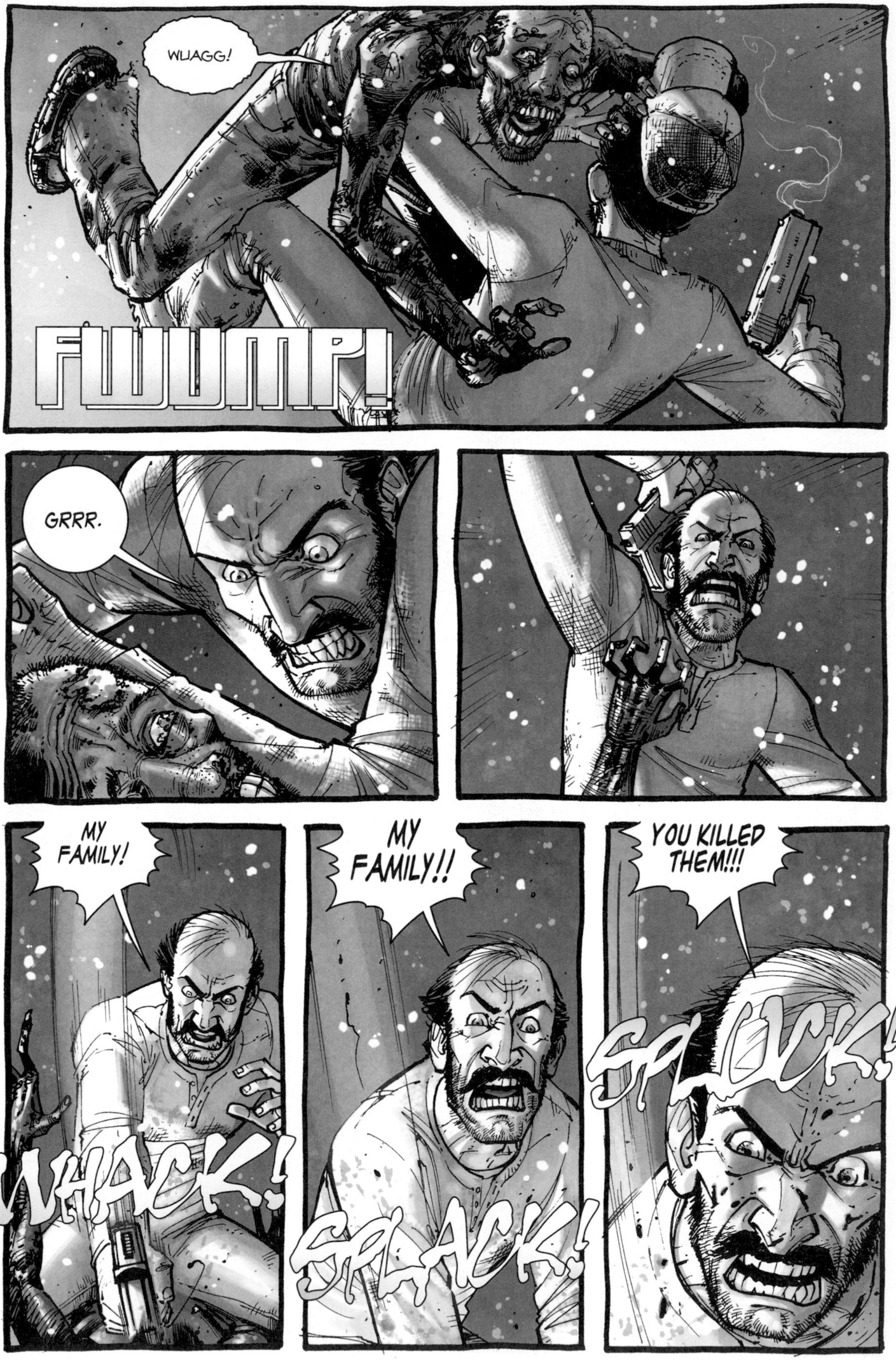
WUAGG!
FWUMP!
GRRR.
MY FAMILY!
WHACK!
MY FAMILY!!
SPLACK!
YOU KILLED THEM!!!
SPLUCK!

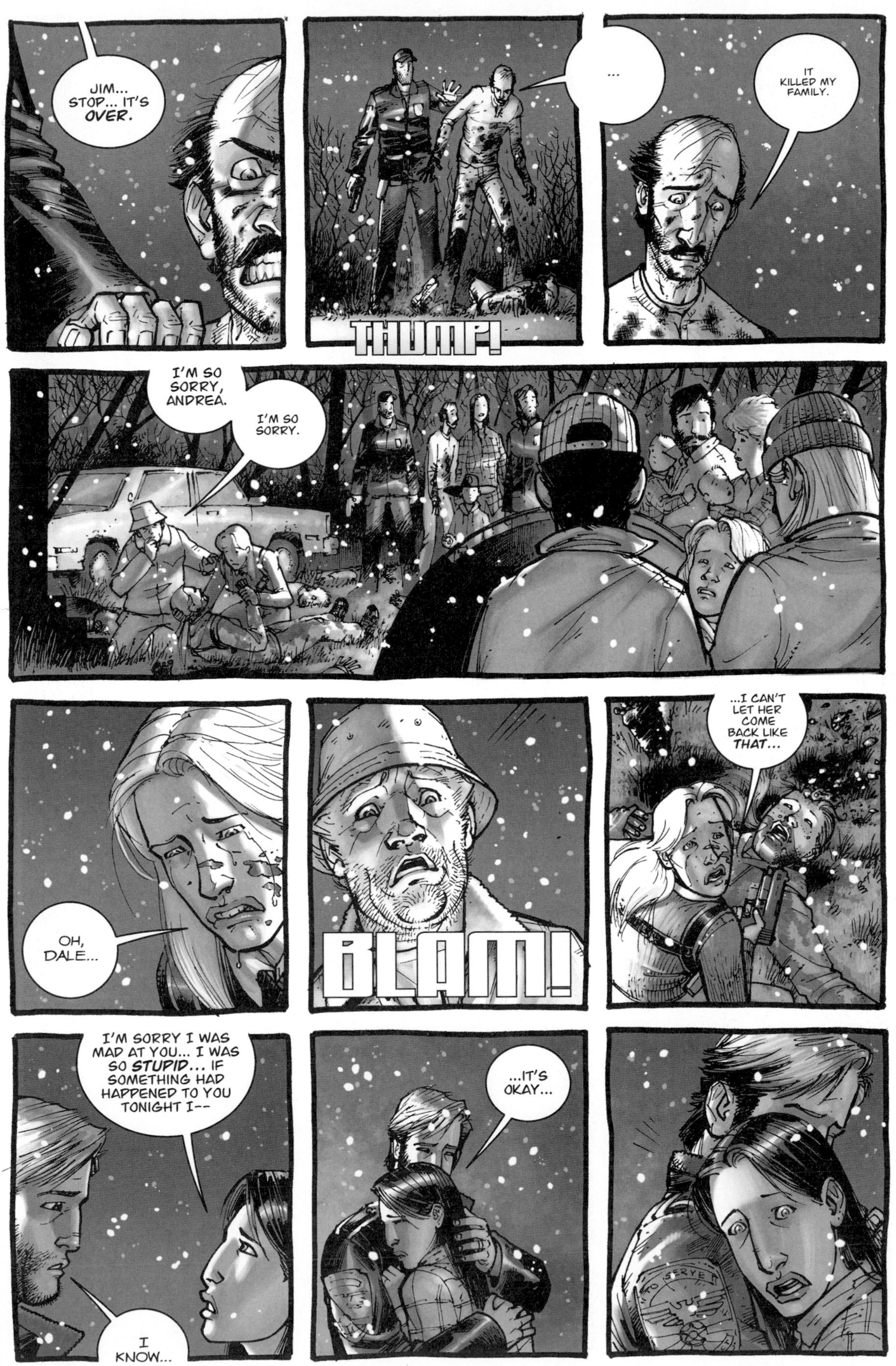
JIM... STOP... IT'S OVER.
THUMP!
...
IT KILLED MY FAMILY.
I'M SO SORRY, ANDREA.
I'M SO SORRY.
OH, DALE...
BLAM!
...I CAN'T LET HER COME BACK LIKE THAT...
I'M SORRY I WAS MAD AT YOU... I WAS SO STUPID... IF SOMETHING HAD HAPPENED TO YOU TONIGHT I--
I KNOW...
...IT'S OKAY...

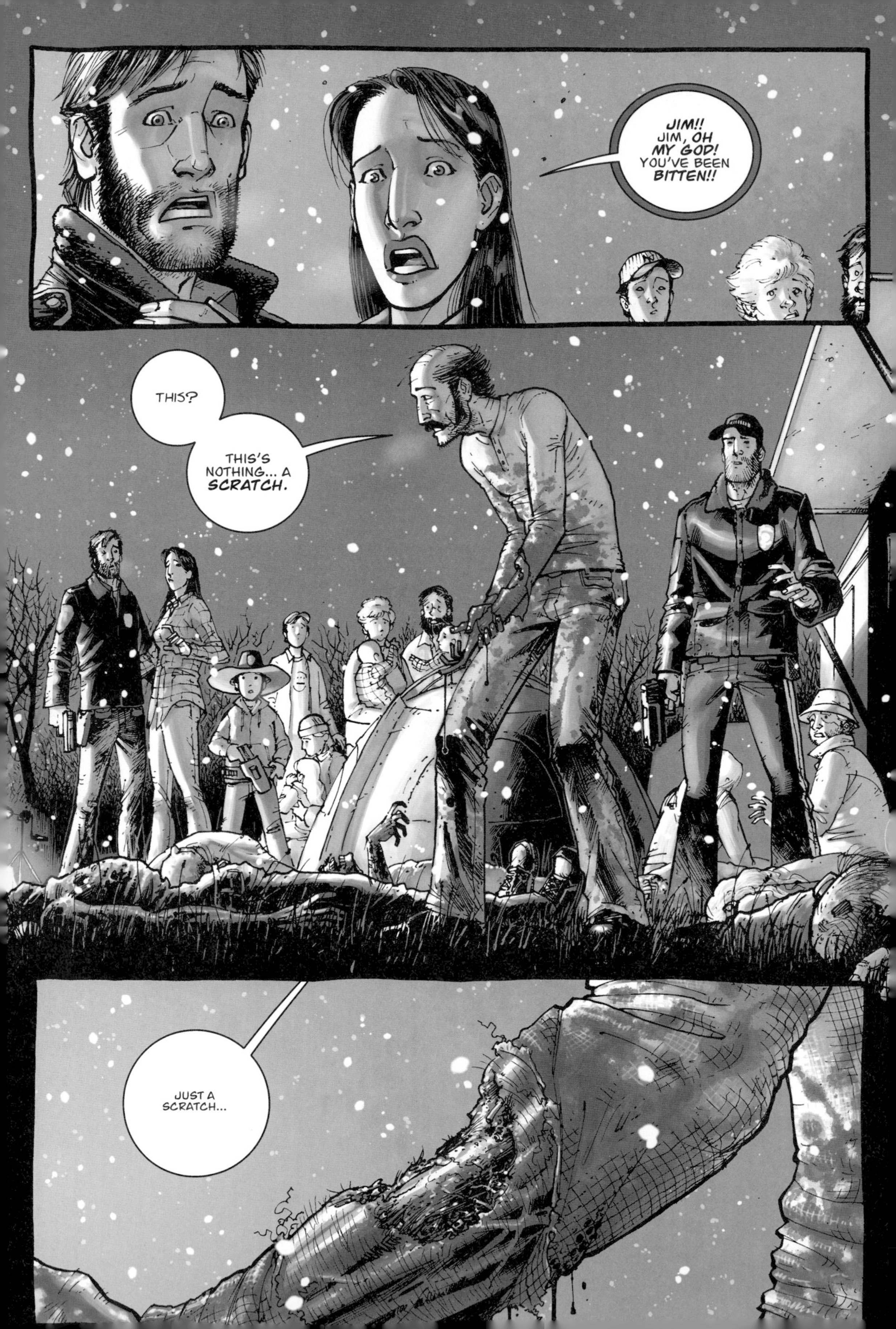
JIM!! JIM, OH MY GOD! YOU'VE BEEN BITTEN!!
THIS?
THIS'S NOTHING... A SCRATCH.
JUST A SCRATCH...

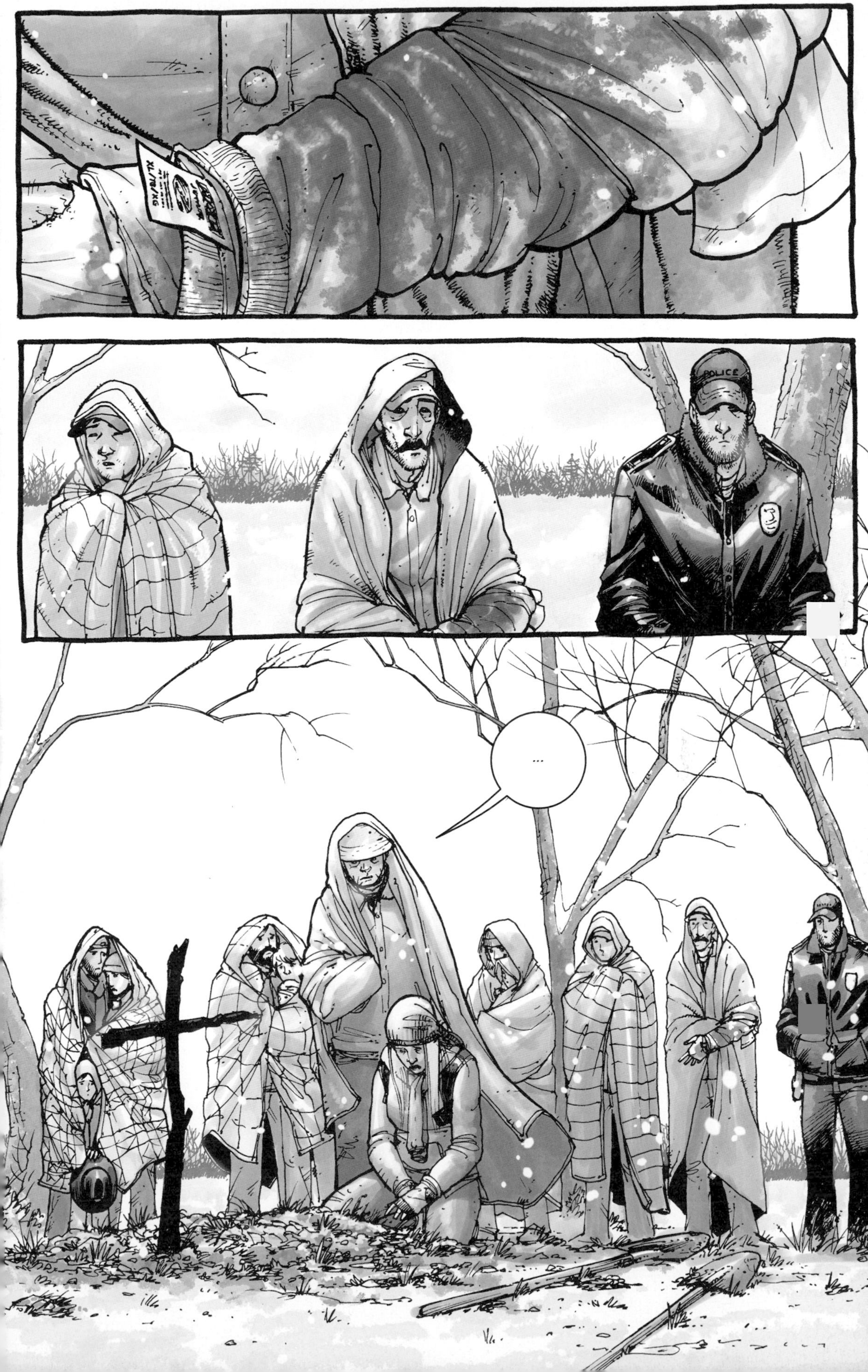
POLICE
...

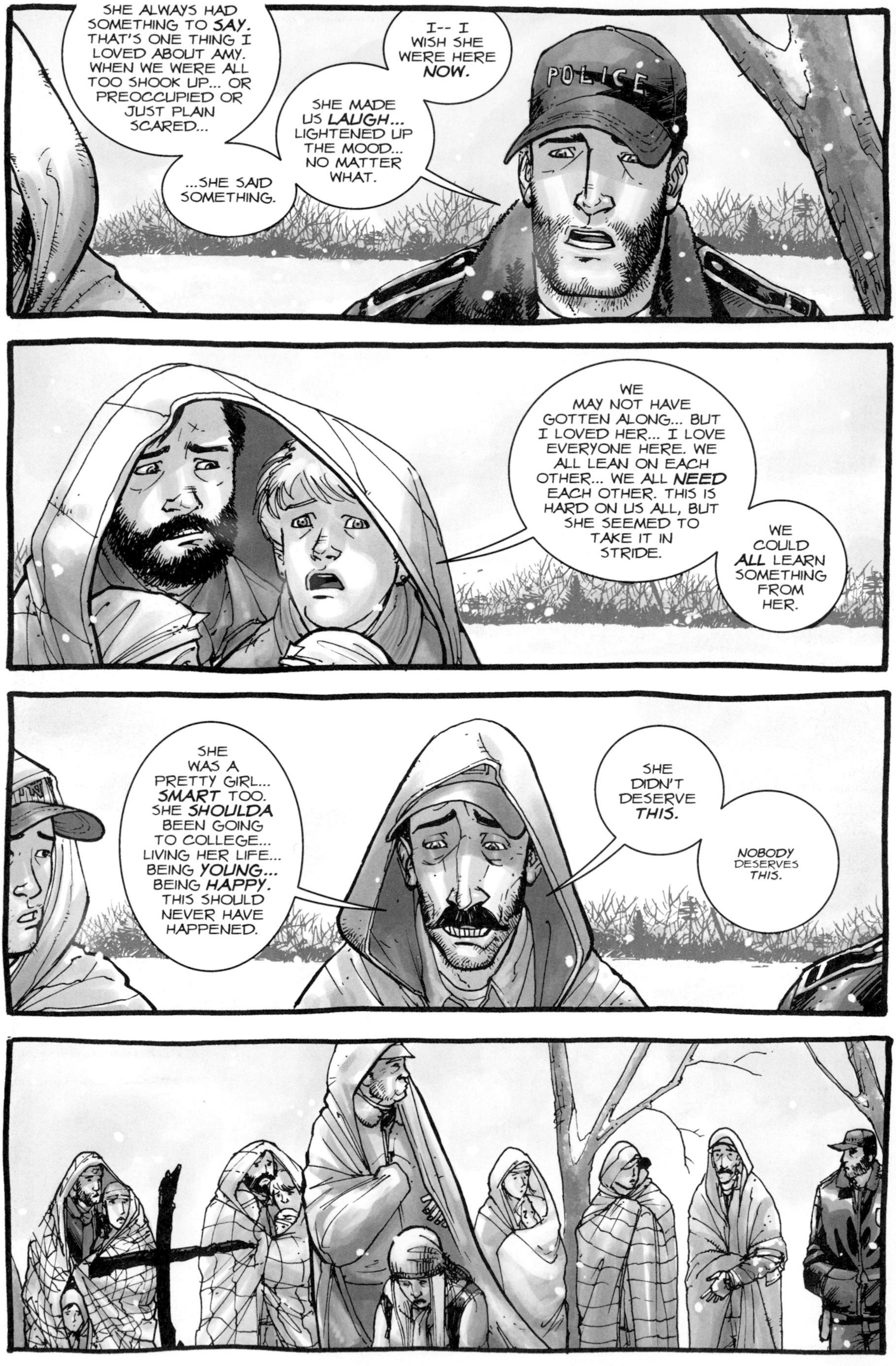
SHE ALWAYS HAD SOMETHING TO SAY. THAT'S ONE THING I LOVED ABOUT AMY. WHEN WE WERE ALL TOO SHOOK UP... OR PREOCCUPIED OR JUST PLAIN SCARED...
...SHE SAID SOMETHING.
SHE MADE US LAUGH... LIGHTENED UP THE MOOD... NO MATTER WHAT.
I-- I WISH SHE WERE HERE NOW.
POLICE
WE MAY NOT HAVE GOTTEN ALONG... BUT I LOVED HER... I LOVE EVERYONE HERE. WE ALL LEAN ON EACH OTHER... WE ALL NEED EACH OTHER. THIS IS HARD ON US ALL, BUT SHE SEEMED TO TAKE IT IN STRIDE.
WE COULD ALL LEARN SOMETHING FROM HER.
SHE WAS A PRETTY GIRL... SMART TOO. SHE SHOULDA BEEN GOING TO COLLEGE... LIVING HER LIFE... BEING YOUNG... BEING HAPPY. THIS SHOULD NEVER HAVE HAPPENED.
SHE DIDN'T DESERVE THIS.
NOBODY DESERVES THIS.

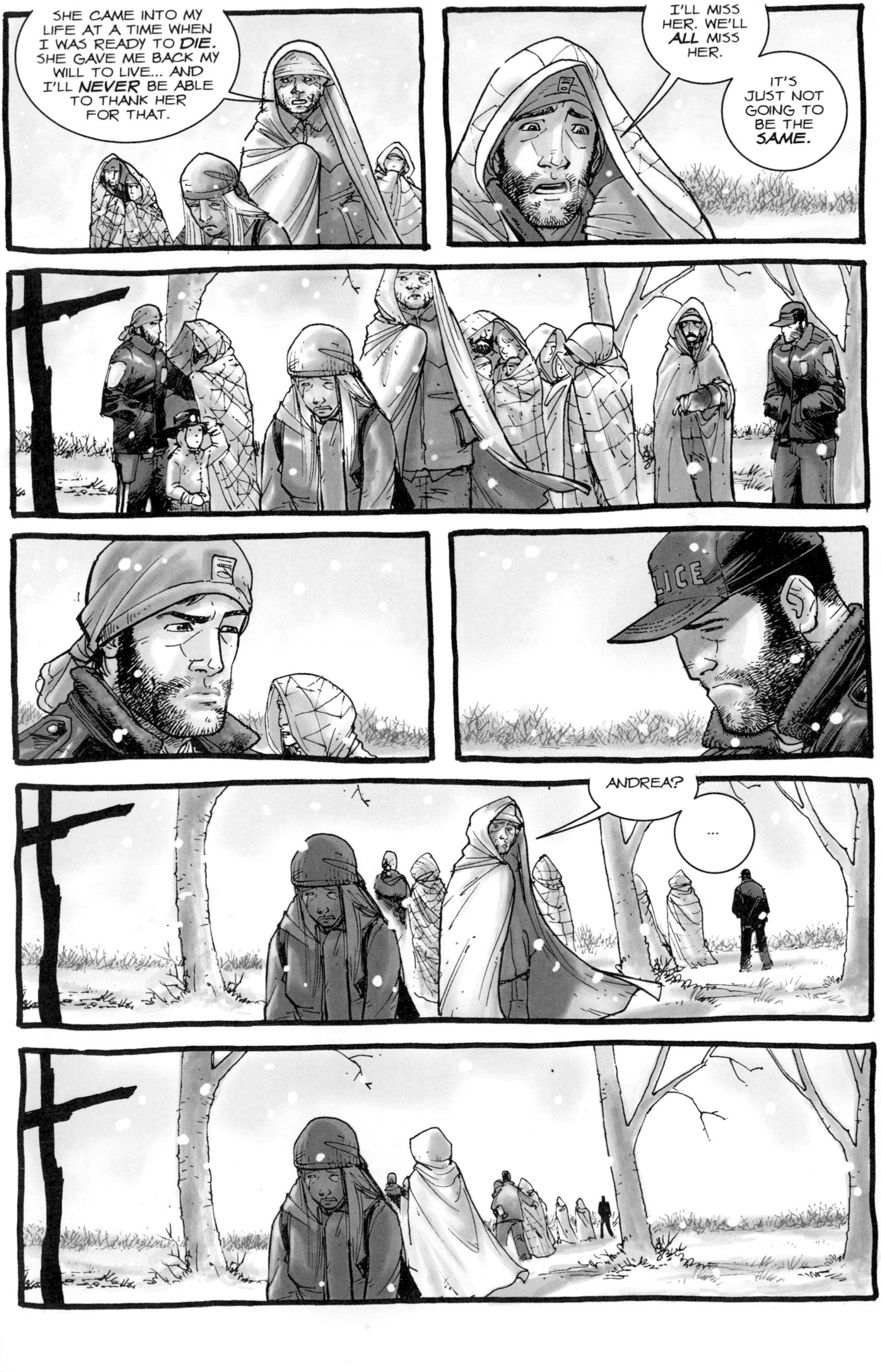
SHE CAME INTO MY LIFE AT A TIME WHEN I WAS READY TO DIE. SHE GAVE ME BACK MY WILL TO LIVE... AND I'LL NEVER BE ABLE TO THANK HER FOR THAT.
I'LL MISS HER. WE'LL ALL MISS HER.
IT'S JUST NOT GOING TO BE THE SAME.
LICE
ANDREA?
...

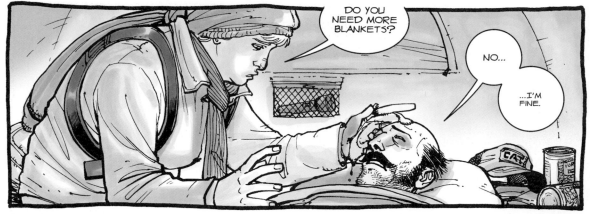

DO YOU NEED MORE BLANKETS?

NO...

...I'M FINE.

THIS SHOULD COOL YOUR FACE DOWN A LITTLE.

THANKS...

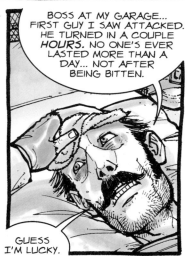

BOSS AT MY GARAGE... FIRST GUY I SAW ATTACKED. HE TURNED IN A COUPLE *HOURS.* NO ONE'S EVER LASTED MORE THAN A DAY... NOT AFTER BEING BITTEN.

GUESS I'M LUCKY.

MAYBE YOU WON'T TURN. NOBODY KNOWS ANYTHING FOR SURE.

YEAH...

IF YOU NEED ANYTHING... JUST GIVE US A *YELL.* SOMEONE WILL COME GET ME IF I DON'T HEAR.

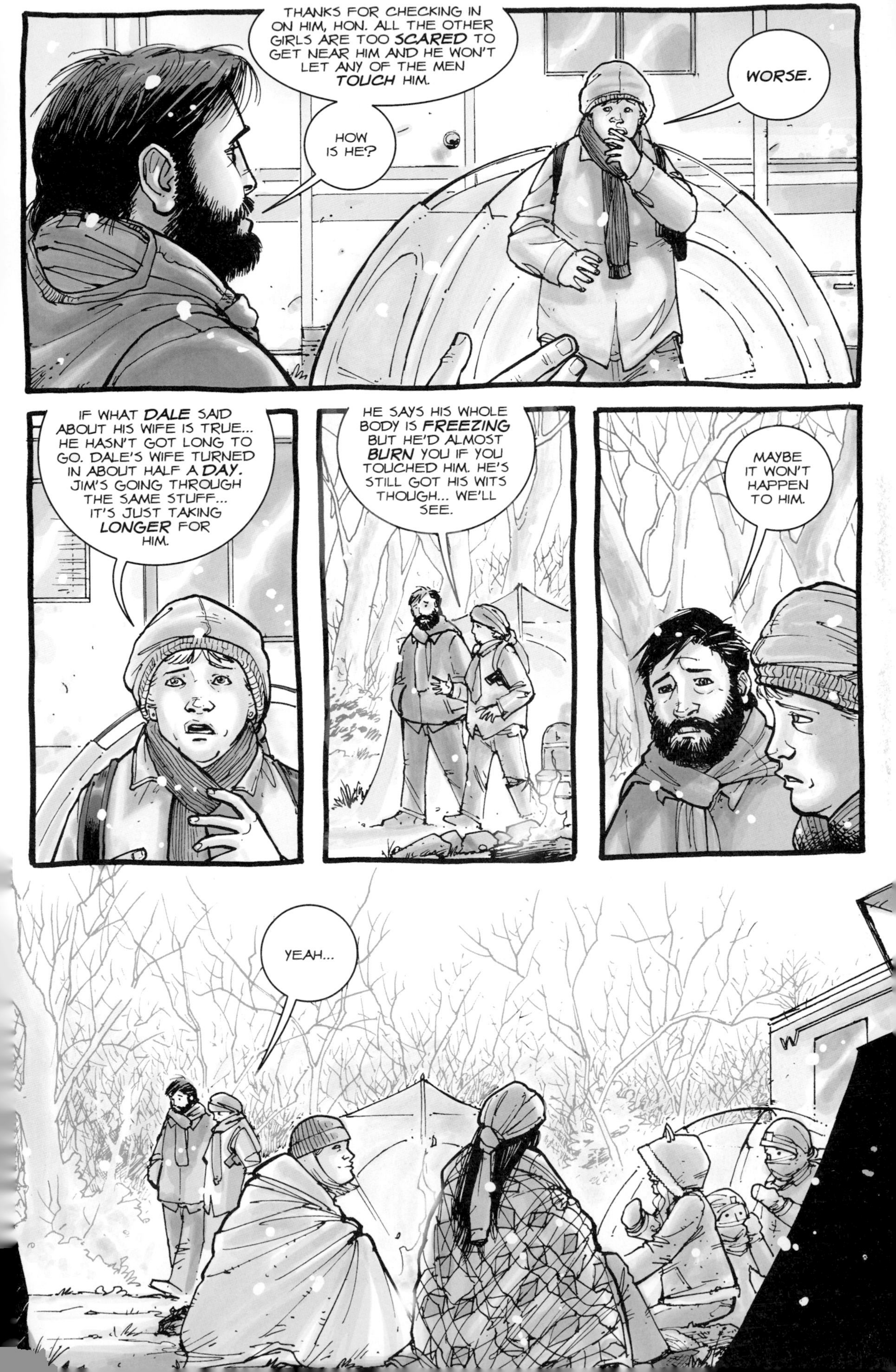
THANKS FOR CHECKING IN ON HIM, HON. ALL THE OTHER GIRLS ARE TOO SCARED TO GET NEAR HIM AND HE WON'T LET ANY OF THE MEN TOUCH HIM.
HOW IS HE?
WORSE.
IF WHAT DALE SAID ABOUT HIS WIFE IS TRUE... HE HASN'T GOT LONG TO GO. DALE'S WIFE TURNED IN ABOUT HALF A DAY. JIM'S GOING THROUGH THE SAME STUFF... IT'S JUST TAKING LONGER FOR HIM.
HE SAYS HIS WHOLE BODY IS FREEZING BUT HE'D ALMOST BURN YOU IF YOU TOUCHED HIM. HE'S STILL GOT HIS WITS THOUGH... WE'LL SEE.
MAYBE IT WON'T HAPPEN TO HIM.
YEAH...

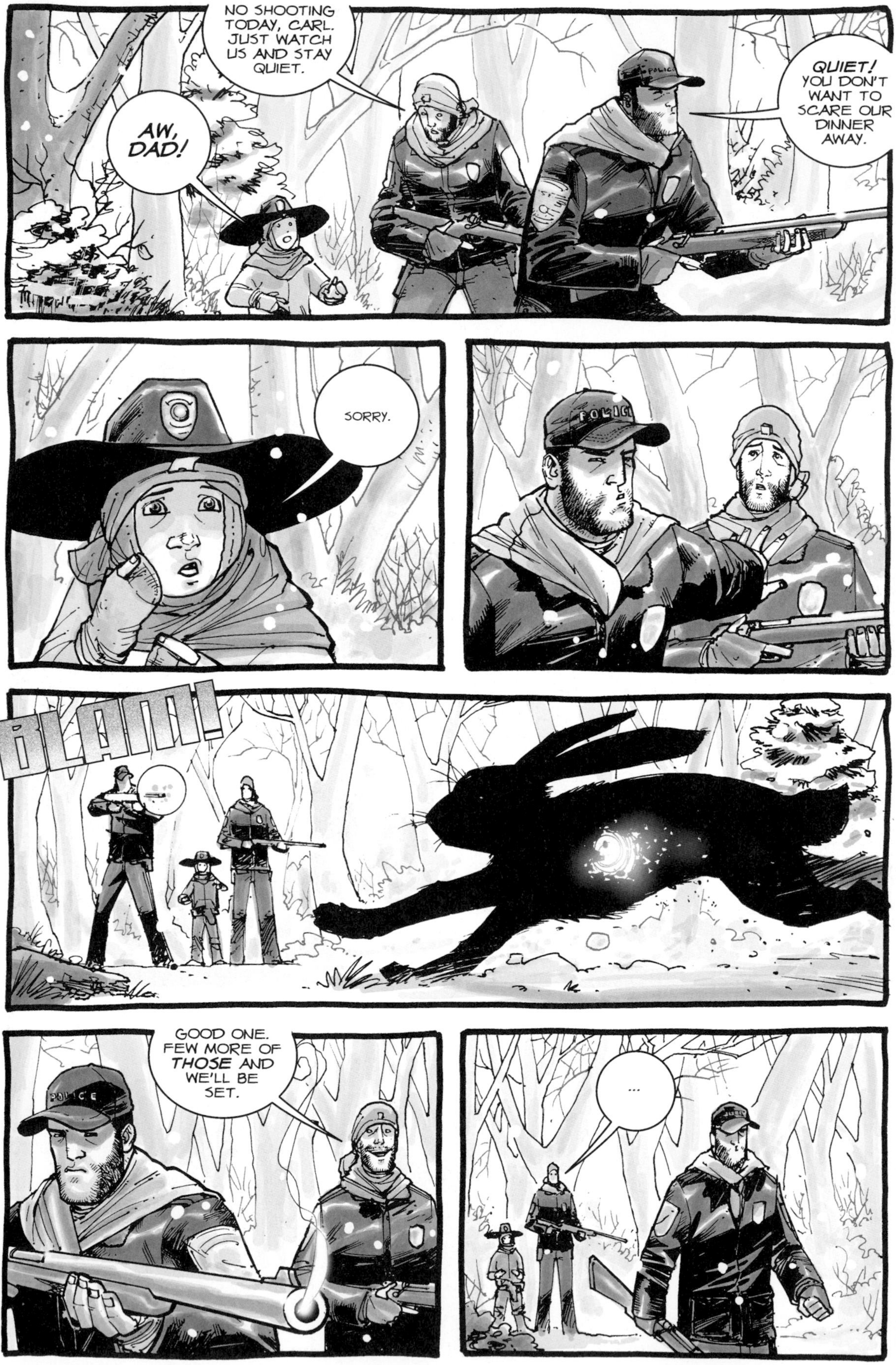
NO SHOOTING TODAY, CARL. JUST WATCH US AND STAY QUIET.
AW, DAD!
QUIET! YOU DON'T WANT TO SCARE OUR DINNER AWAY.
SORRY.
POLICE
BLAM!
GOOD ONE. FEW MORE OF THOSE AND WE'LL BE SET.
POLICE
...

WE DON'T HAVE TO GET AS MUCH AS *USUAL*, DAD. AMY'S *DEAD*... AND JIM'S TOO *SICK* TO EAT.

I KNOW, SON... I KNOW.

GOD DAMMIT, RICK! IT'S NOT MY FUCKING FAULT!!

LIKE *HELL* IT ISN'T! I *TOLD* YOU THIS WAS GOING TO HAPPEN! WE'RE NOT *SAFE* HERE! HOW MANY MORE PEOPLE HAVE TO *DIE* BEFORE YOU *REALIZE* THAT?!

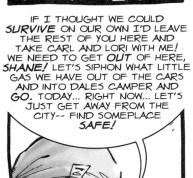

IF I THOUGHT WE COULD *SURVIVE* ON OUR OWN I'D LEAVE THE REST OF YOU HERE AND TAKE CARL AND LORI WITH ME! WE NEED TO GET *OUT* OF HERE, *SHANE!* LET'S SIPHON WHAT LITTLE GAS WE HAVE OUT OF THE CARS AND INTO DALES CAMPER AND *GO*. TODAY... RIGHT NOW... LET'S JUST GET AWAY FROM THE CITY-- FIND SOMEPLACE *SAFE!*

THINK RICK! WE'LL BE *LOST* OUT THERE. THE ARMY IS GOING TO DRIVE THROUGH HERE ANY *DAY* NOW WITH SUPPLIES AND SHELTER AND ALL THIS WILL JUST *GO AWAY*... I DON'T WANT TO *RISK* BEING OUT IN THE COUNTRY... I DON'T WANT TO *RISK* BEING *LEFT BEHIND!*

WHAT ARE YOU BASING *THAT* ON?! WHAT INDICATION DO WE HAVE THAT WE'RE NOT THE *ONLY* SURVIVORS!?! WHAT WAS THAT ATTACK ON THE CAMP? ARE THEY HUNTING IN *PACKS* NOW? WE KNOW *NOTHING* ABOUT THEM!

WE'RE NOT SAFE!!

CARL!!

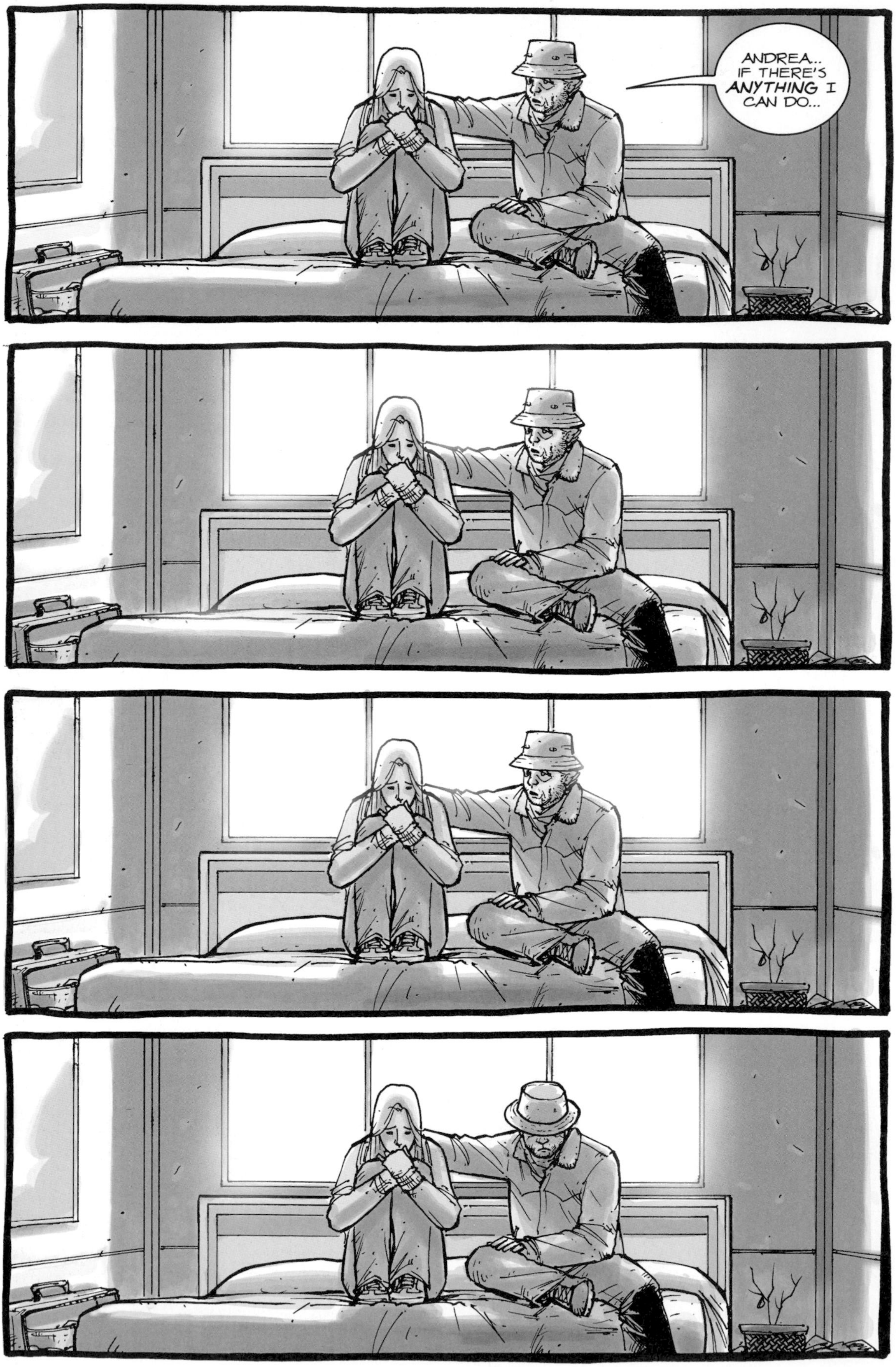
ANDREA... IF THERE'S ANYTHING I CAN DO...

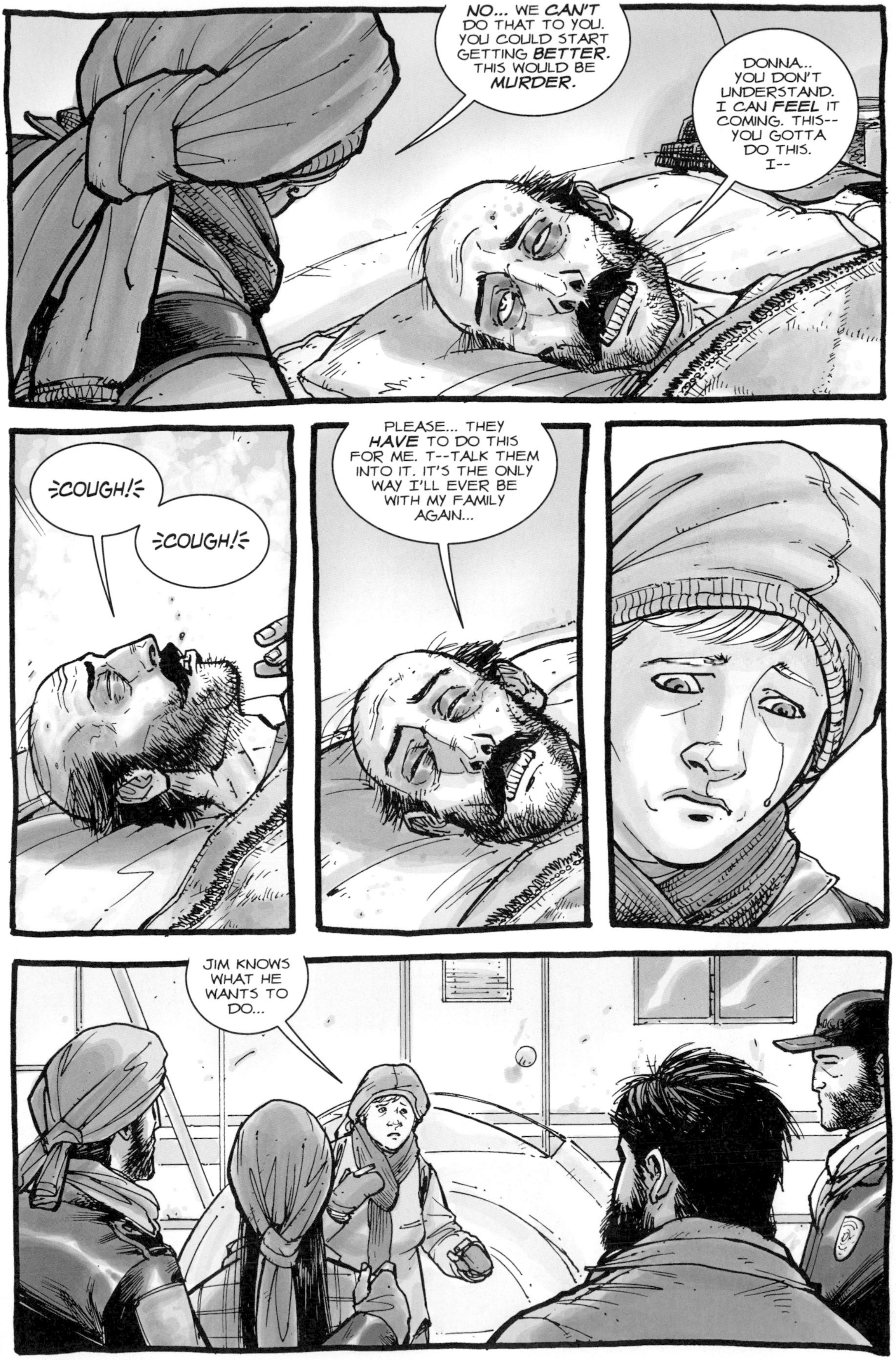
NO... WE CAN'T DO THAT TO YOU. YOU COULD START GETTING BETTER. THIS WOULD BE MURDER.
DONNA... YOU DON'T UNDERSTAND. I CAN FEEL IT COMING. THIS-- YOU GOTTA DO THIS. I--
COUGH!
COUGH!
PLEASE... THEY HAVE TO DO THIS FOR ME. T--TALK THEM INTO IT. IT'S THE ONLY WAY I'LL EVER BE WITH MY FAMILY AGAIN...
JIM KNOWS WHAT HE WANTS TO DO...

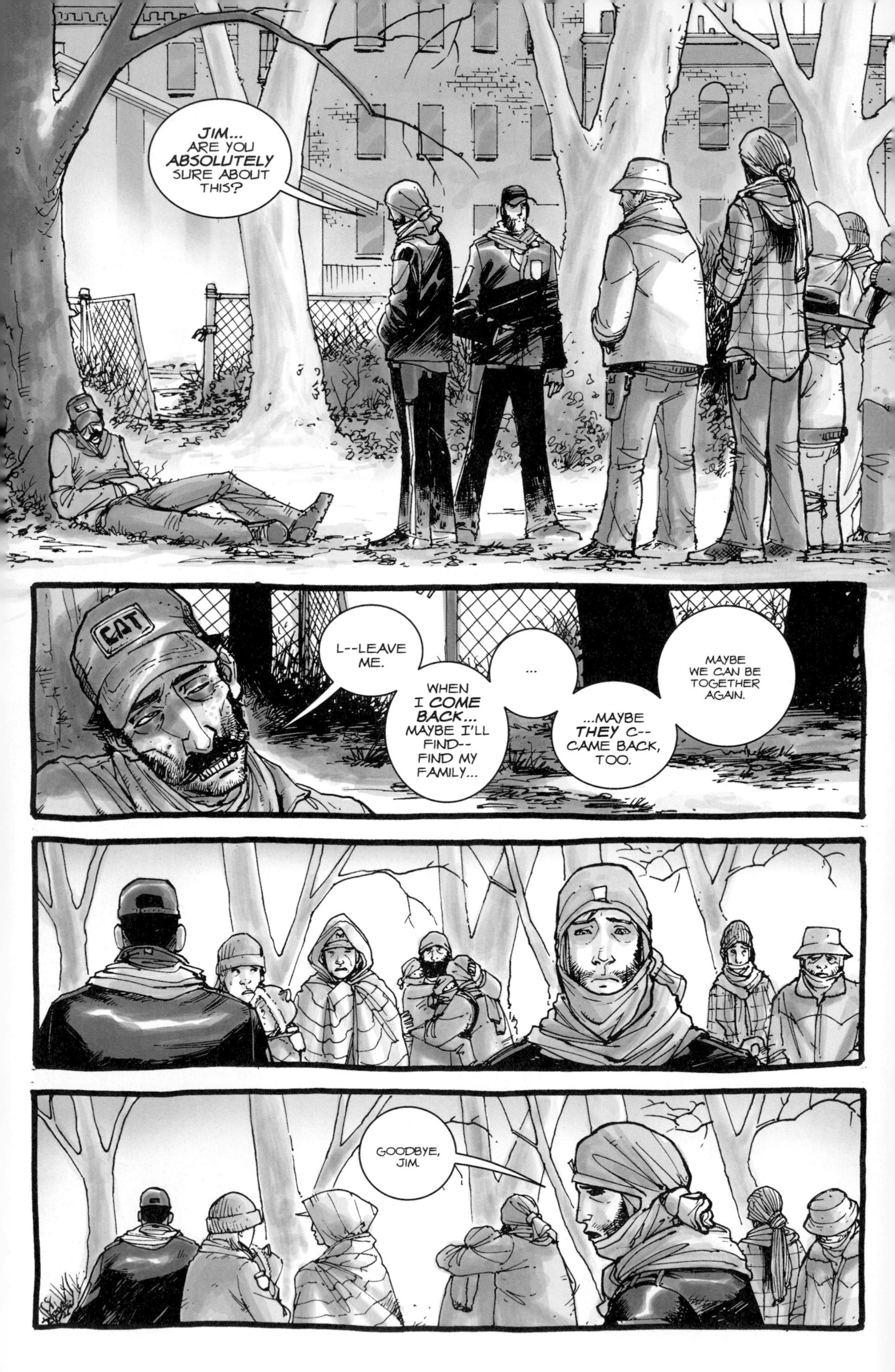
JIM... ARE YOU ABSOLUTELY SURE ABOUT THIS?
L--LEAVE ME.
WHEN I COME BACK... MAYBE I'LL FIND-- FIND MY FAMILY...
...
...MAYBE THEY C-- CAME BACK, TOO.
MAYBE WE CAN BE TOGETHER AGAIN.
GOODBYE, JIM.

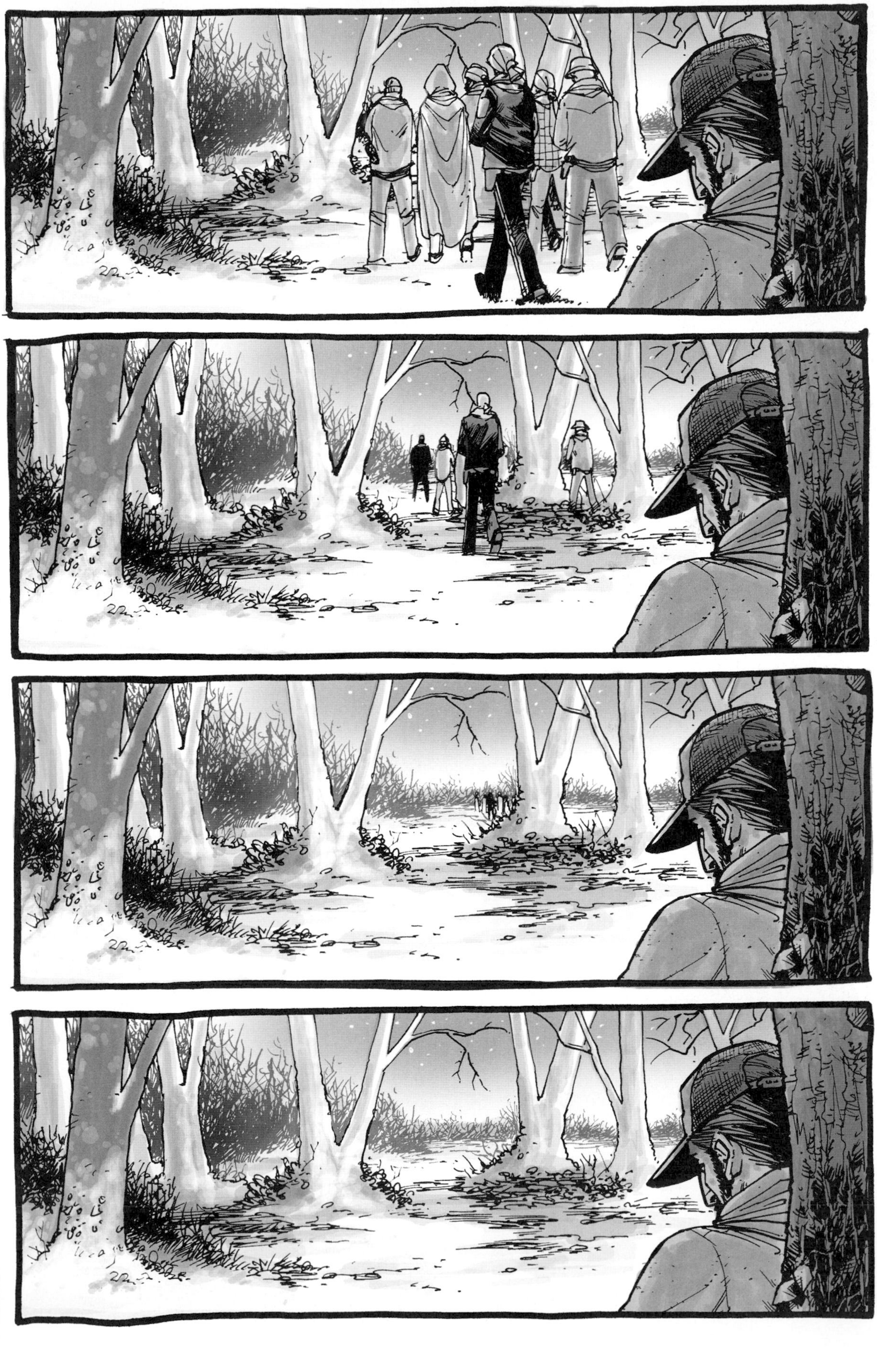

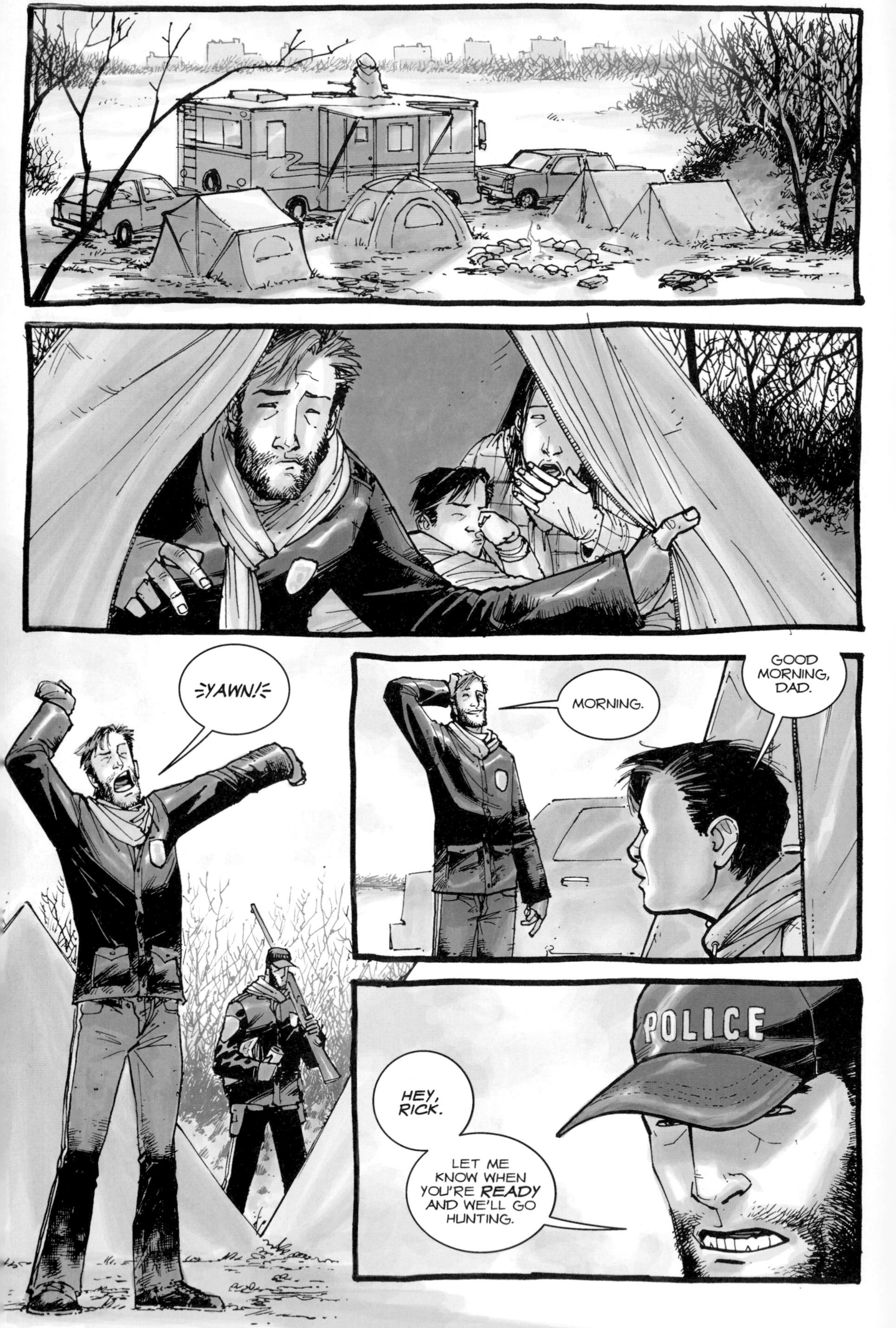

=YAWN!=
MORNING.
GOOD MORNING, DAD.
POLICE
HEY, RICK.
LET ME KNOW WHEN YOU'RE READY AND WE'LL GO HUNTING.

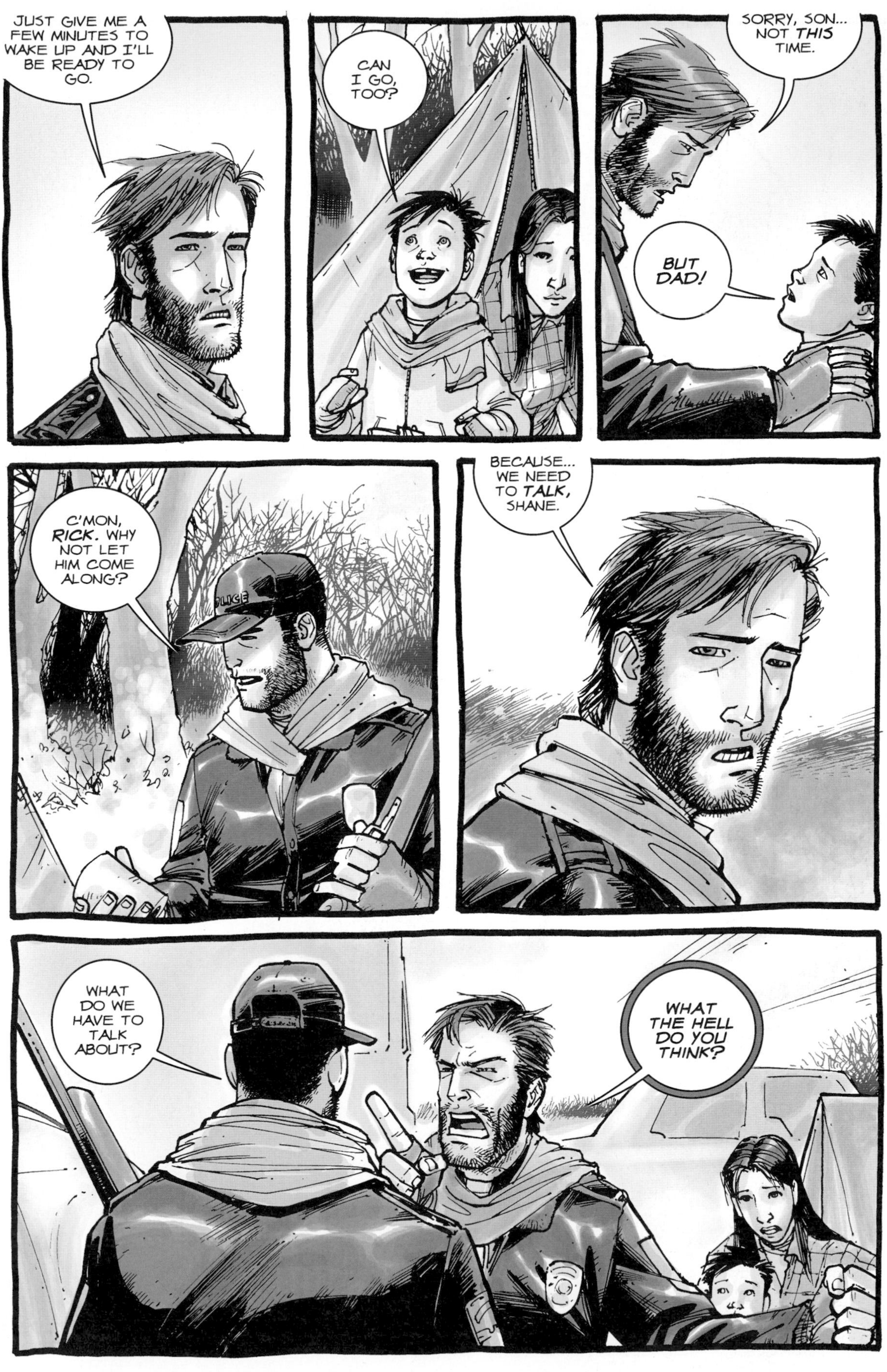
JUST GIVE ME A FEW MINUTES TO WAKE UP AND I'LL BE READY TO GO.
CAN I GO, TOO?
SORRY, SON... NOT THIS TIME.
BUT DAD!
C'MON, RICK. WHY NOT LET HIM COME ALONG?
BECAUSE... WE NEED TO TALK, SHANE.
WHAT DO WE HAVE TO TALK ABOUT?
WHAT THE HELL DO YOU THINK?

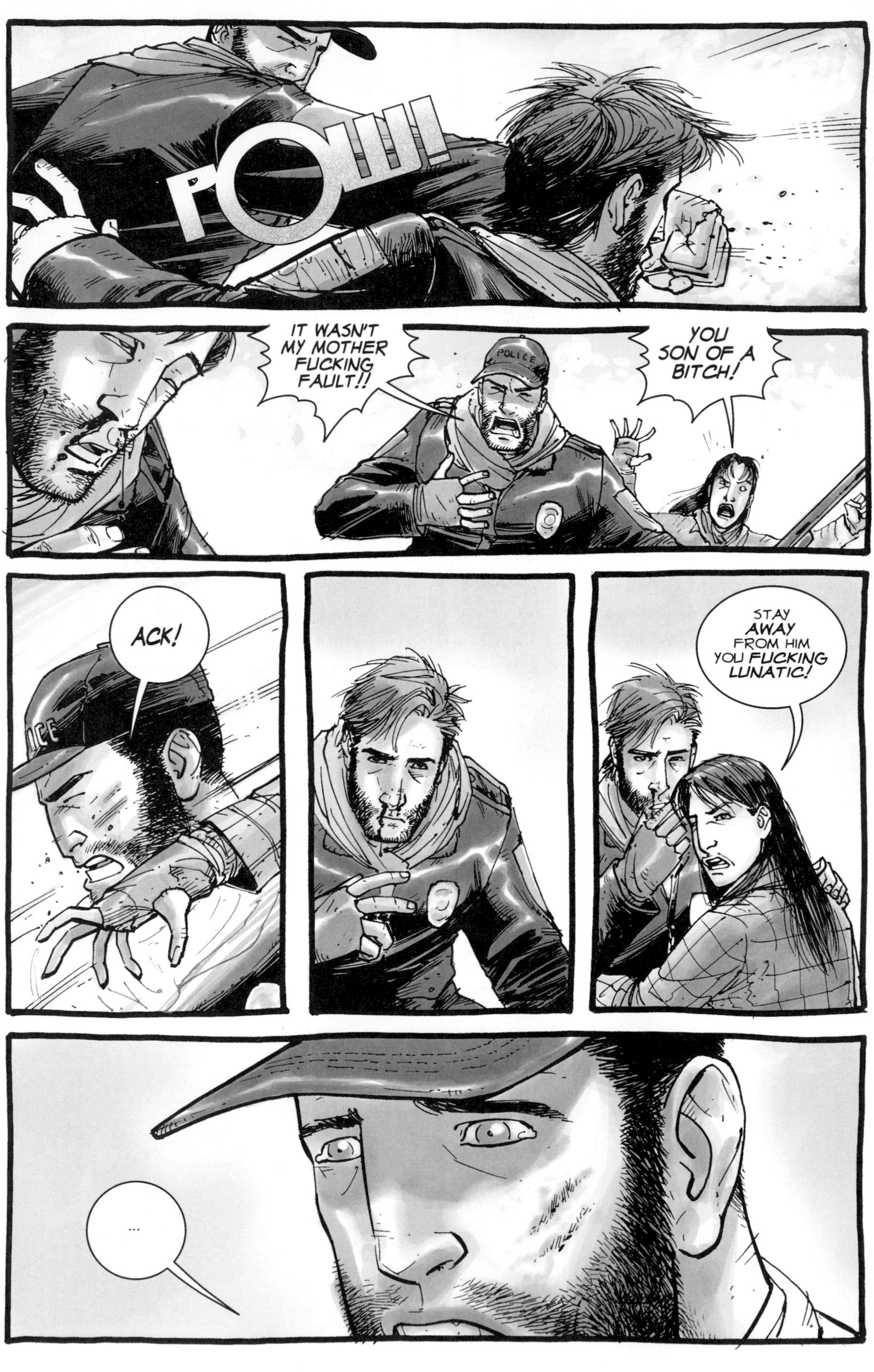
POW!
IT WASN'T MY MOTHER FUCKING FAULT!!
YOU SON OF A BITCH!
ACK!
STAY AWAY FROM HIM YOU FUCKING LUNATIC!
...

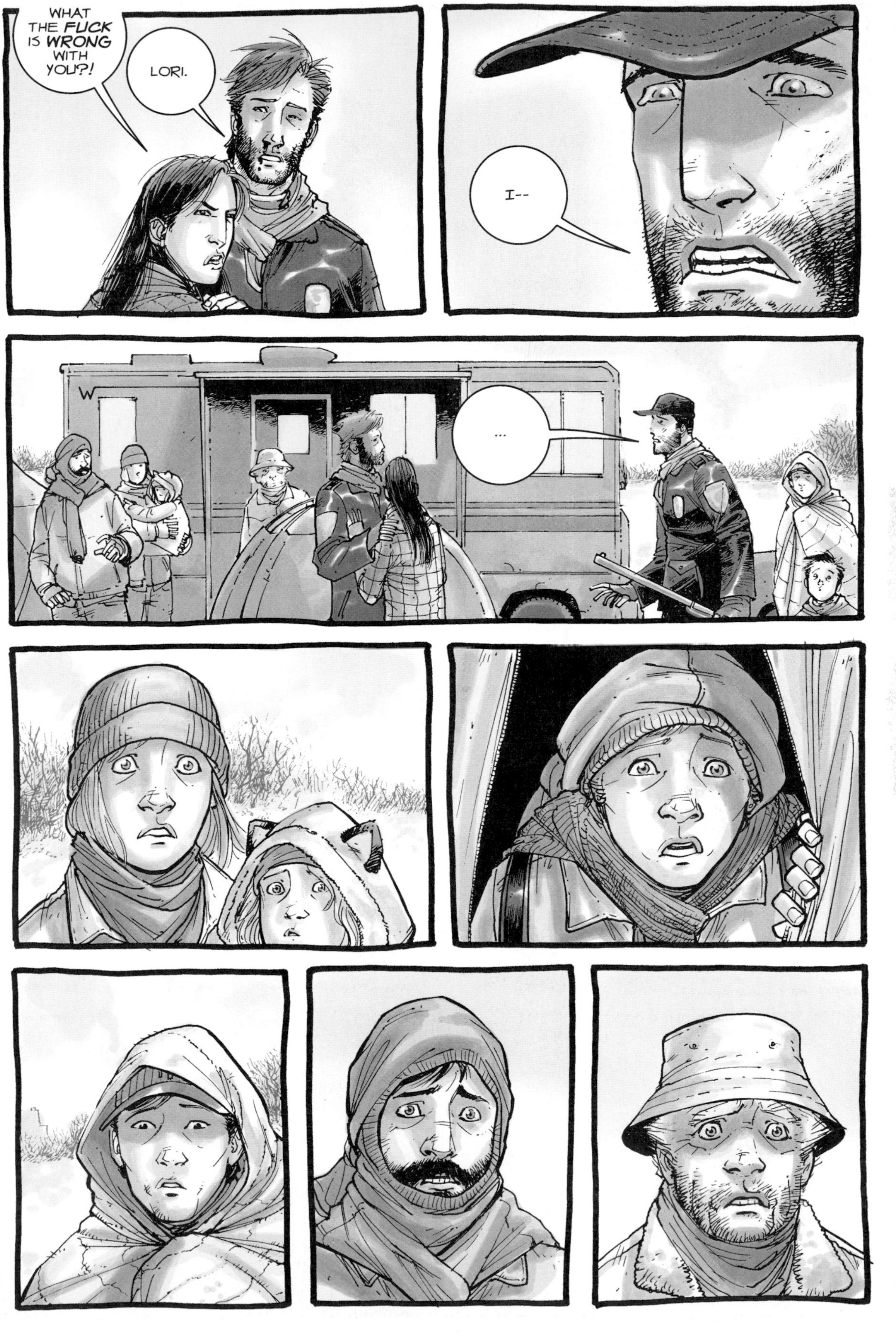
WHAT THE FUCK IS WRONG WITH YOU?!
LORI.
I--
...

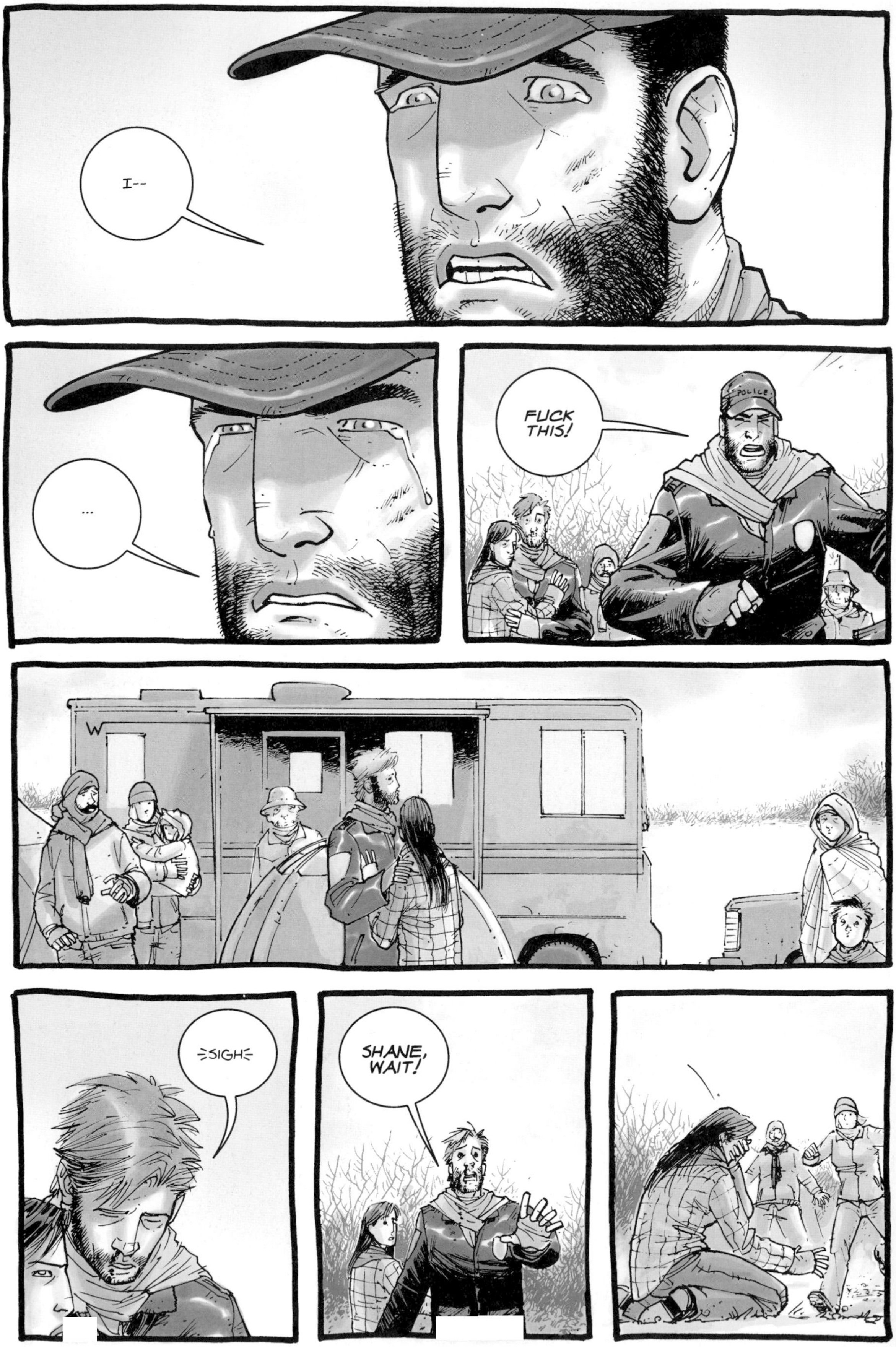
I--
...
FUCK THIS!
SIGH
SHANE, WAIT!

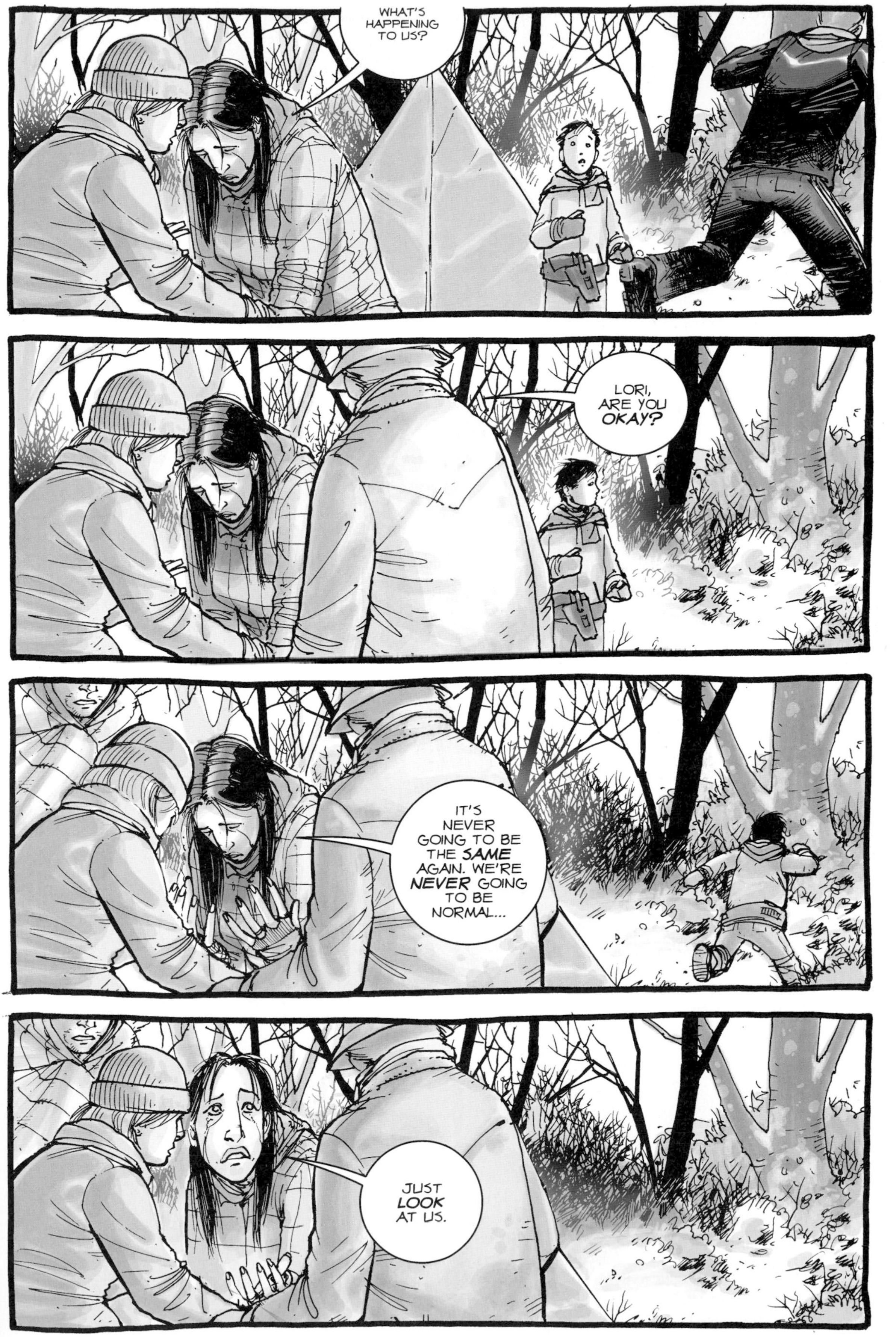
WHAT'S HAPPENING TO US?
LORI, ARE YOU OKAY?
IT'S NEVER GOING TO BE THE SAME AGAIN. WE'RE NEVER GOING TO BE NORMAL...
JUST LOOK AT US.

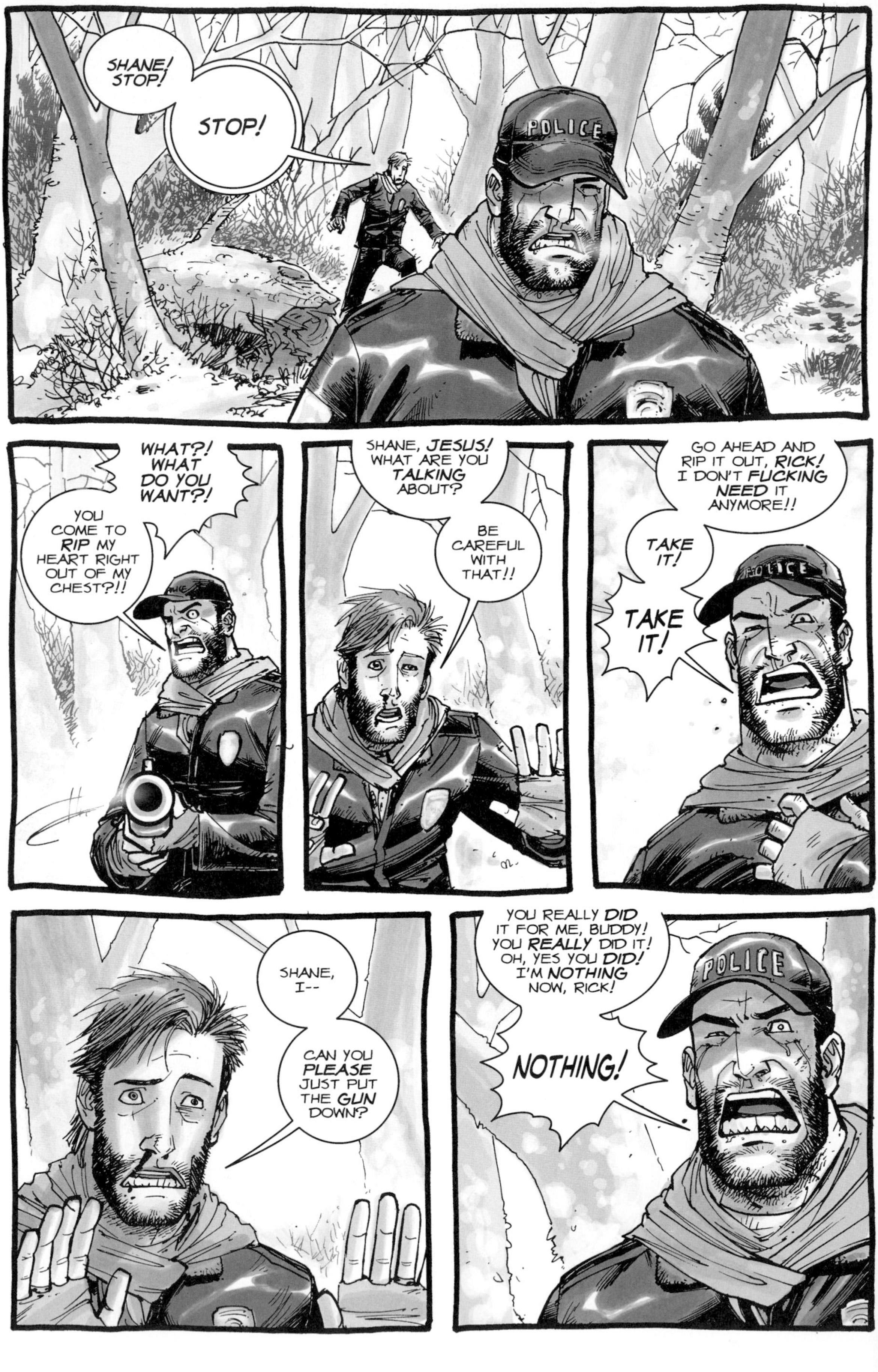
SHANE! STOP!
STOP!
WHAT?! WHAT DO YOU WANT?!
YOU COME TO RIP MY HEART RIGHT OUT OF MY CHEST?!!
SHANE, JESUS! WHAT ARE YOU TALKING ABOUT?
BE CAREFUL WITH THAT!!
GO AHEAD AND RIP IT OUT, RICK! I DON'T FUCKING NEED IT ANYMORE!!
TAKE IT!
TAKE IT!
SHANE, I--
CAN YOU PLEASE JUST PUT THE GUN DOWN?
YOU REALLY DID IT FOR ME, BUDDY! YOU REALLY DID IT! OH, YES YOU DID! I'M NOTHING NOW, RICK!
NOTHING!

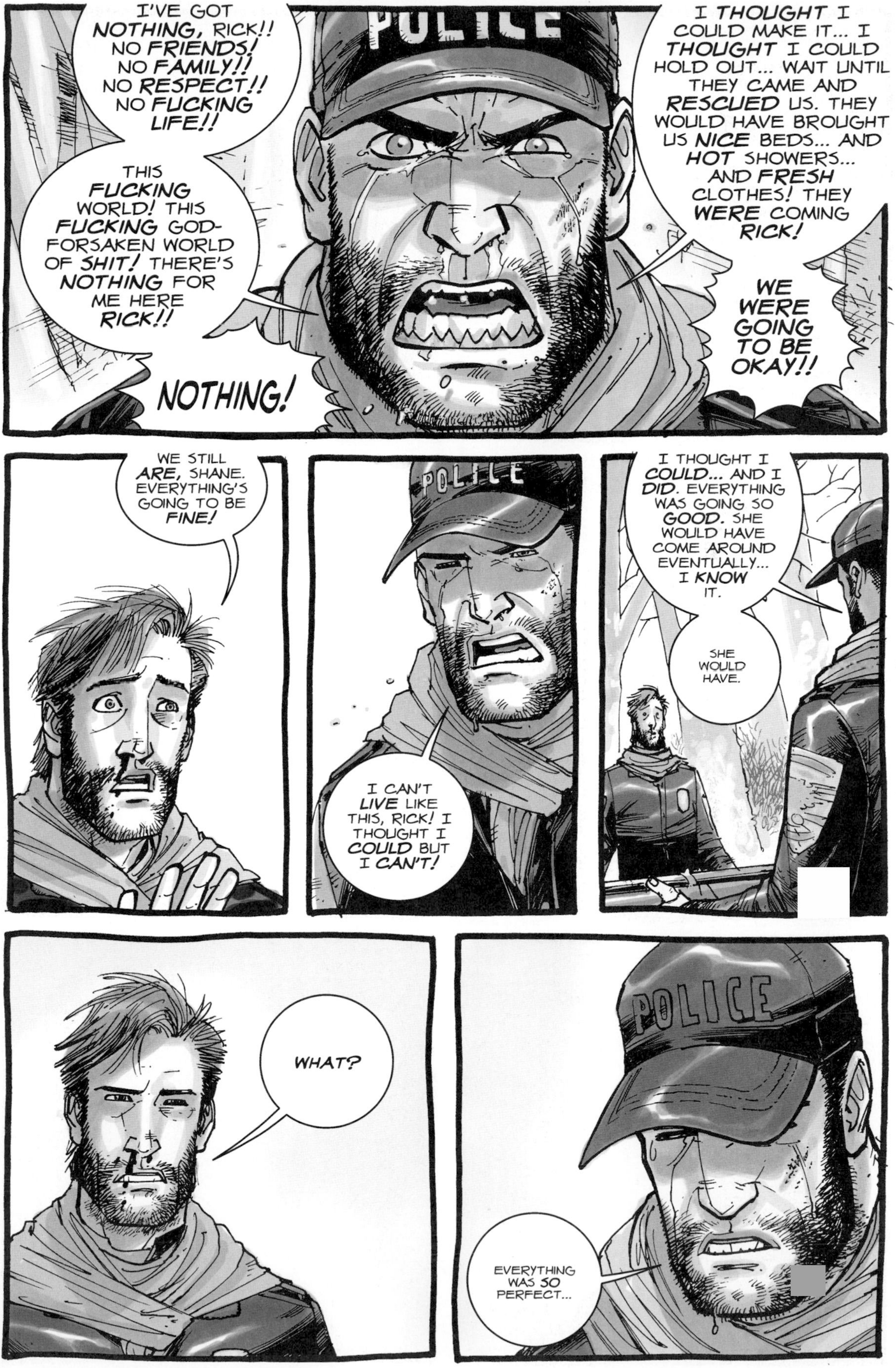

I'VE GOT NOTHING, RICK!! NO FRIENDS! NO FAMILY!! NO RESPECT!! NO FUCKING LIFE!!
THIS FUCKING WORLD! THIS FUCKING GOD-FORSAKEN WORLD OF SHIT! THERE'S NOTHING FOR ME HERE RICK!!
NOTHING!
I THOUGHT I COULD MAKE IT... I THOUGHT I COULD HOLD OUT... WAIT UNTIL THEY CAME AND RESCUED US. THEY WOULD HAVE BROUGHT US NICE BEDS... AND HOT SHOWERS... AND FRESH CLOTHES! THEY WERE COMING RICK!
WE WERE GOING TO BE OKAY!!
WE STILL ARE, SHANE. EVERYTHING'S GOING TO BE FINE!
POLICE
I CAN'T LIVE LIKE THIS, RICK! I THOUGHT I COULD BUT I CAN'T!
I THOUGHT I COULD... AND I DID. EVERYTHING WAS GOING SO GOOD. SHE WOULD HAVE COME AROUND EVENTUALLY... I KNOW IT.
SHE WOULD HAVE.
WHAT?
POLICE
EVERYTHING WAS SO PERFECT...

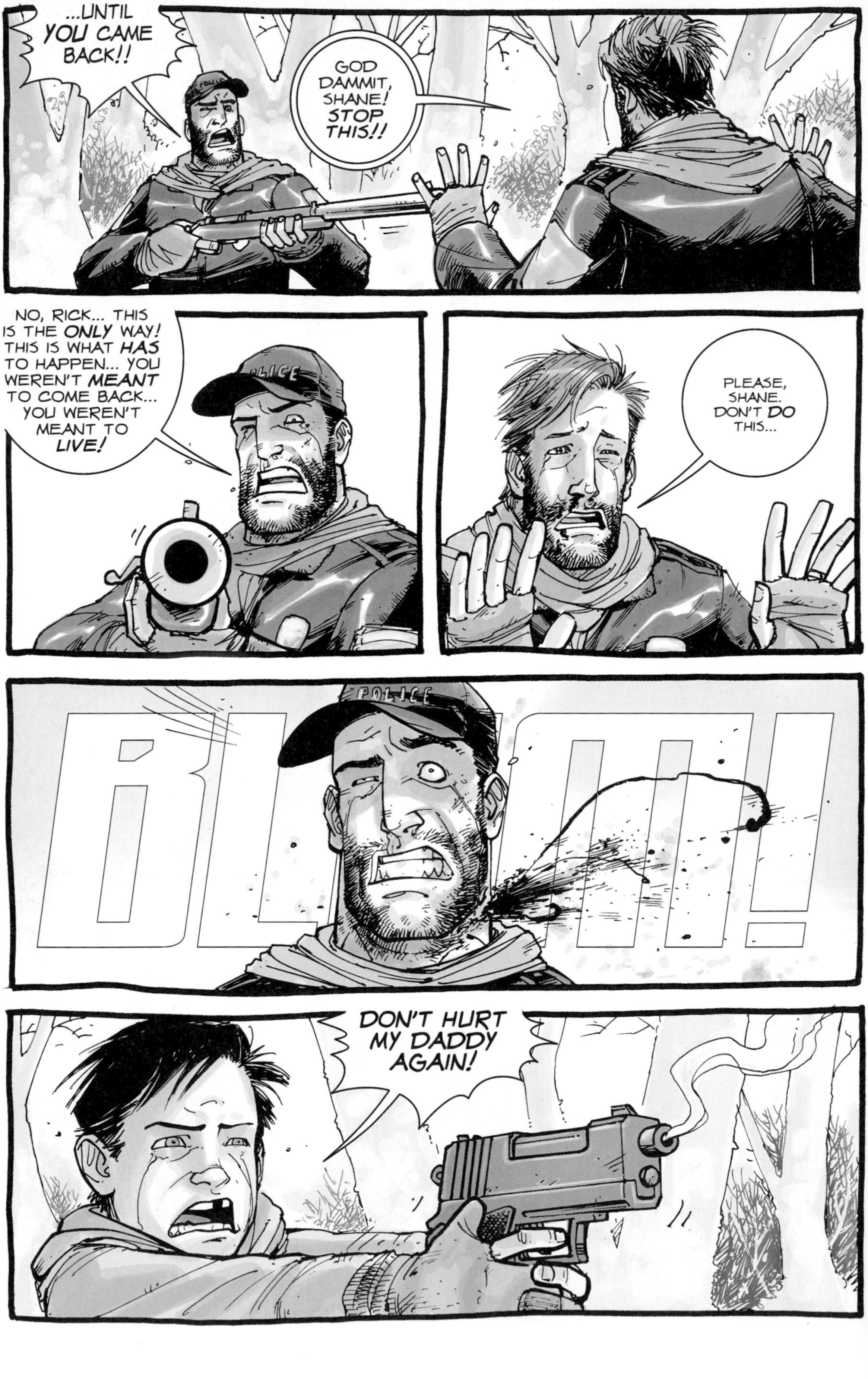
...UNTIL YOU CAME BACK!!
GOD DAMMIT, SHANE! STOP THIS!!
NO, RICK... THIS IS THE ONLY WAY! THIS IS WHAT HAS TO HAPPEN... YOU WEREN'T MEANT TO COME BACK... YOU WEREN'T MEANT TO LIVE!
PLEASE, SHANE. DON'T DO THIS...
DON'T HURT MY DADDY AGAIN!

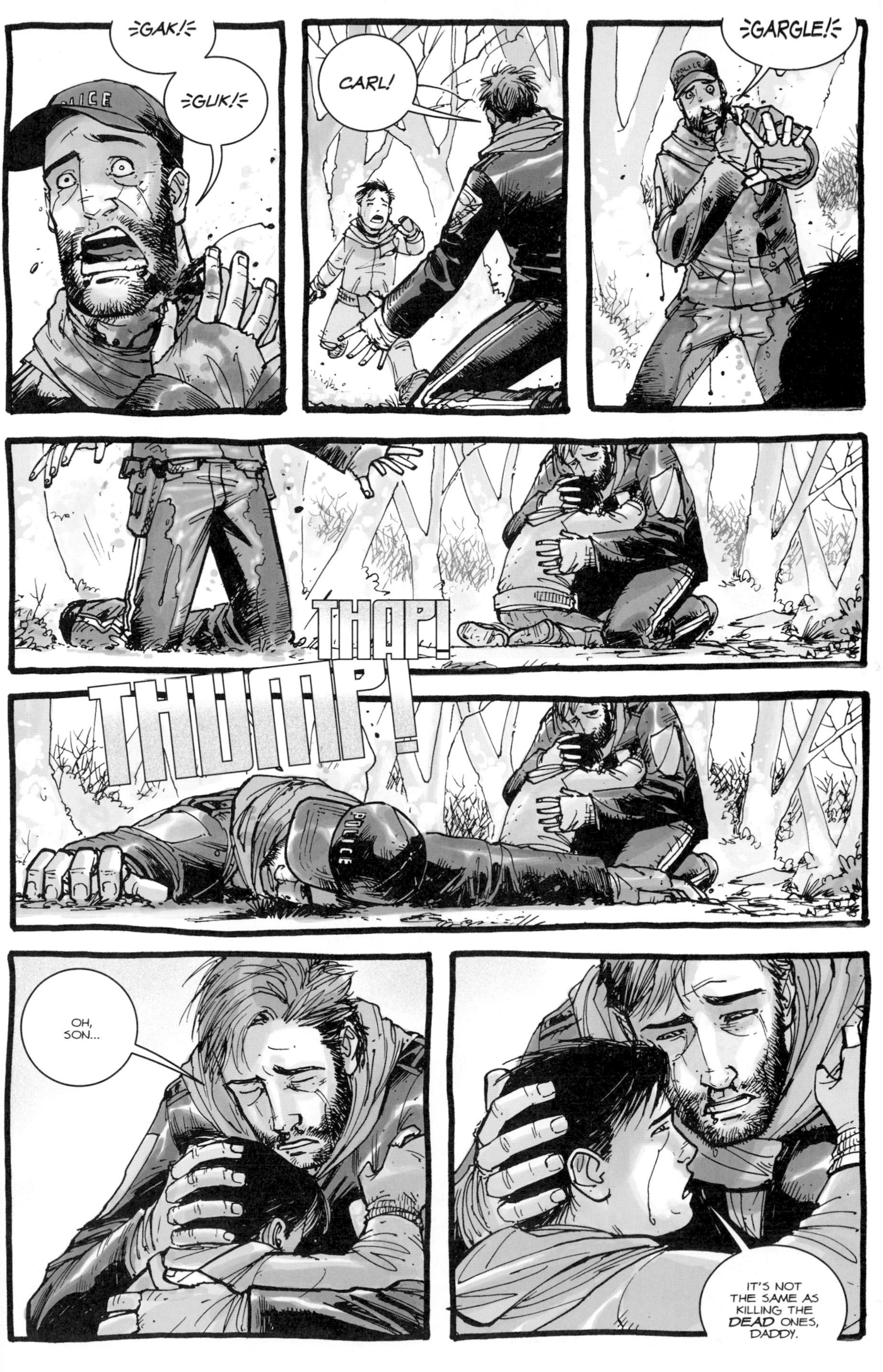
GAK!
GUK!
POLICE
CARL!
GARGLE!
THAP!
THUMP!
OH, SON...
IT'S NOT THE SAME AS KILLING THE DEAD ONES, DADDY.

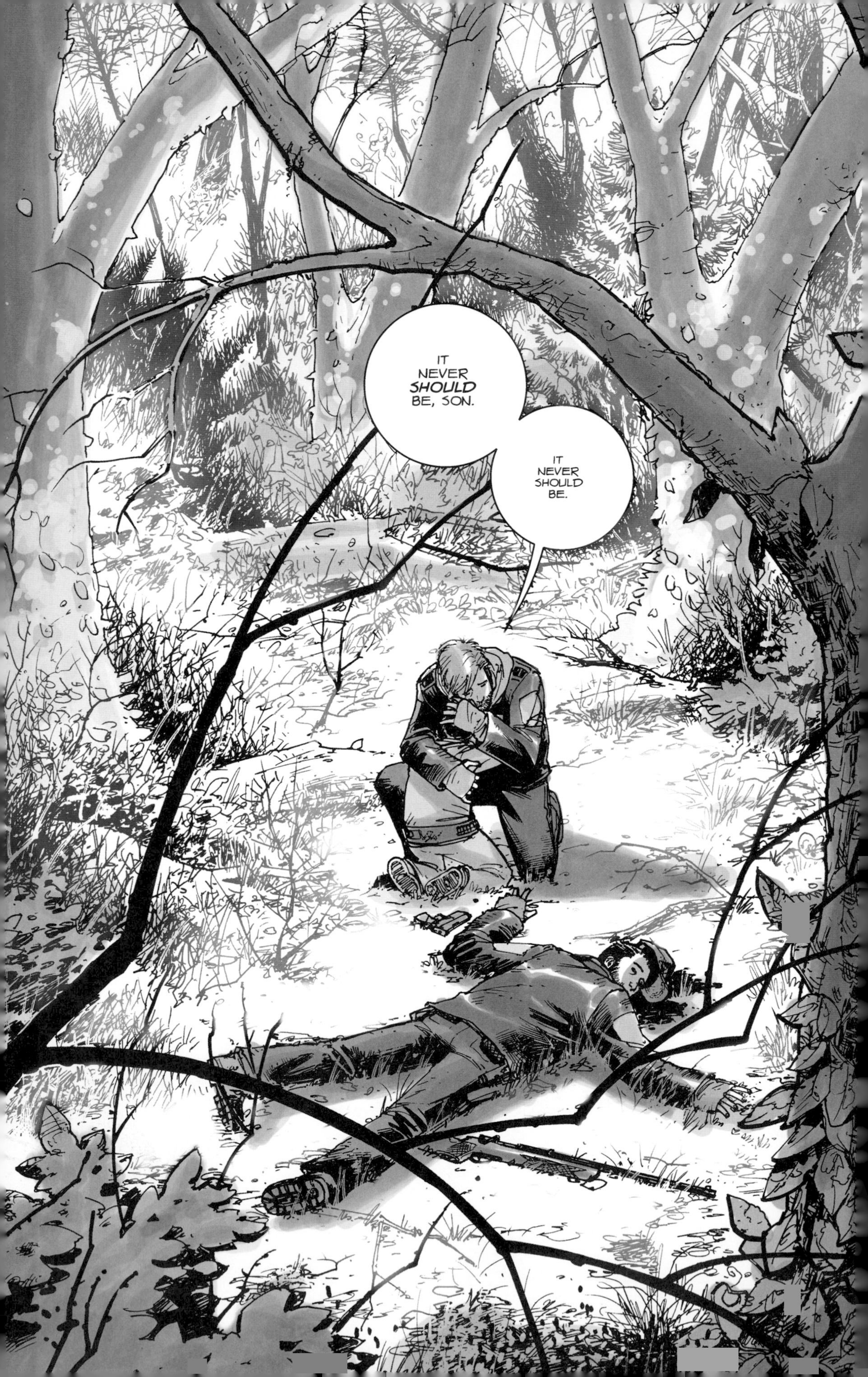
IT NEVER SHOULD BE, SON.
IT NEVER SHOULD BE.

for more tales from ROBERT KIRKMAN and SKYBOUND

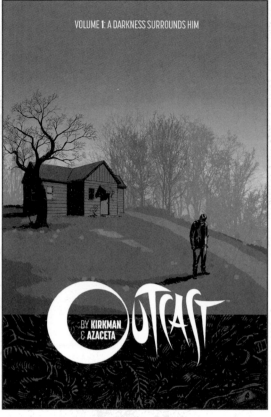

VOLUME 1: A DARKNESS SURROUNDS HIM

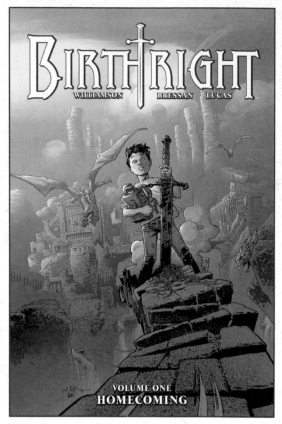

VOLUME ONE
HOMECOMING

VOL. 1: A DARKNESS SURROUNDS HIM TP
ISBN: 978-1-63215-053-0
$9.99

VOL. 1: HOMECOMING TP
ISBN: 978-1-63215-231-2
$9.99

VOL. 2: CALL TO ADVENTURE TP
ISBN: 978-1-63215-446-0
$12.99

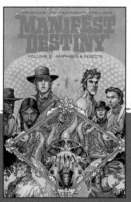

VOL. 1: FIRST GENERATION TP
ISBN: 978-1-60706-683-5
$12.99

VOL. 1: HAUNTED HEIST TP
ISBN: 978-1-60706-836-5
$9.99

VOL. 1: FLORA & FAUNA TP
ISBN: 978-1-60706-982-9
$9.99

VOL. 1: "I QUIT."
ISBN: 978-1-60706-592-0
$14.99

VOL. 2: SECOND GENERATION TP
ISBN: 978-1-60706-830-3
$12.99

VOL. 2: BOOKS OF THE DEAD TP
ISBN: 978-1-63215-046-2
$12.99

VOL. 2: AMPHIBIA & INSECTA TP
ISBN: 978-1-63215-052-3
$14.99

VOL. 2: "HELP ME."
ISBN: 978-1-60706-676-7
$14.99

VOL. 3: THIRD GENERATION TP
ISBN: 978-1-60706-939-3
$12.99

VOL. 3: DEATH WISH TP
ISBN: 978-1-63215-051-6
$12.99

VOL. 3: "VENICE."
ISBN: 978-1-60706-844-0
$14.99

VOL. 4: FOURTH GENERATION TP
ISBN: 978-1-63215-036-3
$12.99

VOL. 4: GHOST TOWN TP
ISBN: 978-1-63215-317-3
$12.99

VOL. 4: "THE HIT LIST."
ISBN: 978-1-63215-037-0
$14.99

BIRTHRIGHT™, CLONE™, GHOSTED™, and MANIFEST DESTINY™ © 2015 Skybound, LLC. OUTCAST BY KIRKMAN AND AZACETA™ and THIEF OF THIEVES™ © 2015 Robert Kirkman, LLC.
Image Comics® and its logos are registered trademarks of Image Comics, Inc. Skybound and its logos are © and ™ of Skybound, LLC. All rights reserved.